Silent Vendetta

BOOK 2 OF THE VENDETTA DUET

KATHY LOCKHEART

Editor: Susan Staudinger
Proofreader: Jovana Shirley, Unforeseen Editing, www.unforeseenediting.com

Cover design:
Model cover design: © By Hang Le
Photographer: Michelle Lancaster (www.michellelancaster.com)
Discreet Cover: Wild Love Designs

ISBN 978-1-955017-25-1 e-book
ISBN 978-1-955017-26-8 Paperback
ISBN 978-1-955017-27-5 Hardcover
ISBN 978-1-955017-28-2 Paperback alternative

Published by Rosewood Literary Press

Also by Kathy Lockheart

Deadly Illusion

Fatal Cure

Lethal Justice

Grave Deception

To the ones who dare to love the villains.

Author's note

The Vendetta Duet contains violence and other content that may be triggering for some readers. I prefer you go into a story without spoilers, but if you would like **a list of detailed triggers**, you can find it posted on my website at KathyLockheart dot com.

Silent Vendetta

CHAPTER 1

Luna

M y boyfriend is the Windy City Vigilante.
And I'm here, in his secret underground lair with him.
Dim amber lights cast an eerie glow that highlighted the rough, moss-covered stone walls. The floor was gritty beneath my shoes, small pebbles and sediment crunching softly with my movements, while the heavy air, cold and dense, clinging to my skin, making it prickle. Every breath I took was laced with the musky scent of damp earth and a faint hint of the lair's sinister purpose.

Franco's bloody figure sat bound to a chair, making my heart launch into spasms.

"You shouldn't have come down here," Hunter said.

I didn't even recognize his voice. Gone were the familiar tones of the boyfriend who loved me, and in its place, a chilling symphony of darkness, possessed with a haunting quality—the low growl of a killer.

How could two completely different people inhabit the same body? Hunter, the man who'd kissed away my past hurts and brought my heart back to life with a love I needed desperately, and the Vigilante, who'd slashed the throats of over fifty men, who'd used an axe to dismember one of his last victims—while the said victim was still alive.

Both Hunter and the Vigilante had claimed they were trying to protect me, but both had lied to me about who they really were.

And most sinisterly, what they were capable of.

I mean, holy shit, look at Franco. *He's missing his ears!* And he's covered in blood, all Stephen King's Carrie style in an underground bunker that looked like a scene from *The Silence of the Lambs*, complete with a blood-soaked floor. Not to mention the wall of weapons that could dismember a small woman in no time.

No. Turns out, I didn't know Hunter at all.

He wasn't a protector—he was a predator. A lethal, violent man.

And I'd just uncovered the one secret that could cost him everything.

My palms burst into sweat, and a metallic tang brushed my tongue, as if I could literally taste the lurking danger surrounding me.

"I'm going to need you to sit over here." Hunter pointed to a spot on the floor, using his bloody freaking knife as his pointer—because this wasn't all sorts of screwed up enough. My heart, once full and vibrant, felt like shattered glass inside me, each fragment piercing deeper than the last.

I looked at the ochre glow of horror stretching through the rock-lined tunnel and focused on the shadow of light at its end—the source, the staircase that illuminated the path to freedom.

Hunter held that blood-soaked knife and took deliberate and heavy steps toward me. Shadows seemed to gather around him, and the room's atmosphere grew thick with tension, making my throat run dry.

"Luna, you need to listen to me." He'd used his soothing boyfriend voice this time.

Listen as in *let me explain why I'm a serial killer?* Or listen as in *obey, so I can kill you easier?*

I wasn't sure, but as he advanced toward me, adrenaline soared through my veins so much, it made my fingers tremble. I needed to get away from him. Run back up that staircase, and make my way through the mansion to the front door, where, soon, the police, who I'd called a minute or so ago, would arrive. They would arrest Hunter Lockwood, capturing the Vigilante who had been slaughtering people for two years.

I took a step, but slammed into the steel arm that snaked around my waist and pulled my back to Hunter's chest. Which sent a jolt of pain through my body.

Still holding that damn knife, he did not say, *Don't worry; I won't hurt you.* No. Instead, he said, "Step with me, Luna."

My breathing quickened.

The blade glistened, painted with a slick coat of crimson—the color so vivid against the metal, it almost seemed alive, like a fresh wound warning me what would happen if I didn't get away. My right hip pinched against the force of his forearm as I put my palms up, pretending that I was going to comply with his orders.

"Good," Hunter cooed in my ear when I began to move with him, like we were in a psychotic slow dance toward my demise. His hot breath against my skin used to elicit a warmth in my lower belly, but now, it felt like a chilling ghost haunting my body—something I wanted to wash off me.

I matched Hunter's pace, giving him no sign that I was just waiting for the right moment to strike as he led me deeper into this underground room.

Hunter twisted me slightly to my left so he could turn me around, but when he did that, the knife shifted away from me just a bit.

I jerked to the left, then my hips to the right, breaking through Hunter's man-made barrier.

My feet slammed against the floor, my breaths echoing off the walls and burning my lungs as I sprinted toward the spiral staircase— while Hunter's footsteps thundered behind me. Each step reverberated in the hollow space, mixing with the sound of water drops falling from the moist ceiling.

The promise of the cold banister met my palm as I jumped up the first step. Then the second.

My shirt yanked me backward though, making me shriek. I

kicked my right foot back, connecting with his chest—not enough to knock him down, but enough to get his hands to release the fabric.

I charged up another step and another—each with its own clank— but Hunter grabbed my right ankle, pulling me down like an anchor, drowning me in my nightmare. My stomach clenched as I screamed and thrashed my leg around, aiming for his face, but his other hand joined my ankle and tugged.

My body flew through the air backward, landing on top of Hunter with a fresh jolt of agony that joined the injuries suffered from the car accident and Franco's torture.

Tears stung my eyes, blurring my vision. How much more could I take?

Any question if Hunter would ever hurt me had just been answered.

Lying under me, Hunter wrapped his arms around my body so tightly, that I could barely breathe, and though I thrashed around, trying to smack my head against his nose, kicking his shins, he didn't seem fazed by it.

It was like a bird trying to escape the jaws of a crocodile.

"Calm down," Hunter growled.

"Screw you!"

I slammed my head back again, but it didn't connect with his nose.

"Luna, you're making this a lot worse than it needs to be. Just calm down and listen to me."

Listen to me. Probably a code word for *I'm sorry, but I can't leave a witness.*

I dug my elbows into his ribs, and when that didn't work, I used my fingernails—clawing at the inches of skin I could get my nails into —but Hunter rolled to his right side and got to his feet. Still holding my damn body.

He shifted his arms so one went under my knees, the other around my shoulders, as if he were the groom on his wedding day carrying his bride over the threshold. Some part of my heart broke at that— that thought I'd found the love of my life who might carry me just like this someday. But this bride kicked and screamed and swatted at his face.

"HELP!" I screamed. "SOMEONE, HELP ME!"

"We're underground and a hundred feet from the main house," Hunter responded casually.

"If I scream loud enough, someone could hear me." Maybe. Hopefully. Then again, this mansion was a long way from another house—my only hope of being heard was once the cops arrived.

Hunter's rigid eyes met mine. "I tortured a man down here one night when you were sleeping. He was screaming, but you never even woke up."

He what?

Jesus.

Bile rolled in my stomach.

But Hunter didn't know what I knew—that the staircase's door and the one in the fake closet, both of which must have completed his soundproofing, were open. He'd left them ajar today, and that's how I found him—following Franco's screams.

If I heard them, the police would, too, once they busted down that front door, thanks to my frantic call to Rinaldi, telling her I'd heard said screaming. Based on my math, they'd arrive in three or four minutes. And they'd find me.

Hunter entered his room and looked around.

The underground chamber created an atmosphere of brooding darkness for whatever horror he was about to unleash with the gleam of deadly blades reflecting the dim light, casting sinister shadows on the walls as if the weapons themselves were conspirators in a dark plot. The one that caught my eye right now was a fiber wire garrote—similar to one I'd seen in a crime scene photo one time, used to silently end a victim. The sight of it set my nerves on edge.

I trembled, the icy air blanketing my skin in dread, as I watched Hunter look around.

Lacking a second chair for a second torture victim, he grabbed a couple of zip ties before setting me on the floor.

Gently. Surprisingly.

"Wrists out," he commanded, holding up one of the zip ties.

Screw that. Fifteen feet to my right, a dozen knives sat perched in perfect holders, waiting to help with my escape.

I lunged for one, but immediately, my ass slammed onto the unforgiving stone, one hand pressing on my shoulder. Worse, Hunter's jaw clenched as he wrestled against my squirms, pinning my wrists together as he squatted down and zip-tied them.

Making my stomach sink. The ties hurt my skin—especially rubbing the already-raw spots from when Franco had tied me up—but what hurt the most was looking into the eyes of the man I'd fallen in love with. Only to be completely betrayed by him.

"Sit," he demanded.

Then Hunter stood up, looking down at me—at the complication that threatened his good name, his freedom, and maybe even his life…

CHAPTER 2

Luna

"Let me go." I hated that my voice quivered.

If any part of the Hunter that loved me was in there somewhere, then maybe I'd be able to convince him to release me.

"I can't do that, Luna," Hunter declared.

I hated that my eyes burned—feelings were not the priority right now, for God's sake. Yet there they were, barbed wires unraveling in my chest, cutting against my insides.

I could still run. Even with my hands tied, I could run—would try to run again. But he was faster, bigger, and armed.

It wasn't lost on me. The tragic irony that he was the person I finally let down my guard with and trusted.

Hunter had been right. I was a magnet for danger. Staying in a cottage owned by the Windy City Vigilante, I'd fallen in love with him and moved into his murder mansion. Just for him to rip off his mask and reveal his true identity: a monster.

A monster—with blood splattered on his bare chest—staring down at me, while I sat on the floor, wrists zip-tied in front of my body, my back pressing to the damp wall of this hellish dungeon.

"You killed Dominic." My voice was a mere whisper on account of this damn lump in my throat.

"We've been over this," he replied in a low, even tone. *We* hadn't been over this. I had talked to a person who I thought was nothing more than a stranger—the Vigilante.

"It was you." I swallowed. "All along, it was you."

How could I have been so stupid? How could I have accepted his innocence so easily? Why? Because he was smaller than the Vigilante? Hunter Lockwood was incredibly intelligent. I should have realized the Vigilante might have taken extra measures to conceal his identity.

"You thought you could take justice into your own hands and get away with it."

"Where justice failed," he said. "I didn't want you to find out this way." It was the first hint of remorse in his tone, the first glimmer of pity in his cerulean eyes.

He stood in his room, surrounded by the weapons he'd used to end people's lives. I wanted answers to all of it—why, who. I wanted to replay the events of the last few weeks with this newfound revelation, but that would have to wait. Right now, I needed to focus on escaping.

"You save her just to do this?" Franco laughed, sitting twenty feet to my right. The guy who'd tried to kill me earlier tonight found this amusing even though his ear holes were leaking down his neck.

"Shut the fuck up," Hunter said.

Franco was right. With zip ties pinching my skin, Hunter had shown he had every intent of hurting me. Or worse…

"What are you going to do to me?" If I knew his plan, I'd have a better shot at disrupting it.

Hunter's eyes snapped from Franco back to me.

I searched for any sign of the man I had known, any remnant of the love we had once shared. But his intense gaze, once a source of warmth and affection, had transformed into something cold and calculating.

"I can't let you go, Luna." His deep voice chilled my skin.

Do not cry. He doesn't deserve it. You will make it out of this.

The cops were probably only a couple of minutes away by now.

Hopefully…this was a busy metropolitan area with a law enforcement agency spread far too thin, so response times could vary.

Let's go with two minutes, so start counting Luna—one hundred and twenty seconds.

One.

"What are you going to do to me?" I repeated.

Two.

Hunter rubbed his jaw and with a deep inhale; his shoulders rose and fell with an unexpected gentleness. His chest glistened with a light sheen of sweat while fresh scratches tore along his midsection from where I'd gotten him.

Hunter shoved his hand through his hair and began pacing. "You really shouldn't have come down here."

CHAPTER 3

Luna

Hunter's bare-footed steps echoed against the floor as he paced, his gaze locked on it as if it afforded him a solution to his nightmare.

I looked around the space, spotting one other small hallway in the far-right corner, but I had no way of knowing what it led to. Escaping through the original hallway to my left was my best bet if the cops took too long.

Which, based on Hunter's frazzled appearance, might be the case.

Hunter's usually immaculate hair was unkempt, strands askew in every direction, and dark circles shadowed his eyes, which darted around erratically. The muscles on his chest heaved up and down while his left fist clenched and unclenched, his right hand spinning the knife's handle.

"Can you hurry it the hell up?" Franco snapped. "I have some stuff to say that you're going to want to hear."

Hunter glared at Franco. "Didn't I tell you to shut up?"

"I told you, I know more," Franco claimed, though I had no idea what he was talking about.

"Be quiet and let me think!" Hunter paced faster, that damn knife blade glistening with crimson smears.

While another drop splatted into a small puddle on the chestnut brown stone, having fallen from Franco's open wounds.

My throat became a desert, but I used his distraction to pull at my wrists, testing how strong the zip ties were. Like I'd have the luck to have defective ones. All it did was pinch my skin.

"Untie me and I'll tell you everything," Franco said.

Glancing at the tunnel, I calculated my odds of outpacing Hunter this time.

Suddenly, he lunged in front of Franco with the blade angled to his face, his eyes wild and unrecognizable. It made me gasp, and it made Franco jerk his head back in surprise too.

"Shut. Up!" Hunter shouted.

Franco's distraction could be the only opening I'd have to make a run for it.

"I'm bleeding, man," Franco whined.

I shifted to my right hip.

"I'm getting weak, and if you take too long, I might bleed out, and then you'll never hear what I have to say. You agree to let me go. I—"

But he never finished his sentence. Hunter kicked Franco's temple with his heel, blood drops flying with the wet splat of contact, and Franco's head fell to the side, dangling from an awkward angle.

His loss of consciousness robbed me of the only hope I'd had to get past Hunter, who looked at me as he began to close the distance between us.

Every step he took resonated in my ears, a grim countdown. The cold glint of the blade in his hand promised a fate I wasn't ready to meet.

CHAPTER 4

Luna

My eyes darted between the small, unknown hallway to my right—the closer one. Or the bigger one to my left that led to his upstairs.

Standing six feet away, Hunter's tall, imposing figure acted as an unyielding barrier, blocking either escape route. The hazy light accentuated the contours of his face, making him look completely different from the man who'd once held me in his arms.

"I thought you loved me," I whispered in a shaky voice.

"I do love you, Luna." His voice cracked with emotion, like he was confessing a painful truth that flowed through his veins in toxins. A truth that would kill me if I ever uncovered his identity.

A tear threatened at the edge of my eye, but I blinked it away. *Do not show him vulnerability, Luna!*

"Why?" I demanded, biting my bottom lip, but releasing it with a cringe. The thing was tender and swollen from getting slapped earlier tonight. "Why did you let me fall in love with you?"

He paused; his gaze clouded with sorrow and regret.

"I didn't intend for any of this to happen," he claimed.

But that was complete horseshit.

"You allowed me to get close to you." My words hung heavy in the air, each syllable drenched in pain and betrayal. "When you knew the consequences if I found out." *That you'd kill me.* I swallowed hard, the sound of it echoing in my head, and when I spoke again, my voice faltered. "If you really loved me, you would never have done that."

Hunter studied me, his head bobbing into a nod.

"You're right," he replied, defeat heavy in his tone. "It was the most selfish thing I've ever done."

I flinched.

Selfish didn't come close to describing the magnitude of his deception. The safety and warmth I had felt in his embrace now felt like the cruelest of illusions.

A lone tear made its way down my cheek as I wondered...

Was any of it real?

CHAPTER 5
Luna

"You don't have to do this." My voice wavered with fear.

Hunter's expression froze; his eyes widened slightly, piercing into me, his eyebrows raised.

"You can let me go and I'll keep your secret," I pleaded. "I swear."

He regarded me with an intense stare, tilting his head.

"If you kill me..." I continued. Why did his head snap back slightly? "No one will fight for my dad's release. So, if I have to choose between ratting you out or him, I choose my dad."

His gaze, which had softened momentarily, intensified again. The lips that had once been pressed between my thighs thinned, the eyes that had glided over my nude body tightened with tension, and the hands that once caressed my breasts clenched at his sides—one still gripping a bloodied knife.

"Kill you." His tone was scathing with pulses of disbelief.

I wanted his anger to be from offense, that the man I loved would never be capable of killing me. But one look at Franco's bloody body and the memory of all his other victims told me otherwise.

After all, my hands were bound, and he was holding me hostage.

"I love you, Hunter. Please. Just let me go."

He hesitated for a moment that stretched on endlessly.

"You can trust me," I added.

For a brief moment, hope surged within me as our eyes locked. There was a flicker of something—doubt, regret, affection? It felt like I might've gotten through to him.

But then the shrill ring of my cell phone shattered the fragile truce. Panic surged as I realized it was in my back pocket.

Hunter lunged for it. I twisted away, trying to protect my only link to the outside, but he was stronger, easily overpowering me and snatching the device.

A voice mail notification beeped, cutting through the tense silence. Hunter scrubbed his jaw, looking at the phone before holding its screen up to my face to unlock it.

And then, he put it on speaker and pushed play.

"Luna!" Detective Rinaldi's voice had lost the calmness she'd learned in police training. "What the hell is going on? I have units on the way to the Lockwood estate, but they're seven minutes out."

My stomach dropped. Emergency response times in Chicago were an ongoing issue—I recalled the mayor even mentioning it at the gala that night. But seven minutes with a serial killer might as well be seven years.

Especially one who looked mad as hell.

"You called the cops," Hunter accused as he glared at me.

CHAPTER 6

Luna

"Why the hell did you come home?" Hunter shouted. My heartbeat skyrocketed in my chest as he pointed the knife in my direction. "You were supposed to be at the hospital."

"You brought Franco to your home. Did you not think that was risky?"

Okay, why the hell did I just say that?

I tried to hide the trembles in my hands.

"How did you find the hidden passage down here?" Hunter demanded.

"I heard screaming." My heart tried to crawl out of my throat as if it could escape without me. "That drew me to your closet, and I found the door to the stairwell."

I hated how cold it was down here—it was hard to hide my shaking, and I was trying to look strong. And I hated how our every word echoed off the stone, because it made the entire situation all the more menacing. But the thing I hated the most was the sound of blood drops splatting to the ground from Franco's head wounds, creating a mosaic of tiny expanding ripples in the puddles of crimson.

Splat.

Splat.

Splat.

His shoulders were still rising and falling, still breathing in his unconscious state, but it didn't make the horror much better.

"And you came down it," he snapped.

"I thought you were getting tortured."

Hunter rubbed his forehead. "And you still walked toward the sound."

His lips twitched upward for a moment before they tightened, his face reddening, veins bulging on his forehead.

"You'd already called the police."

"I was afraid you might be dead before they showed up," I explained.

"You could've walked into an ambush," he retorted.

Was a serial killer seriously giving me a lecture on safety skills while he was holding me hostage?

"I did walk into an ambush," I corrected.

He scrubbed his jaw, staring at the floor.

"You risked your life to try and rescue me." His voice softened with a sigh. "Just like you did with Dominic."

Dominic. Hunter was the one who killed him. Oh God, these realizations hit me like a series of ice-cold waves.

Hunter looked to the ground and paced for a few seconds before crossing his arms and piercing me with his glacial-blue eyes.

"Here's what's going to happen. You're going to call Rinaldi back. Tell her everything is fine."

Everything is fine? Was he freaking serious right now? Did he honestly think I'd cancel my only hope at salvation?

"So you can murder me easier? Fat chance."

"You're going to do exactly as I say," he said through gritted teeth. "Call her back."

My chin rose defiantly. "Gladly. Give me my phone."

"Are you forgetting that I saved your life?"

"Are you forgetting you're holding me against my will? Which is not only a crime, but in case you don't read relationship self-help books, want to know what you're supposed to avoid? Kidnapping."

"Get. Rinaldi. To Stand down."

"Even if I tried, she would never call the dogs off, and you know it."

"You'll convince her."

"I told her I heard screaming. When I'm not there when she answers the door? She'll search your home and find your tunnel."

Hunter looked toward the underground hallway that I'd jogged down. He looked at *his* phone for a moment, and with the soft click of a button—echoed with a metallic clunk from the end of the hall—the tension that had been etched into his features began to dissolve.

"There," he said with a deep exhale. "Both doors are shut again."

My stomach sank. Of course, he'd have an extra feature of security with that thing.

"They could bring in search dogs, and their noses would point them to the hidden doors. They'll find your dungeon, Hunter."

I hoped so, at least. Truth be told, I couldn't be sure they'd find this room, but I had to convince him they would. Or at least make him think it was possible.

"You have roughly six minutes until the cops raid this house." I kept my words measured, attempting to exude confidence while, inside, a destabilization of my vitals took place.

Hunter's jaw ticced.

"Meantime, you'll be trapped down here until they do, and your entire home will be a crime scene. You won't be able to escape with the estate swarming with cops. Cops who *will* eventually find my body. And Franco and his sawed-off ear canals." I was struggling to hold on to my stoic appearance.

Hunter's face contorted into a putrid mix of anger and frustration. He was silent for what felt like an eternity before asking, "What do you want?"

"Let me go," I said.

"You know I can't do that."

"Yes, you can," I countered. "All you have to do is not chase me down and drag me back."

I searched his eyes, hoping to find a glimmer of mercy, but instead, was met with an unwavering, cold determination as he shook his head.

"That won't happen, Luna."

CHAPTER 7

Luna

N ew plan. I was going to stab a six-inch serrated knife into Hunter Lockwood's jugular. I had no other choice. Running had failed, as did my attempt to win Hunter's trust, and now, the police were on their way, creating a ticking clock to the gruesome ending to this hostage situation.

The only question was, who would come out of this alive?

Me, if I had anything to say about it.

I glanced at my only hope for survival. Fifteen feet to my right, the closest blade was polished with a black rubber handle, dangling on a metal hook against the weapons wall.

Getting to it wouldn't be easy. Hunter was still positioned in front of me, and if I jumped up and made a sudden movement, he might stab me before I could ever reach the blade. Further, Franco Hopkins sat in the chair that blocked my most direct route to the knife, and around him, puddles of blood threatened to make me slip and fall on my way.

Not to mention, my wrists were still zip-tied—the plastic ridges biting my flesh, forming an unforgiving grip that refused to loosen. Blood pulsed against the restraints, as if my veins were trying to burst free. And I wasn't exactly operating at full capacity—the night's previous horrors leaving my body aching.

I returned my eyes to Hunter.

"Luna." His voice was low and urgent. "Please. I'll explain everything, but we need to figure out a way to get the cops to back down."

I calculated the odds of grabbing the blade right now. Not good, I decided. I needed to scoot a little closer to it first.

With Hunter now pacing, I used his flustered attention to my advantage, shifting my butt two inches to the right, and biting my lip when a stray pebble jabbed my flesh.

"I don't see a legitimate way to convince the cops it was a false alarm," I said. And even if I did, I would never do it. Not in a million years.

"I'll think of something." Hunter's voice was smooth and deliberate.

I moved another two inches to my right.

He sighed and shoved both his cell and mine into the pocket of his black pants—affording me time to scoot another four inches over. "If you call them, though, they're still going to come and investigate. Especially since they're already en route."

Hunter twirled the knife's handle in his hand, his bare feet patting the cement floor.

"So, calling them is out," he mused.

I scooted three more inches.

"But if I don't answer the door," he continued, seemingly to himself, "and the officers have reasonable belief that someone is in danger inside my residence, then they're permitted to force entry without a warrant under exigent circumstances."

Another four inches over.

"We need to remove the exigent circumstances," he decided.

And then he stopped pacing.

And stared at me.

My damn mouth went dry.

"Killing me won't do that," I argued.

"No," Hunter agreed. "But if they see both of us alive and well, they'll have no reason to enter."

Alive and well. My new favorite words in the English dictionary. Did that mean I had six more minutes to find a way to save myself?

Better yet, did that mean what I think it did?

Hunter grabbed the mask he'd discarded on the ground and used it to wipe away the remnants of blood on his chest—spitting on the fabric to get the last stubborn parts off. He did the same to his dirty feet.

"I'm going to get you a clean shirt," he said. "Yours probably got blood on the back when you fell on me."

Fell? He grabbed me and yanked me off the stairwell, but that wasn't the headline here.

"You want me to go up there and send them away," I realized.

"You and I are going to walk up there together. You're going to answer the door with me, show them that you're fine. We'll explain the screaming that you heard, and we'll convince them to leave."

This was a good thing. Not only would I live for a few more minutes, but if he would put me in front of the officers, I could scream and run out of this building and into their arms.

"How?" I asked, pretending to be interested in his plan instead of pointing out that the cops would never buy any story he came up with, not when I'd called Detective Rinaldi in such a panic. Not when I didn't answer her call just now.

"I have a plan," he said. "I promise you, Luna. I will explain everything to you. I haven't told you everything about my father's death. If you understood that, you'd understand why I became the Vigilante."

Sean's words swirled in my head about the awful rumor that Hunter had been the one to kill his father—Hunter, a killer? As a boy? Hunter's dark tone made me question everything about that night.

There was another reason Hunter being the killer didn't make sense, though. Hunter said he was trying to find the man who killed his father.

Or maybe that was a lie, too. Maybe he was manipulating me from the beginning.

I shook these thoughts out of my head and snapped myself out of it.

This was exactly what he wanted—to distract me into wondering what in the hell happened to him when he was a kid, who had killed his father, and why Hunter had turned into the Vigilante.

To throw me off my game.

Screw him.

How dare he look at me with that tenderness, like he was still my boyfriend? Like I was still his girlfriend and that I would have any interest in understanding why he was doing this.

It didn't matter why he was doing this. There was nothing he could say, ever, to get me on his side.

"But first," Hunter continued, "I need you to do this for me. Help me convince them to leave. If, after you listen to everything I have to say, you still want to turn me in, I will let you go."

I pretended to mull this over, looking forlorn and scared. I even managed to keep my voice meek when I said, "You'll really let me go?"

Hunter hesitated for a second before nodding.

A silent lie with a loud betrayal.

As I locked eyes with Hunter, memories flooded back—the care, the warmth, the love. But it had been nothing more than a cruel mirage.

It was like a person who was wandering around a boiling desert, not realizing how close they were to succumbing to dehydration until they saw a lake. They dove in and swam in the cold water that washed away the burning heat that had threatened to end them. They smiled and laughed, splashing the water and drinking it, overjoyed and never wanting to leave.

But with a secret, lethal identity, the person took that lake away and made me realize it was never real—my eyes welling with tears as I watched it vanish.

"I'm willing to send them away, but only if you give me some answers first," I stipulated, hoping to make it sound believable. If I agreed with no conditions, he'd know I was lying, so I could play the role of the desperate girlfriend who needed closure here.

"Why?"

"I just found out the man I love is the serial killer who I'm working with the mayor to hunt down. I saw you kill multiple people, and we've had mysterious encounters when you claimed to be the Vigilante, but all along were you." I nodded my chin toward him. "I have questions. If you answer them, I'll help you get rid of them."

Hunter stared at me, his gaze seeming to bore into the back of my soul as if sifting through my words, trying to decipher their true meaning.

Splat. Splat...splat...

With the tempo of Franco's falling blood drops slowing, Hunter's face hardened, and his lips tightened as he licked his teeth and shook his head.

"You're lying," he said.

My heart plummeted, and my ribs squeezed around my lungs. Adrenaline rushed through my veins once more, and my thoughts ping-ponged between the knife and Hunter. Maybe he would find some other explanation or legal threat to send the police away. Maybe he was done with me and my betrayals.

Amidst the pungent aroma of mildew and damp earth was the hint of metallic tang that reminded me that blood was already spilled on the floor.

Just like mine might, too, if I didn't do something.

I waited for Hunter's gaze to shift down, and then I bolted to my feet, making it to the knife in just a couple of seconds. Luckily, it was easy to get off the metallic hook, so I spun around. Trying to hide my grimace at the ache of moving so fast—no need to show him even more weakness.

Hunter's eyes darkened with a fiery intensity.

"Stay back!" I held the knife out in front of me, my wrists screaming in pain from the plastic ties.

"That was a very unwise move, Luna." He stalked closer.

Maybe I couldn't make it all the way up to his jugular vein, but a stab to the gut would immobilize him. *I think.* One stab, he would go down in pain, and I could make a run for it.

His eyes fixed on the knife.

"Drop it. Now."

With every ounce of adrenaline fueling my limbs, I bolted into a sprint, the world around me blurring in frantic motion as I aimed my knife at Hunter's stomach. But just as the taste of freedom seemed within reach, Hunter's arm deflected my wrist with a stinging swat.

The hasty shift threw me off-balance, gravity tugging me menacingly toward the ground. Before I could react, an iron grip wrapped around my waist and, with a punishing swiftness, halted my momentum, leaving me reeling from the sudden motion. He spun me around, pulling me into a suffocating embrace, his chest an unyielding barrier to my back, while the chilling edge of a blade pressed against my throat, his breath brushing against my ear.

"You should've chosen differently, Luna."

CHAPTER 8
Luna

"They're here." Hunter's gaze locked on to his phone's video feed.

Adrenaline made my nerves buzz.

Hunter, ever the calm Vigilante, simply shrugged into a hoodie—one I hadn't noticed had been hanging on the other end of the tunnel. And as he did, he kept his steely eyes on me, his determined glint conveying more than words ever could—a silent warning not to try anything again.

Last time, I'd wound up with a knife to my throat. I thought he was going to use it, but he'd let me off with a warning, then spent the last few minutes prepping me for the cops that were now about to swarm Hunter's estate.

Hunter grabbed a T-shirt from the same corner and approached me with it. Probably kept all sorts of clothes down here, presuming he'd thought of every contingency. But he didn't think of me finding this place, now did he?

"In case you get any ideas, what do you think will happen with your father's writ of habeas corpus?"

He wouldn't. That was my Achilles heel. Hunter knew what mattered most to me in my life was getting my father out of prison. I was the only one fighting for him, and surely, Hunter wouldn't punish my *father* by sabotaging his only hope of getting his verdict overturned.

Of course he would, Luna. A man capable of killing people wouldn't blink at using his prosecutorial power to get a motion declined.

Betrayal stung my eyes, and my head struggled to come up with a reasonable plan. I couldn't let those cops walk out of here—allow Hunter to win and continue his reign of terror—but I couldn't let my father pay the price for Hunter's crimes, either.

"You remember what you're going to say?" Hunter's voice was firm and curt.

I nodded. Remembering his script wasn't hard—the hard part was coming up with a new solution that would protect my father while *also* escaping.

Hunter went to his wall and swapped his bloodied knife for a clean one. I stared at that blade, wondering if it was the one he'd used on over fifty victims, and then my gaze drifted to Franco's unconscious body.

I can't go along with Hunter's plan.

And you know what? I didn't have to worry about Hunter interfering with my father's case if Hunter was arrested.

As if sensing my internal thoughts, Hunter also retrieved a small, delicate handgun. It was silver, something that I assumed some grouchy old lady would stuff in her petite purse for protection as she tottered off to church. Not something fit for a large, muscular man.

When he shoved the thing into his hoodie pocket, my intestines dropped to the floor. Was that gun a silent threat to make me cooperate? Or something he'd use against the cops if things went sideways?

Hunter walked up to me and locked his sapphire eyes on mine.

"Raise your hands, Luna."

It took me a second to comply—a tornado of scenarios playing in my mind's eye—but once I did, Hunter gently guided the blade of his knife between my wrists and snapped off the zip tie.

My arms rejoiced with the freedom, but when I stood up, he held up the T-shirt and the knife. In case I had any misconception I had a choice in changing.

Fucker.

I motioned for him to turn around, but he just crossed his arms over his chest.

I clenched my jaw tightly but peeled my old shirt off, and, with grimaces and biting pain in my joints, pulled the fresh T-shirt over my body.

Please let the cops notice I changed. Please let them think it's suspicious, no matter what part of the script explained it.

No. Don't let them grow suspicious—it would endanger them...

Hunter moved toward me, and after pausing at my flinch, he pulled my hip against his, his arm around my waist, while the other still clutched the sharp threat. Reminding me I was still his prisoner as he walked me down the long corridor.

My head pounding from a growing headache.

The cold, damp air pierced my skin as the sinister glint of the knife offered a warning of the fate that might await the poor cops. The walls seemed to whisper stories of sorrow and torment the Vigilante had caused, and as we ventured deeper into the darkness, the unnatural lighting created an unsettling atmosphere that gnawed at my nerves.

Finally, we reached the spiral staircase that I'd naively raced down, trying to save my boyfriend's life.

Hunter positioned himself behind me and guided me up the first step.

"I can't believe I fell for you and your lies," I mumbled.

The metallic clanks of our footsteps ascending the metal staircase rose in pitch with an ominous tension. As did the ache in my body with each step.

Clank.

"I was going to explain all of this, Luna."

Clank. Clank.

"When? On our wedding day?"

I could hear the smile in Hunter's voice. "You've thought about marrying me?"

Okay, the burning in my cheeks wasn't from embarrassment; it was from rage.

I couldn't wait to see him in handcuffs. I couldn't wait to see his name smeared across every news headline like the stain that he was.

"This is what I wanted to tell you before Franco got to you," Hunter said. "I was going to reveal it all, Luna—admit to being the Windy City Vigilante. I didn't want you to find out this way."

Right. His ominous innuendo that he had something to confess. It would have been a softer blow, hearing about it rather than experiencing it—that was for damn sure.

I remained silent as we walked through his hidden closet, where he forced me to wait as he shut all the hidden doors and latched them, blocking any evidence of anything out of order.

As we continued through his master closet and into his bedroom, a piercing wail sliced through the air, a paradoxical symphony that signaled both danger and hope for salvation.

"They're approaching the driveway now," Hunter said, glancing at his phone again before putting it, along with the knife, in his pants and hoodie pocket.

It felt like I was in a trance as we walked out of the bedroom, through the hallway—the walnut floor feeling like walking a plank—and down the stairs. When we approached the foyer, Hunter's gaze—unblinking and intense—captured mine.

"Stick to the script, Luna. If they arrest me, there are plenty of people in the prosecutor's office who *hate* seeing criminals released from prison. It won't take much convincing for one of them to block your dad's motion."

My sore lip quivered. Somehow, this threat was even more painful than holding a blade to my throat.

Squealing tires stopped out front.

"You claimed to love me," I choked. "You call this love?"

Hunter's gaze shifted from my left eye to my right, and I swore I saw a flash of guilt. But it was probably wishful thinking—wanting to see the man I thought I knew one last time.

Car doors slammed with the crunch of metal.

Hunter placed his hand inside his hoodie pocket, presumably clutching the gun.

If I tipped them off, would he start shooting cops?

Bam, bam, bam.

The thick wooden door—with its aged oak adorned with intricate carvings, a testament to the passage of time and the secrets it guarded within—vibrated against each fist pound.

"Police! Open up!"

I swallowed.

He was probably bluffing. Hunter Lockwood wouldn't shoot cops. After all, he swore an oath to himself to only hurt bad men. He had a code for it, he'd told me. Surely, he wouldn't violate that code just to save his own neck.

Then again, people are capable of some seriously disturbing stuff when they're backed into a corner. And those people aren't even serial killers.

My breathing quickened as Hunter swung the door open.

Two uniformed officers flanked Detective Rinaldi—officers I recognized from when they had testified against some of my clients they'd arrested. I recalled tidbits of small talk. The tall guy with silver specs in his mustache talking about his daughter's upcoming wedding and the baby-faced officer with blond hair had a six-year-old daughter and a one-year-old son—pictures he'd shown everyone who would look.

And then there was Detective Rinaldi, who had a toddler of her own at home, waiting for Mommy to return from work.

Behind them were more officers, slowly emerging from their vehicles. More lives at risk.

"Luna." Detective Rinaldi looked at Hunter, then me again, her face unreadable. "Care to tell me what the hell is going on?"

Run. Scream. Tell them Hunter is armed.

What if Hunter wasn't bluffing? *What if Hunter does start shooting and, even though they're armed and will fire back, some of them die?*

As a child, I had lost my father to the prison system. I couldn't sentence those kids to live without their parents, not if there was something I could do to prevent it.

My eyes burned as I realized what I needed to do.

I swallowed the lump in my throat and forced a fake smile.

"I'm so sorry." I recited the story Hunter had fed me. "Turns out the screaming I heard was Hunter. He found out I had been abducted, but hadn't heard the good news that I had been rescued yet."

Rinaldi and both officers looked from me to Hunter, and back to me again as Hunter wrapped his arm around my shoulders, playing the role of relieved boyfriend.

"I can't tell you how grateful I am that you found her," Hunter said.

But Rinaldi's tight eyes looked skeptical.

"You said he wasn't answering his calls," Rinaldi argued, referencing my anxiety as I was being treated in the back of the ambulance. Then she turned her attention to Hunter. "If you were so worried about her safety, why didn't you answer her calls or texts?"

"I'm embarrassed by my behavior." Hunter's voice was full of remorse. "When I found out she had been taken, I threw my cell phone at the wall. The thing broke."

I wasn't sure if Rinaldi believed him, but if she didn't want to risk never going home to her child, she needed to back off. And order all the other cops to do the same.

It shouldn't be too challenging. No one was hurt here. I was safe, Hunter was alive, and that was the threat I had been investigating.

But her face hadn't softened.

My heart was a pendulum, swinging between terror and anger at Hunter.

"And your shirt?" she challenged, looking at my top.

"I was just changing out of my bloody, sweat-soaked clothes," I recited, tossing a thumb over my shoulder. "When you pulled up."

"I tried to call you back," Rinaldi said to me.

"I'm sorry. We...we were just overwhelmed. Relieved, you know?"

Rinaldi's eyes dropped to my wrists, which had red marks, but I'd been tied up by Franco earlier tonight.

Seriously. Who gets held hostage twice in one night?

She then looked past me, peering into the great room before returning her eyes back to us.

"If it's all the same, I'd like to have a look around." Rinaldi glared at Hunter. "Would you have a problem with that, Mr. Lockwood?"

CHAPTER 9

Luna

Eight innocent people, not including myself, were in danger.

To anyone else, Hunter was merely smiling, but the slight stiffening of his muscles told me the prospect of the police poking around his house irritated him.

I doubt anyone suspected Hunter was the Windy City Vigilante, but the police had enough suspicion of something to want a look around.

"Of course." He motioned past the foyer.

Staring at Hunter with tightened eyes that flirted with mistrust—her blonde bun as tight as her posture—Rinaldi stepped into the great room.

The space was a ghost to me, haunted by reminders of a star-crossed romance. The logs in the fireplace that had crackled and popped as we made love next to it now lay cold and gray—the faint scent of burning wood still lingering in the air. Every corner of the space, which once filled with our breathless sighs, echoed with the scuffle of boots on the polished floor, and the grand staircase, where our nude bodies had entwined, now seemed desolate and bare—its banister gleaming coldly as if tensing for a confrontation that could turn deadly.

"Start on the first floor," she said to the officers.

My lips curled slightly, watching the police invade Hunter's space, but fell with the chilling reminder their lives were at risk.

Rinaldi stared at me again, studying me with apprehension.

"I'm going to look around myself."

Hunter's smile wavered. "May I ask what you're looking for?"

She looked from me to him again. "Mr. Lockwood, there was a threat against you tonight. Luna heard screams, and Franco's still missing. We need to ensure you're safe."

She thinks Franco might be holding Hunter hostage.

How darkly ironic.

"I see." He raised his eyebrows like a Boy Scout. "Well, I can assure you, we are safe and well."

"Nonetheless," she said, "I'll look around to cover our bases."

Hunter paused. "Of course."

What a dangerous game. If he resisted her too much, she might gain enough reasonable cause to get a warrant, and then he'd lose all control over this search. But if he let her look around too much, she might find something...

Is Franco waking up? Will he escape and burst in here?

"Luna, you really should go to the hospital." Rinaldi glowered at my arm. Franco had used a knife on it earlier tonight, and while the butterfly bandages and gauze the EMTs had put on it worked well, they didn't replace stitches.

Was she suspicious I hadn't gone yet?

"I will," I assured.

From the corner of his eye, Hunter unleashed a sharp glare at me —a silent warning that only an intimate couple could communicate with each other without anyone being the wiser.

I almost couldn't contain my smirk because I had just created another big problem for him should he choose to hold me hostage much longer. While HIPAA laws in the United States protected patient privacy, hospitals were allowed to disclose minimal information to law enforcement in response to their request about a victim. So, if Rinaldi—troubled enough by the shady events of late—followed up with the hospitals and I'd never showed, well. She'd be worried about my welfare.

And should I turn up dead...guess who'd be first on her suspect list?

"So, Franco wasn't found?" I asked.

Because guess what? While I could not divulge Hunter's secret identity or lead them to Franco without risking their lives, I *could* plant little seeds so that if I died, they might come back and investigate more. Maybe with a swat team.

"Not yet."

"So disturbing." I shook my head. "What about the Vigilante?"

Another glower from the corner of Hunter's eye.

"Nothing yet." She glanced at the officers in the kitchen and dining room. Hands on hips, they scanned every surface, pausing to peer into closets.

I wanted to ask her if she thought the Vigilante and Franco were together, but what if that was too revealing? Too close to endangering her?

Instead, I'd have to shift my verbal warfare.

"That must be so frustrating," I said.

She pinched her lips. "You have no idea."

"I'm sure your IT team is checking surveillance cameras in the area of the warehouse, but they'll probably just see that stupid mask the Vigilante wears."

Hunter's head pivoted toward me.

"You would think a criminal who wants to lurk in the shadows would be smart enough to have an all-black mask." My voice was steady, maintaining a casual air for the officers around us, but there was a biting undertone to my words, laced with veiled sarcasm that would be unmistakably clear to Hunter.

The veneer of calm he presented was betrayed by the slight clenching of his jaw and the barely perceptible narrowing of his eyes.

It took serious effort to contain my grin.

An officer tapped Rinaldi on the shoulder. Whispered something to her. I searched her face for any clue they'd found something but saw nothing.

"Well," she said, "I should get on with it."

Once she walked across the room, Hunter slithered his clammy fingers around mine as if he still had a right to do it. I knew it was all for show, to sell the story of two lovers in front of the police, but the feel of his skin—which once ignited a wildfire of warmth and solace—triggered waves of repugnant nausea. It was like being embraced by a decomposing corpse.

For the sake of people's safety, I'd go along with this charade, but I didn't have to let him touch me. I tried to yank my hand back discreetly, but the motion caught Rinaldi's eye, and she glanced at me with furrowed brows.

I offered her a smile—it didn't reach my eyes, I bet, but it was a smile all the same—and Hunter did as well. Rinaldi glanced between the two of us, some internal thought taking place, and after a slight hesitation, she returned her attention to the search by stepping further away.

"Careful," Hunter whispered in my ear. I could hear that he was smiling for everyone else to see, the heat of his breath invading my earlobe. "You need to cooperate, Little Leopard."

I dug my nails into his skin. *Hope that hurts.* I smiled for the people around us and motioned with my chin for him to lean down, whispering in his ear.

"Don't ever call me by that fucking nickname again."

He pulled away enough to meet my eyes and had the audacity to let humor dance through them like he was the old, playful boyfriend again. He leaned in so that his hot, devil breath once again burned my ears.

"Such a foul mouth on you. I remember when it screamed my name."

I dug my nails in harder, relishing the grimace he tried to hide. He was not winning this. If I was going to be held hostage and maybe even die, he was not winning this battle.

To everyone else, we probably looked like we were canoodling, whispering sweet nothings into each other's ears.

But I was trying to verbally destroy him.

"I faked it all," I lied.

Hunter brushed his thumb along my lower lip. It took serious restraint to not chomp it off, and then he leaned his mouth close to me again, his lips grazing my ear like the touch of a spider's web.

"Bull."

"I'm going to head upstairs," Rinaldi said, snapping me out of this banter.

"I'll show you around," he said, but when he walked forward, he kept his grip on my palm.

Rinaldi's eyes flicked to our joined hands, a subtle shift in her expression.

"You don't need to follow me," she said. "I can search on my own."

"This is my home," Hunter said. "There are valuable things here."

Rinaldi paused on the staircase, her voice curt. "Are you suggesting we might steal something?"

"Of course not," he said in a smooth tone with just a pinch of sharpness. "I would never say that."

Say. An interesting word choice instead of the word *think.* A passive-aggressive accusation.

Rinaldi glared at him. "Luna, can I speak to you for a minute?"

All my humor faded. One wrong word to her and everyone's lives could be at risk.

Rinaldi pulled me off to the side, far outside the reach of Hunter's evil ears. And I bet she noticed Hunter didn't follow the uniformed officers upstairs—poking holes in what he'd just said.

"Look, I'll get right to the point." She kept her voice low, her eyes darting to Hunter, then back at me. "If he's being violent with you, I can help you."

"He's not," I lied.

"I know you're saying that, but I can sense something off with your body language. I have seen my share of DV calls, Luna."

While Hunter's affection could be construed as a boyfriend

relieved I was okay, it could also be interpreted as controlling. Especially by a trained eye.

"Trust me, that's not what's going on."

I wasn't sure if she believed me, though, since her face remained tightened. As more cops funneled up the staircase, she seemed to be waiting for me to confess. But each second she stood here, Hunter was probably growing more anxious.

Trigger-happy.

"Detective?" a cop shouted down from the upper level. "You want to take a look at this?"

Rinaldi looked at me one more time and whispered, "You don't have to do this now, when he's watching. But if you squeeze my hand, I'll know you're in danger, and I will get you out of this."

This offer could save my life. Maybe there was a way I could do it, but before I had the chance to fully process it, Rinaldi ascended the grand staircase.

I didn't want her to leave me—she was my only hope of getting out of this—so I followed her.

What if it could work and I could tip her off without Hunter knowing? What if I could get myself rescued, but in a way that wouldn't endanger anybody? If Rinaldi suspected domestic violence, maybe officers would feign leaving and return discreetly once Hunter's guard was down.

And she knew Hunter had security cameras they'd have to avoid.

I followed her down the long hallway, but when I realized she was heading for the master bedroom, my heart became a storm in my chest. It thundered even harder when I watched her follow the police officer into Hunter's closet. Where the guy pointed to something on the floor.

Something at the base of the secret door.

"Might be nothing," the officer said. "But thought it was odd. Such an immaculate house to see mud like that."

Odd indeed. The warehouse had been dirty, and that didn't even include the parking lot where Hunter must have loaded Franco's body into the trunk of his car. Hunter might have entered his den of evil through a different location, but he had also tromped this way when he'd brought me upstairs to answer the door.

Or maybe the mud was old and had nothing to do with tonight. Who knew, but it piqued their curiosity enough to start looking around the closet more thoroughly.

Hunter appeared in the doorway.

"Do you mind explaining this?" Rinaldi pointed to the small smear of dirt.

Hunter stepped inside and glanced at the mark.

"I run several times a week. About a week ago, it was raining, and my shoes got muddy. I carried them up the stairs, but when I put them on the shelf"—he nodded toward a pair of dirty running shoes that sat among many others along the secret door—"they fell off. I'm afraid my housekeeper hasn't gotten around to cleaning it up just yet."

Hunter's voice was so unconcerned that he'd even convinced me that was how the mud got there.

But the question was, would that satisfy Detective Rinaldi, who had grown more suspicious of Hunter's behavior throughout the search?

As officers searched the other rooms, Rinaldi lingered in the closet. Looking at his collection of colognes, his shoes, his shirts. I don't know what she was looking for or if she was just trying to get under Hunter's skin or maybe give me time to come up and squeeze her hand, but she searched the closet twice before returning to the shelves of shoes.

Staring at the hidden door.

Studying it.

My breathing quickened, and I glanced at Hunter, who placed his hand in his armed pocket.

CHAPTER 10

Luna

Rinaldi turned from the door and walked up to me. She reached down and took my hand. "I'm glad you're okay, Luna."

Her hand was soft and warm, her eyes encouraging me to give her the secret plea for help—a squeeze.

But if I did, what if she didn't handle it discreetly enough? What if Hunter noticed the change and pulled his gun?

In the confines of the closet, the distinct scent of musk cologne clung to the air around us, mixing with the faint, steady hum of air-conditioning. The cool, recycled air touched my lips, and for a brief moment, I could almost taste the freedom that lay beyond the door. Rinaldi's gaze met mine, eyes deep and possibly filled with the promise of salvation.

After a few more heartbeats, she dropped my hand. "My cell is always on."

As she ambled out of the closet, my stomach plunged, and I felt like I'd fallen from a boat, watching my life raft drift away.

What if I was making the wrong decision, cooperating with Hunter? Was there a way out without risking people's safety? If I ran, would that alone cause Hunter to start shooting? What if the cops could disarm him faster than my fear thought possible?

My pulse boomed loudly in my ears, and before I could react, Hunter's hand encased mine, its warmth contrasting with the cold apprehension flooding my veins. His grip shot a hole in my life raft, deflating any hope of getting people away from him safely.

My legs became heavy, my movements mechanical, as a fog of despair clouded my thoughts. I needed to snap out of it—I couldn't give up the fight, but it was like my hope's batteries had drained and needed to be recharged before coming up with another plan.

We followed the police as they finished their search and, with a mixture of relief and horror, watched them leave.

Hunter locked the door behind them and sent a text to his security team who had probably seen the police action on the security cameras, assuring them all was well.

"Come on." Hunter's voice was gentle this time.

I tried to pull my hand from his. I hadn't expected I'd succeed, but it was heartbreaking all the same. My eyes burned as he led me up the grand staircase, through the two secret doors of the closets.

My footsteps clanked on the metal staircase with a hollow finality, soreness and heartbreak spreading through my bones. The tunnel's dim light danced and flickered, playing tricks on my eyes, and the musty scent of the underground stone room hit me as I stepped back into its icy confines.

"Would you prefer to be in the chair?" There was a tender cadence to his words, paired with a faint furrow of his brow.

It took me a second to snap out of my mental torture. "What?"

He nodded toward Franco, who was still sitting in said chair, groaning, regaining consciousness.

"Would you be more comfortable in the chair?"

I blinked. "You're giving me options?"

"If I can make you more comfortable while you stay down here, I will."

So, he was evil enough to hold me captive, but kind enough to care about my last moments of comfort?

"No." I had spent enough time taped to one when Franco kidnapped me. "The floor is fine."

Hunter nodded to a spot in the corner, where a concrete column held up the ceiling.

My eyes traced the dark, foreboding tunnel. Could I make it this time? Could I break free from his grip?

"I'll catch you," Hunter warned.

My gaze dropped, defeat pressing down on me.

I reluctantly obeyed, settling onto the chilling stone floor that seemed to suck warmth from my very bones, making me shiver involuntarily. The surface was uneven with tiny, jagged ridges poking into my skin, but at least I wasn't in a bloody chair someone had just been tortured in.

"Arms in front or back?" Hunter asked.

Tears blurred my vision. "Front," I managed weakly.

My traitorous lip trembled. Hunter didn't deserve to see my despair.

He helped me sit, positioning my wrists in front of the pole as if hugging it. Then he zip-tied my wrists together again, suffocating the last shreds of hope. Hunter Lockwood could do whatever he wanted to me, and even if Rinaldi discovered I was missing later, it wouldn't help now.

This was it.

I can't believe I'm going to die.

At the hands of a man that I had fallen in love with.

I studied him, wondering how someone so ugly on the inside could be so beautiful on the outside—his dark hair tussled yet, even in its messy state, still looking perfect. That sculpted jaw, defined cheekbones, and mostly those mesmerizing sapphire eyes with olive specs. He was like one of those colorful snakes—enchanting people with his looks, one strike away from his deadly venom.

The room's biting cold continued to assault me—each inhale armed with arctic fingers that traced my spine, causing goose bumps to spread across my skin with yet another tremble.

Hunter's eyes softened, brows pulling together in a look of

concern. He stood and removed the gun and phone from his hoodie pocket—setting them far away from me and Franco. Then he undid the zipper, peeled it off his toned body, and wrapped his warm hoodie around my back—taking an extra moment to carefully tuck it over my shoulders so it wouldn't fall.

With our faces only a couple of feet apart, our eyes met once more.

This time, it was the same compassionate stare he'd given me when he'd helped clean blood off my neck at the courthouse. When he held my hand while I got stitches and so many other times.

And it looked genuine—far from a psychotic person prepared to end the lives of innocent police. Making me wonder...

"You were never going to kill them," I started. "Were you?"

Hunter stood up, and his shoulder muscles rounded as he shoved his hands into his pants pockets.

"No." Hunter's voice was low and sympathetic, and his posture was different than it had been before. Softer. Remorseful, even.

He could be putting on an act, but he had nothing to gain by doing that now. Everyone was gone, so there was no threat of discovery—not realistically, anyway. The police search had come up empty, so he was probably in the clear.

I studied him closer, at the gentility pulsing through his gaze, and that's when a sudden realization hit me.

"You were never going to kill me either, were you?" I whispered.

Hunter's chest muscles rose and fell, and his eyebrows softened. When he spoke, his tone was low and full of pain.

"Of course not, Luna. I love you."

A tornado of raw emotion whipped through me. Thank God I was theoretically safe, but why the hell did I have to go through all that terror for nothing? And why in the hell was I feeling this odd comfort —that even after all the pain Hunter had inflicted, our love had been real after all?

"Did you mean your threat against my dad?" My voice quivered. "Blocking his chance of getting out of prison?"

Hunter shook his head slowly, and swiped his lower lip with his thumb. "I wouldn't do that to you."

So, it had all been a bluff, then.

The rope in my gut loosened with the realization that my father wasn't in danger, but I clenched my fists.

"Then why did you say it?" I demanded. Of all the bluffs, why that one?

Hunter looked at Franco, then back at me. "I didn't expect you to come down here and find out my secret like this. I needed time to figure out my next steps and come up with a plan. *Before* exposing all this"—he motioned to the wall of weapons, the blood dripping from Franco—"to law enforcement."

I gritted my teeth, as furious with his mind tricks as I was with myself because, thinking back on it, he never actually said he was going to kill me. He never denied it when I said it, but he never acknowledged that was his intention, either.

I'd made a lot of assumptions, and those assumptions kept me under his control.

"I thought you were going to kill me," I snarled.

Hunter tilted his head. "I could never do anything to hurt you, Luna."

My nostrils flared.

"Aside from holding me hostage, making me believe I was about to die, and tying my wrists together, right?" My voice dripped with venom, each word sharply articulated, cutting through the air like a knife.

He rubbed the back of his neck. "When I saw you here, I reacted on instinct. Self-preservation is a primal force. And like I said, I need you to listen to me."

I raised my bound wrists. "Then why am I still tied?"

Hunter leaned his back against the stone wall and put his hands back into his pockets.

"We need to talk, and we can't do that if you keep trying to run from me."

"Talk." I seethed. "And after we do, you'll let me go?"

His lips thinned. "Let's take this one step at a time."

CHAPTER 11

Luna

"Luna, I'll tell you everything that led up to this. I'll answer all of your questions." Hunter ran a shaky hand through his hair. "All I ask is that you listen. Can you do that?" The depth of his eyes seemed to intensify as they held mine, flickering with a vulnerability that begged for understanding and compassion.

What choice did I have? He wasn't going to let me go until I suffered through his justifications. And even then, it was questionable.

So, fine. I'd listen, but there was nothing he could say to change my mind about him.

I would never ever accept Hunter as a killer. I would never be complacent about his crimes by allowing him to continue them, and even if he didn't continue his crimes, I would not be an accessory after the fact.

I would go to the police and turn him in.

To do that, I needed to escape this dungeon. The dampness of the rock walls clung to my skin with a constant chill, and the faint echo of dripping water somewhere in the distance became a metronome of my grim surroundings.

"Fine." My tone was tighter than I intended.

The floor's jagged texture bit into my skin with every slight movement, amplifying the discomfort on my already-aching body. As if that weren't uncomfortable enough, my stomach unleashed a loud growl.

The sharp pangs of hunger clawed at my insides, their intensity almost burning.

Hunter's eyes drifted to my abdomen.

"When was the last time you ate, Luna?"

"It doesn't matter. So just start explaining," I said.

But Hunter's chest swelled as he ran a hand along the back of his neck, the subtle furrow of his brow and tightening of his lips hinting at an internal debate.

"I'm going to get you some food, Luna."

"I don't want food. I want answers."

"Your body needs nutrients, or you could go into shock."

"I just learned my boyfriend is a serial killer. Trust me, I'm already in shock, so just move it along already. Start talking."

He glared at me, and something inside fired angry shots through my veins.

How dare he hold me against my will like this.

"Here," I said. "I'll even help you. My name is Hunter Lockwood, and I'm addicted to murdering people."

His eyes tightened as he shot me a glare. "Your sarcasm isn't helping, Luna."

"You know what's not helping? Being tied to a cement pole in a dungeon while my first kidnapper is bleeding from ear holes that my second kidnapper created."

His lips thinned. "I'm getting you food. I'll be right back."

"Don't you dare leave me down here!" The panic rose in my throat like bile as his silhouette disappeared down the stone hallway.

This was unreal.

Franco Hopkins let out a muffled, pained groan, a haunting sound that echoed in the cavernous space, breaking the oppressive silence, blood oozing from where his ears should've been. His bindings looked damaged. Had he tried to free himself? If he got loose, with Hunter distracted, he could go after him...

Why did my stomach twist at the thought of Hunter dying? It had to be nerves. That's all it was. And exhaustion at the prospect of another deadly battle.

Plus, if Franco got free, he'd kill me too.

Rising, my arms embraced the cold, rough pole as I strained, the plastic biting my flesh. I lifted my gaze to where the cement column met the ceiling.

Hoping it had hidden cracks, I grabbed the pole with both arms like an angry hug and started yanking against the rough concrete. Grunting and working through the pain of every jerk. Between the accident and Franco's beating, my body felt like a car had run it over. Every tug felt like someone was taking a baseball bat to my bones, but I didn't stop. I tried over two dozen times until I ran out of energy.

When that failed, I scrutinized the walls, the floor, and the ceiling, but nothing helpful was within reach.

I sank to the cold ground again, my eyes welling with tears just before footsteps echoed through the tunnel.

Hunter's silhouette emerged, carrying a water bottle, an orange, pretzels, and something wrapped in paper.

He was seriously going to make us take a damn snack break?

"Time's running out," I said with an edge. "Rinaldi's expecting me at the hospital, and Mayor Kepler is expecting my call to reschedule the meeting I missed."

My last message to the mayor flashed in my mind, saying I thought the Vigilante might be someone I knew. We were to meet, but Franco abducted me.

"One step at a time." Hunter placed the food on the ground and twisted the cap off the plastic water bottle.

As soon as he did, my dry throat screamed at me, begging for relief from this painful thirst. But when he handed it to me, I couldn't get it to my mouth. My wrists were tied in front of the pole, so no matter which angle I tried, reaching my mouth to it proved impossible.

Hunter squatted in front of me, his intimidating presence looming over my weakened body as he took the bottle back and brought it to my lips. I wanted to resist his help, repulsed by his mere existence, but the overwhelming thirst was beyond my control. Reluctantly, I opened my mouth and tilted my head back.

A burst of cold on my tongue soothed the raw burn of my throat.

"Easy," Hunter said, slowing the pour.

I took a few deep gulps before Hunter pulled the bottle away.

For a moment, he hesitated, his gaze fixated on the droplet of water on my lip, and then slowly, he raised his hand. His thumb grazed my lower lip gently, swiping up the fallen droplet.

The whisper of contact sent a jolt through me, making my heart skip a beat, and the warmth of his touch lingered, a sensation that ignited a rush of memories from better times. The surge of longing that came over me was unwelcome; it felt like my body had betrayed me, yearning for the Hunter I once knew, even after everything.

Hunter paused, his hand suspended in the air between us while his gaze deepened, his eyes looking more like a storm than sapphires. Subtle lines creased the corners of his eyes, and a shadow crossed his face, suggesting an unseen burden weighing on him.

His eyes traveled from my parted lips to meet my gaze, searching, perhaps hoping for a hint of the tenderness we once shared. The silence that elapsed between us felt charged, a reminder of the chasm that now lay between us.

"I brought you anti-inflammatories." He opened his palm to reveal four pills.

"Probably poison."

He glowered at me.

"It'll help with your pain."

Right. Which could help me get away should I get the chance. And hell, if he wanted to poison me, he could spray my face with it, and I wouldn't be able to stop it. So fine.

I opened my mouth and let him place the pills in. Let him follow it with a chug of water so I could swallow them better.

The moment he began to peel the orange, a burst of its zest filled the air, the zingy citrus aroma wafting toward me, sharp and intoxicating. My empty stomach churned in response, my mouth watering, longing for the succulence it promised.

But when he brought a piece to my lips, I clenched my mouth shut. Reversing dehydration and reducing inflammation were medical things. Having a snack was different—like a dungeon picnic.

"You need to eat, Luna."

My stomach unleashed a desperate growl, and my eyes betrayed me with tears.

"If you cared for my well-being, you would let me go."

To this, Hunter sighed, sat near me, and crossed his legs.

"I care more about you than I've ever cared about anyone, Luna."

"You have a funny way of showing it."

"I know I might've lost you forever, but I can't bear the thought of you leaving without me at least trying to explain."

"So I won't turn you in."

He shook his head. "I can't exist in a world where the woman I love looks at me the way you're looking at me right now, Luna. Like I'm a monster."

My heart was such a traitor, feeling something other than disgust at his words.

Hunter put the orange in one hand, and with his other, he reached down and pulled something blue from the paper towel: an ice pack, which he pressed to the cheekbone that suffered slaps earlier tonight.

I flinched from the sharp sting of cold, but the throbbing in my face instantly decreased.

"I'm going to tell you everything, Luna. Things no one else knows."

Hunter pulled his lower lip between his teeth and took a deep breath before continuing, "My path to becoming the Vigilante started the night my father died. Something happened that night that I never told anyone, not even my brothers…"

CHAPTER 12

Hunter

The cold, polished wood of Dad's office door sent a slight chill up my knuckles as I knocked.

"Hunter." The soft leather of Dad's journal crinkled as he closed it. The gleaming gold letters of his name caught the muted light, reflecting a gentle glow.

He smiled, but it didn't reach his eyes.

In fact, his smile hadn't reached his eyes for a while. Lines of worry had etched deeper into his forehead, a stark contrast to the father I remembered from just months ago, and sometimes, I'd catch glimpses of him in the hallway with his head bowed, lost in a world of his own.

I eyed the journal on the edge of his desk, wondering if it held the clues to his somber mood.

"How are you feeling?"

"Better," I said. "I think it was the chicken. Everyone else had beef."

"Glad to hear it," Dad said. "What can I do for you?"

"If you're busy, I can come back later."

"Hunter," Dad said, taking his glasses off. "I'm never too busy for you."

Still, I hesitated.

"Well," I started, "today, my teacher asked what we want to be when we grow up."

"*Mmm.*" *Dad nodded.*

"*Everyone else had an answer, and I didn't.*"

Dad smiled. "*Hunter, you're nine. No one knows what they want to be when they grow up when they're nine.*"

"*Everyone in my class knew. Except me.*"

"*They might think they know, but trust me, no one does at your age.*"

"*But...*" *I started.*

"*And what you do for a living doesn't define you. It's what you do with your life that defines you, son. What kind of man do you want to be?*"

I blinked. "*A good man.*"

Every ounce of Dad was one of kindness and strength. He loved his family and helped people every chance he got. Like one day, the news aired a story about a child whose parents couldn't afford cancer treatment. I overheard Dad on the phone arranging to pay their medical bills anonymously.

"*I want to be just like you, Dad.*"

Why did he look at the ground with a sad, crumpled face? And why did he take such a long time to meet my eyes again?

"*Thank you, Hunter. I needed to hear that.*"

"*Why?*"

He cleared his throat. "*I'm about to do something that will be very difficult. But it's the right thing to do. Doing the right thing is important, even if it's harder than staying silent. Do you understand?*"

I nodded.

"*Now, do you still owe an answer to your teacher?*"

"*She said I can turn it in tomorrow.*"

"*How about this?*" *Dad stood and motioned for me to sit at the head of his desk. He had never let anyone sit there before, and I felt so special that he was letting me.*

I walked slowly around his desk and sat down in the leather chair.

Dad took a seat in one of the chairs normally reserved for business guests.

"*You have so many options for your career, Hunter. You could run the business.*" *Dad picked up a picture of Grandpa that was framed on his desk and smiled at it.* "*Like me and my dad.*"

But my heart jumped when something dark moved in the shadows of the hallway behind my father.

The hallway light was off, but whoever it was, was lurching closer to the office's open door.

Inch. By. Inch.

My heart pounded against my chest, threatening to burst out, while a stifling silence trapped my voice.

"You could be a doctor," Dad said.

I gripped the armrests of my father's chair, willing Dad to look up from the photo, to look over his shoulder.

The figure stepped closer to the doorway.

"A firefighter."

My hands trembled, and I tried to raise them, to point in warning since my voice wouldn't work. But I couldn't move.

As the shadow sharpened with each step, the chilling realization hit me: an intruder was approaching, and I was paralyzed with fear, staring right at him. While Dad was lost in the photograph of Grandpa.

"A teacher," Dad said.

The man held his finger up to his lips, silently telling me to keep quiet.

Scream, Hunter!

"A vet."

Look at me, Dad, because I'm frozen, but there's a man sneaking up behind you with a knife, and if you look at my face, you'll see how scared I am, and you'll look over your shoulder to see why.

The man was only a couple of feet away.

"You love animals, just like Grandpa did," Dad said.

I tried to scream, but before the sound could escape, the glint of a blade and a swift, chilling motion silenced everything.

Dad's eyes shot open, staring at me in horror as he grabbed his bleeding throat and spoke his last words in a raspy whisper.

"Run, Hunter."

And then he fell to the ground, just as the figure ran away.

My voice returned with a heart-wrenching cry.

"Dad!" *Dropping to my knees, I cradled him as he struggled for air, his gurgling breaths echoing my terror.*

· · ·

"You saw your dad get murdered." Luna's voice softened, taking on a gentle, mournful quality.

Every time I thought about that night, it felt like my ribs cracked in half and punctured both lungs. Sometimes I wish they would, just to end my suffering.

"I didn't just see him get murdered," I said. "I allowed it to happen. I saw his killer coming up behind him." It wasn't every day that my eyes stung with the threat of tears. "I sat there and watched my dad's killer close in on him, and I froze."

I couldn't even meet Luna's eyes, more ashamed by this than any act I had ever committed as the Vigilante.

When she spoke, she was kind enough to keep her voice low and compassionate, even though I didn't deserve it. I deserved to hear the disgust in her words earlier this evening.

"You blame yourself," she whispered.

"Every night I see his eyes, and all I can think is…if it weren't for me, he'd still be laughing, still be living."

I hated feeling vulnerable like this. This was why I didn't talk about it. I didn't like feeling so small and helpless as I did that day, even though I wasn't helpless. I could have done something; I could have saved him.

"Surely, after all of these years, you can't still think that," Luna said.

I bit my lip, hard enough to nearly draw blood. "When my dad's life was in danger, I did nothing to stop it."

"Hunter…"

"My family knows I witnessed his murder. But they don't know I saw the man coming and didn't even try to save him. I've been too ashamed to tell them we lost him because of me."

"Your family wouldn't blame you," Luna said.

"That's easy for you to say. When you thought somebody was in danger, you jumped into action. Look at what you did with Dominic. You grabbed a shard of glass, prepared to fight off a man twice your size to save him. And when you thought Franco was hurting me, you raced through this underground tunnel, not even waiting for the police to arrive."

I shook my head.

"The weight of that moment presses on me every day. I stood there like a deer in headlights and just...let it happen."

"You were nine, Hunter. If that man came into your house to murder your dad, there was nothing you could have done to stop it."

"I don't know that."

"If you'd done anything differently, you might've been killed, too."

"I wish I had been."

There it was. The truth. For the longest time, each day had been hell on earth, and one of the reasons I fought so hard against my feelings for Luna was because I didn't deserve them. I didn't deserve to feel happy, not then, not now.

I scrubbed my jaw, emotions swirling, threatening to consume me. Each word was a dagger, carving out the raw, brutal truth I'd buried deep.

"You don't know how many days I wished the guy would've just killed me, too."

CHAPTER 13
Hunter

"How did you transform from a witness of your father's death to a killer?" Luna's voice dropped to a hushed tone, each word draped in shadow and intrigue.

They say hell was worse than any suffering a human could imagine. As a kid, I thought hell was in the afterlife, but that was wrong. Hell existed in the tortured soul of a nine-year-old, who kept replaying the moment his dad died and all the ways he failed to save him.

"I'll make you a deal," I said. "I'll talk if you eat."

Luna pressed her lips together. She probably wanted to escape rather than hear me out, but I wanted something else. As selfish as it was, I wanted Luna to still love me despite the monster inside.

But doing that meant baring my soul in a way I had never done with anyone else.

I gently peeled the frigid ice pack from her face and set it on the ground. Then I raised an orange segment, its vibrant color contrasting with her battered lips—how I wished I'd reached her sooner. What if the citrus might sting her wound? What was I thinking, bringing salty pretzels down?

Luna parted her lips and allowed me to place the piece of food inside her mouth—a fresh burst of citrus drifting when she bit down, her eyes rolling back slightly at the taste. My finger lingered on her soft lip, and when she looked at me, my heart ached.

This might be the last time I ever get to touch her.

"As a child," I started, "I couldn't cope with my dad's murder. I felt gutted, keeping this dark secret from everyone that I had let it happen. My mom was so destroyed by my dad's death, and I was scared she'd stop loving me if she found out what I'd done. Especially because my dad's death left my brothers gutted, too."

When she opened her mouth, I placed another bite of food on her tongue, relieved by the sound of a juicy squelch, followed by the subtle grinding of pulp between her teeth.

I wished I could kiss her one last time. I wish I knew the last time she allowed me to hold her fragile body in my arms was the last, so I could have savored it. Just like I had wished I'd known that last morning with my father would be my final one.

"I bore the guilt of my father's death, and seeing the pain in others' eyes, knowing I was its cause…it broke me. I didn't feel worthy of anyone's love anymore, and keeping that secret burned my soul. Imprisoned me in isolation."

Luna's beautiful eyes were locked on mine, and I let myself imagine for a moment that she didn't hate me. My soul was on fire, and her empathetic look was a bucket of water over the flames.

God, how would I go on without her?

Before I met her, I had the blessing of ignorance, not knowing what I was missing out on, but once I got a taste of Luna, her love, her body, her everything, I wanted to possess her soul and chain it to mine.

If living in the aftermath of my dad's murder was hell on earth, Luna was heaven. Right now, my soul was walking the ledge between the two, precariously dangling over each side.

And I knew that if Luna took away my heaven, I would surrender to the grips of hell and never come back.

"I tried burying myself in schoolwork," I continued, my heart clenching. "That didn't help."

As I brought the next piece of orange up, Luna opened her mouth like a little bird, helpless and at the mercy of the bigger animal for survival. I placed it in her mouth and watched her lips close around it, the flicker of relief in her eyes confirming she was hungrier than she had led on.

"I tried sports," I said. "But every night, I'd lie in my bed and stare at my door, knowing my dad would never walk through it again to tuck me in. I pictured him beside me, but then the picture would turn into the killer attacking him from behind."

My gaze dropped to the cracked gray concrete beneath me for a moment.

"I started having this nightmare where my dad came into my bedroom to say good night, but his throat was slashed open and bleeding, and the blood would fall onto my face as he'd say, *Why didn't you save me?*"

Luna stopped chewing.

"Sometimes I have nightmares that I'm in his office again, and my dad looks at me, knowing that I can see the killer. He shakes his head like he's disgusted by me." My chest burned.

"Do you still have nightmares?" Luna's sweet voice rang through the damp air like a melody.

I hesitated before revealing something that had changed my life forever.

"Luna, I didn't sleep peacefully until you slept next to me."

Luna's eyes widened, and each blink slowed.

"Anyway, I became a prosecutor, hoping locking up criminals would give me purpose and closure. But it didn't."

"So, you became a vigilante," she said.

"Not exactly." I cleared my throat. "A while back, I lost a case against a man who had killed a young mother. The DNA evidence had a technical issue with the chain of custody that deemed it inadmissible, but the guy was guilty, and he got off. That case haunted me because there was a three-year-old little boy out there without a mother who would never get justice. And worse, the guy was a suspect in multiple other murder cases, and yet we had no choice but to wait until he killed again so that we could build a solid case that would put him behind bars for good. But only after someone died. It felt...wrong to just let that happen."

The orange gave me a hard time when I peeled off this segment.

"I followed him around every spare moment I had, and I even stayed up all night doing it sometimes, hoping that I'd be able to intercept his next killing. Eventually, the guy attacked another woman, and thank hell I was there to stop it and save her, but, he fought back. And I killed him."

I put the delicate piece of fruit through my Little Leopard's lips and watched her tongue glide over it. Even in the darkness, that image had the power to make me hurt less.

"I thought killing him would feel terrible. I assumed I would get caught, but neither of those two things happened. I felt alive for the first time in my life, like I had saved that woman and saved countless others from being killed, and I'd protected all those children from growing up without a parent who would've been his victims."

I pulled apart another segment of the orange, my fingers growing sticky.

"As the weeks passed, I felt like I was drowning in the ocean again. It made me realize that I'd been drowning since I was nine, and the only time I'd felt like I could breathe was when I'd killed that murderer."

Luna parted her lips for me, waiting as I fed her the piece of food, and this time, I allowed myself to believe she wasn't repulsed by my touch.

"Sadly, there are plenty of people like that man out there, falling through the cracks, and I realized taking the time to stalk them twenty-four hours a day, seven days a week was not only impossible— it was also too risky, waiting for them to attack another victim before I would act. That's when I realized I needed to be proactive, not reactive."

One of the hardest but most liberating decisions of my life.

"So, I got a knife just like the one the killer had used on my father, and I hunted those men down and slit their throats."

The empathetic glimmer in Luna's eyes began to fade, gradually overtaken by a hint of trepidation.

"For the first time, I felt alive and like I had purpose." I paused as pain charged through my veins all the way to my fingertips and toes. "I didn't save my father, but I could save other people from being killed."

When I fed my Little Leopard the last two pieces of fruit—discarding the pile of orange peels on the floor—I noticed tears shimmering in her eyes as she stared at me.

"Until then, I felt like the only thing my existence had done was cause an immeasurable amount of pain and suffering. Ending the lives of killers who slipped through the justice system, saving other parents from being murdered..." I licked my lips. "I guess maybe I felt like I could do some good in this world. That my life would mean something."

Luna studied me. "That's why you became the Windy City Vigilante. Every time you took the life of a killer, it was your desperate attempt to undo the tragic moment your father was killed. The Vigilante represents the hero you wanted to be in that moment, but you don't need to kill people to be a hero, Hunter. You don't need to lock up bad guys by day and kill them by night to be a hero. What you need to do is forgive yourself. Until you do, you won't feel worthy of being loved."

My ribs ached, but I kept my voice steady.

"I failed my father," I said. "And if I'm being honest, my darkest fear is that if you ever found it in your heart to give me a second chance, I would fail you, too."

CHAPTER 14

Luna

H unter cast his eyes downward as if the floor was a more comforting place. His hands clenched tight. "Is there any way you can still love someone like me?"

I shifted, feeling trapped by the weight of his words. Nearby, Franco's shallow breaths provided a muted rhythm, punctuated by the distant sound of water dripping, reverberating gently throughout the chamber that smelled subtly of moss.

"I still have questions." My voice was a whisper. Questions that thrummed through my head like a broken record and refused to be silenced.

"That day at the courthouse when you killed Dominic…" I started.

I wasn't supposed to be there. I'd told Hunter I'd be out in front with reporters, but, "Why kill him there?" It was such a risky move. "Why didn't you kill him somewhere less conspicuous?" Somebody could've recognized him, or he could have been caught.

Hunter ran a hand through his disheveled hair, exasperation in his movements. "I had it on good word that Dominic was going to flee. It was then or never."

"And the day in the prison parking lot?" That was him.

He hesitated. "I was trying to keep an eye out for you. It was an unfortunate slip he got to you."

His lips pressed into a hard line as he continued, "I stayed in the parking lot when you went into the prison, unsure how long you would take. When you came out, you vanished into the parking lot for a few seconds, but it was a few seconds too long."

And then the Vigilante, or I guess Hunter, jumped in the back of that van and killed that guy. I remembered his vow of protection and how angry the Vigilante had been that the man had laid his hands on me.

"But I called you," I said. After the attack, and asked him to come get me. "And you were *home*."

At least, that's what he'd said...

"I had to change my clothing and vehicle."

If he had hit traffic, that wouldn't have been enough time. But looking back, there was well over an hour break between the attack and the police arriving to take my statement before I called Hunter.

"Why were you so angry?" I challenged. "When you came to pick me up, you acted like you didn't know that I had gone to the prison, and you were furious with me."

"When I saw you leave your cottage in Sean's van," he said, "I thought about calling you, but I knew you wouldn't listen, so I followed you instead.

"It took me a few blocks to catch up to you, but I kept my distance and followed you to the prison, where I changed into my Vigilante attire while you were inside. After I raced home, the anger set in that you had almost been killed. That's why I was so angry."

I considered all of this, allowing what felt like an eternity to pass as I digested everything he'd just told me. I thought about the encounter I had with the Vigilante in that alley after the second press conference. When that burglar distracted my bodyguard so the Vigilante could pull me into an alley alone.

"You tried to get me to drop the mayor's hunt for you," I accused.

"Think back to that conversation, Luna. Was that the only thing you took away from it?"

"You offered me proof Dominic was guilty. And you showed me evidence of another guy who had killed a girl," I said. "You told me you don't hurt innocent people, but I guess that was a lie too," I said, motioning to my zip ties.

"We've discussed the restraints, but have I *hurt* you?"

I said nothing.

"When I had you alone and that alley—the woman wreaking havoc on my life—did I harm you?"

My lips pursed.

"The real reason I came to see you that day was to see if there was any hope that you could see my point of view."

"To not see you as a monster," I added.

After that day in the alley, someone had broken into my cottage, and I unknowingly moved in with a serial killer. I had made love to him. But according to him, on at least one of those occasions that I had slept in his mansion, he had slipped out during the night and tortured someone in here while I was none the wiser.

"The guy that you brought down here when I was sleeping—he was Franco's guy, wasn't he?"

Because it wasn't long after I had moved into Hunter's mansion that the Vigilante had paid me another visit, that one in the women's restroom at work.

"Yes."

"You breached your own security and then fired your own body-guard for approaching me at my work."

"He allowed a killer to get near you, Luna. Luckily, it was *me* who'd kill to protect you, but he didn't know that, and he failed at his job, nonetheless."

"Why did you confront me in the bathroom? You could have called or sent a letter."

"Would you have taken it as seriously if I did?"

Well, no. No, I wouldn't have.

After that encounter, I was haunted by who the Vigilante could be. But I had ruled out Hunter.

"You pad your suit," I realized. "And wear bigger boots."

"Listen, I can explain all the details, but the bottom line is this." He gestured around the room, with its earth-scented walls, stone floor stained with Franco's blood, and the wall of weapons. "This is who I am, and now that you know it..." Hunter's fingers twitched at his side, his usual confidence replaced with vulnerability. "Do you think there's any chance you could still love me?"

I struggled to reconcile the man before me with the enigma of Hunter Lockwood—a soul lost in shadows.

"I love you, Luna. I don't want to be in a world without you. It's like asking me to survive without my soul."

I didn't want a crack of empathy to open up for him, but I couldn't deny a sense of understanding. As a child, officers tore me from my father's last embrace. Their cold grip, my screams—it all consumed me.

But it didn't give me a free pass to do whatever I wanted in life.

"Many people experience pain and trauma, Hunter. It's what we do with that pain that defines us. You used that pain as a justification to kill people."

The last glimmer of hope in Hunter's eyes vanished.

"And that's not something you'll ever accept," he said in a low voice.

"No," I said. "I'm sorry, but no."

Hunter couldn't look me in the eye anymore.

My ribs ached, seeing the pain consume his face as solemn silence stretched between us.

Hunter's voice broke, his eyes distant as he whispered, seemingly to himself, "At least, for a moment, with you, I got to feel heaven."

My eyes burned. How could this feel so wrong, pushing him away? How could I still feel love for him when his actions were so deplorable? How could I understand what he had done? He had murdered people!

Hunter stood up and stepped back, creating distance between us. "You deserve better, Luna."

Hunter's posture slouched, and the light in his eyes dimmed.

Watching Hunter's soul collapse in on itself was like witnessing a devastating crash in slow motion.

How could I want to condemn him and hug him all at the same time? This was so confusing.

But then, it was confusing because the love we shared was real. Hunter was in there somewhere behind the mask, but it didn't change that he was also a killer.

"Mmmmmm," Franco groaned, his eyes threatening to open.

As Hunter glared at the man who'd abducted me and driven a knife into my now-bandaged forearm—the man who'd intended to kill me in a heinous way—his jaw ticced.

"Let me ask you this." Hunter tilted his head, challenging me with his gaze. "Do you believe Franco Hopkins deserves to live after what he did to you?"

CHAPTER 15

Hunter

"That's not a fair question," Luna said. "Do I think he deserves to live? No. But do we have the right to end his life? No."

It would seem that Luna and I would forever be in a stalemate. I didn't feel an ounce of remorse for Franco Hopkins, who still sat bleeding in that chair. Matter of fact, I looked forward to killing him after what he did to Luna, but my eyes swept over the love of my life, my stomach wrenching from the sight.

Look at her. Gashes beneath that bandaged arm, split lip, bruises, eyes red and swollen from tears of terror. She looked so damn fragile right now, so exhausted from the trauma she went through with Franco. And then what do I do to her? The man who promised to protect her?

I tied her up, terrorized her, and imprisoned her in a cold, damp room, zip ties digging into her soft flesh.

I clenched my fist until my nails stung my skin.

"Once I let you go," I said, my voice heavy with resignation, "police will have me dead to rights, and I'll be stuck in a prison cell for the rest of my life. Before it's all over, I need to do two things."

She straightened, eyes sharp. "Which are?"

"One, I need to find my father's killer." I clenched my jaw, memories rushing back.

"You've been hunting for him for years. You may never find him."

"I have to try."

"You've been trying. You can't hold me here forever!" She tried to keep her voice level, but terror crept into it on the last word.

"Not forever," I agreed. "But I believe I have the right guy to find him. I just need a little more time."

She took a shuddering breath in. "So let me go. You can hunt for him after you release me."

"You'll turn me in."

"No, I won't."

I smirked, sensing her insincerity. "If I let you go and you don't run straight to the police, you'll be an accessory after the fact. I won't put you in that position."

"So, you're what, my knight in shining armor, saving me from that? Seriously?"

"It's in your best interest."

"Oh, well, as long as it's in my best interest, then by all means continue to hold me hostage!"

"I'm sorry, Luna. I'll go as fast as I can."

"You can't keep me hostage. People will notice I'm missing."

"One step at a time."

Her mouth gaped open. "So that's it? I just have to wait around while you have one last kill?"

I looked over at the piece of shit bleeding on my stone floor. The wooden chair creaked beneath his weight, the modest pools of crimson already starting to crust around the edges.

"Two, actually." I returned his gaze to her. "But first, Franco says he has some information about your father's case. I am going to find out what he knows."

Her eyes flickered with both hope and caution. "And what makes you think he'll tell you the truth?"

"I have my methods." I cast a sharp look at the tools on my wall. "If there's only one thing I can do for you before you walk away from me forever, I'm going to help solve what happened to your father, Luna."

She swallowed hard. "Then what? Will you turn yourself in?"

CHAPTER 16

Hunter

F ranco, with sweat streaking down his pallid face, his shirt darkened by blood and perspiration, struggled against the raw, chafing restraints that held him. Each movement caused a faint rustle to reverberate through the chamber while the scent of his sweat merged with the metallic tang of blood and dirt.

Adrenaline surged within me, every nerve taut with anticipation as I plunged my knife into the meaty part of his thigh.

Listen to him squeal like a pig. *Totally awake now, asshole.*

Luna's voice trembled with a mix of fear and determination. "You can't do this to him."

I'd blindfolded her and put on noise-cancelling headphones to shield her from the unnecessary trauma of witnessing this, but she pushed her ear against the pole, dislodging the headphones.

"He said someone else hired him to kill you," I said. "The same person who sent the letter demanding you stop looking into your father's case. Whoever wants you dead is so worried about that case that they're willing to kill you for it."

"We already knew that." Her voice cracked, her chest rising and falling rapidly. "And he's probably lying."

I scratched the side of my temple with the base of my knife.

"He might be." A momentary pause elapsed while my mind raced. How could he know of the letter's existence?

"I'm not lying," Franco said. "I know stuff, man. More than I told you before, but I won't tell you unless you let me go!"

I couldn't help but laugh.

"You think you can negotiate in your position?" The blade gleamed. Its sharpness promised swift but painful vengeance as I brought it to his ear in case he forgot it was missing.

"Hunter, stop," Luna pleaded.

The scent of vengeance clung to the back of my throat.

"Kill me, and her enemy remains free. How will you protect her, then?" Franco barked out.

For a fleeting moment, I imagined what it would be like to record this, to capture his agony and relive it over and over. My grip on the knife tightened, and with a swift, decisive motion, I drove it into his cheek, feeling the resistance before it gave way.

"Stop!" Luna screamed.

"Luna." Irritation ground against my nerves. "Please be quiet. I'm trying to focus."

"I won't be quiet." The raw desperation in her voice hid behind its firmness. "I will not let you torture someone to death."

"Fuck you," Franco said. "I ain't telling you nothing until you let me go."

"You're going to tell me what I want to know, or I will cut off every single finger, every single toe, and I will remove your flesh inch by inch until there's nothing left of you but bones and muscles."

His eyes darted around, pupils dilated with raw terror. His Adam's apple bobbed, a visible swallow betraying his mounting fear amidst the facade of bravado.

Good. I was growing impatient. I wanted to kill this guy already.

"Who hired you?" I demanded.

"Untie me," Franco said.

I stabbed his arm, making him groan.

"Hunter, don't do this!" Luna shouted.

"Give me a name."

"Untie my hands," Franco shot back.

"Why does he care about the case?"

No answer. I stabbed his hand.

"You'll bleed to death if you don't start talking," I advised. "Why is someone so up in arms about a cold case?"

Franco jerked around in his chair as if his sudden burst of anger had the power to rip through his restraints.

"Is he afraid of getting arrested?" I pressed.

"Fuck you."

"Last chance. You talk, or I start removing skin."

"I hope he kills her," Franco said.

Well, if Franco Hopkins had any hope of a quick death, he just destroyed it.

"Suit yourself." I walked over to the array of weapons—knives with serrated edges, pliers cold to the touch, and bolt cutters, their sharp edges promising excruciating pain—rubbing my jaw.

"What are you doing?" Luna asked with a shaky voice. The silence must have been too much for her.

"I bet the bolt cutters snap through bone pretty easily," I mused, picking them up.

"It doesn't matter what you do; I won't spill."

"You've made that clear, Franco."

I walked over to Luna. "Headphones back on, Little Leopard. And this time, keep them on. You don't want to hear this." I shifted them back over her delicate ears.

"Hunter…"

With his wrists tied behind his back, Franco could do nothing but squirm as I positioned his left middle finger between the blades of the weapon. "This is for scaring her."

I slammed the two handles together, hearing the resounding crack of bone mixed with the howled screams of Franco as his middle finger fell to the floor in the fresh pool of dripping blood.

"You're fucking crazy!" he shouted.

"Most likely," I agreed.

Luna squirmed her head against the pole again.

"This…" I grabbed his left thumb between the blades next.

"Don't do it, man!"

"This is for causing her car accident."

I let the metal chomp through his bone and snap his thumb clean off.

Again, his screams echoed off the damp walls.

Maybe I'd played my hand too soon to Luna, assuring her I wouldn't hurt her, because she, once again, disobeyed my command and dislodged her headphones.

"Fine, fine," Franco cried. "I'll tell you, just stop!"

I aligned his right middle finger this time, holding the blade against his digit.

"Start talking."

"Someone hired me to kill her because he doesn't want her looking into that case against her father."

"Why?" I demanded.

"Because he knows her father is innocent."

"How does he know my father is innocent?" Luna asked.

Franco tried to look over his shoulder toward her.

"Uh…he said something about evidence that proves that your father didn't kill that kid or whatever. But look, the point is, that dude hired me to end her."

"What was his name?" I asked.

"He claimed it was John, but I think he was lying."

"How did he pay you?"

"Cash. Half up front, half when she's dead."

"Even if the courts found my father was innocent," Luna pressed, "why would this guy care about it? It's nearly impossible to try a person for a crime they already found another person guilty of."

"I don't think the dude was, like, worried about prison time or whatever. I think, like, he didn't want his friends and family to know he'd done something."

Luna's spine stiffened, but this was awfully convenient.

"And this man supposedly spilled all of this information to you," I said. "You expect me to believe that?"

"For all I knew, he was a cop, so I had my boys shake him down for some answers until I was satisfied he was legit."

"If you're lying, I'll cut your dick off and feed it to you," I warned.

"I ain't lying, man!"

I added one more person to my list. This man, whoever he was, would die, too, but I needed something to find him. A name, a phone number, a description, an address, or a meeting point to get the second part of his money.

"What did he look like?" I said, pacing in front of the bleeding asshole.

"Uh, like, older. Like, dark hair, average height."

"Skin color," I pressed.

"Some white dude, man."

"You have a cell phone number?"

"No, man."

"Then how were you going to get in touch with him when the job was done?"

The job. The word left a bloody taste in my mouth that anyone would refer to ending Luna's life as a job.

"I was supposed to leave her body in a public location, so he'd watch for it in the press."

"And then?"

"And then he'd drop off the rest of the money."

"Anything else you can give me on this guy? A car, license plate, anything he might've dropped?"

"No, man. I swear if I did, I'd give it to you!"

"So that's all you have?" I snapped.

"It's everything I got!"

I exchanged the bolt cutters for my favorite knife, irritated that I was having to rush through this. I wished I could savor killing Franco, but if there was somebody else out there who wanted Luna dead. I needed to find him.

Fast.

If I didn't find this man before the cops returned to check on Luna, he could come after her, and I wouldn't be able to protect her.

"Don't move this, Luna," I said in a stern voice as I put the headphones back over her ears.

"Hunter, don't," she said.

"Please, man, don't..."

His words were cut off by the gurgling blood spilling from his neck as I dragged the blade from his left ear to his right.

I didn't even get to appreciate it, savor it as much as I'd dreamed I could when I first brought him down here. And it irritated me that I'd have to cut his hands off and tongue out *post*-mortem; I'd been looking forward to doing that while he was still alive, punishing him for having laid hands on her, and the vile things he'd said to her.

As Franco's heart took its last beat, the room fell silent, save for the soft drip of blood on the cold cement floor. Time seemed to stretch, and then, with a sense of resignation, I retrieved my cell phone and dialed.

"It's me," I said. "I need you. How fast can you get here?"

CHAPTER 17

Luna

"Don't leave me down here." I hated the pleading tone in my voice.

Hunter's silhouette paused as he turned his chin over his shoulder to look at me.

Franco Hopkin's corpse sat beneath a white satin sheet draped over him to protect my eyes from the carnage, but his form jutted against it, crimson spreading through the shiny fibers, like an infection reaching for me. The smell of his blood was now so pungent, that it lingered in my mouth and swirled bile in my stomach.

"Please don't leave me with a dead body."

"I'll remove him shortly."

He took another step.

"Look, I'm not sure how long you plan to keep me, but I can't sit on this stone floor any longer. I need to use the bathroom, and I'd like to clean off my sweat and dried blood." Ideally, ice my aching body more, too.

Franco Hopkins's blood stretched another half inch outward.

Hunter turned around and stared at me, his fingers twitching at his sides as distant waterdrops splatted on the concrete.

I wondered if he thought I was plotting an escape, but this time, I wasn't. I just wanted to get out of this hellhole of blood and death.

He stepped back into this room, retrieved a knife, and locked his cold, unwavering gaze with mine. Before delicately drawing the blade between my wrists. It wasn't lost on me how one change of the angle and this admitted serial killer could end my life, but he yanked up, snapping the zip tie.

My wrists jolted apart in freedom.

Hunter towered over me with his deltoids, watching me try to stand up.

Not an easy task, it turned out. The hell that my body had been through was catching up to me, my bones and joints aching with every move. I was exhausted and beyond done with this entire situation.

"You're in pain." A crease formed between Hunter's brows as I finally rose.

Hunter scrubbed his jaw, his lips tugging up before he nodded his chin toward his dungeon tube.

"Come on."

The dampness of the tunnel settled around us, making the hairs on my arms stand on end with the chilling draft that whispered his secrets.

As I trudged along behind Hunter, my body ached with each step from the car wreck. Hunter stopped, his eyes lingering on my wincing face.

"I'll try to go faster," I assured.

With a steadying breath, his body, previously coiled with the predator's readiness, relaxed, replaced by an almost-imperceptible lean toward me. If I didn't know better, I would swear it wasn't from impatience; the softening of his gaze looked like he couldn't stand seeing me suffer like this—like it yanked at the invisible threat tied around his heart. And that he also yearned to close the space between us.

"Don't fight me on this," he said.

"Fight you on wh—"

In one swift movement, Hunter scooped me up. His muscular arms cradled me, one sliding under the bend of my knees, the other wrapping around my back, the sudden motion and unexpected intimacy it created leaving me breathless.

Especially with his face only inches from mine and him looking down at me like this. Like...nothing had changed between us.

As I stared into his eyes, memories of our shared laughter, whispered secrets, and stolen glances flooded my mind. It was tempting to fall back into my feelings for him—my heart at war with my mind—but they were now tainted with the grim reality of his actions. Thirty feet away, a bloodied corpse lay as evidence of the true man that Hunter Lockwood was.

Hunter began walking down the tunnel, but he didn't take his eyes off mine.

His intense gaze was like a tornado you couldn't look away from despite the danger lurking in their winds, and his heartbeat...I could feel it strong and steady, beating with the rhythm of my own. Which was terrifying and beautiful all at once.

His scent—sandalwood masking a hint of sweat—triggered the memory of our first kiss and the electric spark that ignited between us. I didn't want to remember that spark, but there it was, rekindling, making me question everything.

And as we walked through the dark tunnel, time seemed to slow, allowing warmth to cascade throughout my body. It was shocking how, despite being surrounded by death and darkness, the closeness between us could feel so natural.

Yet foreign all at once, familiar but seductive.

His muscles strained with my weight, but he didn't falter as he carried me with the same determination he'd always had, the same strength that drew me to him in the first place. It was that strength, his unwavering determination, that made me fall in love with him.

And, though I struggled to understand why, those feelings were resurfacing now.

Maybe it was because of the vulnerability in his eyes—a knowing look that he was doomed to lose me forever. Or maybe, with Hunter's arms around me, I felt safe.

And loved.

Despite all that had happened, I knew deep in my heart that Hunter would stop at nothing to protect me even if that meant protecting me from himself—his alter ego, the Vigilante.

I hated how much I needed his love, how much I wanted him and the love that still lingered between us.

Hunter's breathing grew uneven, and for a moment, he seemed trapped in the pull of some unseen force. Then, with a visible shudder and a sharp exhale, he managed to ground himself back to the present, breaking the spell that had momentarily ensnared us both as he set me down by the staircase.

It was too narrow to carry me up, so he guided me, step by step, making sure I didn't fall.

The change of scenery helped me refocus on the fact I was still being taken against my will and needed to do something.

He had my cell tucked into his pocket—of course he did. He'd never leave it to chance that I could break free and call for help, but it now butted against my hip as he carried me through both closets.

Trying to take it was probably totally doomed, but I had to try.

As we passed through a doorway, I pretended to adjust my posture and bumped my foot against the frame—hard. The jolt let me snatch the phone.

"Stop fighting me," Hunter demanded.

I pretended to widen my eyes in fear and had to seriously work hard at not saying a sarcastic comeback. Because I got it. The phone was in my hand.

The relief was immense when he began walking again, guiding me through the hallway before finally depositing me on my feet in the guest bedroom.

Where I stood with my hand behind my back, hiding my cell phone, my only hope of escape.

"Thank you," I said. "I'll be a lot more comfortable in here."

"You can shower." He nodded his head toward the bathroom. "I'll bring you up some food soon."

I nodded.

Hunter turned to walk out the door, my heart fluttering at the victory I gripped in my hand. He stopped, clenched his fists, and turned around.

His face was full of pain and hurt that made me paranoid. What if he knew I'd grabbed the cell phone and this was a test to see if I'd let him leave when I had it?

"I'm sorry for all of this, Luna. When it's over..." Hunter held the back of his neck, looking at the ground. "Don't let my mistakes stop you from the path you're on." He raised his pained gaze to meet mine. "You're too beautiful of a person to not spread your love around. The world would be robbed if it didn't get your light, Luna. Don't put it out because I screwed up."

Damn it, my eyes were blurry now.

This was the selfless Hunter that I had fallen in love with, who never wanted me to suffer.

"I don't deserve you," he said. "But it doesn't change the fact that I'd burn the world down for you."

His words, laden with emotion, left me reeling. How was it possible to feel so cherished by someone like him?

He stepped a few feet closer to me, my body aching with a different pain. The pain of not embracing my former love.

"All your life, you've felt people don't love you enough to fight for you." Hunter stepped closer. "Know this, Luna: I'd kill for you. I have killed for you. When I'm gone, never forget how much you're worth fighting for."

Hunter brought his hand up to my cheek, making me gasp at the spark created by his touch.

"Remember," he said, "so long as your heart beats, there was one person out there willing to stop any heartbeat that ever hurt you."

I should not want his words to sprinkle inside me like seeds and grow. But they did. And I wanted to water them and nurture them and allow them to consume my body. To replace my cells with nothing but those words.

And I should not be devastated by the word *was*. There *was* one person willing to end anyone that hurt me. Was—past tense.

"I love you, Luna. Nothing will change that."

But everything was changing. And I couldn't control it, nor did I know how badly I'd be damaged when this car accident stopped flipping.

"I don't know how I feel," I admitted. "I know how I *should* feel. But everything just feels so…muddy right now."

Hunter's eyes brightened, but after a few seconds, the corners of his mouth drooped, and he shook his head back and forth.

"You deserve somebody better than me, Luna." He swallowed. "I'm a monster. I relish enacting justice when justice isn't served, and I enjoy inflicting pain on the men who've inflicted it on others. I want them to suffer, just as they've made their victims suffer, and I want them to feel the same fear, too."

I shuddered at the confession he got off on his kills, and then my chest burned because after everything he'd confided, I realized I probably knew him better than anyone else. I mean, look at the brokenness etched across his features right now. I bet the real reason he'd never gotten close to anyone was because he didn't feel worthy of being loved.

In the expanding silence, the familiar chime of my cell phone reverberated through the room like a dangerous toll.

The color drained from Hunter's face, and his features darkened.

"Give me the phone, Luna."

Fight or flight. Flight won. I sprinted toward the bathroom—the cold touch of the cell phone's screen clutched in my palm—where the subtle scent of lavender was invaded by his distinct musk scent when he caught me.

Embarrassingly easily.

He wrenched the phone from my grasp, its smooth surface scraping my skin. Then, towering over me, he stood rigid, every line of his body radiating a sense of betrayal.

CHAPTER 18

Luna

H unter gave me one last look before storming out of the bedroom and slamming the door behind him.

What the hell was that click?

It better not be what I think it is!

I ran and tried to turn the doorknob to open the ancient beast, but it wouldn't budge. Instantly, all my confusing emotions washed away, as did my fear, and the only one that was left was hot, boiling anger.

I hadn't given much thought to *how* he'd keep me here, but this? This was too far.

"It's locked, Luna," Hunter said from the other side.

"Thanks for mansplaining that to me," I snapped. "Why the hell does your door lock from the *outside*? How many other hostages have you had in here?"

The A-hole had the nerve to chuckle. "You're my first one, Little Leopard."

"Stop calling me that, you freaking snake! Why is there a door lock on the other side? How long have you been planning this?"

"I installed a bidirectional door lock when you started staying here. I knew there might be times I'd sneak out at night, and I couldn't afford for you to wake up and discover things you weren't supposed to."

Like the night he evidently brought somebody here and tortured them.

"I see. And you thought if I discovered I was locked inside a room, I would what, never have asked any questions?"

"It was a precaution."

"A stupid one," I said. "Have you forgotten I need stitches? What's your plan there, Hunter?"

Silence. "I'll figure something out. Meanwhile, get some rest, Luna."

"Go to hell, Hunter."

I pressed my back against the door, assessing my surroundings.

Somehow, this room looked so different from how it had when Hunter and I first made love in here. The vintage chandelier had looked soft when he'd kissed me, but now it looked like a possible weapon. Maybe I could bust it into pieces and stab Hunter in his ear to escape. Or maybe I could use the antique furniture to break down the door. Or better yet…the floor-to-ceiling window that overlooked the mansion's lush backyard garden.

I walked over to the glass window and looked down, my hope of escape disintegrating. Even if I could bust out the glass and didn't get sliced up from it, Hunter's mansion had tall ceilings, resulting in a high fall from a second story. One I doubted I could pull off without snapping my spine. Especially since a stone courtyard sat below me.

I pawed through the desk, and when I found paper clips, I bent the cold metal and battled with the door lock. But when the repeated scratches didn't produce a loud click, I flung them away in utter defeat.

Running through other potential options, I sprinted to the bathroom, searching for any way out, but there was nothing.

I plopped on the bed, grabbed a pillow, and screamed into it. Having no choice but to bide my time until that door opened again, and once it did, I'd make a run for it before Hunter had a chance to close it.

Meanwhile, I was covered in dried blood and sweat, feeling so disgusting I couldn't take it for another second, so I walked into the bathroom and stripped away my clothes, each layer peeling off the traumas I'd endured.

Standing before the grand marble shower, I turned the handle, and water flowed generously. The great thing about a billionaire holding me hostage was that he had seriously good water pressure. The water, initially cool, began to warm, cascading over my fingers in a reassuring embrace, its heat slowly seeping into my chilled skin. I closed my eyes for a moment, trying to focus on the sensation and the sound of the water splashing, when an unexpected click of the bedroom door jolted me back to stark reality.

Hunter stepped into the room, carrying a basket, but stilled when he saw me.

Completely nude.

CHAPTER 19

Luna

I froze into a statue, as if my muscles were immediately incapable of moving, not even an inch.

Hunter's gaze felt predatory as it swept down my body, lingering on intimate spots before settling back on my face.

Then he shut the door behind him—with him *inside*—and this time, the click of the lock was deafening.

The shower's water now burned my skin, so I yanked my hand away, backing up, wishing the calming scent of lavender could stop my throat from becoming a desert.

The old Hunter—the one I loved—would never harm me. But this man? He was unpredictable.

He moved closer. Each step accelerated my pounding heart, and evidently, my hormones had compartmentalized the awful things I'd learned about Hunter tonight because they fixated on how gorgeous he looked. His hair, a midnight black, was untamed, messily scattered over his forehead, and his rounded shoulders, exposed chiseled chest, and arms looked as though they were carved from marble.

His cerulean eyes seared into mine, making my breath hitch.

I hated how my body responded to him, how my pulse quickened at his proximity. I hated how desperately, how completely, I was drawn to him. Every stolen glance, every lingering touch sent ripples of confusion and longing through me. He was a storm of passion and danger, and I, like a sailor entranced by the song of a siren, was willingly walking into his eye.

Damn him for being the magnet that pulled at my every fiber, and damn me for my undeniable attraction. Because maybe, just maybe, part of me craved the chaos. Perhaps, in some twisted sense, I didn't want it any other way.

As he closed the distance between us, he allowed his gaze to sweep over my body once more.

I crossed one arm over my chest and held my hand in front of my sex, shrinking in on myself. It was too intimate a moment to share with him.

But—never breaking my gaze—he reached out and slowly, gently, pulled my arms away from my frame.

You would think he'd find me repulsive, covered in bruises and injuries sustained from the car accident and beating, but beneath his flare of anger over what had been done to me, his eyes softened, tracing each mark as if they were stardust and not scars. To him, every blemish seemed to only enhance my beauty, as if each wound were a testament to a strength he admired. There was a reverence in his stare, an unspoken promise that he would always see me, not for the imperfections, but for the radiant—and in his mind, perfect—soul beneath.

Part of me wanted him to see how beaten and battered I was because the outside was a mere reflection of how I felt on the inside. And I wanted him to really *see* me. I squared my shoulders, wanting him to realize that despite it all, I wasn't broken.

And I would go down fighting.

Hunter brought his hand up to my face, making me shudder at the touch of his knuckles running along my jaw.

It shocked me that earlier tonight, when we had been with the police, his touch had felt like a corpse, because right now, it was a wonderful sparkler on the Fourth of July, crackling against my skin.

Maybe my earlier reaction tonight was because of my shock and betrayal over Hunter being the Windy City Vigilante. And maybe now I could see, at least part of him, was still the man I'd fallen in love with.

"I should keep you here forever, Little Leopard." His voice was low with a grainy growl that reminded me of his Vigilante voice. "I wonder," he said, allowing his fingers to drag down my throat, "if part of you still feels something when I touch you."

I do. I didn't understand it, didn't want it, but the chemistry between us, the pull he had on me, was still strong—very much yearning for him. All our breathless moments threatened to consume my logic in its wildfire, begging me to surrender to this desire rather than to reason.

"I don't," I lied.

But when the crack in my tone gave my deception away, Hunter's lips tugged up.

Maybe my hormones were a survival skill. Feel turned on, want Hunter to throw me down on the bed, and abracadabra, I couldn't fixate on the horrors that had happened tonight.

"You're still attracted to me," he accused, looking at my peaked nipples as evidence.

"Physical attraction means nothing."

But his face sparkled with victory; it meant everything to him.

His knuckles grazed my collarbone, then my breast, and though my skin came alive with his touch and begged for more, begged for me to submit, I forced myself to remember who he really was.

And what he'd just done in that basement.

I slapped his hand away, but he caught my wrist and held me there, towering over me while the gentle touch of warm steam enveloped us, causing tiny droplets to form on my bare skin. The steam snaked its way to the mirror, coating it in fog and amplifying the fragrant blend of lavender from the air freshener with his intoxicating sandalwood scent, making every sensation more pronounced.

I tried to shove aside the warped feelings of gratitude that he'd done it all for me. That standing in front of me was a man who had literally killed for me, because that wasn't a healthy thought. A healthy relationship was finding a man who never broke the law, without an alter ego who took justice into his own hands.

This man was lethal, and there was no guarantee someone as dangerous as him wouldn't turn on me.

I didn't want to feel excited around him like this, and I didn't want to imagine, even for a moment, what it might be like to surrender to his darkness.

He tightened his hold on my wrist and pulled me against him, my breasts swelling against his chest as he stared down at me.

I gulped, trying to shove down this inappropriate arousal.

It was like Hunter had been more reserved before, but now that I'd seen him—all of him—he was letting his inhibitions go.

"You can't have me," I uttered, hoping my voice wouldn't give away my growing attraction to him.

His gaze flickered with something wild and primal.

"You like to challenge me," he said.

"I don't know you well enough to challenge you." Did I? He was a completely different person than I thought he was yesterday. Yet he'd confided his hidden truths.

"On the contrary. You're the *only* person who knows me," he said, emphasizing each word.

Again, I had to push aside the allure racing through my heart at being the *only* person who knew his darkest secret. There was something forbidden and intimate that strengthened our bond to a level most people never experienced.

"You know me," he continued, "and you know the monster that dwells within. And even though you won't admit it, maybe both of them thrill you."

I shook my head. "You're the only one who gets off on murder."

To this, he smirked.

With his free hand, he trailed his fingertip down the base of my throat, down my collarbone, down my breast, and I couldn't help but gasp at its radiating warmth.

"If you were repulsed by me, your breathing wouldn't increase under my touch." He cupped my breast, and I inhaled sharply.

This intense desire was wrong—missing the feeling of him on top of me, buried inside of me. Probably some kind of mental breakdown on my part.

"Tell me to stop," he dared, trailing his fingers to the other side of my chest.

"Stop," I whispered.

"Is that really what you want?"

No. My body, maybe even part of my heart, wants this. But my head...

"Yes."

A challenge erupted in his eyes. "And if I sink to my knees and bury my tongue inside of you..."

Holy shit.

"Would you push me away?"

How is it possible that my throat can be this dry?

"Yes," I breathed.

A mischievous grin tugged at the corner of his lips, and when his hand twitched, it was clear that he was seriously considering putting that theory to the test. But then, with a resigned sigh, he let me go.

"You will love me again, Little Leopard."

"I do love you," I admitted. "It's the monster inside of you I can't love."

He grazed my lower lip with the pad of his thumb. Like a traitor, my mouth parted for him.

"Maybe instead of fighting against the monster, you should embrace it. Because the same man who will open your car doors for you will also annihilate anyone who ever harms you. If anyone ever lays a finger on you, I will fucking kill him."

I swallowed and stared at Hunter, his stare a tempest of fierce determination and raw emotion. I'd always known he was protective, but this was darker and more powerful, like a tornado brewing on the horizon.

"You don't mean that." My voice wavered, betraying the emotions raging within me. "You have a code."

His fingers brushed against my jawline, eliciting a tremor of warmth.

"You're my code now," he murmured. "And there's nothing in this world that could stop me from protecting you."

I swallowed hard, my heart racing as my mind told me to pull away, to put an end to this madness. But the raw passion in his gaze, the fervent promise in his voice—it was intoxicating. It was a kind of love I'd never experienced before, wild and unyielding.

"Why?" was all I could manage, my voice a whisper.

"Because," he murmured, "I love you with an all-consuming intensity."

Tears welled up in my eyes at the weight of his confession. As much as I wanted to deny it, there was a primal allure to being loved with such an intensity that he was willing to kill for me.

"It's still not right, Hunter."

His eyes searched mine. "Love isn't always rational. Sometimes it's wild, fierce, and dangerous."

His thumb breached my mouth, touching my tongue.

"These aren't just words," he said. "I've shown you what I'm willing to do for you."

"Murder isn't love," I said. "You can't romanticize it, Hunter."

"Tell me it doesn't feel good. To have a man who'd snap the neck of anyone who harmed you."

It does, but it shouldn't. It's wrong.

But I wouldn't act on these unwanted emotions.

"And if I can't love you? What then?" I asked.

His face fell as he considered this, his voice a mere whisper. "Then I will hide in the shadows and protect you for the rest of your life."

I blanched. "You'll be in prison."

Hunter looked at me for several moments before taking a step back and clearing his throat.

"I brought you food." He looked at my injuries. "And a first aid kit. Take a shower and rest."

After a few more empty seconds, Hunter stepped away.

"Wait, where are you going?" I asked.

"I have something urgent to attend to."

CHAPTER 20

Hunter

I had roughly forty-eight hours to solve two decades-old cases. Any longer, and the police might come looking for Luna. And once that happened, all hell would break loose, and any hope I had to solve anything would go up in smoke.

Including my ability to save Luna from whatever asshole was out there, threatening her over her father's case. Thankfully, I had the best PI in the country, eager to solve my father's murder.

"Mind if you tell me what this is about?" Barry Mansfield asked.

I'd thrown on a T-shirt so I looked as normal as possible, since what I was about to say was anything but.

"I appreciate you meeting with me on such short notice," I said.

"I'm happy to drive over." Barry's face monopolized my twenty-seven-inch computer monitor via a video call.

No way I could risk him coming into the house. With Luna hidden here, I'd told my staff to stay away to give her privacy after her ordeal. They didn't complain since they were still on my payroll.

"That's unnecessary, and this is too urgent to wait for you to drive over."

Barry fiddled with the pen between his fingers as my cell phone buzzed.

"I have a visitor joining us shortly," I said, looking at the text.

Barry furrowed his eyebrows. "And who might that be?"

"We'll get to that in a moment, but first, let me explain why I called you." I leaned my elbows in front of the monitor, looking sternly into the video camera. "Our timeline just escalated. Now, I know what I'm about to say may sound extreme, but I need you to listen to me."

Barry's gaze was unwavering, showing that he was paying close attention.

"We have forty-eight hours to solve two cold cases."

Barry sat back in his chair with an unreadable expression.

"And what cases would those be, sir?"

Fair enough. I had hired Barry to work on solving who had killed my father, but then I pulled him into helping me chase Franco and his team down. For all Barry knew, I was going down another rabbit hole here.

"The first is my father's case."

Barry scrubbed his jaw. "Your father's case."

"Yes."

"The one no one has solved for twenty years."

"That's the one."

"You want me to solve it in two days?"

"I *need* you to solve it in two days. Three, tops."

Barry set his pen down on his table, clasped his hands together.

"What happens in forty-eight hours?"

"I turn into a pumpkin," I said.

"Meaning?"

"Need-to-know basis, Barry."

The slight pucker to Barry's lips revealed his offense. "All due respect sir, as much as I want to work your father's case, I don't appreciate getting jacked around. So, either tell me what's going on or this will be the last time we speak."

Shit.

I couldn't tell him what was going on, obviously. But maybe I could speak in generalities and allow Barry's imagination to fill in the blanks.

"I'm in trouble," I admitted. "I've got a day or two before the shit catches up to me, and once that happens, I might not have access to my funds." Or be here anymore. "My window—our window—just shrank, so if we don't solve it within the next couple of days, it may never get solved."

Barry had admitted this case was one he'd hungered to get his hands on; letting it slip through his grasp shouldn't be something he'd do without a fight. He stared at the computer monitor, his eyes flicking down to the floor. After a few moments, he scratched the skin above his upper lip.

"Please don't ask me any more questions about it," I advised. "It's best if we keep this separate for now, for your sake."

That warning alone would probably make a strait-laced PI run for the hills. I could only hope Barry had the slight edge I'd sensed when we'd first met—a man who might be willing to bend the rules or look the other way—and hope that he'd still work with me on this.

Barry's shoulders rose with his inhale.

"You said two cold cases. What's the other?"

Did that mean Barry was on board with my father's case? Or was he just fishing around for clarification?

"You remember my friend Luna?" I said.

"Franco and his men are after her."

Were. Franco's corpse is rotting in my basement right now, but I digress.

"You remember Luna's father? Nineteen years in prison for a crime he didn't commit."

"And she was sent a letter, warning her to drop the case trying to free him," Barry recalled.

"Right. She has an important court hearing next week. A writ of habeas corpus. It's the first step to requesting a new trial."

"And you want to help her? How?"

"I have it on good word that there is evidence her father is innocent. Perhaps evidence of his innocence exists and was missed in the first trial. His public defender was fresh out of college and was up against a high-profile prosecutor with a team of people."

"Do you mind sharing where you got this tip about the evidence?"

"It's best if you don't know," I said.

Barry frowned.

"Now, I can fill you in on all the particulars. I can call my office and get you access to any files and evidence and any records you need and help escalate this. But we need to resolve both in the next two days."

Barry scratched his jaw. "Sir, I heard what happened last night from some of my cop buddies. That Luna was abducted. Shouldn't finding Franco be the priority?"

If only I had an assistant who could come drag Franco's carcass into the lake for me.

"Police are looking for Franco," I continued. "No one is looking for this mystery man, which makes it easier for him to get to Luna."

Barry tapped his pen on his desk, his voice bordering on irritation.

"Sir, even if I wanted to help you, solving even one of those cases is difficult. Impossible in that time frame."

"Let's assume for right now that there *is* evidence in those case boxes that could exonerate Luna's father. If you or your men left this second and went to the evidence locker, got every piece of evidence, and then boarded a private jet and flew to a lab who'd be willing to immediately process it..." Money helped you cut in line at private for-profit labs. I'd checked when I'd gotten desperate one time about my father's case. Matter of fact, I even had a list. "And you sat down with the analyst as they did it, I would have the results quickly, yeah?"

Barry stopped clanking his pen.

"That's not how labs work. They would make us wait in line, just like anyone else."

"Not if we flashed $200,000, they wouldn't."

Barry pursed his lips.

"I don't have time to get in line. What I do have is money—and plenty of it. I can fund as many private jets as necessary, as many bodies as you need. I can pay extra fees—"

"Bribes."

"Compensation for a rush job, to get this done."

"Sir, aren't you worried about how this will look? You're a prosecutor. Someone gets wind of this…"

"I can pay a lab analyst a hundred grand for a couple of hours of
their time. Money is no object. Arrange what you need, call who you
need to, and get this done."

I expected him to push back even more—even I could hear how
unreasonable this timeline was—but he scrubbed his face and sighed.

"You looked into her father's case already, didn't you?"

We had talked about him looking into it, but I didn't know how far
he'd gone.

He cocked his head. "I've done a cursory look."

"Did you find anything?" I pressed.

"I found some…inconsistencies, but I didn't look into them
deeper."

"Well, look now. Do a deeper dive and get your hands on all the
evidence."

Barry shifted. "You're presuming that there's evidence we can test.
What if there isn't?"

"We run parallel plays. Have a team investigate witnesses again.
And, I have a private medical examiner that I used to review my
father's autopsy in the past. I'll call him and ask him to do an independent review of the autopsy of the boy that was killed. I'd like a fresh
set of eyes on it to see what else we might be looking for."

Barry twisted his pen. It had to be a good sign. If he was going to
say no, he wouldn't look so stressed out.

"And what about your father's murder?"

"Same rules. No budget. No expense spared. I've had many autopsy
reviews of it, and all conclude the same thing—that he died how I
remembered—so nothing to be gained by doing that, but if you have
enough guys, go for it. The bigger thing to chase down is motive. Find
out what was going on in my father's life around the time of his death.
There has to be something in the case files—a statement, something—
that will point us in the right direction."

"If there was something, wouldn't other PIs have found it?"

"They weren't you," I said.

Barry's silence weighed on the room. Each passing second made my palms sweat and my throat tighten.

"I will make this worth your while, Barry. For the next forty-eight hours, money is no object. Pull every favor you have out there. If you pull off these two cases, I'll write you a check in two days for $100 million, *plus* expenses."

Barry tried to hide the widening of his eyes, but I saw a flicker of it for just a moment. He cleared his throat.

"Sir, this isn't about money. These things take time."

Still trying to be rational. Reasonable.

"Barry, if you pull this off, you'll be set for life." Or maybe retiring was too boring for a guy like him. "Or think of all the career-making cases you could solve with a hundred million dollars. You could pick the ones you *want* to work, not just the ones that pay."

Barry's face softened. Wheels turned in his eyes, and while he probably still thought this was impossible, Barry got off on solving things no one else had been able to. The thrill of it enticed him, and this was no different.

"You've already been sifting through my father's case files, so you have a baseline to jump from," I reminded him.

Barry rubbed his jaw.

"You have other people helping look into it too, don't you?" I pressed.

Barry was known for his contacts with highly skilled specialists in investigative circles.

"I asked *some* people to look into a few things, but a two-day turn-around isn't going to happen."

"Check in with them. See what they've found so far and offer them an incentive to dig faster."

Even if Barry didn't succeed, he had all-you-can-consume expenses to see what was possible. This was a treasure hunt, too delicious for him to pass up. But he shook his head, set the pen down in front of him, and folded his hands.

"I'm sorry, but—"

"Please," I interrupted.

The room seemed to grow quieter, and time seemed to stretch as Barry was caught in a silent battle between his logic and the plea in my eyes. The weight of my single word hung in the air between us as he chewed the inside of his cheek, his gaze never leaving mine. Every tick of the clock heightening the tension.

After a few seconds, Barry let out a deep sigh and frowned.

"I can't make any promises," he said. "Our chances of success are low, you know that, right?"

I cleared my throat.

Eventually, Barry spoke again, his tone laced with caution. "Tell you what. I do have to return a voice mail from a colleague who was helping me look into something. I'll see what he has to say, and as for Luna's case, I'll head to the evidence locker. But even if we do find evidence," he continued, "there is no guarantee people will drop everything, no matter how much money we throw at them."

"Which is why I'm sending you help."

He paused, his voice sounding offended. "You're sending me help."

"I know someone who I think can be…encouraging when people need a shove."

I leaned back in my seat, steepling my fingers.

"Speak of the devil." I paused, my attention snapping to the doorway. "He just walked in."

CHAPTER 21

Hunter

"The hell is going on?" Grayson's silhouette darkened my office doorway. He was a stark contrast to the summer sun outside, draped head to toe in black.

I hesitated, weighing each word before speaking.

"Barry, get started," I said, and just before hanging up, I added, "I'll call you back in a few minutes."

I pushed off my desk to approach my brother, but Luna's cell phone cut through the tension with its insistent chime. I'd been monitoring Luna's communications, ensuring no complications arose from Detective Rinaldi or others. Once I'd used Luna's facial recognition to unlock her phone the first time, changing her password had been easy.

My eyes skimmed the message, its contents pulling at my stomach. This wasn't about her whereabouts.

In Luna's eyes, it would be even more devastating.

"Damn it," I mumbled under my breath. "Wait here."

Grayson threw his hands in the air as I stormed past him. "You told me this was urgent."

From my first-floor office, I made my way up the mansion's grand staircase, glancing back to ensure Grayson hadn't followed before unlocking and opening the door.

Luna sat up in bed, eyes widening at my intrusion.

Even with everything going on, I couldn't stop my eyes from dragging over the soft contours of her freshly showered body. Again, rage pulsed through my veins at the sight of her injuries, but I swallowed it, not wanting to upset her more than I was about to. Instead, I forced myself to notice how stunning she looked, wearing nothing but a pair of boy shorts and a fitted white T-shirt she'd kept in the drawers during her stay here.

"Hey," I said, looking over my shoulder to ensure we were still alone before shutting the door. "What's on your docket Friday?"

She glared at me. "It appears I'm being held hostage against my will."

"I mean case-wise."

"If you want to know, you can make some phone calls." Her tone was tense.

"No time for calls. Which case on Friday is the most important?"

"Why?"

"Because I need a viable excuse for your absence for something."

Dammit, Luna smirked and raised an eyebrow, realizing the power shift that had just happened. I needed her to cooperate.

Sure, I could email, but I needed a damn good reason she would miss the most important meeting of her life. Otherwise, it would sound the alarms.

She stood up and crossed her arms over her chest.

"You know I don't quite remember," she said dramatically. "I would have to think on that long and hard."

"Luna," I warned, stepping closer. "Do not test me. I don't have time for this."

"I have court cases in a few hours. Not to mention, I never made it to my appointment with the mayor. Have you thought about that?"

Crap. I hadn't gotten that far yet. I needed an assistant. A hostage assistant to help me reschedule her entire calendar in a believable way. But first, I needed to deal with this nuclear bomb.

"Friday. Tell me the most important case you're working on."

Luna examined her fingernails. "I'm quite hungry."

"I'll get you more food then. Now, give me a case."

"You know what sounds delicious right now?" She wiggled her fingernails in the air. "Filet mignon. Medium well, covered in blue cheese with a side of asparagus. Could Maria bring that up to me?"

"This isn't funny, Luna. Tell me now or—"

"Or what?" She stepped even closer, and her eyes blazed, a fiery tempest of wrath swirling in their depths.

"I can just look at your schedule," I snapped.

"But that's just data. Without understanding each case, you won't have a *believable* reason that I would miss it."

"I'll guess," I snapped, my patience breaking.

"Good luck with that. Want to place an over/under wager as to when the cops show up here today when you guess wrong? I'm guessing..." She wiggled her hand in the air. "Tonight. What do you think— before or after?"

"You know I'm trying to help you!"

"By holding me hostage. Yeah, welcome to Reverse Stockholm Syndrome 101. That isn't going to work with me."

I took her chin in my hand, holding her gaze as her breath caught.

"Give me a legitimate reason you can't show up on Friday. Now."

"Why?"

I gritted my teeth. "Because the judge just emailed you. The court date for your writ of habeas corpus got moved up."

Her eyes ping-ponged between mine. And all humor fell from her face. "What?"

"It seems the judge's daughter is going to have her baby sooner than expected, so he's rearranging his calendar next week."

"He bumped up the date to Friday?" She jerked her chin from my grip.

I waited.

"As in three days from now?"

In order to be ready for that court date, she would need to spend the next two and a half days preparing both herself and her father for that hearing. Obviously, she couldn't do that while she was here.

"Why would he move me up? Why not push me back?" She began pacing.

"Best guess, your buddy, the mayor, pulled some strings to make this happen faster." Thanks to her being his little puppet in his hunt for the Windy City Vigilante. "But it doesn't matter. Point is, give me a legitimate reason you can't make it Friday so I can email him to push it back."

"You can't do that!"

"I have no choice."

"If you do that, it sends the message to the judge that this case isn't important enough to me."

"Legally, that doesn't matter. The judge will still hear your case loud and clear when he's back."

"We both know what a huge pain in the ass it is for a judge to move a case up in his schedule. If I don't accept the updated time, he's going to be irritated as hell, and we can both argue what's legal or not, but you know as well as I do that a judge's opinion weighs *heavily* into some of his verdicts!"

"We'll have to cross that bridge later."

My Little Leopard marched up to me and grabbed *my* chin this time. Holy hell, the fire from her grip made me want to throw her on the bed and ravage her.

"You will not take this from me," she snapped. "I am showing up to that court date. I am going to prepare for it. This is the most important thing in my life, Hunter! If you care about me at all, you will not do this."

"We've talked about this. I can't let you go."

"If I have to choose between looking the other way—*not* reporting you to the cops for three days—and having the first legitimate shot at getting my father out of prison, I choose my father. I don't even care if that makes me a bad person. The police will catch up to you soon enough. So, I swear. I'll say nothing, Hunter. I won't tell a soul. Let. Me. Out."

She didn't see it now, but I wasn't robbing her of the chance to get her father out of prison. I was just making sure she was safe *and* helping him at the same time.

"The best chance of getting your father out is having my private investigator work it."

"So have him work it. But in the meantime, let me go."

I couldn't do that. When it came to her father, all of Luna's rational thinking went out the window. She might be okay with spending years in prison for being an accomplice after the fact by not turning me in, but I would not let that happen to her.

Her cries and pleas grated on me, challenging my resolve, but I would protect her. Even if she hated me for it.

And she was forgetting one very important point.

"This isn't just about your father," I reminded her. "Franco said someone hired him to kill you over your dad's case. We have to figure out who that is and why they'd be willing to kill you over it."

"I don't trust Franco Hopkins, and I'm not letting something that lunatic said scare me into *not* freeing my dad!"

"It wasn't just what he said, and you know it. Someone sent you a letter, telling you to drop the case or you will be killed. I can't let you out of my sight until I get to the bottom of that threat."

"I've worked my whole life to get to this moment, Hunter. I will not back down now. Not out of fear, not out of love, nothing. Nothing will keep me from the courtroom on Friday."

"I'll come up with an excuse by myself." I decided.

As I turned to walk away, she grabbed my wrist, spinning me around, her eyes welling.

"Don't do this!"

Seeing those tears, a torrent of emotions crashed over me. Each drop was an accusation, tempting me to surrender to her raw pain.

But doing that risked her life.

"I'm sorry, Luna."

I carefully pulled my wrist out of her fragile grasp and walked toward the door.

She made a break for it, but I managed to grab her, the lingering

trace of vanilla in her freshly damp hair meeting my nose. Her determination surged through every kick and punch she threw, and I had
to focus my grip on her soft skin to be firm yet cautious so I didn't
hurt her further. With a focused effort, I lifted and redirected her
struggles, our tangled dance culminating with her landing softly on
the bed.

Where I gently pinned her down.

She pounded on my chest with her tiny fists, but it felt like the
flutters of a hummingbird.

"You need to trust me, Luna."

But those hazel eyes—light brown with specks of green—tightened, and I hated that they began to shimmer.

"Let me go, or so help me," she said, "I will get revenge, Hunter. I
will tell everyone what you've done. I will make it my personal
mission to ruin you."

Her words struck deep, a pang of unexpected hurt coursing
through me, and right behind it, guilt—holding her against her will
like this wasn't how it was supposed to be.

"I'm going to keep you safe, Luna. If it's the last thing I do."

I shoved off the bed and locked the door behind me.

But this time, Luna wasn't quiet. She banged her fists against the
door, screaming, "Let me out! Hunter, Let me out of here!"

Wonderful.

Grayson was going to hear that.

I was already going to have a hard time explaining to my brother
what I needed him to do, and now he could probably hear my hostage
pleading for her release.

CHAPTER 22

Hunter

"What the hell is going on?" Grayson's eyes darted to the ceiling, where, upstairs, Luna pounded on the guest bedroom door, shouting profanities. "You've got her locked up in there?"

Understandably, Luna was upset that her father's court case needed to get pushed and that she wasn't allowed to leave just yet. But hopefully soon, she'd want to digest everything else I'd told her. Each confession that had tumbled from my lips had been a vulnerable piece of my fractured heart, and I hoped she'd at least try to understand.

Every fiber of my being yearned for her acceptance. In a world full of chaos, she was my anchor, and if she didn't at least try to process my most intimate revelations, it would cut me to the core. No matter how irrational that might sound.

My hand tightened as I raked it through my hair and sank into the chair, exhaling heavily.

The sun was starting its ascent in the sky, like a burning reminder that just twenty-four hours ago, it had risen with Luna in my arms. Before Franco had taken her, before she'd stumbled onto the scene last night.

Just like when my father had passed, I wished I'd had a warning at that moment that it could be the last time she'd ever look at me like I wasn't a monster. So I could have savored her adoring gaze one last time.

"I'm in trouble, Grayson." The ticking clock on the wall seemed louder than ever, each second echoing my growing desperation. "I only have two days to get some shit done, and I need your help to do it."

It wasn't surprising that Grayson narrowed his eyes; I had never uttered words like this to him before.

The first rays of dawn crept through the window, painting the room in soft, golden hues—a stark contrast to the chaos ravaging my head. I needed to reschedule meetings, and let my team know I wasn't showing up to work today. Or tomorrow.

If Detective Rinaldi was keeping tabs on me, she would notice that both me and Luna were absent. But I'd have to worry about that later.

Bam, bam, bam. "Let me out, asshole!" The sound of her voice made my stomach churn with guilt and anxiety. Luna's fists would be bloodied if she kept this up much longer.

As Grayson folded his arms over his chest, I tried to gauge his expression. Hopefully, my instincts had been right—that I could trust my brother with this.

His voice held a hint of that protective older brother from our childhood.

"Hunter, what's going on?"

I explained how Franco had tried to kill her and had said someone hired him to end Luna because she was working to get her father's conviction overturned. That others would likely come after her, too.

I hesitated, the weight of my secret identity pressing on my chest, but I held back, giving Grayson only half the story. Grayson would find out who I was soon enough, but anyone who helped me *after* they uncovered my identity might have the book thrown at them. I also left out that Franco Hopkins was decomposing in my basement right now. It was bad enough that I was asking Grayson to get involved in something that might get him in trouble; I didn't need to make him an accomplice to homicide after the fact.

"You're holding her to keep her *safe?*" Grayson pressed skeptically.

"That's one of the reasons, yes."

"And another?"

I cracked my knuckles. "Let's just say I obtained that information in an illegal way." *By torturing a man.* "And if anyone finds out what it is, I'll be staring at prison bars."

Grayson glared at me, and looked up. "And the girl knows this?"

When his eyes met mine again, I nodded.

"If you let her leave, you go to prison?" he clarified.

"When you say it like that, it sounds more sinister than it is."

Grayson looked up at the ceiling again. "What are you going to do with her?"

"I'll let her go when she's safe," I said.

My brother studied me.

Bam, bam, bam. "I'm going to snap your dick off and throw it in the lake, Hunter!"

"What do you need from me?" he asked.

I sighed in relief, because with that one question, my brother had pledged his support.

"Whoever wants her dead is about to find out last night's hit failed and that the timeline shrank. The hearing got moved up to this Friday, and while I'll try to get it pushed back, the person's likely about to get more desperate."

"You need my help to *protect* her?"

Bam, bam, bam, bam. "I'll tell the blogs you have a little tiny penis! Like a baby carrot!"

Her shriek was interrupted by my cell phone ringing. If it were anyone else calling, I wouldn't have answered, but when Barry's number flashed on the screen, my entire body tensed.

"If you're about to say you've reconsidered..."

"No, sir," he said.

Thank hell.

"I just returned that voice mail I mentioned." Barry's voice was tighter than earlier. And that was saying something. "For the record, this was set in motion *prior* to your accelerated timeline, but it's *possible* we have a clue." He elongated the word *possible* to diminish whatever he was about to say. "It's most probable that it's a dead end, to be honest, but it's worth digging deeper."

"What kind of clue?"

"Or a dead end," Barry repeated. "I have a colleague who's an excellent forensic accountant. When I started reviewing your father's case, I asked him to look through the company's official financial records, filed the year of your father's death. Figured it was a long shot," Barry continued, "but he specializes in untangling complex financial data. And he found something...curious."

I stilled. "You have my attention."

"It seems some money went missing that year."

"Missing money?" Grayson and I locked eyes. "I don't remember reading about this in any of the police reports. And I don't remember any of the private investigators coming across this."

"I don't know that any of them utilized a forensic accountant. And like I said, it could be nothing. Could be as simple as a poorly documented accounting transaction, but with your permission, I'd like to request more information about that transaction from the accountant. You're a large shareholder of the company, correct?"

I leaned back in my chair. Upstairs, it sounded like Luna was trying to dismantle my door, piece by piece.

"I am."

"Shareholders, particularly those with a significant stake in the company, have the right to access financial information and can request additional details to assess the company's financials."

"I'll call the lead accountant now. He's our personal accountant as well, so having him send you whatever you need shouldn't be an issue."

Bam, bam, bam. "Hunter Lockwood!"

"Everything okay over there?" Barry questioned.

"Fine. Let me try to patch in the accountant."

And so I did, introducing them to each other.

"Jeff," I said, "I want you to give detailed financial records to Barry Mansfield. Specifically, more details about an accounting transaction that took place the year my father died. Barry, send him the transaction in question; I'll provide you his email."

Jeff hesitated. "I...sir?"

"It's possible money went missing the year my father died. Jeff, do you recall any unusual accounting transactions?"

"I..." Jeff hesitated. "It's been a long time, but I can look into it and give Barry what he needs if that's what you want."

"It is."

I ensured both men had each other's contact information before I disconnected the call.

Grayson widened his stance, staring at me as I steepled my fingers. "You still haven't explained exactly what you need from me."

"The PI is going to be talking to some people. He may need help... motivating them to speak."

Grayson's jaw tightened. "What the hell?"

I leaned forward, resting my elbows on the desk.

"I know you're into some bad shit, Grayson," I said, noting the narrowing of his eyes. "And after you vanished that first time and made it clear you didn't want to talk about it, I haven't asked you about what you do since. Because I never wanted you to ask what screwed up stuff I'm involved in. But I get the impression you're the type of guy that could motivate people if they needed it, yes?"

I remembered Grayson as that giggling kid, chasing me through the house with our toy guns. But after Dad's death, darkness settled in him, erasing traces of that joyful boy.

Mom had been so damn worried about him, and then he really took a turn. Got involved with some shady characters. She tried to hire all kinds of therapists and who knew what else to try to help Grayson, but he slipped further and further through her grasp.

Hardening to stone in front of her eyes.

As an adult, he had no job that I knew of. Though that wasn't terribly surprising, given he was a billionaire like me, but I knew he was up to something. His absences were frequent and mysterious. No explanations, no trace, just sudden reappearances with that guarded look in his eyes. Whenever I asked him where he'd been, he'd always been evasive.

The guy was always alone. No friends, girlfriends, or dates.

"What are you asking me to do, exactly?" Grayson pressed.

"Barry will be asking some people to pull off the impossible over the next couple of days. I will throw all the money I can to encourage them, but if anyone still won't cooperate, I may need you to"—I tilted my head—"convince them cooperating is in their best interest."

Grayson scrubbed the side of his face. "And how encouraging do you want me to be, exactly?"

"Non-lethal." Not sure if I needed to clarify that. Better safe than sorry, I guess. "But whatever motivation you use, it has to be quick. We don't have time for someone to be motivated slowly." In other words, torture.

"This isn't what I normally do, Hunter."

"And what is it that you normally do, Grayson?"

"You really want to have this conversation?"

"Do you?"

He licked his lips. "You're asking me to get involved in this and won't even tell me everything that's going on?"

Grayson looked up at the ceiling as Luna's pounding ended. Finally.

"Look, I'm into something deep, but like I said, accomplice after the fact is a nasty charge. Will you help me or not?"

"Are you going to kill her?" He pointed up.

I blanched—both at the casualness of his tone and the horrific thought.

"No. I love her."

A deep sigh escaped Grayson's lips.

"Two days of work?" he clarified.

See—most people would probably go on a rant about a moral, ethical code, not worried about how much time this would eat out of their life.

Would I ever find out what my brother was up to?

"Two days."

Grayson scratched his temple. "And Barry?"

Hmm. My gut said he probably bent the rules from time to time to get what he needed, but for now, I couldn't assume he'd go along with this.

"Keep your *tactics* discreet from him. Tell him you have billionaire connections or something. I don't care, just…get it done."

CRASH.

I shot up from my chair.

"What the hell was that?" Grayson asked, but I was already running out of my office. Upstairs.

"Luna!" I dug the keys out of my pocket. "Luna?"

She didn't answer. Instead, another crash erupted.

I opened the door to a fluttering curtain and shards of glass scattered on the floor. My heart sank just before she leaped out the window.

CHAPTER 23

Luna

My voice cracked with desperation as I yelled, "Open this door!" The rawness in my throat betrayed how many times I had already screamed, and my hands were seriously aching from pounding for so long.

In return, all I got was a haunting silence, wrapping around me like a frozen grip, emphasizing the vast distance between Hunter and me.

This couldn't be how this all ended for my father.

The moisture in my eyes blurred my vision, distorting the door into a painfully familiar scene from my past.

"No!" I cried.

I clutched my father tighter.

"It's okay, Luna." Dad's voice was choked with emotion. He kissed the side of my head, my racing heart momentarily calming from his familiar scent. It bore the deep, musky undertones of classic aftershave—a mixture of old leather and spicy tobacco that blended with fresh-cut grass from mowing the lawn. "You can let me go."

My voice broke, tears flowing freely now. "Don't take him! He's innocent! My daddy...he's never hurt a soul."

Neighbors were gathered on their lawn, women clutching their chests at the scene before them, but no one was helping. They were letting these men take my dad.

The officer yanked me one more time, so harshly, it hurt my ribs while another one grabbed my dad and slammed him to the ground.

Dad groaned as the guy twisted Dad's arms behind his back and locked his wrists with handcuffs.

"Let him go!" I begged.

I kicked the officer's legs and punched his arms, but he didn't let me go. Instead, Mom helped hold me back while the officers yanked my dad into a standing position and shoved him in the back of a squad car.

Dad looked over at me through the little window. He tried to smile reassuringly, which broke my heart—that he'd try to make me feel better when he must be scared. His eyes started to shimmer as he mouthed the words, "I love you."

As one of the two squad cars pulled away, Dad stared at me, at Mom, at the house, and the life that he may never see again. I used to hide behind Daddy's legs, knowing he'd protect me from anything. But now, he looked vulnerable, shrinking in that cold, mechanical vehicle, and as the car began to take my daddy away from me, the world shattered.

"Don't go..." I whispered.

When the officer finally set me down, I ran after the squad car, my little legs pounding against the pavement, but I couldn't keep up with the car.

"Daddy!" I cried.

The harsh wail of the squad car's siren faded, replaced by the gut-wrenching quiet of our neighborhood. I stood there trembling, struggling to breathe.

What if they never realize they made a mistake? What if they never bring him back?

I thought police officers were supposed to help people. Why are they hurting Daddy?

I balled my little fists and picked up a rock. I threw it as hard as I could

at the last place I'd seen the police car—watching as it landed unsatisfyingly
on the empty road.

In an instant, my anchor was gone. The world seemed to loom larger,
every shadow deeper, making me feel like an insignificant speck in a universe
that had suddenly turned dark and unfeeling.

Tears spilled down my cheeks as I gazed at the empty road in front of my
house, my heart heavy with sorrow too great for my little shoulders to bear.

I promised at that moment that I would do anything to get my father
back, and now here it was, the one court date that could change
everything for him.

But any second, Hunter was going to contact that judge and jeopardize everything.

I needed to get the hell out of this room before he could do that.

And there was only one way to do it.

I stripped the bed of its sheets, tied the fitted one to the flat one,
and secured one end around the ancient headboard that I hoped was
sturdy enough to support my weight. The makeshift rope wasn't long
enough to reach the outside courtyard, but it would make my drop a
hell of a lot shorter.

With my heart pumping, I grabbed the writing chair, swung it
back, and crashed it into the window. Glass shattered outward, a glit-
tering downpour of razor-edged confetti, the high-pitched symphony
of destruction echoing in my ears.

In the distance, the rhythmic sound of Lake Michigan's waves
softly crashing against a jagged bluff whispered promises of freedom.
The water itself was a deep shade of cobalt, shimmering with reflec-
tions of the dawning sun, stretching endlessly until it met a pastel
morning sky that was just beginning to light up in hues of pink and
orange.

Within seconds, footsteps came running up the grand staircase.

The hole in the window wasn't big enough for me to get through,
so I swung the chair again, cracking against the broken shards.

"Luna!" Hunter snapped from the other side of the door. "Luna?"

Unfurling the sheet rope I'd created, I hurled it through the opening and out into the daylight.

The click of the lock preceded the door swinging open.

Hunter entered, his eyes wide with shock as he watched me grab my rope and launch myself through the jagged window.

Beneath me, the uneven cobblestone was encased by a vibrant border of flowers, whose colors burst with vivid reds, yellows, and purples. Their delicate fragrance—a mix of sweet petals and fresh morning dew—offered a soothing contrast to the metallic tang of blood that had tainted my senses all night.

As I clung to the rope, the fabric was so silky, that I had to tighten my wavering grip. An overwhelming vertigo took hold as the ground loomed closer—a vast expanse of stone—yet I couldn't help but smile with a wild, triumphant glint that I was free.

But as I ran out of rope and looked down, my stomach plummeted. I was dangling from the edge of the bedsheet, but the stone ground below me was much farther than I thought, a menacing abyss threatening to annihilate me if I jumped.

And the rope...the knot I'd tied loosened as the fabric shifted beneath my sweaty hands.

"Luna!" Hunter's frantic voice came from below me this time as my legs dangled in the air, nearly twenty feet above an unforgiving landing.

Unable to let myself drop, I tried to pull myself up, but my lack of upper body strength made it all but a joke.

"Luna!" Hunter said.

"Hold on!" a voice shouted from above me.

Grayson dangled his upper body through the window. He grabbed the makeshift rope and tried to pull me up, but the knot loosened once more. The little tip of fabric was now only an inch away from slipping through the middle of the binding and sending me into a free fall.

I gritted my teeth, my fingernails stinging from gripping the fabric, my feet kicking around wildly, trying to find a position to help me.

When I reached up again, time seemed to stretch infinitely. The tip of the sheet hesitated at the edge of the knot, leaving me suspended in fate's hands for an eternal second. Then, as if the universe had made its decision, it slipped free.

The world became a blur, colors and shapes melting together in a dizzying whirlwind. I braced for the jarring impact, but instead, a warm, solid embrace halted my descent.

Gradually, the chaos ebbed, and I became acutely aware of the rhythmic heartbeat against my chest, the comforting grip of strong arms encircling me.

My vision cleared, and I was met with Hunter's intense blue eyes, full of concern and something deeper. His hand cradled my cheek, his thumb grazing my skin.

"Luna," he whispered, his voice hoarse with concern. "Are you okay?"

Hunter's steely gaze was filled with alarm as he scanned my body.

"Did you break anything?"

The intensity of our combined stares sent a flash of heat down my spine, and I shook my head, unable to find the words.

He sighed in relief, his gaze softening as his lips grazed my temple, sending sparks through me before he pulled back and allowed me to stand up on my own.

"Hunter, you got her?" Grayson shouted from above.

Hunter looked up and nodded and then locked his eyes with me. It was haunting, really, watching them darken like this—from relief to boiling hot anger.

"What were you thinking, Luna?"

I clenched my fists. How dare he snap at me like that after all he'd put me through. And did I seriously need to point out that my only chance of helping my dad was if I got away?

I pivoted and took off running to my right, ignoring the screaming pains of my body, but Hunter snared me in his arms and turned me around to face him.

"You could've been killed!" Hunter snapped.

"What choice did I have?"

"If you died hurling yourself from that window"—Hunter swung his arm toward the broken glass—"what would happen to your father, then?"

I bit my lip, my throat swelling.

Hunter's bare chest heaved up and down as a gentle breeze wiggled his dark hair, carrying the scent of freshly cut grass. He stared at me silently, putting his hands on his hips, and looking at the ground.

A bird's happy song sliced through the air between us, and after a few seconds, Hunter swung his gaze back to my face. He licked his lower lip and pulled it between his teeth before finally asking me a question in a frustrated tone.

"You're just going to keep trying to escape, aren't you?"

Silence.

"Come on," he sighed, motioning toward the mansion.

CHAPTER 24

Luna

T he morning light, filtering through the sheer curtains, cast a gentle luminescence on the white marble counter I was sitting on as dust particles danced in the sunbeam, like frozen remnants of the close call I'd just had falling from that window.

Hunter and I were in his bathroom, where he'd laid out a first aid kid next to me. His gaze raked over my body, each glance leaving a trace of heat on my skin, making me more aware of every bruise and cut—his brow furrowing deeper with each discovery. Then he delicately picked up both of my wrists, turning my arms over, his lips thinning when he saw a handful of fresh scratches along my skin.

"You saved me," I choked out, the weight of gratitude and surprise tangling with the pain in my voice.

For a brief moment, Hunter locked eyes with me before he snapped them away and retrieved a fresh washcloth from the drawer, wetting it with water and soap.

The scent of fragrant lilies mingled as drops of water fell with a rhythmic patter into the sink, as if echoing my heartbeat.

"I'm the only person that knows your identity." I literally held the keys to his freedom, if not his life, in my hands, and he didn't even need to do anything to make that problem go away. I had jumped out of that window of my own accord. All he had to do was let me drop, and if my skull had hit the stone below, this might've been over for him.

"You could've let me fall," I said. "Your complication would have been over."

Hunter shook his head.

"If you think for a moment I'd ever allow something bad to happen to you, then you still don't understand the depths of my feelings."

He gave me a slight frown, like he realized how holding me hostage was giving off all sorts of mixed signals on that.

With the sharp sting of antiseptic biting into my scrapes and cuts, I watched him. His furrowed brow, the tightness around his eyes, his mouth drawn into a thin, grim line. All of it was evidence of Hunter's deep conflict, as if he was battling demons of his own while trying to heal mine.

The room fell silent, save for our shared, ragged breaths, and eventually, his grip on my arm loosened, his touch lingering just a moment too long before he retrieved a roll of white gauze, wrapping it around the cut he'd just cleaned up.

None of my new wounds were deep, luckily.

But the ones from Franco...those Hunter studied with a frown, cradling my arm tenderly.

"They stopped bleeding," he said. "But you still need stitches for the skin to repair properly."

"You should get the one on your shoulder checked out, too," I said, nodding toward it with my chin. "You're hurt."

Hunter glanced at it but shook his head.

"Hunter, let me see how bad it is," I insisted.

"Not until every cut on your body has been attended to."

Hunter moved on to the next wound, applying antibacterial ointment and covering it with an oversized Band-Aid. He moved on to another one on the back of my arm.

Each touch was gentle, and caring, yet with an undercurrent of something forbidden, lighting up pathways of sensation I wasn't ready to understand. Its warmth defied time and logic, as if Hunter's affection remained imprinted on my soul. He looked over my arms, and my legs, examined my scalp with his fingertips, the back of my neck.

"Okay, that was the last one," I said. "Now let me see your shoulder."

I tugged at Hunter's pants to pull him closer to me, widening my legs so he could stand between my knees, waiting for him to pull his shirt off.

For a moment, I became mesmerized by the gorgeous muscles blanketing his torso. His lined abdomen was just inches from my reach.

"I need you to be shorter," I said.

Hunter hesitated before slowly sinking to his knees.

It wasn't lost on me, the position we were in. Under different circumstances, this could be sensual, his face so close to my inner thighs.

Just as it had been when he'd held my legs apart on the hood of his car, just as it'd been when he'd pulled my body to his mouth on that staircase.

I forced myself to ignore the intimate memories drifting through my head and instead reached for a cloth, dunking it in soapy water before using it to clean his shoulder.

"I'm sorry." The tone of his voice made me freeze, his agony piercing my heart as Hunter dropped his gaze. "I'm sorry. The choices I've made in my life have hurt you."

It took me a second to find my voice. "Hunter…"

He held his palm up. "I'm not saying this to play with your emotions or convince you to stay with me. I just…" He took in a deep breath. "You deserve an apology after what I've put you through."

I believed him. His words were as sincere as his profession to always protect me.

Silence stretched on between us, eclipsed only by the sound of the bandage wrapper I forced myself to retrieve from the first aid kit. I don't know why this kit contained both normal and child Band-Aids, but somehow, the hot-pink Hello Kitty Band-Aid seemed like the perfect choice. I placed antibacterial ointment on it and gently secured the thing to the serial killer's muscular shoulder.

Hunter looked at the cartoon cat with her pink bow and shot me an irritated yet amused glare.

Before standing up.

I remained frozen on the counter, unsure of what I was feeling, unwilling to let this moment go. He looked to be wrestling with the same thing as he brought his warm hand up against my cheek.

"I failed my father," he whispered, "but I won't fail you. I can't allow anything to happen to you, Luna."

My eyes stung.

"I'm sorry, but I can't let you leave. It's too dangerous."

I shut my eyes, fighting back tears. "Hunter…"

"Sometimes judges just want a public setting to decline motions. Don't get your hopes up."

"He's willing to listen. That's a huge step. Why are you being so negative?"

"I know this judge. It's unlikely he'll let you plead your case for a new trial on Friday."

"I know that. He'll set another date to listen to the evidence for a new trial, but to do that, he needs to hear a reason. Friday is about moving the ball down the field while a judge is allowing it to be in play."

Hunter's lips turned down. "I can't let you go, Luna. Not with those men after you, but I can't have you jumping out of two-story windows, either."

I shifted back an inch. "What are you saying?"

Hunter's eyes met mine. "Let's negotiate."

I studied the contours of his jawline. "Negotiate what?"

"I'll give you the tools and resources you need to prep for the hearing."

Hope swelled within me. "You didn't already postpone the court date on Friday?"

"I hadn't gotten to it yet. You'll stay here. But I'll give you access to a computer and anything else you need to work your father's case."

I narrowed my eyes. "How do I know you're not trying to trick me?"

"Into what?"

"I don't know. But if I have a computer, I could fire off emails, sending the cavalry," I said.

"First of all, if you do that, you and I both know you'll sit in the interrogation room for the better part of three days. Instead of being able to prepare for Friday. Second of all, you still have criminal deniability in not turning me in. I'm still holding you hostage. Surely, you're terrified of making a move against me." He raised his eyebrow.

Unreal.

My lip curled up slightly, and my voice attempted to maintain a semblance of neutrality but betrayed it with a playful undertone as I questioned, "And if I say no?"

"Then I'll have to find somewhere else to keep you where there are no windows. And no paths of escape."

The murder room. Where Franco was probably decomposing.

Hunter was going to hold me against my will, no matter what I did. The only thing up for debate was what kind of amenities I had.

But most importantly, if I'd be able to help my dad.

I chewed the inside of my cheek, trying to rush through possible scenarios.

"Fine," I said. "But if you screw me on this, I'll push *you* out a window, Hunter Lockwood."

A small smile crept across his face.

In that suspended moment, our eyes locked. It felt like the world had shifted on its axis, bringing us to a crossroads neither of us could have anticipated.

Before I could digest the unexpected intimacy, a cell phone buzzed —my cell phone, I realized, once he pulled it out of his pocket.

Whatever its contents, his lips thinned, and his teeth clenched.

"What?" I asked.

He snapped his eyes to me. "Whoever sent you that letter must have heard your court date was moved up."

He handed me the phone.

Unknown: I warned you to drop the case. Guess you need proof I'll follow through with my threat. Ticktock, Luna. The time is ticking.

CHAPTER 25

Luna

"It was a burner phone." Barry's voice crackled through the line. Hunter, restless, traced a path around the room, each step mirroring the drumbeat of tension while Grayson, in contrast, slouched against the wall.

I was impressed that it had only taken Barry a couple of hours to come back to us with this.

"I'm having my team trace it now, but if it's the same guy that sent that threatening letter to Luna, I'm not optimistic we'll find anything."

"Get optimistic," Hunter snapped.

Gone was the vulnerable man I'd caught a glimpse of in the bathroom, replaced by the fiercely protective alpha I both feared and admired.

"He hid all traces of himself with that letter, and I suspect he did the same thing here," Barry said.

Hunter's eyes darkened, voice firm. "Then find out who's slipping him info from the courthouse. Someone there knows more than they should. Check with the clerks, their significant others, and family members. Work your way outward from the judge. Someone who has access to his calendar."

"Leaving the evidence locker now," Barry said.

Hunter paused. "Have you found anything else with Mr. Payne's case that might help us?"

Barry let a long silence pass. "I may have found something, but it's premature."

"Tell me anyway."

"Sir, it might not—"

Hunter's impatience was palpable. "Minutes matter, Barry. Spill it."

Barry took a measured breath. "There was one piece of evidence that caught my eye," he explained. "The pants the victim was wearing the night he was killed."

"What about them?" I asked.

Barry hesitated. "When you asked me to look into the letter that threatened Ms. Payne, I'd pulled the case files, just so I could be thorough and to get my bearings," Barry said. "At the time I'd read the file, I was just trying to familiarize myself with the case, but I'd made a note of something. I wondered why the pants hadn't been tested."

"And?" Hunter asked impatiently.

"It seems there was a small amount of paint on the jeans," Barry said.

My heart thudded, hope and anxiety waging a war.

"It could be nothing," Barry cautioned. "Like I said, it's premature to presume anything."

"But you think it means something."

"I think it might," Barry clarified. "My guess is, the police were focused on finding the murder weapon, so the items sent off for testing were objects they'd found around the body and in that alley. A pipe, a large rock, a beer bottle. But no one tested the kid's jeans. It surprised me they didn't rule out what kind of paint it was and how it got there."

"Why didn't they test it?" I asked.

Barry cleared his throat. "I can't be sure, but I think the police were under pressure to move fast and neglected it. The prosecutor focused on evidence that would support his case."

"What do you think the paint means?" I asked.

"I'd rather not speculate," Barry said. "That's what got your father into this mess to begin with. But I have a lab lined up ready to test it today."

A surge of optimism took flight, wings fluttering like a trapped butterfly.

"Meanwhile, I left a message with an M.E. to have a second review of the autopsy. Told him it was urgent, so hoping he calls me back soon."

"Good," Hunter said. "If you get any pushback on the evidence, you call me right away. I'll pull strings. Same thing with the M.E. And while you do that, send several of your guys to the courthouse. Find out who had access to the judge's schedule or this case file."

"I will, sir, but I want to caution you again. The time frame we're working with…"

"I know," Hunter said. "Call me as soon as you have an update."

Hunter ended the call.

"I need to call my dad, and get him prepped for court on Friday," I said.

Hunter's jaw clenched, veins prominent against his temple.

"Hunter, I'm not debating this again."

"The threat…"

"Doesn't change anything. Except for the urgency," I amended. "I'm doing this no matter what, so the longer it drags out, the more time whoever this guy is has to come up with threats or whatever else they plan to do. The faster this resolves, the less time they have to act. So, speed is our asset, not theirs."

Hunter must have seen the determination on my face, because he thinned his lips and didn't argue further. Instead, he leaned down so his mouth was next to my ear, his breath tickling my skin as he whispered for only the two of us to hear.

"I can survive never finding out who killed my father if I have to. But I cannot survive if anything happens to you, Luna."

Hunter tilted his head so his gaze could caress my own, and it was there—a silent assurance that he meant every word. I melted in the depth of his eyes, my heart swelling with the shift in my emotions.

Memories of Hunter's chilling actions battled against his warmth, the sharp edges of horror blurring, overshadowed by the tenderness radiating off of him.

And as he continued to stare at me, the reasons I couldn't, shouldn't love Hunter began to crumble like a fragile sand castle before the crashing waves. His words lingered in the air, vibrant and heavy. I had told myself that feeling this way again was impossible, that I could remain immune to his love. But here I was, heart pounding, drowning in a wave of affection.

Transporting me back in time, back to our moments of laughter and whispered promises. The pain, the heartache, the emptiness— they were all there, but beneath them surged a powerful tide of love that I had believed I could bury too deep to resurrect.

And in the deafening silence that followed, I realized something with a terrifying clarity: I could never stop loving him.

But it was as shocking as it was tragic, because what realistic future did we have together?

"I wish I could talk you out of this, for your own safety," Hunter said. "But I know how much this means to you." Straightening up, Hunter looked every bit the protector. "Tell me what you need, Luna."

He was with me, every step of the way. A lump lodged in my throat, making my voice waver.

"I need to speak with my father."

CHAPTER 26
Luna

"My dad will call within the next ten minutes," I said. So far, everything was going smoothly. I rescheduled all of my appointments for the rest of the week. Yes, Grayson and Hunter stood there to ensure I said nothing that would signal I was in trouble, as they did when I called the prison and lined up a phone call between me and my father, but whatever.

Things were moving in the right direction, and Hunter was actively working with Barry, getting all the dominoes lined up in my father's case.

I was set up in Hunter's dining room, reviewing all the material to prepare for the hearing. Grayson had been kind enough to go to the cottage and retrieve the boxes I had stored in my living room, which were now spread out on the table.

Grayson set my laptop and phone down with a warning glance, and when he moved against the wall behind me, he kept me locked in his gaze.

I opened a blank email on my phone, my heartbeat accelerating.

Could I fire off a quick email before Grayson could stop me?

My fingers hesitated over the keys. Did I want to? Technically, I was still being held against my will, but after that time with Hunter in the bathroom and the moment we'd shared earlier, the energy had changed. Plus, Hunter was helping me with my case—a lot—so turning him in meant hurting my dad.

Did hesitating make me a bad person?

"Don't do something stupid, Luna," Grayson said sternly.

I looked over my shoulder at him—wondering what all he knew about Hunter and why he seemed so...dangerously intimidating.

He pulled his buzzing cell from his pocket.

"Yeah?" he answered, and a few seconds later, asked, "Who is it?" Silence. "I'll get her away from the..." Grayson paced. "Right." He fastened his eyes onto me. "And if he refuses?"

Grayson pinched the bridge of his nose and exhaled through clenched teeth. He shoved his phone back into his pocket with a scowl.

"We have a problem," he said.

I followed his gaze out the window, seeing the car ambling up the driveway. It parked, and when the door opened, Sean stepped out.

What the hell is Sean doing here?

"You need to say whatever you need to, to make him leave," Grayson warned.

As I met his glare, I couldn't shake the sinister vibe he was giving me, a dread filling the pit of my stomach. I wondered what threat lay buried in his words, but something told me I didn't want to know the answer.

I stood, putting my cell into my back pocket, and as I tentatively walked to the front door and opened it, Grayson put a hand on my lower back like a looming force.

"Sean," I said. "What are you doing here?"

It was times like this that Sean's massive size overwhelmed me. When you had a body that was six foot four and built of solid muscle, you don't shy away from fighting with other men. Today, he sported a fitted Cubs T-shirt that emphasized his broad chest, paired with faded jeans and worn tennis shoes, and his sandy-blond hair was styled as usual—tall and voluminous on top, tapered to a neat buzz on the sides.

"Jesus." Sean closed the distance between us and tilted my chin up to the side to get a better look at my face. "I heard Franco hurt you, but holy crap."

His blond hair danced in a breeze.

"You heard?"

Sean glared at the man invading my space.

He reached down and took my hand, walking ten feet from the front door, where Grayson remained a sinister statue, watching Sean's gaze slowly take in every detail of my appearance.

"Are you okay, Luna?"

"I'm fine. But I'm swamped. My dad's court date got moved up to Friday, so I'm in a mad scramble, preparing for it. I appreciate you coming to check on me, but I can't talk right now. I'll call you later, okay?"

"Luna, wait."

The severity of his tone made me freeze. I turned around and looked at my longtime friend, remembering what he'd said to me the last time we spoke.

I was in the car on the way to work, about to get kidnapped by Franco and his men, and I had called Sean, stressing that Hunter was keeping something from me. That was before I knew Hunter was the Vigilante, but Sean had said he was out of town.

But just before he hung up, I had heard the "L" train in the background. Which meant Sean had been lying about where he was, and now here he stood, looking stressed as hell.

"There's something I need to tell you." Sean looked at the doorway where Grayson was glaring at him.

"What is it?"

"Can we go for a drive?"

"Can it wait?"

"No," he said. "It's important, Luna."

I searched his eyes for a hint at whatever this was.

Sean rocked from his left foot to his right, looking from me to the mansion and then back again. "I lied to you when I told you I went out of town."

"Why?"

"Because I didn't want you to know what I was looking into. I honestly figured it was a dead end. I get a lot of bogus tips that I need to check out with cases, and I've learned over the years to keep some of that to myself. Especially if it will upset someone I care about, because nine out of ten times, tips lead to nothing. I didn't want to hurt our friendship by making an accusation."

"What kind of accusation?"

Sean bit the inside of his cheek. "I still should have told you I was looking into it, especially since you were fishing around..."

"Looking into what, Sean?" I tried to hide my nervous impatience.

"Luna, you encouraged me to try to find the identity of the Windy City Vigilante."

Oh shit.

"I was on my way to meet with a source who said they had a compelling theory about who the Vigilante might be. Before I met with them, all they said was that it was somebody close to law enforcement, so I worried it was one of your coworkers or something."

"But you met them."

"Yes."

"And they laid out their theory," I said.

"They don't have anything rock solid."

Obviously, otherwise, they would've gone to the police with it.

"Look." Sean guided me by the arm further away from the front door—the soft summer breeze contrasting with the hardening of his muscles, his veins bulging around his thick forearms as birds chirped warning sounds to each other. "Police are focusing on people with criminal backgrounds, but I think they're wrong. I think whoever this is, he's smart enough to know how to evade police, because I think this source is right: I think it's someone who works with law enforcement."

"You think the Vigilante is a cop?" I kept my voice calm to hide the hope that he was on the wrong track.

Sean bit his lip. "Don't you find it strange that the Vigilante was there to rescue you in the prison parking lot? And again last night? Almost as if he's keeping tabs on *you*."

"What are you saying?" Could he hear the dryness in my throat?

Strange, how a few hours ago all I wanted to do was out Hunter, but now I was panicking over it.

Sean looked back up at the expansive home, and I wondered if Hunter was up in one of the rooms, looking down on him right now. Grayson remained in the doorway, his arms crossed over his chest, glaring at the unwanted intruder as we stood fifty feet away, out of earshot.

"Luna, I don't think you should stay here. I don't have enough evidence to go to the police yet, but I think the Vigilante may be..." He paused. "I don't have proof," Sean hedged. "Not yet."

I glanced over my shoulder at Hunter's surveillance camera. Did it have sound? If it did, were we far enough away that he couldn't hear this conversation? I needed to get Sean out of here before he said something he—

"I think the Windy City Vigilante is Hunter."

Holy shit.

My mouth fell open. Sean probably thought it was from the shock of the revelation—maybe even assuming it was ludicrous to me—but it was from the shock that he'd pieced this together.

And dread. If Hunter and his brother were willing to hold me against my will, what would he do to Sean—a guy he loathed?

I shifted my gaze over my shoulder again, this time studying Grayson. What was that guy capable of and just how far would he go to protect his brother?

I had so many questions for Sean—what evidence was out there, and who else held his theory? But this conversation...this couldn't happen today. Sean had to leave now.

The problem? How the hell could I get him to walk away?

The answer came in the form of my cell phone ringing.

"I have to take this," I said.

Sean opened his mouth to protest but was cut off with the automated greeting on speakerphone.

"You have a call from an inmate at Stateville Correctional Center. To accept this call, press one."

"We need to talk about this, Luna."

"We will, I promise, but let me make progress on my dad's case, and I'll call you, okay?"

"Luna!"

Was I making a mistake, by not leaving with Sean? For hours, I'd wanted to escape Hunter's mansion. I had even broken glass and risked my life to try, and now here Sean was, with a working vehicle, prepared to whisk me away to safety.

But my safety wasn't the only one in play here...

"Luna, you can't stay with him!" Sean said.

"I'm fine," I repeated over my shoulder.

Unwavering in his resolve, Sean sped up his steps and reached out to grab my arm, but Grayson stepped forward and shoved a hand on his chest—looking hauntingly calm and collected in the process.

His voice was guttural. "She told you to leave."

Sean glared at Grayson. "Take your hand off me."

"Get in your car," Grayson said. "And get out of here."

"Grayson!"

When Grayson turned to look at me, a chill coated my spine. Something dark and dangerous swirled within his gaze.

"I'll call you later," I promised Sean in an upbeat tone, as if that could downplay Grayson's ominous one.

Sean hesitated for a few more seconds, his gaze pinballing between me and Grayson before he took a step back and glared at me like I had just betrayed him.

I watched with barbed wires ensnaring my heart as Sean stalked away from me, got into his Uber, and drove off.

"Luna?" Dad's voice came over the phone. "Is everything okay?"

CHAPTER 27

Hunter

"Care to tell me what the hell is going on?" Uncle Alexander stormed into my bedroom, where I'd just finished tying my tie.

I turned away from the mirror and eyed his fingers flexing with a fleeting panic that he might've uncovered my secret double life.

"Regarding?" I asked.

My uncle pulled up his phone and turned the screen to my face. "Some whistleblower talking about embezzlement."

What the hell? I had no idea what he was talking about, but this was the last priority right now. "Embezzlement?"

"An inflammatory word for an accounting discrepancy."

I took his phone and skimmed the article, shocked by many parts. One of which clarified an open question for me...

"So the missing money meant something?"

Alexander's eyes tightened. "What missing money?"

I handed his phone back, my mind racing with this information.

"I've been looking into Dad's murder," I reminded him.

There was that look of pity Alexander always gave me whenever I brought this up. I knew what he thought—that I was letting this Moby Dick of a goose chase hold me back in life.

"And what does that have to do with this whistleblower?" Alexander pressed.

A dread tugged at my gut. "Whistleblower, no idea. But missing money..." This was important, so important, I needed time to process what it meant.

"Look, I can explain later, but right now, I need to go."

"You have something more pressing than reporters slaughtering your father's reputation?"

Dad's honorable image had been important to Alexander. Guilt snared my bones at what Alexander might think when he found out *my* real identity.

"I have court."

Actually, that was inaccurate. *Luna* had court.

Over the last two and a half days, Luna had buried herself in preparing for this hearing. She prepared her father, secured him a suit to be arranged at the courthouse, and had been reviewing all of his files in addition to having conversations with Barry about his ongoing investigation—which, by the way, had officially breached the forty-eight-hour window, but he assured me he was close.

Meanwhile, there were so many times in the last couple of days I almost pulled Luna aside again, begging her to tell me how she felt. Sometimes, I'd catch her looking at me with love, but sometimes, it was with something darker—as if something weighed on her mind, something she wasn't sharing with me. But I'd resisted the temptation to confront her.

Until today. After court, I hoped to find out where she stood with her feelings.

But today's court hearing posed another complication.

I wasn't sure what Luna would do once it was done. In a courthouse full of armed security and law enforcement officers, she would have every opportunity to escape my confinement and turn me in.

I was still protecting her from criminal prosecution to the best of my ability, anyway. That's why I was going with her, so if she didn't turn me in, she could claim she was still under duress.

Plus, I wanted to be with her during her most pivotal moment. I hoped all her dreams would come true, but if this didn't go her way, I didn't want her to be alone.

"Isn't this more important?" Uncle Alexander asked.

"How did reporters catch wind of this?" I wondered.

"You tell me."

"Who is the whistleblower?"

"They're staying anonymous. But whoever it is, is saying the accounting discrepancy was some kind of cover-up."

So, the missing funds turned out to be a very big deal, then.

"A cover-up of what?" I wondered, but Alexander merely shrugged, reading the article on his phone as if each word was a bullet to our family legacy.

It pissed me off that someone had gone to reporters over this rather than coming to me first. Especially since there was only one person that I could think of who might have done it.

I looked at my watch. Eight minutes until we needed to leave, which gave me time to make a quick call.

I dialed my accountant, Jeff, and put him on speaker.

"Mr. Lockwood," Jeff started.

"Was it you?" I snapped.

Jeff was quiet.

"Why did you do it?" I snarled.

Jeff's hesitation was grinding against my nerves. I began pacing in my bedroom, clenching my fist. When I set out to solve my father's murder, the last thing I wanted was to drag his name through the mud. He was the victim here.

"I'm sorry," Jeff said. "It weighed on my conscience back then. I managed to get past it, but to get involved again...I can't do it anymore."

"What weighed on your conscience?"

"You'll have my resignation by the end of the day."

"If you're going to make an accusation, tell me what the hell you're accusing my father of!"

Jeff hesitated.

"The damage is done, Jeff. So, spit it out."

The asshole took the time to sigh before answering me.

"Improper use of company funds."

I froze. "Elaborate."

"I don't know everything," Jeff hedged.

"And yet you went to reporters to ruin his reputation."

"You don't need to get curt with me."

"Don't I? I specifically asked you about this accounting transaction, and instead of telling me what you knew, you went to reporters with it."

"To clear my conscience, because I was afraid you might cover it up."

"Explain what happened back then, already!"

Silence.

"Look, all I know is that company funds went missing. And then your father took money out of his own bank account and deposited it into the business account to compensate for it."

Why would Dad do that? "How much money?"

"Five million."

"What was the money used for?" I asked.

"I never knew back then, and I don't know now, because they moved the business money to an offshore account. From there, it could have been moved anywhere, and it would've been untraceable."

"So, someone stole five million from the business."

"It would appear so."

A rock dropped into my intestines.

"My father was a billionaire. My whole family was a billionaire by that point. If someone had stolen from the company, it wouldn't have been my father. And if he *did* steal, he wouldn't have reimbursed the company back."

"My brother was a good man," Uncle Alexander chimed in, his neck red from frustration. "If he had any kind of mismanagement of money, it would have been an innocent mistake on his part."

Jeff sighed. "Look, your dad wouldn't tell me the exact reason he refunded that money. But, if you ask me, he might've had an inkling about who took it. Embezzlement—it's no small matter. Maybe he was trying to cover for someone. He was adamant, you know? Told me in no uncertain terms to keep it under wraps. Even made me promise not to breathe a word about it to anyone."

"And keeping that secret weighed on your conscience."

"It did."

I tugged at my tie. "If this bothered you so much, why didn't you tell me?"

No response.

"Or say something about this back then?" I demanded.

Jeff let out a long breath.

"I did consider turning your father in, but..."

He stopped talking.

"But what, Jeff?"

I squeezed my phone tighter.

"But three days after he moved the money," Jeff said, "he was dead."

CHAPTER 28

Hunter

A sharp, cutting edge crept into my voice, making each word pointed. "And you didn't think that was something the cops should know about?"

In all the police reports, never once was anything mentioned about missing money.

"If his death was linked to the financials..." Jeff started.

"*If!* Are you fucking serious right now? Of course his murder must be linked to that missing money!"

"Keeping my mouth shut was your father's last wish."

"And yet you're breaking it now! And it was his last wish because he was fucking murdered over it, Jeff! Three days after my dad moved the money, he wound up killed, and you said nothing. You know what it's called when you withhold key information about an active crime investigation? Obstruction."

"I never felt good about it, Hunter. I reconsidered confiding in the cops many times but..."

"You waited twenty years. And let's be clear. Coming forward now is not clearing your conscience, Jeff. If you wanted to do that, you would've told the police, not reporters. If you really cared about my father as much as you claim you did? That would not have been your move."

"Hunter, I did try to—"

"You're fired, Jeff."

I hung up and began pacing, clenching and unclenching my fists so hard, that it stung my palms.

"I can't believe that guy." Uncle Alexander shook his head.

My head was spinning, processing everything I had just found out. I needed to talk to Barry ASAP.

Alexander's hand on my shoulder felt like an anchor in the hurricane that erupted around me.

"This will be okay," he reassured, his voice a steady and a familiar balm. "I'll talk to the reporters to clear your father's name. Your father was a good man, Hunter. If there's talk of embezzlement, it wasn't him."

I swallowed the guilt welling up. His steadfast determination to preserve the Lockwood legacy had always seemed like a thorn in my side. But standing here, with the weight of the world pressing in, I was grateful—for the protection he was about to give, a fortress standing between my father's reputation and the hungry wolves outside.

A torrent of gratitude came over me.

"Thank you," I said, hoping he'd hear not just the words, but the depth of emotions behind them.

"What's wrong?" A crease deepened in Luna's forehead as a cloud of concern passed over her gaze.

We were now sitting in the back of the sedan.

I wanted to tell her what my uncle said about the missing funds. And also, how his fear—of my father's name getting smeared—reminded me that my secret identity could hurt my family.

Every choice I had made was fueled by good intentions, right? Justice for the innocent, avenging my father.

But in all of it, collateral damage scattered around me like broken fragments of a mirror. Reflecting back to me my choices and how they hurt the very people I cared about.

I never meant to tarnish my father's name in the process of seeking justice. And I never meant to hurt Luna.

"Nothing," I lied, straightening my tie.

She took my hand in hers, a gesture I didn't deserve, but I was greedy, unable to resist the warmth of her touch.

I met her gaze, the veil of unease softening into a gentleness. Even after all I had done, she somehow managed to look at me like I wasn't a monster.

"I can tell something is upsetting you," she said.

Outside the window, the ground flew beneath us, just like the last few years had flown by in my life.

"With Barry digging into my father's past," I hedged, "I have this fear creeping in..." I bit my lip. "What if my dad wasn't as perfect as I thought?"

What a hypocrite I was to need him to stay up on his pedestal. When I'd fallen into a dark chasm, I wanted to believe the good parts of me were all him. And the bad parts were me.

I needed my dad to stay my hero. Otherwise, it rocked the foundation of my world, and if it cracked beneath me, I wasn't sure how much darker I could become.

"Did something happen?"

I shook my head and lied, "Just thinking a lot."

And that's where I'd leave it. I shouldn't have said anything about my problems, but I would bite my tongue about the rest of it—how my world was crashing around me.

Today was the most important day in Luna's life, and I was not going to do or say anything to ruin this for her. If she knew what I'd just found out, she'd worry about me.

Because that was Luna—someone who could still worry about a person, even after she'd seen the most awful parts of their soul.

"I know my dad is innocent," she said in a hushed tone. "But over the past twenty years, I'd be lying if I said I never once had dark doubts creep in." She looked out her window this time, her face falling into sadness. "What if I dedicated the last two decades of my life and my dad was actually guilty?" She pulled her lip between her teeth. "And then I feel like a terrible daughter for letting those doubts seep in. Because in my heart of hearts, I know he's innocent, and I'm the only person he has left who believes him. Imagine how he'd feel if he found out I'd ever doubted him."

I wanted to pull her against my chest.

"Luna, you wouldn't be human if you didn't at least wonder sometimes."

She was silent for several seconds before whispering, "I just want to be a good person my dad would be proud of."

"Your dad is lucky to have you, Luna," I said. "And I'm lucky I met you."

I'd never meet anyone like her again, nor would I ever feel this deeply for another. My love for her was so profound, it shook me to my core; her very presence was an intoxicating melody echoing within the chambers of my heart.

Each time I looked into her eyes, a myriad of stars gleamed back at me, reflecting a universe of possibilities. And yet, none of these possibilities included me anymore. I was an unwelcome silhouette, basking in the brilliance of a luminous soul.

Not that I could blame her, the twisted and scarred man that I was.

The gentle curve of her fingers under my thumb sent shivers down my spine, and in a moment of selfishness, I pressed my lips to the back of her hand.

It was a desperate, primal act, one that betrayed my uncontrollable passion and feelings for her. She let out a soft gasp, her lips parting in surprise, her breath mingling with mine.

It was an intense moment, an eternity folded into seconds.

Her eyes were a kaleidoscope of sorrow and resignation.

I understood then—the haunting look she'd been giving me the past couple of days, that she'd been wrestling with a decision. One she'd made. That at some point before or after this hearing, she was going to turn me in.

There was a bitter sweetness to the revelation, a pain that stabbed deep and twisted, yet amidst the heartache, I loved her still.

It wasn't her fault. I didn't blame her; if anything, I was proud of her strength, her courage, and her integrity, even though it meant my own undoing. She was radiant in her unwavering conviction, an epitome of everything good and just in a world that had proven itself to be anything but.

I memorized the curve of her cheek, the softness of her lips, and the familiar scent of her skin that had become my lifeline. I ran my fingers through her hair, each strand a promise, a memory, a farewell. The hum of the car's engine became a metronome to my final moments of freedom, each rotation of the tires a reminder of the impending end.

I could stop her. Deny her access to the exit, hold her captive in this bubble of time that was ours and ours alone.

But I wouldn't, couldn't. Not her. Not when she had the most important moment of her life. My love wouldn't rob her of that, not even if it cost me my freedom.

I could drop her off, board a private jet, and leave the country.

But I refused to be a coward. Not with Luna. Even if I'd destroyed any chance of being with her, I'd own my sins and take my punishment. I'd be the man Luna wanted me to be.

The gravity of her decision hung between us, every silent moment heavy with unspoken words. Her tears were a reflection of my inner conflict—of love battling against inevitability. I blinked away my own tears, wanting to be the stronghold she could lean on.

The memories we shared, the moments where our hearts beat in tandem, all flooded my mind.

My hand squeezed hers once, twice, a silent message that I hoped she understood. *I love you. I'll always love you.*

Our burning love was now reduced to dying embers, but there was a beauty in its destruction, a selfless adoration that withstood the impending fire, even if it was to be its ruin.

A single tear slid down her cheek, marking the end of an era, the beginning of an end.

I wiped the tear from her soft skin and hoped she could see the sincerity in my eyes.

"It's okay, Luna," I murmured.

"We're here." The driver's announcement jolted us back, an unwanted intrusion. I released her hand, warmth lingering, as we braced for the truth—where I was her monster, and she was about to turn me in.

CHAPTER 29

Luna

Alone envelope sat ominously on the defendant's table, my name boldly etched in black cursive. It was the only thing capable of interrupting the stifling guilt and doubt whipping through my heart. How could I turn Hunter in—the very man who stood by us through this trial prep?

Amidst my curiosity and inner turmoil, a pivotal moment was about to occur.

Any second, my father would enter the room, and a judge would render his decision: deny the request outright or agree to listen to arguments for a new trial—either today or at a later date.

I picked up the white envelope and glanced around the courtroom. Ahead, the judge's towering bench loomed, its gavel symbolizing the impending gravity of judgment. Overhead lights buzzed, casting stark shadows that cut through the muted rays from a window draped in crimson—dust particles floating in the room's musty-scented atmosphere.

Behind me, the old wooden doors groaned with each new entrant, their whispers joining the murmurs of those on the worn benches. Mayor Kepler himself was among them. Maybe the letter was from him, an annoyance that I had yet to reschedule my meeting with him?

I opened the letter.

Ms. Payne,

It's unfortunate you haven't heeded my warnings. When the judge arrives, withdraw your motion. Surely, your father's life means more to you than his freedom.

Do not alert anyone to the contents of this letter. If you do, I'm afraid you'll force my hand.

A cold chill raced down my spine as I desperately scanned the crowd, searching for a hint, a clue—anything that might betray the author of that venomous threat. A man with bushy eyebrows, wearing a business suit, looked at me sternly. An older lady with white hair pursed her lips. There was a man standing in the back, leaning against the wall, his ankles crossed over each other, his balding head glistening in the courtroom lighting.

Had one of them left the note?

Hunter caught my eye, concern evident in his furrowed brow. Leaning forward, he mouthed, "You okay?"

"All rise."

The only thing capable of snapping me out of this trance was the vision of my father entering the room.

As the light illuminated his groomed hair and fresh shave—a stark contrast from his prison days—I was consumed by guilt. It was Hunter who had orchestrated this transformation, meticulously styling my father's outfit. The black suit, the white shirt, and the blue tie—all elements of the designer outfit Hunter had procured—had erased the visual reminders of his imprisonment.

How could I have let Hunter do all this for him? Only to spend this morning preparing to betray him?

Dad smiled at me, knowing this was the moment I'd been waiting for my whole life. I seriously wondered if it meant more to me than him—a selfless man who'd wanted me to move on with my life rather than waste it on him.

But his smile faded when he saw my bruises. I'd filled him in on the basics, but hearing your daughter was attacked and *seeing* the evidence were very different things.

After a few minutes, the judge got to the heartbeat of this hearing.

His voice held a firm edge, each word enunciated with a commanding authority.

"Your filing requests a chance to argue for a new trial. Is that correct?"

I glanced at the letter that warned me to withdraw my motion and clenched my fists.

"That's correct," I managed.

"This isn't a matter the court takes lightly," the judge said in a tense tone. "And you, as a criminal defender, are arguing ineffective counsel. Is that right?"

"That's right," I said as calmly as possible, my gaze flickering between him and the letter.

"If we deemed every lawyer fresh out of college as inadequate, imagine all the criminals that could come forward and have a case for dismissal."

Focus, Luna.

"As you can see from my filing, it's not just the lack of experience, Your Honor. I laid out the different objections and the different procedures that should have been followed and weren't. In addition to that, new evidence is coming to light that I believe will exonerate Mr. Payne."

"This is your father, yes?"

"It is."

"Do you not believe you may have a biased slant?"

"I believe I'm the only person looking at the evidence with enough passion to care if it's correct."

By the tightening of the judge's jaw, I could tell that offended him. Judges and lawyers didn't like it very much when we claimed other people screwed up. It left a stain on the justice system when somebody inside of it pointed out its flaws.

"Your Honor"—I cleared my throat—"a man has been in prison for over nineteen years for a crime he did not commit." I pulled my eyes away from the damn threat and straightened my spine. "I've laid out the specific points where counsel was ineffective in that hearing, and I

have shown a reasonable probability that, but for the counsel's unpro-
fessional errors, the result of the proceeding would have been
different."

The judge looked at the clock that ticked away on the wall. "Are
you prepared to lay out your evidence today?"

That's not a dismissal.

Hope took flight, but I tried to tame it; the judge could be going
through the motions here.

"I am, Your Honor, but I am waiting on one lab report that should
arrive shortly."

The judge's annoyed stare snapped to me.

"You didn't have the results *before* you filed the motion?"

"The evidence came into my possession two days ago," I said, my
heart jumping into my throat. The testing was taking longer than
Barry hoped, as was the second review of the autopsy findings, but he
was close. The problem was, I still didn't know if it would give us
anything definitive. "But I'm prepared to proceed without it if
needed."

The judge's chest puffed out as he continued examining the papers
in front of him. With how quickly this got moved up, maybe the judge
hadn't had time to review everything as thoroughly as he normally
did.

"This is extensive." He glanced at the clock again, his lips pursed.
His caseload had to be considerable today, what with his sudden time
off next week.

Time that might give the person threatening us more runway. I
stared at the envelope, biting my lip.

"There's something else, Your Honor." I lifted the letter. "I've been
receiving death threats, warning me to drop this case. This is the
second letter I have received. This one threatens Mr. Payne's life."

My dad's eyes widened, his pupils dilating as concern surged
through them, quickly followed by a fiery glint of anger.

"Why didn't you tell me?" he whispered.

"I didn't want you to worry, but now they're threatening *your* life,"
I whispered back.

The rustling of people shifting behind me, including Hunter, signaled them sitting up straighter.

The judge motioned for the bailiff to bring him the letter and looked it over.

After a couple of tense minutes, the judge cleared his throat, looked at me, looked at my father, and said, "I will grant the hearing to explore these arguments for a new trial."

Oh my god.

"Bailiff, hand this note back to Ms. Payne so she can get it to detectives," he said. "In the meantime, for the defendant's safety, he shall be incarcerated in solitary confinement until such a hearing can commence."

A knot of unease tightened in my intestines. I wanted Dad to be safe, so solitary was the right answer. It was also psychologically damaging to be alone in a cell, though, separated from all the other inmates, twenty-four hours a day, seven days a week.

"Court will set this hearing for a week from Monday."

The judge's first day back from leave.

The gavel came down with finality. I turned and looked at my father's face, the wrinkles symbolic of the years that had been taken from us. And then I wrapped my arms around him.

"Luna, the threats…"

"We can talk about that later," I said, my throat swelling. "Please, let's just have this moment."

And he did. He let me focus on his arms around my ribs and the inviting scent of the fresh soap on his neck—which bore a clean and slightly medicinal scent. Before pulling back.

"In just over a week, you could be sitting at my dinner table," I said.

"Luna, even if we get a new trial…"

"I know." There was a good chance he'd have to stay in prison, pending it. But a girl could hope.

That glimmer in his eyes, that unfamiliar warmth that had dimmed through the years, made my heart waver.

It was unethical to worry that doing the right thing about Hunter might mean never getting the test results that could clear my father's name. I'd gone over that part in my head repeatedly this morning and convinced myself I could still get my father out—even without them.

But what if I couldn't?

And, by the way, Hunter had been the one to find those paint chips to begin with, through his PI. Hunter had funded it all without expecting anything in return.

A pang of guilt twisted my insides, thinking of turning him in. The very act felt like a betrayal—not only to Hunter, but to my father's newfound hope.

Was I being selfish? Or was it selfless to consider the bigger picture?

A cyclone raged inside me, blurring the line between right and wrong.

CHAPTER 30

Luna

Mayor Kepler approached, a tight smile on his lips. His gaze darted past me briefly, lingering on the spot where my father had just been escorted out.

"Congratulations."

"I get the sense I owe you a thank-you for the hearing getting moved up." I smiled.

"It was nothing." The mayor waved his hand, but the lingering intensity in his stare hinted it came with expectations. "I have to confess, I'm not here to wish you luck." At that, he raised both eyebrows. "I'm here to talk about your email."

Lord, that felt so long ago. I'd almost forgotten where the mayor and I had left off in our conversations. It was right after the Vigilante had confronted me in the women's restroom at work. After which, I'd emailed Mayor Kepler, saying I was starting to suspect that the Windy City Vigilante might be someone I knew.

And that I wanted to meet.

It shouldn't have surprised me he'd turn up here today to talk; Mayor Kepler had staked his entire reelection campaign on uncovering the identity of the Windy City Vigilante so he could lock him up. And here I was, holding the information.

All morning, I'd convinced myself I *had* to turn Hunter in, no matter how bad it felt. I'd planned on calling Rinaldi, but here was the mayor—the man who wanted him the most, standing in front of me. Like the universe had served him up on a silver platter.

Tell him.

"Right, the email," I said, my voice wavering slightly.

Hunter leaned against the far wall, his sharp suit making him stand out against the drab courtroom. But it was the resignation in his stare that held my gaze.

Mayor Kepler cleared his throat, glancing briefly at the bruises on my face, a flicker of concern—or was it impatience?—crossing his features.

"I heard what happened." The mayor looked at my bandaged arm, stitched by a physician Hunter brought to the house—paying extra for discretion. "Heard you were lucky to make it out alive."

Every time I touched the tender skin of my cheek, flashes of that night surged back—the fear, the helplessness. And the relief that Hunter had saved me before it was too late.

"My bodyguards weren't so lucky. They died trying to protect me." My chest clenched, especially when I'd heard they had families. Having Hunter fully fund their funeral and make generous donations to their loved ones didn't take away from the suffering they'd endured.

"Can you believe he got away?" The mayor's jaw clenched.

"I'm sure Franco will turn up soon." Wherever Hunter had disposed of his body.

"Not him," the mayor snarled. "The Vigilante."

His words were a sword slicing my gut, revealing the brutal truth. The real tragedy to him wasn't that the murderer—who had killed three innocent bodyguards, tortured me, and almost taken my life, too —had gotten away.

But that the *Vigilante*—who had saved my life—had slipped through his grasp once more.

It was ridiculous to feel hurt.

"I heard about that goddamn stunt the Vigilante pulled at your office." He tugged at his tie. "You know what a PR nightmare and slap in the face that is to the Justice Department? The Vigilante breaking into the building where we keep criminal records?" Mayor Kepler's face reddened. "This damn guy."

A flash of dread coursed through my veins.

I twisted my fingers together.

"When you catch him," I said, "what do you plan to do with him?"

The mayor's eyes tightened, his tone clipped. "What do you mean?"

I shifted nervously. "I mean, from a prosecutorial standpoint, once you apprehend him, what are your plans?"

"If I had it my way, we'd put him in front of a firing squad. People like that don't belong in this world. They're a deadly virus that needs to be eliminated. Because it's not just him that's wreaking havoc. I'm starting to get pop-ups of copycat killers," he said. "This guy is starting to convince other criminals to take justice into their own hands. If I don't stop him, the city is going to be infested with these people."

Life imprisonment was a given with the body count, but there were other things he could do to make a prisoner's time even more insufferable. Namely, influence the prison he'd be sent to.

Mayor Kepler tilted his head, a ripple of frustration bubbling through his features.

"You're not having doubts, are you?" His voice, though soft, carried an undercurrent of a threat.

"No," I lied, the word a stone in my throat.

"Because that would be a big problem," the mayor snapped. "Your email said you're convinced the Vigilante is someone you know."

"I never said *convinced*," I replied hesitantly.

Veins pulsed on his reddening forehead. "What prompted that email?"

I bit my lip nervously, trying to enter the confession pool at the shallow end.

"Well," I started, "when the Vigilante confronted me in the ladies' room, I wondered if perhaps I'd met him before."

"What made you wonder that?" he asked.

I shrugged. "It was just a…feeling that I got."

"You have any idea who the Vigilante might be?"

The mayor's shadow seemed to envelop me, his demanding presence making my heart race, each beat mirroring my moral struggle. This morning, watching the sun rise over Lake Michigan, everything seemed so clear. I had to do this.

The air in the courtroom was thick, clinging to me like a heavy fog while my stomach churned with anxiety. Each beat of my heart sounded like a warning in my ears, a signal of imminent disaster.

Moments with Hunter flashed through my mind. His smile, the feeling of his hand on mine, the look in his eyes when he vowed his protection, and the one when he'd said he loved me.

It was like a flood, drowning out the certainty.

My tongue tasted bitter with my impending betrayal, a mixture of guilt and heartbreak.

The words sat heavily on my lips, a confession waiting to spill like an unstoppable tidal wave. Just one whisper. That's all it would take. One whisper and the man I loved would become a criminal in the eyes of the law—worse, the target of Mayor Kepler's vendetta. One whisper and I would become his betrayer, sentencing him to prison for the rest of his life.

The thought twisted my heart in knots.

The mayor pressed impatiently. "Who jumps out as a possibility?"

There it was, stuck in my throat like a jagged piece of glass, the words that would cast me into a world of darkness. My heart ached, a burning, wrenching pain. How could love and justice demand such a price? A sacrifice that tasted of ashes, one that felt like the damning winter to forever settle into my soul.

It felt like a death sentence, not for him, but for me. A chasm of darkness that threatened to swallow me whole.

His question hung in the air, and in the silence that followed, the answer that had eluded me became painfully clear.

"After thinking about it some more..." I paused, searching for the right words, my voice cracking slightly as I finally spoke. "I think I was wrong."

I couldn't turn Hunter in.

Because not everything in life was black and white—sometimes, we have to navigate through the gray. What Hunter, as the Vigilante, had done was wrong legally, but that law wasn't always right or just; it was a legal system fraught with inequities, and sometimes innocent people went to jail. Like my dad. Other times, the guilty were free to commit further crimes. As misguided as he was, Hunter stepped in to do what our imperfect legal system failed to do. He no longer straddled the line between right and wrong—he crossed over it into the gray.

He wasn't a monster; he was a good man with a good heart, who lived to right the wrongs by seeking justice for those who deserved it.

"Yet you felt so sure of this a few days ago that you called a meeting with me," Mayor Kepler said.

"I shouldn't have sent that email. I'm sorry."

The mayor's chest swelled as he evaluated me. Did he sense I was lying?

"Trust your gut, Luna. Maybe it's time we take a closer look at the people in your life."

CHAPTER 31

Luna

"You didn't turn me in." Hunter's voice was low with just a hint of hope, quiet despite the partition between us and the driver.

In the sedan, a rich aroma of leather blended with the chill of the air conditioner while our shared secrets seemed to suffocate the space around us, and as we drove closer to Hunter's mansion, the purr of the engine became a whispered warning that everything was about to change.

"I was going to," I admitted.

"I know," he said. "I could see it in your eyes when we parked."

There was something so intimate about his declaration—that with a simple look, he could see my intentions. Had he also seen the anguish my intention had caused me?

"What changed?" Hunter's voice skated over my skin, embracing me in a warm hug that only cemented my decision to back out.

A better person would have pushed aside their heartbreak, their love for him, and would have been courageous enough to speak up. Maybe I wasn't as good of a person as I thought.

"I don't know what'll happen to you." I twisted my fingers in my lap. "But I just couldn't be the one to turn you in."

The sedan took a right turn, pulling my body closer to Hunter's like a devil tempting me.

"Mayor Kepler's planning to look into everyone in my life," I said. "Before I knew you were..." I glanced at the driver, then back at Hunter. "I told the mayor I thought the *person* might be someone I know. I tried to backpedal but..."

Shame froze my words, guilt that I'd had a hand in Hunter's likely demise. It was one thing if he got caught. It was another if I was the one that pointed the arrow at him.

It would put me in a prison of my own for the rest of my life.

Hunter placed his hand on mine.

That simple touch set off a cascade of feelings I had been desperately trying to fight. It was like a dormant volcano suddenly erupting, a seismic shift that set off a tidal wave of affection surging through me. Raw and powerful, overwhelming in its intensity—and I knew I had no hope of controlling it.

His eyes found mine, those beautiful orbs that held galaxies in them, brimming with profound gratitude, yet the corners of his eyes crinkled, a shadow passing over his face.

"You shouldn't have backpedaled, and you shouldn't have lied for me," Hunter said.

"Wasn't that the plan? To conceal your identity from everyone?" I whispered.

"Not if it put you in danger or got you into trouble, no."

Hunter's blue gems were unreadable, but I thought I caught a glimpse of resignation in them.

"Sean suspects you, too," I said.

This elicited a lick of his bottom lip. I suspected it had less to do with someone questioning him and more to do with the idea that Sean would be the one to take him down.

"I don't know what evidence he has, but I can call him and find out."

"No," Hunter said sternly. "You're not going to do anything that could get you in trouble."

"Between Sean and the mayor, it feels like just a matter of time before they put it together," I said. "What's your plan?"

"My plan is to get your father out of prison."

My throat swelled. "Why are you staying here to help me? You could be fleeing the country to save yourself."

"Luna, I would never abandon you when you're in danger." He brushed a fallen hair behind my ear. "We're going to talk about that second letter," he said, looking from my left eye to my right. "But even if you weren't being threatened, I'd stay."

"Why?"

His suit jacket swelled up on his chest. "Because you deserve to get justice for your father, and I'm going to do everything in my power to make sure you do." He reached out, hesitating just a moment before entwining his fingers with mine, gripping firmly, as if he feared I'd slip away. The warmth of his touch sent a jolt through my skin—a moment we stayed in, lost in, neither one of us speaking or wanting to break our connection.

Who loves someone so much they'd be willing to damn themselves to prison forever?

"And if we get my dad out of prison? And the threat against me ends? What then? What are you planning to do?"

Hunter was silent for several anguished heartbeats, and I watched his mouth, waiting to hear what his future held.

"Sir?" the driver's voice interrupted us, the partition sliding down with a hum. "Looks like you have company."

With arms crossed, Grayson stood before the mansion beside a man clad in a gray suit. I wondered why they were waiting outside for us like this and why they exchanged glances as Hunter opened my door.

"Barry," Hunter said. "What's going on?"

The guy in the suit held up a folder.

"We did it, sir. I have proof Mr. Payne is innocent."

CHAPTER 32

Luna

"I wanted to wait until I had all the information back before getting your hopes up," Barry said.

We stood in Hunter's office, the golden light streaming through the window like a beacon of optimism, while I tried to remind myself that hope was a dangerous force.

Grayson stood along the far wall—his hands in his dark jean pockets, a black shirt fitted against his bulging muscles—while Hunter remained next to me, his gaze flickering between me and Barry, as if fearful I might not be able to withstand whatever Barry was about to say.

"I'll start with the paint chips." Barry spread out an assortment of papers and X-ray photographs on Hunter's desk. "The paint chips were from a vehicle," he continued. "Paint used for automotive manufacturing—specifically, a Jaguar."

"A Jaguar?"

"As you know, an autopsy involves examining the body and all other evidence from the scene. Anything that can determine the cause of death."

"Which was deemed a homicide," I said.

"And I would agree with homicide," Barry said.

I clenched my hands. How could he get my hopes up like this?

"I thought you said you had proof my dad didn't do it."

"The second medical examiner we hired took a close look at the reports. Specifically, the injuries the victim sustained. The victim had several broken bones which were, at the time, believed to have been caused by a beating. But if you look closer at the leg bones, they tell a different story."

"Which is?" Hunter asked.

Barry pointed to a break in the bone. "The kid was hit by a car."

A cold wave of shock washed over me, my breath catching in my throat.

"How can you be sure?" I asked.

"You see this break right here?" Barry pointed to a gap in the white bone against the black backdrop. "This is a break you see when someone is struck by a car. It's on both of his legs," he said, adding a second X-ray to the table.

I studied the pictures more closely.

"Why didn't the medical examiner notice that in his autopsy?"

"He did. But he concluded the breaks were part of a beating since the victim's arms and skull were also fractured."

"So, what makes you think he wasn't beaten now?" I asked.

"The paint chips. Broken bones are one thing. But when you combine it with the paint chips found on his pants in the same area of the breaks?" Barry scrubbed his jaw. "This kid wasn't beaten. He was struck by a vehicle."

My mouth turned into a desert, and Hunter leaned down and squeezed my hand, as if anchoring me to this new reality so I wouldn't fall into the depths of shock.

There was a lot to unpack there—how was he found in an alley, then? Was it wide enough for a car to get through? Even if it was…

"My dad didn't own a car," I said. "Neither did my mom. We were struggling financially, so he walked to work every day."

"I know," Barry said.

"There's more." Grayson pushed off the wall with a grave expression. "Barry thinks someone knew this kid got hit by a car and let your dad take the fall, anyway."

The news tore through me like a sledgehammer, every word a crushing blow threatening to unhinge my stability. The room darkened, edges smudging like a watercolor painting left in the rain.

"Luna." Hunter gripped my elbows—the warmth of his hand piercing through the sudden chill that consumed me—and guided me to a chair. Where he helped me sit down and squatted in front of me.

"Breathe." He cupped my cheek.

I was overwhelmed, but I didn't want to miss whatever Barry said next, so I forced myself to take steady breaths until the edges of the room lightened.

"Why would someone do that?" I asked through stinging eyes.

"To get away with whatever they did to that kid."

"My dad saw someone else in that alley," I remembered. "The police didn't believe him."

"I believe him," Barry said. "And if it's all right with you, I would like to speak with your father. I'd like to hear firsthand what he remembers about the person he saw in that alley."

I shook my head. "I don't know if they'll allow it, since he's in solitary for his own protection. And even if they do, I don't want to risk his life for a phone call."

Barry scratched his temple. "Even without talking to him, this is enough evidence to prove that your father is innocent."

"The judge could challenge the findings," I said. "You have conflicting conclusions by two different medical examiners, so there's no telling if the judge will rule in favor of the new one."

Hunter's gaze lingered on mine, gauging the steadiness in them and assessing whether my legs might give out the moment I tried to stand.

"Barry, how confident are you that the second medical examiner is correct?" Hunter asked sternly.

He kept his hand on my shoulder, his thumb rubbing up and down.

Barry scratched his jaw, taking a moment before speaking. "In all my years working cases, I've seen my fair share of accidents," he began. "Everything about this scene...the injuries, your father's eyewitness account...it all points to a hit-and-run. Your dad? From what I've gathered, he was trying to help, not harm the kid."

"I can't believe this is actually happening," I whispered.

It was this strange mix of disbelief and euphoria, for I finally had the answers that I sought. But also, heartbreak and anger, because my dad had been sitting in prison for almost twenty years, and there was at least one person on this planet that knew he was innocent.

The person who'd hit that kid with a car. Who never stepped forward or did anything to stop it.

"I'll fund more independent medical examiners to review these autopsy findings and paint chip analysis," Hunter said. "If we have more corroborating conclusions, the judge won't be able to deny it."

"That's expensive." My eyelids burned as I met his gaze.

"Luna," he said softly, "I would spend every dollar I have if it means you'll finally have the evidence you need to prove your dad's innocence and set him free."

His eyes held a depth that radiated with authenticity, and at that moment, we were the only two people in the world. A soft gasp stole my breath, and I found myself sinking into the ocean of his love, lost in its depths. With him, I was cherished, adored, and loved, beyond everything else. Beyond his freedom. Beyond his money. Beyond his own happiness.

"Barry," Hunter said, an edge to his tone that wasn't there before. "I think it might be beneficial for Grayson to have some conversations with the people who built the case against her father."

I tilted my head back. "What role does Grayson play in this?"

He'd kept an eye on me when I was captive, but he'd also taken a lot of calls. I'd been so immersed in court prep, that I really didn't *care* what he was doing, so long as he stayed out of my hair.

But the look Hunter exchanged with his brother? The weight of that stare was heavy, like a storm cloud ready to burst. And Barry shifted, his face tightening. Glancing between the brothers, whose eyes stayed fixed on Barry's.

As if gauging his reaction.

That's what Hunter was asking, wasn't he? For Grayson to be some sort of hired muscle for Barry, not intending to play by the rules. He didn't intend to have polite conversations; he would get answers the hard way if that's what it took.

And the thing that shocked me even more was that Barry didn't storm out in offense. Instead, he eventually offered a slight nod.

Sparking a silent exchange between the brothers. Perhaps specific boundaries would be flushed out more when I wasn't here, but that wasn't the point.

Was I the only one who wanted to play by the book?

"We already have proof that my dad is innocent."

Barry scrubbed his jaw. "Ms. Payne, it's *possible* investigators and prosecutors simply got this one wrong."

"But?" I pressed.

When Barry took a long breath, I got the sense he didn't want to get my hopes up. But eventually, he said, "My gut says there's something more going on here."

"Such as?"

Barry put his hands on his hips. "It's just a gut feeling," he hedged. "But I'd like to rule out that there wasn't something more nefarious going on here."

"Someone's been threatening me. I think that proves it," I reasoned.

He said nothing.

I sat up straighter. "You think someone set him up back then."

"I'd like to rule out the possibility that someone didn't stack the cards against your father."

I looked over at Grayson.

And I was suddenly facing a moral test.

I had always been a good steward of the law, dedicating my life to preserving it. It was bad enough that I had bitten my tongue, withholding Hunter's name in my conversation with Mayor Kepler. But could I really do this? Could I give Grayson permission to extract information from people in an illegal manner?

The files sat neatly on the desk, missing the key information we needed.

The vengeful part of me wanted to do it. If there was someone who'd done this on purpose, who'd stolen a father from his family, who robbed us of our peaceful world, who took everyone and everything from my father, I wanted them to burn.

I wanted to annihilate them, and I wanted them to suffer at the hands of whatever Grayson was capable of to extract said information.

A better person wouldn't want that, but I didn't care.

The problem was, I couldn't do it. I couldn't give Grayson the green light, or I'd be no better than the people who may have stolen everything from my dad.

I wouldn't cross that line, no matter how tempting it was.

I had evidence that my father was innocent, and that's all I ever wanted in life—to get him out of prison.

"No," I said. "Let's validate this evidence and take it to the judge. If the other medical examiners corroborate this, there's no way my dad won't get a new trial."

"Ma'am, if someone put your father behind bars on purpose, they could be behind the letters threatening you."

I considered this while the eyes of everyone in the room were fixed on me.

"Detectives are looking into the latest letter," I reasoned. "Whoever left it for me had to have been in that courtroom sometime prior to the start of the hearing." So, in theory, they'd be easier to find.

But even if they weren't, I couldn't fall down the rabbit hole of illegal activity.

"Investigate what you can legally," I said. "But that's where I draw the line."

Hunter pursed his lips.

"Line up the other medical examiners," Hunter said to Barry. "Spare no expense. We need to get this done in the next two to three days so we can present this in court."

"I'll get started on the medical examiners," Barry said. "In the meantime, I've also been digging into your father's case, Mr. Lockwood." Barry's stare locked on Hunter. "And I found something significant."

Hunter's spine stiffened, and he and his brother exchanged a glance with tightened eyes.

But before Barry could continue, my cell phone chimed so loudly, I jumped. I pulled it out, intending to put it on vibrate.

Until I saw the text.

And a cold sweat broke on my forehead when I read it.

Unknown: Your father might be out of reach in solitary, but you're not. You should've made a different choice.

CHAPTER 33

Luna

Hunter yanked my phone from my hand, clutching my screen so tightly, I thought he might break it.

"Grayson, go with Barry. Lean on whoever you need to get answers."

"No." I stood up. "We're not doing it this way. I'll take the text to detectives."

But nobody was listening to me. It was like I was nothing more than a shadow in the room as the three men performed some silent secret handshake, united in a goal to find out who was threatening me.

"Wait!" I demanded.

But neither Grayson nor Barry so much as turned around, let alone stopped walking out of the room.

"Who are you going to talk to?" I pressed, watching with wide eyes as the two men approached the front door.

But they didn't answer. And I didn't have time to chase them because Hunter was charging up the grand staircase.

Two steps at a time.

"Hunter, wait."

But he didn't wait. I had to jog up the stairs and trail behind him, each step echoing my rising anxiety. The hallway seemed longer than I remembered, shadows casting eerie dances on the walls, and his master bedroom was saturated with a palpable tension. We wove through his closet, a labyrinth of expensive suits and colognes that lingered in the air, to the Vigilante closet hidden behind the facade of his daily life.

"Hunter," I said.

But he was already through the second fake door, and as we descended the spiral staircase, each twist took us deeper into the heart of his secrets. The amber glow from sconces illuminated the stone tunnel, revealing the moist beads that clung to the walls, sending a chill across my skin.

But when we made it to his weapons room, it took me off guard that Franco wasn't there, nor was a single drop of his blood. The stone was pristine, reflecting the soft glow of the room, washed of all its dark history, and the once-foreboding chair had vanished—almost as if nothing in here had ever happened, any hint of it a figment of my imagination.

"Where did you put him?" I wondered aloud.

Hunter grabbed a knife from the wall.

Making my stomach sink.

"I won't make you an accomplice after the fact." His tone was sharp, his words slicing through the air with authority.

He stormed down the tunnel again so quickly, that I had to jog to keep up with him, my calls for him to stop going unanswered. His footsteps were so loud on the metal staircase, their clanks hurt my ears, and once he reached his closet, he yanked a Vigilante shirt off so hard, the hanger flew to the ground. All the while, he kept hold of the knife.

"Don't do this." My voice was rising and shaking.

When he grabbed a pair of boots, blood pumped through my veins so quickly, my limbs weakened.

"You have a choice, Hunter. Do you want to be the Vigilante? After everything we've been through, is this the man you want to be?"

His blue eyes locked with mine, cutting through false pretenses and exposing our inner truths, and when he stormed up to me, he released the shirt and boots and grabbed my chin.

Making me gasp.

"I'll kill anyone who even whispers a threat against you, Luna."

I swallowed, unsteadied by the feral look in his eyes.

It was wrong to feel adored, loved, and protected in this moment. I should have felt disgusted, but I didn't. Not even a little. I knew, without a doubt, that Hunter would carry through with his threat if I allowed him to. He would seek out the owner of this letter, and he would kill them.

There was something primal and protective about that, which chipped away at the wall I had built around my heart.

But I couldn't let him do this, whatever *this* was. I needed to find a way to stop him, and poking holes in his plan seemed like a good first step to get through to him.

"And how are you going to do that?" I challenged.

"Whoever left that note was at the courthouse today. I'll start looking there."

Hunter was normally methodical with these things. But when it came to me...

"You have no idea who this person is or where to find them. What are you going to do, prowl the streets, hoping he walks past you?" My voice was nearly a shriek. "You're being reckless."

To this, he leaned down so close, I could smell the toothpaste on his breath.

"If there's one last thing I can do, I'm going to end the person who's threatening you."

Good God, there were a lot of layers to unpack there. One last thing—as in one last thing before turning himself in? Or going out with a bang, even if it meant dying to protect me?

I wasn't sure, but my eyes stung from fear. It wasn't until this moment that I allowed the prospect of him dying to enter my thoughts.

Hunter *would* die to protect me—of that, I had no doubt. But he needed someone to protect him from himself. I mean, my God. Look at the rage pumping through the vein on his forehead and his whitened knuckles around the knife's handle.

I pressed my palms on his chest. He was still wearing the suit he'd worn to court this morning. The fabric was smooth beneath the pads of my fingers as his heartbeat smashed into them.

"Drop the knife, Hunter."

Hunter's chest ballooned. "No."

He released my chin and tried to walk around me.

I stepped in his way. "Drop. The knife."

Clenched teeth. "Move, Luna."

"No."

He tried again, and again, I blocked him.

It wasn't lost on me that I, an unarmed woman half his size, was obstructing a killer brandishing a blade with one hand, fist clenched with the other. A killer whose eyes were wild.

This time, when he stepped past me, he almost made it, and I had to grab his belt buckle to jerk him back. A man of his strength could have easily yanked free, but doing so would've sent me to the ground, so here we were.

Chest to chest, in a standoff.

When he grabbed my chin again—a soft breath escaping my lungs—his gaze darkened into a cobalt blue.

"You're playing a dangerous game, Little Leopard."

"Your recklessness could get you caught or killed, and I won't allow either."

I tugged at his belt again, making it clear I wouldn't let him leave without a fight. His gaze dropped down to my hand, then slowly dragged back up.

Hunter twisted the knife's handle.

The atmosphere in the room shifted as his piercing eyes devoured me as if they held the antidote for his fury—the air between us crackling like a live wire, charged with electricity that ignited a fire through my body, pooling between my legs.

Especially when he looked at my mouth and then crashed his lips to mine.

I moaned, aching to forget the chaos around us, to lose myself. I longed for him to claim me, to smother me with his weight, and for a fleeting moment, let the world outside cease to exist while our bodies entwined.

His anger pulsed through his touch, his mouth pressing so harshly against mine that it hurt.

I missed this.

I missed him.

I needed this. I needed him to make me forget all of this again, just like he did on the hood of his car, just like he did when he bent me over the guest bed and claimed me from behind.

And I needed him, the man I was in love with, no matter how wrong our love might be.

My lower belly was screaming for him to take me, my skin alive, craving to be touched everywhere, especially between my legs.

Hunter's kiss became harder while the soft clips of his buckle coming undone preceded a swift glide of it.

Hunter grabbed a fistful of my hair and pulled my mouth from his —his jaw clenched as he glared down at me.

"You have any idea what it would do to me if something happened to you, Little Leopard?"

I couldn't free myself from his grip, even if I wanted to. But I didn't. There was something…intoxicating about his anger, for the source of it was the threat to my life.

Hunter released my head and pushed my wrists together, wrapping them with his belt. It stung, the wound beneath it still not healed, and for a second, I worried he might tie me up so he could go off and kill the man who'd threatened me, but instead, he picked up the knife.

And brought it to my chest.

He lightly dragged the blade of the knife down my torso to the bottom of my shirt. He pulled the fabric away from my flesh and slowly—carefully—cut it away from my body.

Inch. By. Inch.

I'd never imagined something so dark would be so sensual, but when he tossed my shirt to the ground, my mouth watered, watching him move onto my pants. Still angry. Tugging, making sure the blade never touched my skin, he cut through it all. Leaving me standing before him in a red bra and panties.

He drew the tip of the blade near my sternum, and with a pop, my bra sprang open. Two more cuts of the straps and it was off me.

I panted, watching the blade delicately trail my skin until it reached my panties, and this time, Hunter stretched them away from my skin, but looked me dead in the eyes as he cut them free.

Leaving me naked. Wrists bound. Standing in front of a violent killer.

He was chivalrous enough to set the knife down now as he took a step back and growled, "Get on your knees."

Holy heat between my thighs.

I gladly obeyed, and as he stripped himself free of his clothes, I couldn't help but salivate at the sight of him.

He grabbed the back of my hair.

"Open your mouth."

I looked up at him as my jaw went slack.

This time, Hunter Lockwood wasn't gentle. He plunged inside me and made me choke, pulling back to thrust in again. And again. Holding the sides of my head, he used my mouth to take his anger out.

I loved the look on his face. His teeth clenched in pleasure and frustration. I loved the sounds of his groans and how he'd hold himself in for a moment, only to pop free and start again. He began moving faster and faster, his growling rising in pitch like he was getting close.

And then he popped out of my mouth again and stepped back.

"Stand up."

My legs were slow to rise after being in that position, so he reached down, grabbed me, and slung me over his shoulder.

He carried me like I weighed nothing into his bedroom and tossed me onto the bed.

With one long end of the belt still unraveled, he grabbed me by the hips and pulled me to the center of his bed, where he secured the other end of the belt to his headboard until my arms were pulled above my head, my nude body exposed and vulnerable to anything he wanted to do to me.

Hunter stood at the foot of the bed, his eyes roaming over my body like a hungry man ready to devour a feast. His every muscle was tense with anticipation as he looked at my legs, my mouth, and my breasts, appearing to debate where to start devouring his meal first.

"Spread your legs," he demanded.

I let my knees fall open, and he stared at my center, managing to look even hungrier than before as he crawled up and lay on his stomach in front of me.

His tongue wasn't gentle this time—it pressed apart my folds as it licked a torturous path up my center, and when it hit that sweet spot of nerves at the top, I moaned, arching my back. Hunter sucked on the apex of my sex. Hard, nipping at me with biting stings, mixing with pleasure before he drew his tongue back down again. Firmly. Roughly.

With my moans echoing off his bedroom walls, he repeated this over and over, and then he elicited a gasp when he breached my entrance with his tongue.

Once.

Twice.

Three times.

I began to squirm, but he abandoned my sex—hovering his mouth so close, I wished I could just grab it and bring it back.

"What are you never going to do, Little Leopard?"

I looked down at him as he stared up at me between my thighs, waiting for me to answer. Unwilling to give me what I wanted until I did.

"I'm never going to let anyone take me from you," I whispered.

I wasn't even sure what I was committing to—wasn't sure what this meant for the future of our relationship, if we even had one. Because right now, it didn't matter.

He rewarded me with a long, thick lick of his tongue, sucking at the top, making me quiver so hard, he had to hold my thighs down.

Our eyes locked again as he licked and circled my sensitive nub, building a fresh wave inside of me. He circled and circled—alternating between a flat, soft tongue and a tight, sharper one—and then added a flicking that nearly sent me over the edge right then and there. As he worked my core, he took in my every gasp, every quiver, like a compass on a map, directing his tongue to hit the right turns. My arms tugged at the leather bindings, which bit into my skin as I began to rise higher and higher.

"You taste so damn good," he murmured, the vibrations of his words pulsing off my skin.

I wanted to grab his hair, push him to me, hold him in place. This man, who'd literally kill for me, had his mouth on my center. With only one purpose.

Hunter's cerulean pools latched on to mine as he worked his tongue, a devilish delight dancing through them as he groaned, "Come for me, Luna."

His words made me come undone, my back arching so hard, Hunter grabbed my thighs and pulled my center against his mouth, swirling his tongue to ride every last moment of the wave until I was panting and breathless, spent on his bed.

Only then did he climb on top of me and position himself between my thighs.

"Tell me what you want," he demanded.

I lifted my gaze, locking on to his sapphire depths that were brimming with a storm of desire and love. I entwined my ankles around his waist, drawing our bodies closer, seeking solace in his embrace.

"I want you, Hunter."

His skin was hot against mine as he sank into me, inch by inch. Stretching me, watching my mouth fall open once more, until finally, he pressed himself all the way inside of me.

Where he stilled, filling me.

Before slowly pulling out and making my breath catch as he thrust all the way back in.

He began to move, hard and deliberate, my skin burning with pleasure as he hit the bundle of nerves inside my body and out, all at the same time.

I felt myself falling further into him.

Sparking a stronger wave to build inside of me, only this one would make me come undone, having it happen around him.

Hunter grabbed my breast and squeezed so hard, the pain laced with pleasure, his thrusts becoming angrier.

I wondered if I'd have more bruises tomorrow with how hard he was slamming against me, but I didn't care. Instead, I locked my ankles firmly together, pulling him closer, arching my back and groaning his name so he could push further.

This felt right. Being with him like this, surrendering to him physically, and if I were being honest...

Emotionally, too. I reveled in giving up control to Hunter, surrendering my body and heart to him. Because I was always in control, and it felt great to let go of it, even if only for a little while.

Every time his name slipped from my lips, he groaned and pounded harder and harder until the wave rose so high, it finally crashed around me.

"Hunter!" I screamed.

He growled like an animal and pounded into me, watching my face as he rode every wave of my orgasm.

Before roaring from one of his own, stilling on top of me.

Breathless, he kissed me, but this time, it was gentle, and when he pulled back, he had a softened expression, smiling slightly as he released the belt from around my arms.

This was the Hunter I recognized.

But what about his other part? Could it ever be tamed? Did he want to tame it?

I let him pull my head onto his chest, listening to the beating of his heart.

"Hunter?" I started, trailing my fingertip along his toned stomach.

His fingers trailed along my hair. "Yes, Little Leopard?"

Nerves tangled around my words. "Do you *want* to stop being the Vigilante?"

CHAPTER 34

Luna

He froze beneath me for several beats of our hearts. Eventually, he murmured in a tone riddled with emotion, "What do *you* want, Little Leopard?"

I wasn't sure if I could choose him, be with him fully, but...

"I want you to give up this lifestyle."

"Because you can't be with a killer."

I wasn't sure that was true. Somehow, in the music of our time together, the beats of understanding created a melody of trust. I trusted Hunter would never hurt me, never hurt anyone I loved. The only people in danger from him were killers.

Hunter held my chin between his finger and thumb and tilted my head up to meet his stare.

"Do you still love me? Despite everything I've done?"

The weight of my feelings almost choked me, but I managed to whisper, "I love you so much, it scares me."

His lips brushed mine softly, teasing out my fears. "How so?"

I rested my ear on his chest again, looking at the window's cloudless sky.

"Because you being a killer doesn't scare me for the *right* reasons."

He let me collect my thoughts, dragging his fingertips through my hair.

"I should be afraid of you," I said. "I should be afraid of the lives you would take if you continued being the Vigilante." That was the moral thing to fear. Yet, while I didn't condone his actions… "When I look deep, that's not what I'm most afraid of."

Hunter kissed the top of my head and asked gently, "And what is it that scares you the most?"

I placed the palm of my hand on his warm skin, feeling the ridges of his chest muscles.

"This Vigilante life has two outcomes: prison or death. I don't want that for you, and selfishly, the thought of another person I love being in prison forever…" My lip quivered.

Outside, a flight of birds soared through the sky, free and limitless. Inside, I was caged with guilt at not finding him repulsive.

"What if I vowed to never get caught?" he mused.

I knew what he was asking me: could I look past all his crimes—if they were *ongoing*?

As disturbingly unafraid of Hunter as I was, the only thing tethering me to this life was my moral compass. And while the thread of it was definitely fraying, tempting me to do things that were immoral and corrupt…

"I can't be with someone who murders people."

Hunter seemed to consider this.

"Let's say someone hurts you," he said, his knuckles trailing down my neck to my chest. "Mugs you, for example. May I murder him?"

I couldn't believe my mouth hitched up slightly, threatening to smile.

"No."

Hunter frowned.

"Can I ask you something?" I said.

Hunter trailed his fingertips over my belly, the skin coming alive with his every touch.

"If you find your father's killer, what will you do to him?"

Did *he* want to change? Or was his urge too strong?

Hunter was quiet for a bit again before sighing. "Honestly, I don't think I'll ever find him."

"You're giving up hope?"

"I'm accepting reality," Hunter said. "Should've done it a long time ago."

Hunter's fingertips swirled around my hip.

"What about you?" he asked. "It's looking like the new trial is virtually a guarantee. Which means after all your years of hard work, you will have saved your father. Where do you go from here?"

I stared at the ceiling, sifting through my confusing thoughts.

"You know, I thought the only thing I would feel would be happiness and relief," I said. "But...saving my father won't change the injustice going on in the world. I'm realizing that I can't save everyone. I'm exhausted trying."

Hunter's fingernails trailed up my chest to my neck. He cupped my cheek and shifted my head so I would look at him.

"I think I want a normal life for a little while," I said.

The pad of his thumb brushed my lower lip.

"If I could give you normal," he said, "could you look past everything I've done?"

CHAPTER 35
Hunter

"I found something, sir," Barry began, his voice hesitant.

In the dim light of my home office, Grayson leaned against a shadowed wall, his gaze intent on me. Barry's intense eyes hinted at the weight of his revelation.

The air was thick with tension and the musk of Barry's aftershave.

"Before your accountant left, he did provide the details we requested about that financial transaction. It took a little time for the forensic accountant to sift through it, but he prioritized it, given our tight schedule."

Tight was a kind word; it had been less than four days since we'd spoken last about the funds.

"And?" I pressed, trying to keep the desperation out of my voice.

"He found who the money went to," Barry said.

I sat back in my chair, looking at the closed manila folders he'd laid out on my desk, wondering if the name of my father's killer was inside them.

"Did he trace the full five million?" I asked.

Barry nodded.

"Was he an employee?" I asked.

"No. It wasn't an inside job. Nobody related to the recipient had connections with the company."

Grayson and I shared a puzzled look.

"If he didn't work for the company, how did the guy get the money?"

"Someone from the company paid it to him," Barry said.

My mind raced, trying to piece it together. "For what?"

"That, I don't know," Barry said. "But whoever paid him went to a lot of trouble to conceal where the money went. You don't do that unless you have something to hide."

"And this is the same money my father reimbursed?"

"Yes."

I rubbed my jaw. "Do you know *who* paid this guy that five million?"

"My forensic accountant is still digging, but whoever it was knew how to hide the trail."

I stood up, walked to the window, and looked out at the simplicity of the landscaping—the emerald lawns, the birds chirping, while in here, a complex cyclone of problems was unraveling.

"And this money vanished days before my father was murdered?"

"Yes."

"Which means this guy's likely involved in my dad's death." My neck hardened with tension.

"That would be my take, yes. I haven't found anything else in your father's life that was out of sorts before he died."

My heart launched into a rhythmic warning. My sixth sense told me this guy didn't just have the answers that eluded me my entire life. He probably knew who killed my father. Hell, he might be the killer himself, even if I hadn't pieced the motive together.

One thing I'd learned as a prosecutor was how often humans get tangled up in motive. If we can't understand the why, we're tempted to dismiss it.

But this couldn't be dismissed. This was the key to everything. I could feel it.

I needed to go there, shake the guy down for answers, and if he was the man who killed my father?

I would slit his throat.

Luna wanted me to stop my ways, but would she forgive me if I did this one last thing?

Doing so would be a tremendous risk, not just to my possible relationship with her, but also because Mayor Kepler was looking into everyone in her life, trying to uncover the identity of the Vigilante. Maybe even having them watched.

Now wasn't the time to confront a man who may have murdered my father, because I doubted I'd be able to control myself.

Yet the Moby Dick I had hunted my whole life was within my grasp.

"What's his name?" I asked.

Barry opened up a file and inched it across the desk, waiting for me to read it.

Why does that name sound familiar?

It took me a second to place it. Out of context, it made no sense, was never connected to this case, but now, a terrible dread overcame me, drying my throat.

My voice broke in disbelief. "This…it can't be."

"It's real, Mr. Lockwood."

Holy shit.

There was no way in hell I was *not* heading to this guy's address. Right. Now.

CHAPTER 36
Hunter

I charged out of my office.

"What is it?" Grayson followed me.

"Barry, I'll be in touch," I said, opening my door and seeing him out.

The man looked at me and hesitated before leaving.

I shut the massive wooden door, and I turned my attention to Grayson.

"I need you to stay here and keep an eye on Luna for me. Can you do that?"

I walked toward the staircase.

"I'm not letting you confront some asshole alone, Hunter."

"Grayson." I stopped. Looked at my brother deadpan with a look that said, Don't. Ask. Questions.

It wasn't fair to evade them, but I'd have to explain later; I didn't want him to come with me in case I went the murder route, and I needed to confront this guy and find out what the hell happened all those years ago. Before it was too late. I still didn't know what it all meant, especially given who the man was, but my gut said it was bad.

Worse than I ever imagined.

Bam, bam, bam.

Grayson and I looked at the front door curiously.

"Mr. Lockwood," Rinaldi's voice shouted from the other side. "I need to have a word with you."

Damn it all to hell. Now what?

When I opened my door again, I tried to hide my glare from Mayor Kepler and Detective Rinaldi, as well as my immense irritation that Sean was standing next to them on my front porch.

"Now is not a good time," I said.

Luna wandered out of the dining room, where she was preparing for her next court date.

She was smart enough to keep a poker face on, smiling at the sight of the three people who could take me down.

And judging by the suspicion in their tightened eyes, they might do so right now.

"Mayor." She smiled. "I'm surprised to see you here." She glanced at Sean with curiosity, then settled her eyes on Rinaldi.

"Did you find something with that letter?" Luna asked.

Rinaldi's brows furrowed. "The letter?"

Luna's lips thinned. "The one that threatened my father's life."

"Oh, not yet," Rinaldi said.

Other people might not have noticed Luna's slight facial change, but I did. She was frustrated, not only that the cops hadn't found anything, but that Rinaldi had to be reminded of its existence.

In Luna's mind, the threat to her father was everything, but Rinaldi clearly wasn't here to talk about her father. You don't drag the mayor along for something like that. Whatever they were here for was bigger, but Luna wasn't going to let them off that easily.

"Have they looked through surveillance footage?" Luna crossed her arms over her chest.

"We're working on it," Rinaldi said. "But that's not why we're here. We would like to talk to you, Mr. Lockwood."

"Actually," I said, "I was just heading out for an errand."

"What errand would that be?" Rinaldi asked.

I swear to hell, if Mayor Kepler and Rinaldi weren't standing here right now, I'd deck Sean in his jaw for looking at me like he'd just made a chess move that was about to ruin me.

"A private one," I said. "Do you mind telling me what this is about?"

"Sean, what are you doing here?" Luna asked.

Sean glared at her. How dare he look at her like that? The next chance I got, I'd slam my fist into his teeth for giving her that look.

"You and I need to talk," Sean said to her.

How dare he speak to her in that clipped tone? It was everything I could do to keep my arm at bay.

Grayson stood to my left, his tight gaze sweeping methodically from person to person.

"We need to ask you some questions in private," Rinaldi said to me.

"I'm happy to answer questions. But as I said, now is not a good time."

"We can be quick," she said. "May we look in your garage?"

I blinked. "My garage?"

"Yes."

Shit.

"For what purpose?"

"We received an anonymous tip," the detective said.

Sean smirked.

"An anonymous tip," I said. "In regard to what?"

They said nothing. Which pissed me off even more—did they think a criminal lawyer wouldn't protect his rights?

"You expect I'll allow you to search my private residence without so much as an explanation? Or a warrant?"

"We don't want to drag your name through the mud in front of these people." The mayor nodded to Luna and Grayson.

I held the mayor's gaze, a menacing growl rising from deep within my chest.

"But you *are* accusing me of something then," I said through clenched teeth. "Of what, exactly?"

"Accusing is a strong word," he muttered.

I didn't have time for this. If he had the balls to show up at my front door, the least he could do was tell me what the hell he knew. Their hands were void of paperwork, so they didn't have a search warrant. If they'd had that, they'd have shown up with an army of police officers, but it was just these three.

This is a fishing expedition.

"Since when does the mayor accompany the police on searches?" My voice strained for composure, even as my jaw clenched in suppressed anger.

"Do you really want me to say it out loud?" Mayor Kepler's eyes narrowed as he glanced at Grayson and Luna, then back at me.

"I have nothing to hide," I lied, keeping my voice firm.

The mayor tightened his lips, a sign of irritation dancing through his face.

"We received an anonymous tip about the Vigilante."

"Did you find him?" I dared him to answer.

If I didn't win this battle with the mayor, they might take me into police custody, and then I might lose the opportunity to interrogate the man who had something to do with my father's death.

The man who played a bigger role in our lives than I ever could've imagined.

Sure, I could send Grayson. He was the guy I trusted to get answers after all, but when I saw that name, I wanted to—no, needed to—look him in the eyes myself.

"We're getting closer," Mayor Kepler answered.

He looked at Luna, who was still doing a damn good job of keeping her poker face, even though she was probably panicking on the inside.

"We would like to check out your vehicles," Rinaldi said.

"My vehicles."

Silence stretched until they must have realized their only hope of me agreeing to a fishing expedition was to tell me what drew them here.

"Luna, when you were attacked in the prison parking lot, the Vigilante rescued you," Rinaldi said. "After reviewing the footage, there was one security camera that caught something."

Shit.

When Luna told the mayor that she thought somebody in her life might be the Vigilante, clearly, they had been busy. Pulling footage of the Vigilante rescuing Luna was a smart move, one I should've anticipated.

But I had been careful at the prison. At least, I thought I had been.

"A security camera on the far end of the parking lot caught the Vigilante climbing into a vehicle and speeding away."

Double shit.

I kept my face calm. "Great. Run the plates and find him."

Rinaldi and Mayor Kepler looked at each other. "The footage was too grainy to get plate numbers."

They were fake anyway. I changed out the plates every single time I used that car, but I was trying to fish for how strongly they suspected me.

"We know the make and model, though. If you'd be so kind as to let us look in your garage."

Dammit, I loved that car. Now I'd have to get rid of it.

"You still haven't answered my question. Why are you *here*, wanting to look in *my* garage?"

Sean's lips curled into the perfect target for a fist.

"There's someone who has been researching the Windy City Vigilante case for quite some time," Sean said.

"An armchair detective," I said with a raised brow. "I guess you've been busy then."

Sean's fists clenched. "They found something interesting."

"Please tell me you didn't convince the city's *mayor* to drop what he was doing based on some armchair detective's conspiracy theory."

Sean's face reddened. Whether it was from embarrassment or rage, I couldn't be sure, but it was satisfying all the same.

"You know what they found?" Sean narrowed his eyes.

"Nothing significant, or you'd be at the *correct* house with a warrant."

Sean took a step toward me, the asshole. He was baiting me into a fight, and my fingers were twitching at my side, begging me to oblige.

Luna laced her hand in mine.

Sean looked down at our clasped hands, his glare growing angrier.

"The day Dominic Hopkins was killed at the courthouse, no one saw the Vigilante, or anyone else for that matter, fleeing through the parking lot after the murder," Sean said.

"If you can get to your point, I have things to do," I said.

I had been trying to keep my tone respectful with the detective and the mayor, but I didn't intend to do that with Sean. In fact, doing so only made me look more suspicious.

"The Vigilante went back inside the courthouse," Sean said.

I looked at my watch to make a show of it. "What does that have to do with me?"

"Mr. Lockwood." Rinaldi stepped forward. "You're a very prominent figure with a busy social calendar. And yet, when we cross-referenced the dates that the Vigilante struck against your social commitments, they don't overlap."

"In a city of three million people, I'm sure many of them weren't seen in public at the times in question. You talking to all of them, too?" I asked.

Rinaldi's lips tightened. Maybe she couldn't give me everything—suspect 101—but I wasn't stupid, and I knew they had to have more to show up here like this. If they wanted access to anything, they were damn sure going to lay out the broad strokes that led them here.

"We believe the Vigilante has knowledge of law enforcement, based on evasive tactics and lack of forensics. Obviously, you have that knowledge, Mr. Lockwood."

"As does the entire Chicago Police Department."

"There was *one* social commitment that did overlap, though," she continued. "You told a coworker you'd be at a charity event the night of one of the Vigilante's attacks but never showed."

"For a person who was evading law enforcement, that would be a pretty dumb move, to no-show at an event," I countered.

That asshole took way longer to kill than I'd planned.

"You have similar motives as the Vigilante."

"Do I?"

"You want to hold people accountable for their crimes, and these victims were all accused of violent crimes."

"I spend my days working within the legal system. It's a pretty far leap to say I'd suddenly break all the laws I was spending my days to uphold."

"You have a traumatic past, with your father's death."

"You searching the home of everyone who had a rough childhood?"

Rinaldi's posture stiffened, her eyes narrowing as she took a sharp breath.

They had done limited research to see if I had an airtight alibi on any of the nights in question without asking me, which, of course, I didn't. Some person came up with the hypothesis that the Windy City Vigilante was someone inside the courthouse and probably plucked well-known people inside that day as possible candidates. Then Rinaldi caught a glimpse of the Vigilante's car through a grainy security camera. None of this would be grounds for even an informal search, let alone a warrant. And certainly not incriminating enough to justify the mayor coming to my door.

That was until Luna planted the seed in his ear that she thought the Vigilante might be someone she knew. Narrowing the list of suspects from Chicago's three million residents to a handful.

"If you would allow us to look in your garage, perhaps we could exclude you," Rinaldi said.

Son of a bitch. I wanted to deny them access out of principle alone. This was insulting to come to my home on such flimsy grounds, but if I refused, it would only heighten their suspicions.

Sean had clearly egged them on, and Mayor Kepler's reelection campaign was going into overdrive next week. So here he was, trying to catch the Windy City Vigilante just in time to look like a hero. So desperate and pressured for time, he was making mistakes.

I wanted Sean to look like a complete dumbass at this moment. So, there was that, too.

I sighed, playing the role of someone who had nothing to hide.

"If you could be quick," I said, motioning for them to follow me.

All three of them looked away quickly, but I saw the unmistakable brightness in their eyes before they did. Clearly, they weren't sure that I was going to cooperate, but I led them through my foyer, through my kitchen, around the back hallway, and into the main garage.

Where I turned on the lights so they could see my vehicle collection.

None of them were the Vigilante's car. That one was parked in my underground garage on the back of the property.

The mayor and the detective walked around, looking at each vehicle, their face growing more discouraged with each passing minute.

I shoved my hands in my pockets and glared at Sean, who was staring at Luna, as if waiting for an opportunity to say something to her.

Meanwhile, Grayson stood in the doorway like a statue, watching this all unfold. No one else knew him well enough to see that his look was haunting—one that made him appear like a predator ready to strike if it came down to it. Making me wonder what, exactly, my brother was capable of...

"Do you have any vehicles parked in a parking structure in the city?" the detective asked.

"No."

"Do you have any other vehicles parked at friends' or your family's houses?"

"No."

They frowned. They didn't ask me if I had another vehicle parked in the secret underground garage.

Shame.

Mayor Kepler and Detective Rinaldi locked eyes and glanced at Sean.

"He probably has it hidden somewhere," Sean pressed.

"Yeah. Probably buried it in the backyard," Grayson said flatly. "Why don't you go look?"

I bit back a smile.

But I could tell by the downward slope in the corners of their mouths that this didn't rule me out in their eyes. They were onto my scent, and the sand in the hourglass was falling before they might find something that would put me away for good.

"Thank you for letting us look around," Detective Rinaldi said.

A few more pleasantries were exchanged before I escorted the three of them back to my front porch.

"Why is there a squad out front?" I asked, noting the police cruiser.

"It's for your protection," Rinaldi claimed. "We still haven't found Franco."

"I have my own security," I reminded them, pointing to my cameras.

"Better safe than sorry," Rinaldi said.

Bull. They were putting me under surveillance, under the guise of protecting us against Franco. The problem was, there was nothing I could do about it. How could I claim I didn't want protection from Franco when he was still missing?

"Have a good day, Mr. Lockwood. When we have more questions, we'll let you know."

When. Not *if.*

Wonderful.

I eyed the police cruiser at the end of my drive with disdain.

I needed to go find this man who had received five million dollars and interrogate him, but with police watching me, the risk was too great they'd follow me. I could go to the tunnel, go to my secret garage, but there was a chance another squad car could be parked along the road I would emerge from, and if they saw me, they might trail back and find my secret garage. My everything.

And even if they didn't, there would be an APB on that make and model car.

Son of a bitch.

I'd evaded police for years, but never with this much heat—never with them this close, literally parked on my property looking for anything suspicious.

As painful as this was, the smart move would be to bide my time. Just for a very short while.

I'd think of some way to get away from them.

"Luna," Sean said. "Can I have a word with you, alone?"

CHAPTER 37

Luna

"Do you know who he is?" Sean's voice, tense and cold, came from behind me. This time, in the courtroom, the first place I'd seen him since he tried to talk to me in Hunter's foyer.

Here, hushed whispers of spectators mingled with the creaking of wooden benches.

Dimmed lights cast an ethereal glow upon the polished oak panels, which seemed darker in anticipation of the judge and defendant soon coming in.

In this crucible of justice, a flicker of hope shimmered: perhaps today, my father would be freed.

I could not afford any distractions, and yet Sean approached me from the front row of the audience like he couldn't wait to talk to me until another time.

"What?" I asked, turning around.

"Do you know?"

His tousled blond locks hinted at his frustration, likely raked through numerous times, and his black tie was loose around the white collar shirt, like he'd been tugging at the knot, while his brown eyes seemed so dark, they almost looked black.

I nodded to the side of the room, where we could talk in private, waiting for Sean to follow me there.

"Know what?" I asked.

"You know what I'm talking about," he said.

I glanced out at the sparse audience, spotting Hunter.

Sean's gaze hardened. "Eight days, Luna. Not a word since we showed up at Hunter's. And that doesn't even include the time I came before that, warning you of my suspicions."

His words pressed down on me, every syllable a reminder of the weight I'd been carrying, the distance I'd put between us.

"I told you, I was working on my dad's case, and I didn't have time for anything else."

"You could have talked to me for two minutes when I was at Hunter's place." Every line on his forehead was etched with hostility.

Lord, I was a terrible friend. Was this how it would be if I chose Hunter's side? Hunter had asked if I could live with his past crimes, but if I did, I'd be going against my only friend. Could I live with that?

"Do you know who Hunter is?" Sean pressed.

"Why do you think he's the Vigilante?" I hedged.

"You heard what Detective Rinaldi said."

"All of which was circumstantial and weak at that."

"That's not what I asked," Sean said, taking one step closer. "Do you know if Hunter is the Windy City Vigilante?"

If. A very telling word. They still didn't know for sure, thank goodness, but this still felt terrible, staring into the eyes of a friend who had always been good to me.

I wanted to be honest with Sean—he deserved my honesty after all he'd done for me, after being my only friend for years—but honesty sentenced Hunter's fate.

Sean was a great guy, but he was also someone you didn't want to get on the wrong side of. He could hold a grudge like no other.

Once, Sean's sister had her college entrance essays stolen, copied, and sold online. When she got her rejection, it came with a big fat accusation that she'd plagiarized her own damn essay. With Sean's sleuthing skills, he figured out what happened, but by that time, the school had already filled all their seats, and she missed out on her dream college.

So, what did Sean do? Let it go?

No. No, he didn't. He tracked down the kid who'd stolen it, found out which college the kid was going to, and drove twelve hours to meet with the dean. With all his evidence. But he didn't stop there.

He created a webpage optimized for search engines, so anytime someone googled the kid's name, his plagiarism and the deceitful act of selling it online was the first thing you saw. Second thing? Disgraced expulsion from college.

And he still didn't stop there. He pulled favors from some of the local reporters he'd developed relationships with by that point—Sean was older than his sister and was well on his way to working full-time as a true crime podcaster—and they ran stories in the local news, newspapers, and blogs, further disgracing him.

The guy was ruined. Completely. No other colleges would accept him, no one would hire him, and no one wanted to date him. Sean ensured his life was completely destroyed.

If he found out who Hunter was, Sean would do everything in his power to make his already-ruined life even worse. Serving a life sentence wouldn't be enough. He'd ensure every prisoner hated the prosecutor even more than they already would, not just to endanger him, but to make him a target of unspeakable acts.

Every. Single. Day.

"Sean, I was the one that told you to hunt the Vigilante. Why would I do that if I were trying to protect him?"

"Maybe you said it before you knew."

Look at the veins about to pop on his temple. "I've never seen you this riled up over a case you're working."

"This one's personal."

"Yeah, but"—now that I was thinking about it—"you've been getting more upset with each case you work on," I said. "Why?"

A troubled expression crossed Sean's face, his teeth catching his bottom lip.

"In all my years of podcasting, I've reported on countless crimes but never actually solved one. I'm just a glorified reporter, and that was never my goal. My goal was to make a difference...and this is my chance to do it." He jabbed his finger toward the ground. "I can stop the Windy City Vigilante before he hurts anyone else—including you."

I wondered if he could hear my veins thickening with guilt and fear.

Lying to him made me feel like a traitor.

The secret threatened to crush me. It wasn't just mine anymore; it was a living, breathing entity, wedged between Sean and me.

"The only person I'm in danger from is whoever threatened me and my dad, trying to stop this hearing."

Sean's chest puffed out in an almost-paternal manner. "If you're lying to me, Luna..." Sean glowered at Hunter, then back at me. "I won't let that go."

CHAPTER 38

Luna

I n a heartbeat, our world could shatter or shine.

My father approached my table, wearing the same suit as he had at the last hearing.

"You look great, Dad," I whispered, holding back tears. My stomach churned, and I forced a smile, swallowing the rising bile from my nerves.

"Did push-ups every day." The corners of Dad's eyes crinkled as a weary smile spread across his face.

"I'm sorry you spent the last few days in solitary."

Nine days, to be exact, but I was beyond grateful the judge scheduled the hearing for *today*. Normally, it could have been weeks or months. Thankfully, Mayor Kepler, despite his suspicions about Hunter, hadn't interfered with the original favor he'd called in to have the judge hear our case so soon.

"Spending your birthday outside prison walls would be a dream come true," I said, my voice choked with emotion.

Dad's fingers fiddled with the cuffs of his suit, avoiding my gaze.

"Luna, I love your optimism, but let's just take this one step at a time."

"I've been daydreaming about your birthday all week."

I could imagine this Saturday in my mind's eye. Dad opening up a menu and getting to pick whatever he wanted to eat for the first time in two decades. He could pick the restaurant. He could pick the time of day. He could pick the meal. He could pick out what he wore.

"I don't know that I can get my hopes up that high," Dad said, his lips curling down. "It's been so long."

"Get your hopes up, Dad. This terrible chapter in your life is about to be over. You have the next thirty years ahead of you to be a free man and do whatever you want."

And there it was, that glistening in his eyes that told me he was allowing the hope to break through.

"All rise," a voice echoed through the vast courtroom, making the high ceilings and cold marble walls seem even more imposing.

Throughout the beginning of the proceedings, my throat got drier, and my hands began to tremble.

Especially when the hearing rested on my shoulders. I had talked a good game with my dad, but truthfully, I was terrified that this might not go our way. Countless nights spent meditating and manifesting this moment played in my head, but nothing truly prepared me for the weight of it.

Barry had secured the additional autopsy findings and lab results, just as he promised. And they all said the same thing.

But there was no guarantee. Judges didn't take too kindly to releasing convicted murderers. And now, the time was upon me to say my part—the moment in my life I'd been preparing for since I was that little girl, being ripped out of my father's embrace.

The judge was perched high on his bench, looking down at us, my client—my dad—and me.

My fingers traced the frayed edges and dog-eared corners of the case file, each mark a testament to the fight I had waged for two long decades.

"Your Honor," I began, my voice steady despite the butterflies in my stomach, "I stand before you today to present new evidence, evidence that will illuminate the truth that has been hiding for two long decades."

Judge Whitfield, a man with a reputation for being tough but fair, peered at me over the rim of his glasses, nodding for me to continue.

"With respect, I submit new findings from a recent review of the autopsy by new medical examiners." I slid the files to the clerk. "Which reveals that the victim's cause of death was not, in fact, from a beating as initially reported. Instead, it was the result of a vehicular strike."

A restless rustling shifted in the courtroom from the handful of people, whispers colliding and bouncing off the walls.

"We've also found new evidence on the victim's clothing. Paint chips," I said, presenting a sealed bag containing the pants, carefully preserved.

"These paint chips, Your Honor, match the color and type of paint used in vehicles. They were embedded deeply in the fibers of the victim's pants, consistent with the force of a car hitting a pedestrian."

The judge looked down at the evidence before him, his brow furrowed in contemplation. The silence was deafening, a stark contrast to the cacophony of heartbeats thundering through my chest.

"Your Honor," I pressed on, my voice echoing in the silence, "this new evidence turns the whole case on its head. A man has lost two decades of his life for a crime he did not commit. The defense respectfully requests that all charges against my client be dismissed."

Rumbles cascaded over the onlookers behind me.

The judge's eyes bore into mine, his raised eyebrows a silent challenge.

"Counselor," he began, "you were asking for a retrial, and now you want dismissal?"

"The defendant did not own a vehicle. Nor did he have access to one, so there is no way this defendant could have been the one to strike the victim. Further, video surveillance from my client's work shows him leaving on *foot* before the victim was killed. This is a second and third independent lab confirming the paint found on the victim was from a vehicle. Specifically, a Jaguar."

I shuffled the files in my hand to retrieve another piece of paper—

the new evidence that bore the possibility of freedom for Dad—and handed it off, waiting as the judge looked it over.

"And these tests were carried out by accredited laboratories, Counselor?" he questioned, finally breaking the silence.

"Yes, Your Honor, they were conducted by three accredited and recognized forensic laboratories," I confirmed, "They've also provided a statement attesting to the reliability and accuracy of their testing methods."

With a sigh, the judge leaned back, removing his glasses to rub at the bridge of his nose.

"You've made some compelling arguments. However, why were these autopsy findings not presented at the initial trial?" he asked.

"Your Honor, the initial autopsy report was, unfortunately, incomplete and did not account for some crucial details," I explained. "The subsequent analysis, completed by three different forensic pathologists, reveals that the original report overlooked critical evidence consistent with a vehicular accident."

"And these paint chips found on the victim's clothing," he continued, holding up the sealed bag, "why weren't they discovered sooner?"

"Regrettably, Your Honor," I said, swallowing hard, "the original investigation didn't scrutinize the victim's clothing to the extent necessary. The discovery of the paint chips came only when we sought to re-examine all physical evidence."

"Well, Counselor," he began, his voice grave and deliberate, "this evidence was available at the time of the original trial."

The statement hung heavy in the air, echoing the judge's reluctance to acknowledge the possible miscarriage of justice.

"Your Honor, while the paint chips were indeed present at the scene and collected during the initial investigation, the technology to accurately identify and match these specific paint chips was not available twenty years ago," I explained, the crisp edge of my voice slicing through the courtroom's silence.

The judge waited for me to explain.

"The forensic paint analysis technology has significantly advanced in the past two decades. This report"—I motioned toward my copy of the document in front of him—"verifies that the paint chips match those used in automotive manufacturing. This evidence exonerates my client."

As the judge took his time to peruse the report, the room was gripped by a tense silence. Each tick of the courtroom's grand clock struck like a hammer to my heart, echoing the agonizing wait for justice.

The silence was thick, suffocating. When the judge finally sighed, removing his glasses again, my heart skipped a beat.

"Counselor, I will adjourn to review this evidence in detail. This court will reconvene after lunch to deliver a decision," he declared.

While my dad was taken into holding and Hunter stayed in his seat —presumably to give me space—I stayed in the courtroom, unable to eat lunch or do anything else, until finally the judge returned, and the hearing resumed.

Everyone seemed to hold their breaths as the judge steepled his fingers, his gaze sweeping across the room.

"Upon careful examination of the new evidence presented," he continued, his voice reverberating through the courtroom, "it has become apparent that the death of the boy was not due to a physical altercation, but rather, he was tragically struck by a vehicle."

I wanted to reach out and grab Dad's hand, but I refrained. Irrationally terrified that one wrong move would stop where this was headed.

"That said," the judge continued, "the boy was not found in a street, but rather in an alley, suggesting the boy may have tried to flee from the accident, or his body may have been moved."

Maybe that's the guy my father saw all those years ago—the man who'd moved the body.

"Vehicular homicide is something that should be explored further. In light of the fact that the defendant, Mr. Payne, was confirmed to have no vehicle at the time of the incident and was indeed seen on foot shortly before the occurrence of said incident, it has been determined that there is enough doubt as to his involvement, that this case needs to be re-examined."

As the judge's words sank in, the brick that had been on my chest since I was a small girl began to lift.

"Justice," the judge continued, "is not about rigidly adhering to past decisions, but about ensuring that the truth prevails, no matter how late it comes to light. It's evident that the original trial was incomplete in its assessment and, therefore, the verdict."

He paused for a moment, letting his gaze sweep over the silent spectators.

"I have carefully reviewed the evidence and arguments presented. While I am not convinced that a dismissal of all charges is warranted at this juncture, I do find sufficient grounds to grant the defendant a new trial."

My eyes burned with tears of joy. While it wasn't a complete dismissal of charges, it was damn close.

"After considering the circumstances," the judge continued, "and in light of the upcoming new trial, I hereby order that the defendant be released on their own recognizance, pending the proceedings. Conditions for release will be set forth by this court, and I expect the defendant to adhere strictly to them."

Dad's eyes shimmered, and as he swayed, I grabbed his elbow—both of us on the verge of something we'd dreamed of for decades.

The judge's gavel came down with a resounding crack, and the words we had waited two decades to hear echoed.

"You are free to go."

Warmth spilled down my cheeks, each tear a testament to the years of heartache, relief, and disbelief etched on my father's face. I grabbed my dad and pulled him into a bear hug. Everything else around me seemed to fade away, and the only thing that existed was the relieved whimpers of my dad, his tears brushing against my ear.

"You did it," he choked. "You actually did it."

"I told you I would never give up, Dad."

The minutes that followed became a blur of faces and congratulations. Sean. Detective Rinaldi. Elizabeth Wood, Hunter, Grayson, Rodney, and his daughter, Charlotte, not to mention other well-wishers.

"Sir," Hunter said, extending his hand, "congratulations. It's an honor to meet you."

"Hunter, this is my dad, Dad, this is...Hunter." I almost said *my boyfriend.* The term lodged in my throat, and I swallowed it down, unwilling to let my confusion over Hunter cast a shadow over this victory.

"The media are out front," Elizabeth said.

I raised an eyebrow at her.

"Someone might have tipped them off that an innocent man who has served twenty years in prison might get exonerated today."

My lip quivered. My whole life, I had felt alone, but I wasn't alone, was I? Faces filled with warmth smiled, hands reached out, squeezing my shoulders, or patting my back. Every gesture whispered, *We're here for you.*

"Do you want to give a statement, Dad?"

Dad shook his head. "I'm done trying to win people over. I just want to celebrate with my daughter."

I smiled.

"What food have you been daydreaming about for the last twenty years?" I asked.

His eyes were still red, though he was doing a better job composing his emotions than I was.

"A rib eye," he said.

"Then that's what we're going to get."

"You take the car." Hunter smiled. "You and your father could use some time alone."

"No," Dad interjected. "I wouldn't mind getting to know my daughter's significant other."

My cheeks blazed with red. "Dad..."

"It's written all over your face. Now come on. You and your boyfriend are going to buy me a steak. And then I have to figure out where I'm going to live."

"There's a gorgeous cottage that I'm hoping will be free," Hunter said, looking at me—his implication clear.

He hoped I'd choose to be with him. And stay.

"But even if it's not, I have plenty of other options, sir. The last thing you need to worry about is having a place to stay."

Dad raised his eyebrows. "I like your boyfriend."

"Dad, he's not my...never mind."

I wrapped my arm around my dad's waist and began leading him out of the courtroom.

"Is it really over?" he whispered in disbelief.

"The new evidence is rock solid, Dad. I doubt the DA will even pursue that new trial once he sees it."

Dad shook his head. "It's going to take some time to get used to thinking about what I want to do tomorrow. Next month, next year. Maybe I'll go back to school and get a degree."

Finally, Dad was allowing his freedom to sink in. It dawned on me that, in all of these years, accepting his injustice must have been a coping mechanism. A dark one that was now gone.

When we arrived at the front doors, Dad's lips turned down into a frown when he spotted the reporters waiting to ask questions.

"We can go around back," I suggested.

"No," Dad said. "Let *them* not feel heard for a minute."

I smiled. Dad had tried to get them to listen to him back then, and now the tables were turned.

He straightened his tie and held his chin up as we emerged onto the front steps of the courthouse.

Flanked by Hunter and Sean, we kept our chins up, ignoring all the reporters who wanted our time as we made our way toward the black sedan fifty feet in front of us.

We made it down the steps and another twenty feet when...

A sharp pop exploded in my ears.

Screams pierced the air, followed by pain, when something heavy slammed into me, and the warm pavement hit my body. My ears, still ringing, began to pick up other sounds: the frantic shuffling of feet, and muffled cries.

Hunter's weight on me was both reassuring and terrifying. His breath, ragged and quick, echoed my own rising panic. But his presence was momentarily forgotten as my gaze landed on the stillness next to me.

"Dad!" I screamed.

I bucked against Hunter's weight.

"Luna, stay down," he urged.

Dad was lying there, unmoving. His eyes stared blankly into the sky, the light that had danced within them only moments ago now extinguished.

As a slow trail of blood dripped from the hole in his forehead.

With fingers trembling, I reached for him, desperate for some sign, any sign, that this wasn't the end of our story.

"Let me go!" I squirmed until I broke free and made it to my dad.

Where Hunter hovered his body over mine again, shielding me, should a second bullet strike.

"Daddy," I whispered, cupping his cheek.

Just like all those years ago, my father had been taken beyond my grasp while I sobbed helplessly, my tears soaking into his button-down shirt.

The words he'd spoken when I'd sobbed as a little girl, ripped from the sanctuary of his arms, echoed through my heart like a torturous metronome.

"It's okay, Luna," he had said. *"You can let me go."*

"No!" I screamed so loud, that my voice cracked as I clutched the fabric of his shirt.

CHAPTER 39

Luna

"Luna, don't do this."

I sat in the front seat of a funeral home, waiting for the service to begin, while Hunter stood along the far wall, giving Rinaldi a chance to talk me out of this.

This place reminded me of a home in the 1800s. Thick, white trim, lace fabrics, peach walls, as if that could soothe away the pain of losing their loved one whose casket was displayed front and center.

As if to say, *Here, come look at the dead person who's now a translucent version of the warm flesh you once hugged. It will give you closure.*

"They haven't found who killed him," I said in a monotone voice that bordered on hopeless frustration.

We had done everything we could within the legal system. We showed up at police headquarters every day, putting pressure on detectives so that the case would remain a top priority. I had called Mayor Kepler and asked for favors. I had asked for favors from old colleagues. I had put out a news press. Sean had done an emergency podcast. I had done everything I could, and yet we still had no leads.

"It's only been a few days," Detective Rinaldi said.

I pulled the tissue I was holding into a tight line and twisted it around my finger until the circulation cut off.

"A few days is everything with an investigation, you know that. If a murder isn't solved within forty-eight hours, statistically, it's not going to get solved."

"Luna..."

I whipped my gaze to hers.

"If you're asking me to hold on to hope and keep fighting this fight for the next several months or years or decades, you've come to the wrong person. I told you guys my father had been threatened. Where was the police protection? Not just for my dad, but you knew that Franco had threatened Hunter. And me. According to you, we were supposed to be under police surveillance."

Maybe it wasn't fair to take all my anger out on Detective Rinaldi, but I didn't have it in me to care about that right now.

"A police officer did follow you guys to the courthouse, and he was in the courtroom. He was twenty steps behind you when this happened."

I was furious at myself for walking out the front door of the courthouse.

I mean, how naive and reckless of me to assume that whoever had been trying to stop the hearing from happening would have nothing to gain by following through with those threats after the hearing had taken place.

I guess if I were being honest, the person I was most furious with was myself. I could've asked Hunter for an army of bodyguards around my father, and he would have given it to me. I could've taken Dad out the back door. I could've done a million things differently, but I hadn't.

I had failed him.

And now the legal system was failing him.

Again.

"The police don't even have a lead. They have many cases, and they might not prioritize a convicted felon's death."

"That's not fair."

"Isn't it? Because I haven't seen a huge uprising like there was when that kid was killed twenty years ago. Granted, that was a teenager, and my father was a grown man, but still. This took place right outside the courthouse, where judges and law enforcement officers spend their days."

"Look, I understand that you're upset, but putting yourself—"

"Upset isn't even in the same hemisphere as what I'm feeling."

Rinaldi's lips tightened.

"Look, I'm sorry for being rude," I managed. "But I've run out of energy to be polite. We both know how this is going to go, so please. Save yourself the energy of trying to convince me otherwise."

"Luna, if you do this, you might put yourself in danger."

"From the person that killed my father? According to the *multiple* threats I handed over to you, I already am."

"Luna, listen to me. Whoever killed your father clearly believed he was still a threat."

"Yeah, and I think I know why," I said. "You'll hear it in my eulogy."

Tense silence thickened the air between us.

"Be that as it may, they probably think that threat died with your father, or you would have been shot, too."

"Or I was shoved to the ground so fast by Hunter, they failed to finish the job."

"But if you declare war on them, they'll see you as a threat, too."

"I underestimated the threat against my father. So, I know full well doing this might poke a beehive, but whoever did this tried to control me and my dad through fear. I'm not going to let them control me anymore."

I watched the people taking their seats, wondering if the murderer was among them. There were colleagues of mine, lawyers, including Elizabeth Wood. Mayor Kepler made a brief, cursory appearance and had already left. Then there was Hunter's family—his brothers Grayson, Jace, and Bryson, as well as Hunter's uncle Alexander, making small talk with other funeral patrons. Sean sat one row over, having given me a hug and profuse apologies that we had an argument right before Dad was killed.

"The only thing that matters now is finding my father's killer. If you'll excuse me, I have a eulogy to give."

The funeral started like any other, I suppose. Hunter sat to my right, lacing his warm fingers through mine in a warm reminder that I wasn't alone in my hell.

No matter how much it felt like I was.

When the time came for me to give my speech, I walked to the little white podium and looked out at the too-small crowd.

Relatives of my father sat in the back row with my mother—who I couldn't stomach talking to just yet. I wondered if they sat in the back because they felt guilty for having believed in Dad's guilt for two decades. The angry part of me hoped they felt like crap because of it. The compassionate part of me was grateful they had enough respect for his life to say their goodbyes.

The beginning of my eulogy was typical for a funeral, recalling stories of my father's love for me when I was a little girl. I branched into the pain that he had suffered over the last two decades, being imprisoned for a crime he didn't commit.

And then...

"Dad..." At the sight of the casket, I had to force the lump in my throat to shrink so I could speak. "I'm glad that in your final moments of life, you had finally found the joy that had eluded you for twenty years. I'm grateful that you were excited about your future."

I looked at the audience, keeping my face stern just in case the murderer sat among them.

"Someone took my father's future. My guess is, it's because my dad could identify the person he'd seen in that alley shortly after that teenage boy was killed."

Hushed whispers of shock rippled through the attendees.

"The person must have realized that during the prep for a new trial, all evidence would be re-examined. Closely, especially with the new evidence we uncovered."

More murmurs.

"They got away with it two decades ago, but that was all about to change, wasn't it?"

Concerned glances.

"I was going to let the threats go when Dad was released. But now?

I promise, Dad, I'll never stop hunting the person who took you from us. They won't escape justice."

While the audience shifted in their seats, Hunter flattened his black tie, his face full of resignation.

When the ceremony concluded, Hunter held my hand in silence in the back of our sedan as our parade of vehicles crawled along the roads to the cemetery.

There, my father's black casket was placed above the hole in the earth where he would reside forever.

Under a shroud of obsidian clouds, I stood, swallowed by the same merciless darkness that consumed my heart. I clung to Hunter's hand, the silent warmth of his grip the only tether to my shattered world.

Tears leaked from my eyes, tracing warm paths down my cheeks, the moisture evaporating into the summer air. Hope was a distant memory, a mocking demon as a stinging wind swept through the cemetery, whispering broken promises through the bare trees.

Trees like the ones we'd had in my backyard as a kid, bringing back a memory.

"And we'll have tea parties and read books in here!" I squealed, twirling a pigtail with my finger.

Dad's grin widened as he took another long nail and started whacking it with his hammer.

"Once it's done, we can go to the library every week if you want," Dad said.

"And we can make art! We can draw with crayons in here!"

"I can hang up any art you make." Dad wiped a bead of sweat from his forehead and pointed next to me. "Can you hand me more nails?"

I reached into Dad's metal toolbox and handed him another handful that he shoved into his jeans pocket.

"Every nail we drive," Dad said, stilling with the hammer in his hand, "every wooden board we place, we're not just building a tree house. We're building dreams and a place where we'll make memories. No matter how big

you get, always remember that the strongest foundations are built with love and patience, and if you hold on to that, anything is possible."

"You okay?" Hunter asked, though he already knew the answer.

"No," I admitted, my voice a husky whisper torn from the depths of my soul. My eyes were transfixed on the polished wood box holding the remains of my beloved father—wood that reminded me of the boards of our unfinished tree house. The finality of *this* wood gleamed in the faint light as though mocking my sorrow. "I'm not okay, and I don't think I'll ever be."

His hand squeezed mine a little tighter, the unspoken vow to do whatever he could to make my life less painful resonating through the thin layers of our skin. He couldn't promise me that things would get better, that the wound would eventually heal. He was silent, respecting the enormity of my grief.

And I appreciated the hell out of that.

The funeral workers began to lower the casket—the dreadful sound of the straps creaking a deafening roar in the silent graveyard. Every inch it descended into the abyss was a reminder, an echo of the finality of death, of a life stolen too soon. My heartbeat drummed in my ears, a haunting sound that matched the tempo of my heartbreak.

"It's not fair," I growled, squeezing Hunter's hand. "Who did this to him?"

My words were punctuated by the thud of the coffin hitting the floor of the grave, a sound that reverberated through the bleak surroundings. It echoed in the hollow space inside me, hollowed out by a loss that fractured my soul.

The heartbreak was there, a dull throb that pounded in time with my heart, but above it, a new sensation overtook the emptiness: rage. My free hand curled into a fist, my nails biting into my palm, and my tears stopped, replaced by a hardening resolve that crystallized in my chest.

I wanted to find who had taken my father from me, and I wanted them to hurt, to feel even a fraction of the anguish that was ripping me apart.

"I understand now," I whispered to Hunter. "I finally understand your vengeance."

It wasn't lost on me how similar our tragedies were. I, too, witnessed my father's murder. I was with him. I watched him die, and I was helpless, powerless to stop it.

"My dad has only been gone for a few days," I whispered. "I can't even imagine what this must've been like for you, to spend years living with this awful mix of hopelessness and rage."

Hunter pressed his hand to the palm of my back, probably knowing from firsthand experience that there was nothing he could say to take away any of my pain.

"I can't imagine what this has been like for you," I continued. "To go as long as you have without getting justice. I've only had to live with it for a few days. If I had to live with this for the next few years, I don't think any good parts of me would survive."

They would be eaten up with bitterness and hate.

Someone purposefully and maliciously took my father's life. My father, who had already been robbed of twenty years of his freedom, was executed like an animal, as if his life meant nothing.

And while it might not be fair to feel enraged that the police hadn't found any leads—not a single clue—that's exactly what I felt. How dare this person treat my dad like a disposable piece of garbage? How dare someone end his life—just when it was getting started, no less? How dare they put so much forethought into murdering him that they covered their tracks?

"They can't get away with this," I said. "Going about their life like ending Dad's is inconsequential."

I wouldn't *allow* them to get away with it.

Maybe it was ethically the right thing to do to leave this in the hands of law enforcement and pray that they'd miraculously get a lead. A clue. Something.

Screw that.

"Hunter?" I clenched my hand into a fist. "I want you to find who killed my father."

Hunter studied my eyes, looking for any sign that I was saying this only out of grief. But he must have realized how deadly serious and unwavering I was, because after a few seconds, he tightened his lips and offered me a silent nod.

I realized at that moment that I no longer loved Hunter *despite* the lengths he went through to protect people; I loved him more because of it.

Maybe it was a twisted love, but Hunter would do anything for me —protect, lie, even end someone's life.

Hunter would find the person responsible.

And he would kill them, just because I asked him to.

CHAPTER 40

Luna

I stood on the edge of Lake Michigan at the back of Hunter's mansion, the vast, tranquil body of water before me glowing in the colors of the sunset. Hues of pink, lavender, and soft peach stretched across the heavens, the lake's surface sparkling in the fading light, a mirror to the sky above, the gentle lapping of the waves at the shore keeping rhythm with my heart.

The beauty of the sunset was a bittersweet reminder of the man who was no longer here to see it.

But as my tears spilled onto my cheeks, a strong arm wound around my waist.

Hunter. He pressed his body against mine, a living, breathing anchor in my ocean of grief. He was my beacon of hope in the hurricane that had consumed my life, my lighthouse guiding me through the dark waters of my despair.

"Hunter," I whispered, finding solace in the sound of his name. He squeezed me tighter in response, his silent promise of unwavering support.

"I'm here." His warm breath ruffled my hair. His voice was firm, and resolute, a testament to the strength of his love for me. A reminder that although I had lost much, I hadn't lost everything. I had him.

And for that, I was grateful.

I met his steady gaze—a moment of quiet understanding, a promise of support and shared sorrow.

I leaned into him, resting my ear against his chest, the steady beat of his heart a comforting rhythm.

The sun finally sank beneath the horizon, the last remnants of its glow fading into the darkening night. But I knew that the sun would rise again. And with Hunter by my side, I was ready to face whatever the new day would bring. Yes, beauty often masks horror, but love, I realized, heals it.

"I would do anything to end your pain," Hunter said.

He would—more than anyone would do for another soul.

Without hesitating, I said, "I know. I can't tell you how much that means to me."

We stood silently for a few more minutes, listening to the sounds of the water, before I angled my face so I could stare into his eyes, which were as blue as the lake.

"I want to be with you."

His eyebrows fell, and the time that stretched on filled me with dread. I didn't like the way he looked down, nor the heartbreak in his voice when he next spoke.

"I've been doing a lot of thinking," he started. "You deserve a man who takes responsibility for his choices." My heart clenched as he swiped his lower lip with his thumb. "I'll find the man who did this to your father, and I will end him, but after that…" Hunter's gaze cascaded over my features, as if drinking me in like a thirsty man afforded one last glass of water. "I'm going to turn myself in."

I pushed off of him. "You can't do that."

"Luna…"

"I know I'm being selfish and immoral, but I don't care. I've spent the last twenty years trying to do the right thing, and look where it got me—my father is in the ground." My throat clenched. "And I have all this fresh resentment toward my family, my mom, for not being there for him. I'm done doing what's noble, and for *once,* I want to do something that makes *me* happy. So please." I turned to face him. "Don't. I can't go through having someone else I love stuck in prison again."

Hunter's chest sank, and he shook his head in agony.

"Luna, even if I don't turn myself in, Sean, the detectives—they're onto me. It's probably just a matter of time."

"So, burn the evidence. Get rid of the car, burn your weapons room. Burn everything. Everything they have is circumstantial right now. Arresting a prominent prosecutor and charging him with being the Windy City Vigilante will give Mayor Kepler and the police a huge black eye. They won't do that unless they have airtight evidence against you."

"We don't know that."

"Yes, we do."

"They could arrest me, anyway."

"Maybe," I said. "But don't make it easier on them. Please."

Hunter's lips curled down. "I can't let you get yourself involved in a crime, Luna."

"I'm already involved. I know your identity, and I will never tell anybody."

His face softened into pity. "Look, you might feel this way today, but you just lost your father. I'm sure once you have time to think about this—"

"I won't change my mind." I jutted my chin up, staring at him defiantly. "I love you. You're all I have left, and if you get taken from me and put in prison, I'll have nothing."

My words landed a blow to his features, which fell into agony.

"Don't do this," I pleaded.

"Luna..."

"I finally fell in love with someone so deeply that I can't imagine spending one breath away from you, Hunter." My vision blurred. "You said you would do anything for me."

His lips thinned into a hard line.

"We could leave the country," I suggested.

He shook his head. "And rob you of any hope of ever reconciling with your family?"

My heart burned. "I don't want to reconcile with all of them."

"Maybe not all of them, but what about your mom?"

I frowned.

He stroked my jaw with the back of his knuckles. "I'll never take that from you." I was about to protest, but he continued, "Besides. A life on the run is miserable."

"Then do what you have to, to not get caught here."

Silence.

"This is what I need. Burn your house down if you have to. Stop being the Vigilante, not because I reject it morally, but because I don't want you to go to prison. I need to be with you, Hunter. Now and always."

The muscles along Hunter's jaw flexed and twitched, each clench betraying a battle of emotions roiling beneath his composed exterior. Like he was fighting an internal war between being the man he thought I deserved and the man who would be around to love me and cherish me all the days of my life.

With sorrow tumbling through his features, he cupped my cheek, and after a few seconds, he offered a slight nod as he whispered, "I would do anything for you, Luna."

My heart rejoiced at his words, at the resolution on his face. There was no guarantee Hunter would get away with his crimes, no guarantee we had a tomorrow together.

But at least he wasn't going to turn himself in.

At least the future wasn't doomed.

I brushed his cheekbone with my thumb, then gripped the back of his head, pulling his face closer to mine. His mouth lingered above my own, his quickened breaths that smelled of peppermint thick with hesitation.

"Luna..."

"I want you."

Hunter inhaled a shaky breath, and his eyes locked on mine with a laser intensity unmatched by anyone else.

"You just suffered a terrible loss."

Yes. I was drowning in heartache, and my only life raft was him—the hope of our future and the possibility that I could focus on something other than this sharp agony piercing my heart. If only for a few minutes.

"Make me forget," I whispered in breathless desperation. "Make me feel something other than pain."

Hunter's eyebrows fell into empathy.

Would he deny me this? Desire pulsed through his features—with his moistened lips, his tightened muscles—and I wanted him to stop fighting it.

Surrender to me, Hunter.

I pulled his face closer to mine again, his body taut with indecision.

I wanted his mouth on mine. I wanted his hands on my body, and I wanted to feel him inside of me—stretching me and filling me until it consumed my every breath, every thought.

I needed this...

Especially now. This man was willing to kill for me. Not just to save my life, but to hunt down an enemy who stole my father and broke my heart.

I'd never known a life this good, and after everything that just happened, this energy between us was wonderfully new and explosively heightened at the same time.

"Please," I stuttered.

Hunter's hot breath bounced off my lips as a gentle breeze tossed his dark locks into his forehead and mixed the scent of his musk cologne with freshly cut grass. The sun warmed my face, but it wasn't as warm as his palm as it trailed down my cheek—his thumb and finger pinching my chin and lifting it higher.

His mouth hovered over mine, pausing there for a torturous few seconds before he finally surrendered.

His lips were soft as they ensnared my lower lip between them, but the energy that exploded was unbreakable. Instantly, all the complications and the hurt and the fears drowned, and the only thing that surfaced was his body touching mine.

My breath quivered as I opened my mouth, and when Hunter slid his tongue inside, a hot flash of energy shot between my thighs. Making my sex throb for him.

I snaked my fingers through his hair, tilting my head to the left as the waves of Lake Michigan lapped against the rocky shore below. While up here, our breaths became louder and more urgent, the heat in my belly intensifying.

Hunter's hand pulled my lower back, my breasts pressing against his chest, making me whimper when his growing erection pulsed against me. His lips curled into a smile at the sound, and his hand slid from behind my back to my stomach, inching up slowly, making me wait for it until his large palm cupped my breast.

A fire engulfed between my thighs, demanding urgent relief, and I slid my hand over his suit pants and rubbed the bulge waiting for me.

I loved that I could make him growl with one touch. I loved that I could make him grip me harder, like an uncaged beast, my nipples hardening at the touch.

"Tell me what you want," he whispered over my lips.

"I want you inside of me."

With a groan, Hunter hoisted me up around his waist as if I weighed nothing and walked me backward. I thought he was going to walk me inside his mansion, which was empty of staff and people, but instead, he gently placed me on an oversized boulder that was part of the landscaping.

The smooth rock was waist high for him, and as he looked down at me, he greedily began inching up my dress. I tugged at his belt, remembering what he had done with it before, but he seized my wrists and stopped me.

His grip around my wrist flashed down my body and shot between my legs once more, which was now pulsing with need.

Hunter's blue eyes silently commanded me to obey him, his dark locks shimmering from the sun. He looked like he was glowing, his black designer suit almost shimmering with rays as he sank to his knees in front of me.

Watching me pant as he pulled my panties down my ankles with such a torturously slow speed, I whimpered, Hunter's lips curling as he tugged them over my high heels and balled them into his pocket.

This ache in my sex was unbearable as he inched up my dress higher to my hips, exposing me in front of him—legs spread wide as he stared at my center, his every blink seemed reluctant, not wanting to miss a single moment of my beauty.

My breath came quicker with anticipation, longing to feel him. But Hunter made me wait for it.

He placed his lips on my knee, leaving a trail of delicate kisses along my left inner thigh, and just before he reached my sex, he stopped, locked his knowing eyes with me, and began the same agonizing path along my right leg.

The kisses grew closer and closer to where I needed them to be, where my body screamed for relief.

But he stopped just inside my thigh.

"Please," I whimpered.

"I like to hear you beg," he mused.

I was more than happy to oblige. "Please, Hunter."

"Tell me you're mine," he demanded, kissing inside my thighs, punishing me with how close his mouth was to where I needed it.

"I'm yours," I said.

"For how long, Luna?"

He kissed the space between my leg and my center—the closest his mouth had come to the pulsing heat screaming for his tongue.

"Forever," I said.

Hunter rewarded me with a long lick up my sex. I moaned and leaned back on the boulder, gripping the stone as he repeated the process, swirling his tongue along the bundle of nerves at the top.

The heat became an inferno, my hips squirming as he flattened his tongue against the sensitive bud, moving it ever so slowly.

Hunter was capable of being rough, but right now, he was being gentle, meticulous, and working at the core of my body, triggering a wave that began to quiver in my lower stomach.

Oh, what we looked like right now—with me, my dress hitched up to my hips, lying on this rock with my legs spread, Hunter Lockwood in his designer suit, kneeling on the grass, his face buried between my legs, bobbing up and down as he licked my body into a frenzy.

But the hottest thing was watching Hunter. He wasn't looking at me. He was focused on the space between my thighs, working it like a hungry man devouring a delicious dinner. He began to swirl his tongue again, just like he knew I loved, and then he brought his hand up and—pausing to lock eyes with me—lined up two fingers at my entrance.

I groaned as he pushed slightly up to the middle knuckles, pausing as he watched me squirm. He pulled back and then slid them deeper, until he pushed them all the way inside of me.

I arched my back so high, that my scalp scraped across the unforgiving surface as Hunter hit that internal bundle of nerves.

Then he lowered his mouth to me again and circled my apex with his tongue.

I longed to feel every inch of him inside of me, yet this felt so damn good, I wanted to feel this forever, too, so I grabbed his hair and tugged, holding him there.

Which motivated him to go faster, moaning. His voice vibrated against my delicate skin as he became more determined with his licks. Every lick felt better than the last, pushing the wave to climb higher and higher, the heat burning hotter, and the closer I got, the more desperate I became to keep his face between my thighs.

I trembled against his mouth as the heat that had been burning became an incineration, shooting up from my core to my spine. With his fingers pulsing inside of me, curling, I began to shake and squirm.

Holding the back of his head as I came undone.

"Hunter!" I let out a desperate gasp for oxygen, my orgasm so intense that my thighs pressed against Hunter's head, nearly dislodging him as the world around us faded to nothing.

All that existed was this burning ecstasy, the space between my thighs consuming my soul as it writhed with pleasure.

He pushed his fingers deeper inside, riding every last quiver of my climax with his tongue.

He waited for my quivers to subside, lifting his gaze to mine, slowing his licks until he finally stopped.

Stood up.

"Take off your dress," he commanded as he unbuttoned his shirt. I sat up, the rock smooth against my ass, as I looked around, making sure no one had come back unexpectedly that could see us before I tugged the dress up and over my head. Then I removed my bra and lay down on the boulder like I was on an altar, preparing to be worshipped.

Staring into my eyes, he positioned himself at my entrance and said, "You're mine."

He pushed, making me gasp as he began to fill me inch by inch. Stretching me. He pulled back, only to go deeper this time, my lower belly quivering as he worked himself completely inside of me.

Hitting the bundle of nerves in my center.

When my eyes started to roll back, he really began to move. Gently at first, the passionate thrusts of two lovers professing their love for one another, no matter what.

He filled me, physically, and emotionally.

As Hunter made me his own, I became locked in his gaze. He began to work harder, his hips rocking back and forth as my high heels scraped against his hips.

"I love you," he growled as he thrust deeper.

"I love you," I echoed.

I could already feel a rising wave, but I was trying to fight against it. I wanted this to last as long as possible, wanted to feel him consuming me, filling me. I wanted to feel Hunter like this every day of my life.

His hips beat against the inside of my thighs, his body going deeper, while also hitting that sensitive area of flesh.

When my head fell back against the rock with a moan, Hunter clutched my hand and dragged it between my legs.

"Touch yourself," he demanded.

I gladly obeyed, working the sensitive tissue while he watched my fingers.

Clenching his jaw, he moved more frenziedly, and heat shot up my lower belly again, my thighs trembling as the world around us became a vortex of pleasure.

"Hunter!" I screamed, the all-consuming ecstasy crashing around us.

His fingers dug into my flesh as we groaned through our orgasms.

CHAPTER 41
Luna

"How are you feeling?" Hunter asked.

The morning light cast a golden promise across the bedroom, as if whispering, "Today could be better." But despair anchored me, my soul teetering between hope and its cold embrace.

"When will the pain start to fade?" I wondered.

Hunter walked deeper into his bedroom, stopping at the foot of the bed, his hands tucked into his cotton pants, his T-shirt clenched around his biceps.

"It doesn't fade, exactly," he said gently. "More like you learn to weave your life around it."

His words stung, but there was a raw truth in them that I appreciated.

"Maria is going to make you breakfast. I'd like you to try to eat it."

I took a deep breath and offered a sad smile.

"I've asked her to leave after breakfast to give you some privacy, but if you prefer for her to stay, I—"

"No," I interrupted. "I'd rather be alone."

Hunter sat on the bed, which tilted under his weight.

"I'm sorry," I said. "I'm trying to snap myself out of this."

Hunter rubbed my leg over the blanket. "Luna, you have nothing to apologize for. You buried your father yesterday, and you're not just grieving his loss; you're grieving the loss of the last twenty years and the hope that evaporated before it even started."

My chest warmed as his words wrapped around me—how did he always know just what to say?

But I couldn't stay in bed all day. I needed to get some fresh air and walk around to take my mind off this pain—otherwise, I would just wallow in it.

"Grayson is coming by soon," Hunter said.

I threw the covers off my legs and sat up.

Hunter's voice dropped to a near whisper, a shadow crossing his face. "And I need to leave for a little while today."

I stared into his cerulean gems.

"Where are you going?"

He scrubbed the side of his face. "It's better if you don't know. But when I'm gone, I want you to stay inside. There are security agents positioned around the mansion, in addition to the surveillance, and, of course, a nearby team that can rush over if we need anything. But…"

Hunter cleared his throat, staring at me with such severity, it almost made my throat run dry.

"In the unlikely event anything happens and all those fail-safes don't work, I want you to sneak into the weapons room. Close the closet door behind you. And hide there until I retrieve you. You understand?"

Whoa. I thought back to that night Rinaldi and the mayor showed up. After, Hunter said their scrutiny had thwarted his ability to follow up on a lead he'd gotten about his dad's death. With the surveillance, then my dad's murder, Hunter hadn't looked into it yet. Was that what this was about? Or…

"Do you have a lead on who killed my father?" I asked.

"I'm still gathering information. When I have something concrete, I'll let you know."

A knot tightened in my stomach. "I don't want you to get hurt."

A hint of amusement danced in Hunter's stare as one corner of his mouth lifted. "Your lack of confidence in my ability to protect myself is a little offensive."

"I want to know who killed my father, but not if it comes at the expense of you, Hunter. If anything seems dangerous, I want you to stop immediately. You understand? I meant it when I said I can't live without you."

Hunter stood up and positioned himself in front of me, looking unworried.

"I promise," he vowed. "Now come on. Let's get you cleaned up."

I hadn't showered yet today, hadn't cleaned myself off since Hunter made love to me on that bolder yesterday.

He gently took my hand and guided me to his master bathroom, where a massive shower was lined with glass and stone. When he turned the silver handle, the powerful waterfall filled the air with a fresh scent, steam gradually fogging the glass.

Hunter walked back over to me, and as he slid the fabric of my T-shirt over my head, his knuckles brushed along my skin, my nipples hardening in response. He tugged my boy shorts, along with my underwear, down next and bent down on one knee so he could help free the fabric from around my ankles.

I locked eyes with him, seeing the hungry desire flirting through the edges of his gaze as he looked from my face, down my bare breasts, my stomach, to the apex between my legs.

Mere inches from his mouth.

A greedy need took over me.

Yesterday, making love was the only time this imaginable pain had paused. I had only been able to focus on the flick of his tongue, the sensation of him grinding against my body.

I wanted that now. I *needed* that now. The pain would still be here when we were done, but at least I'd be exhausted with pleasure.

"Get in the shower with me," I said.

Hunter's eyes traveled up my body to my face again.

"And don't be gentle."

CHAPTER 42
Luna

I drew Hunter up by his shirt and brought his mouth to mine. Next to us, the sound of the shower's water cascaded to the ground, the steam swirling through the confined space, heightening the smell of his musk cologne.

I was more aggressive than normal, licking his bottom lip and plunging my tongue inside his mouth, inciting a growl.

"Make me forget my pain," I whispered over his lips.

"Luna," he cautioned.

I didn't want to hear that this might not be healthy. There was only one thing I wanted, and there was only one person who could give it to me.

I grasped his wrist and slid his palm down my stomach, sliding it lower until it dipped between my thighs.

Hunter moaned, surrendering deeper into the kiss as his finger slid over my sex, feeling how ready I was for him. But first, I wanted to return the favor that he had given me yesterday, when he'd sunk to his knees and buried himself between my thighs.

I pulled Hunter's shirt as high as I could, waiting for him to yank it off and step out of his pants and boxers. Before I took his hand and guided him into the shower.

The water was so hot, that it stung my skin as it drenched my hair and spewed down my nipples, my stomach, and between my thighs, where Hunter's fingers had dipped between my folds again.

This time, curving and sliding inside of me.

I clutched Hunter's biceps and dug my nails into his flesh as he worked me from the inside, my forehead pressing against his chest. Just like I had asked him to, he wasn't gentle, thrusting harder and harder, and after a minute of working me into groans, he brought his thumb up, swirling it at the apex of my sex.

I could already feel an orgasm starting to climb in my lower belly, and I wanted to feel its release, but I needed to feel it with my body stretched around him. All of him. I clenched my thighs, trying to resist it, but his fingers curled and hit that spot in my core while his thumb worked that sensitive flesh on the outside. I was thrilled when Hunter's warm lips pressed against mine once more.

The water drenched us as Hunter thrust two fingers deeper, then drew them all the way out to the tip, only to thrust them in again. He repeated this movement multiple times, making my orgasm climb higher. Until it crashed.

I grabbed his arms so tightly I was probably hurting him, my lips meeting his chest as he cooed his praises through my shudders.

Panting after its end, I gripped his hand and pulled him out, stepped back until I hit the wall behind me, and then, keeping my eyes locked on his—the water sliding down his hungry face—I sank to my knees.

Slowly, making a show of it.

Watching his chest begin to rise and then fall faster.

I looked down at his throbbing shaft in front of me, and I held it at the base, swirling my tongue around the tip.

Hunter groaned and grabbed a fistful of my wet hair.

With water droplets on my eyelashes, I looked up at him again as I opened my mouth as wide as I could, relaxed my jaw, and drew him into my mouth.

The look on Hunter's face was one of pure, unbridled passion. His jaw clenched, and his lips curled tightly, as I drew him back out and then pushed him back inside until I gagged.

My eyes watered, but I didn't stop.

This was too intoxicating, pleasuring the billionaire who'd literally annihilate anyone who wished me harm. He was ruthless and powerful, but right now, I held all the power.

I grabbed the base of him and began massaging up and down as I pulled him in and out of my lips. I pushed through the gag reflex, and I kept pushing even as my throat tried to tighten. I focused on relaxing the muscles, opening my jaw, until finally, all of him was inside my mouth.

"Oh fuck," Hunter groaned, his head tilting up.

I held my position, which wasn't easy. Hunter was big, and I wasn't sure how long I could do this without choking again, but I drew him out a few inches, and then I thrust him back in.

Inciting another feral roar from Hunter's throat.

I began moving then. Working up and down, licking the bottom with each pull and push. With each movement, Hunter's fingers tightened in my hair, and his thighs quivered.

"Fuck, Luna." Hunter's voice was raspy. "That feels so good. Don't stop."

I would not stop. I looked up at him as I pulled him all the way out, then back in again, watching his desire grow as I found my rhythm, bobbing up and down. But I wanted more.

I wanted to surrender to him.

I wanted the power to shift back to the man who'd do anything for me.

So, I pulled back, grabbed both of his hands, and placed them on either side of my head, staring up into his eyes as I opened my jaw and waited for him.

Realizing my silent permission, Hunter's teeth clenched with desire as he lined himself up to my mouth and then held me still as he plunged inside my throat.

He found his rhythm, holding my head and taking my mouth just like he had taken me on that rock. Pushing deep, then pulling all the way back up to the tip, and then sinking deep inside again.

I gagged a few times, but with the tensing of his muscles, I knew he was getting close.

So damn close.

He groaned, his head tilted back up again, but suddenly, he pulled back, releasing his grip. He yanked me up to my feet, turned me around, and pressed his hand between my shoulder blades, pushing down as he pulled my hips back.

Then he lined himself up and thrust inside of me with one forceful motion.

Making my eyes roll back in my head. Feeling him deep inside sparked the fresh build of an orgasm, and when he found his pace, he hit that sweet spot inside my body.

Hearing my groans, Hunter changed his rhythm, and adjusted his angle to make sure he hit that precious spot over and over. Filling me, stretching me, burying himself inside of me.

Water continued to assault our bodies, our skin turning red from its heat, but all I could focus on was his girth working me from the ideal slant. The first quiver made my muscles tremble, and, as he grabbed my hips harder, warmth radiated through my lower belly.

I put my forehead against the stone, moaning as I grabbed Hunter's wrists and clawed at his skin.

Sensing my climax, Hunter began pounding harder, his hips smacking against my ass.

The sound of his flesh hitting mine mixed with the sound of the water splashing around our wrinkled feet while the smell of his cologne mixed with the aroma of our lovemaking.

The peak of the orgasm was even higher than the one I'd had yesterday, making me wonder if each time we made love, it would be better than the last.

Hunter worked every wave inside of my body before slamming himself deep and stilling his movements with a roar. He stood there, both of us panting, until finally, he pulled back and turned me around. Cupping my chin.

Before planting a sweet kiss on my mouth.

"When you get back," I said against his lips, "I need this again."

Hunter's mouth curled up, his thumb tracing across my lower lip.

"Little Leopard, I'll take you anytime you want. Anywhere you want. Any way you want."

CHAPTER 43

Hunter

"How is she?" Grayson asked.

The gentle breeze from Lake Michigan ruffled the edges of my shirt as we stood in the backyard of my ivy-clad mansion. The faint scent of grass mixed with the rich earthiness of the surrounding gardens as I watched a white sailboat drift along the cobalt water.

"She's grieving. Looking for any distraction she can. She took two weeks off work, so at least I can keep her safe inside for a while, while I figure out this mess."

Grayson nodded, and ran a hand through his hair, his charcoal-colored T-shirt stretching from the movement.

"You still haven't explained what happened a couple of weeks ago," Grayson said. "With them questioning if you're the Windy City Vigilante."

I licked my teeth.

"I'm not asking if you're the Vigilante," Grayson clarified. "I won't ask you that." He shoved his hands into his pockets. "What I'm asking is, do they have enough evidence for this to be a problem?"

I studied my mysterious brother. These were the things he said that made me wonder who he really was. Grayson would always have my back, without question, but he wouldn't grill a family member who'd just been accused of being a serial killer?

His only question was if I'd get caught?

There was an odd comfort in knowing he'd stand by me no matter what, but a nagging question remained. Why wasn't he pressing for answers?

"You heard the evidence," I said. "That's all they have, and it's flimsy."

We walked in silence, save for the birds chirping around us as if an almost-confession wasn't lingering in the air between us.

"Listen," I said. "The reason I called you here is because I need some help." I spotted the security guard only a hundred feet from us. Probably a safe distance away, but I jerked my chin in the direction of the north side of the property, motioning for Grayson to walk with me.

Along the back of the property, a stone path etched its way through colorful gardens that my mother had planted. I made sure the landscaper kept up those gardens, because it was the last thing I had living of my mom. Pinks and yellows weren't my vibe, but she loved them, and when I was a kid, I'd often see her attending to her flowers with a sun hat and a smile.

"Why do you keep looking around?" Grayson asked.

"I'm looking for any hidden police."

Grayson's eyebrows rose. "Aren't they here for your and Luna's protection?"

That's what they claimed, yes—protecting us from the guy who shot her father, and Franco, of course, who still hadn't been found.

"They pose a complication."

"Is this about the Vigilante shit?" Grayson asked.

"Not exactly." I mean, yes, they were *here,* in part, to keep tabs on me. But my leaving wasn't about the Windy City Vigilante. "I need to sneak out. Undetected."

Grayson swiped his nose with his thumb. "Do I want to know why?"

"I'll get to that in a second, but when I leave, I'd like you to meet with Barry. Finding the gunman is a long shot, but see if there's anything you can do, anyone you could talk to, to help him get to the bottom of it."

My brother looked at the stone pathway.

"And what will you be doing while I'm off chasing a dead end with Barry?"

"It might be a dead end with the cops, but with you and Barry, it could be a different story."

"Any shooter that good at evasion and brazen enough to kill someone outside of a courthouse swarming with law enforcement—and not get caught—is probably a hired professional. You and I both know that if they haven't found the shooter by now, they likely won't."

I sighed. "I know. But we need to try."

My brother looked out at the expanse of the property. We were leaving the main area and heading into a heavily wooded section that flirted dangerously close to my hidden garage.

"This have something to do with the name Barry gave you?" he asked. "The guy that got the missing five million? Because before Mayor Kepler and Detective Rinaldi showed up, you were on your way to confront him."

I nodded. "You know how Luna's father was convicted of murder?"

Grayson waited for me to continue.

"He was convicted of murdering a teenager named Oliver Weiss."

I scratched the side of my face, my fingernails digging into the bristles of my whiskers.

"The missing payment went to Stanley Weiss."

Grayson stopped walking as the words probably rumbled through his head like puzzle pieces, trying to find a home.

"He's related to the teenager that died?"

"He's the kid's father," I said.

Grayson's neck tightened so much, that his veins popped out. It took a lot for my brother to look bothered, but this definitely succeeded.

"What the hell does it mean?" Grayson asked.

"I don't know yet," I admitted. "I'm going to pay Stanley Weiss a visit later today. Problem is, I need to get off the property to do it."

I looked around my private grounds with disdain.

It was well within my rights to demand the police leave, but I couldn't do that without raising suspicion. Which would only put *more* police eyes on me.

"Keep walking with me," I said. "I need to see where police are positioned so I can avoid them."

We started strolling again with Grayson lost in his thoughts, just like I was.

"Why would Dad pay the father of that kid five million dollars?"

"I don't know," I said. "If it weren't for the accounting cover-up of the transaction, I'd have assumed it was an act of a Good Samaritan or something, trying to help that family in need after their loss."

I raked a hand through my hair, clearing my throat. "There's only one guy that can tell me what the hell happened all those years ago. Stanley Weiss received the money, so he knows something."

"Take me with you," Grayson demanded.

"I need you to help Barry track down the shooter at the courthouse."

"Barry's perfectly capable of doing that with his own team. Take me with you. There's a good chance he's involved in Dad's death somehow. There's no telling what he'll do when you go knocking on his door."

I clenched my jaw.

"Hell," Grayson continued, "if this is all connected, he could be the one that hired the hit on Luna's dad."

In which case, I'd kill him.

"If that's true, you don't want to go with me," I said.

"Why's that?"

"Don't ask me a question that could incriminate you after the fact."

Grayson stared at me. "Who says I care about being incriminated?"

CHAPTER 44

Hunter

This didn't look like the home of a man who had received five million dollars.

It was an eyesore in the pristine neighborhood. Faded yellow paint peeled away in patches, and the wooden porch showed years of neglect. Each window was coated with decades of grime, staring out like the sunken eyes of a cadaver, while the front yard was a chaos of overgrown weeds and thistle.

I stood on the sidewalk, looking at it, dressed in a casual outfit—not donning my Vigilante attire for two reasons. First, there was too much heat on me right now, so if a police officer *had* seen me leave my property, no matter how discreet I thought I had been, that would be the end.

Second, the conversation I was about to have with Stanley Weiss had nothing to do with the Vigilante and everything to do with my father. So, I came as myself.

I gripped the handle of my knife in my hoodie pouch—I'd worn this unforgivingly hot top because it concealed my weapon—and glanced around the neighborhood, making sure no one was looking at me. No kids playing outside, no one riding their bikes. Hopefully, that meant I could slip in and out undetected.

As I approached the front porch, movement inside from the front window caught my eye. A male figure stood with his back to the glass, so I couldn't see if his face matched the one I had looked up online.

A shiver ran down my spine, an uneasy feeling I couldn't place.

Was it the fact that all his windows were closed despite no sound of air-conditioning on a hot summer day? Was it possible that the people threatening Luna and her father had also come back and threatened *him* and he was now being held hostage?

I scanned around his house for any evidence of another person. And while I saw nothing, there was no guarantee he was alone inside.

Standing a mere ten feet from his front door, so close that one glance over the guy's shoulder would reveal my position, I watched as he turned.

That's when I could finally see his face.

It was, in fact, Stanley Weiss.

The only person who could explain what the hell happened around the time of my father's death. This man held the secrets that had been buried for decades, secrets that had haunted my soul.

It felt surreal that I was finally about to get some answers. And not just about my father's death, but also, how in the world it connected to Luna's dad.

I studied him for a few more seconds, watching as he reached down, his hand returning with something metallic.

He brought the barrel to his temple.

My heart stopped.

"No!" I charged up his front porch, nearly tripping in my desperation. Banging my fist on the door, I shouted, "Don't do it. I need to talk to you, Stanley! I want to talk to you about your son!"

The door was locked, so I continued pounding, praying the mention of his son would make him pause.

"Please!"

Maybe I should go around back, and try to break in. Maybe I should try to break through the window. But before I could do any of those things, the lock clicked, and slowly, the front door creaked open.

CHAPTER 45

Hunter

Stanley Weiss stood before me, holding a loaded pistol.

"Do I know you?" Stanley's voice was as rough as a chain-smoker's, his skin prematurely wrinkled with deep lines around his sunken eyes, which had an unhealthy yellowish tint to them. Like someone who had abused the bottle for years. The pungent stench of stale tobacco and unwashed sweat hit me, stains saturating the armpits of his worn-out gray T-shirt that accentuated his unnaturally thin shoulder bones.

"I was hoping I could talk to you, sir." I kept my tone calm, on account of the loaded gun. "I know about your son."

Not as much as I needed to, but the mention of his dead kid made his eyes flicker with heartbreaking curiosity.

"This about Payne getting killed?"

A cold shiver raced across my chest. "You know about Payne?"

"Course I know about him," he said.

My left fingers clenched into a ball. I couldn't allow this guy to kill himself. Not only because of the information he held about my dad, but also, if he had anything to do with Luna's dad getting killed, I'd made her a promise that I'd deal with him.

I gripped my knife's handle tighter, my muscles tensing to strike.

Could I overpower him and get the gun faster than he could fire off a shot?

"What exactly do you know about Mr. Payne?" I asked.

Stanley looked over my shoulder, his paranoid gaze sweeping over his jungle of a front lawn before settling back onto me.

"Doesn't matter now. Go away."

His twitching finger threatened every second, and Luna's voice echoed in my mind—a desperate plea to not let myself get killed, a promise I couldn't break. Not now.

He tried to shut the door, and again, I blocked it, my foot wedged between it and the frame.

"Why are you here?" The guy's voice was laced with as much impatience as anger for keeping him from his suicide.

"Answers."

The guy looked me up and down like a disgusting wart. "Who the hell are you?"

"Hunter Lockwood."

The guy's eyes widened, and his Adam's apple bobbed up and down.

"You're the Lockwood boy," he whispered, almost to himself in a tone of despair.

"Every night for almost twenty years, I've replayed the moment he was killed. It haunts me, having no idea why it happened or who did it, but I think you might have some of those answers."

The guy's chest rose, as if he was trying to grow another pair of balls.

"Doesn't matter anymore." His voice broke slightly, hinting at regret.

"Does to me."

The only sound was that of my breathing as I leaned forward, about to strike.

"I'm sorry for it all." He brought the gun up and pushed the barrel beneath his chin, and when he did, he exposed his forearm.

Time froze, dragging me back to the haunting night of my father's murder. A buried detail from the shadowed recesses of my memories came surging forward.

As the man brought his knife around my father's throat, I saw something on his forearm.

Something that I didn't register at the time, too fixated on the blood and the open gash and the sound of my father struggling to breathe and the chaos and the crying and screaming and police lights. And death.

Something that remained entombed behind the thick wall of trauma, even throughout all the police interviews asking if there was anything I could think of at all that might point us to the suspect.

A tattoo. A unique one of a child's hand grasping his father's in black-and-white ink.

The same tattoo I was staring at right now.

He clenched his eyes shut, bracing for the bullet to end all my hope of finding out *why*.

I yanked the guy's wrist and knocked the gun to the side.

"You're the man who killed my father," I said.

Stanley stared at me blankly, like his soul had died long ago and the only thing that remained was a lifeless zombie. Regret sagged his shoulders, and after several tense seconds, he whispered, "I shouldn't have killed him in front of his child."

CHAPTER 46

Hunter

I wasn't expecting the shove. That's why it knocked me off-balance. That's why Stanley was able to gain the upper hand. And regained control of the weapon as he placed it beneath his chin again and said, "I'm sorry."

I shoved my shoulders into his torso and pushed him back.

Stanley spun off me and aimed the gun at me.

"Get out of my house."

"Why did you kill my father?"

"Leave, or I'll shoot you!"

"Why did you kill him? Why did you do it right in front of me?"

"Last warning." He pressed the barrel against my chest, right over my heart.

My skin prickled with an electric mix of fear and adrenaline, each heartbeat echoing loudly in my ears, a cruel balance between existence and oblivion. As I stared into the haunted eyes of the man who held the power of life and death.

Just as he did all those years ago.

"What kind of monster slashes a guy's throat right in front of his kid?"

A flicker of shame came across Stanley's face, a flicker of humanity returning.

"You weren't supposed to be there," he said.

"How did you know that?" I was supposed to leave with my brothers and my mom so my dad could work, but I had gotten sick and stayed home.

Stanley looked at the gun. Looked at me.

One squeeze, and I would break my promise to Luna.

"How did you know my dad was supposed to be home alone when you killed him?"

"I can't talk about any of this." A hint of fear danced through his words.

"You were about to put a bullet through your brain. What difference does it make if you answer my questions first?"

"They could come after my other son! Look what they did to Payne when he was finally set free."

I bet I could grab that gun, and yank it from his hand before he could pull the trigger.

"What exactly do you know about Payne?"

"The guy finally got out of jail. Finally. And what happens to him? He gets killed before he could even get into his car."

"You knew he was innocent," I realized.

"Course I knew. You know what that's like? Living with that, knowing some guy is in jail and you didn't stop it? I never thought he would get convicted."

"How do you know Payne was innocent?" I demanded.

"Because I know what really happened!" Stanley's eyes shimmered. When he spoke again, his brokenhearted tone was softer. "I know what happened to my boy."

"How? How do you know what happened?"

Stanley hesitated, his shoulders softening after a few seconds.

"A kid on the street caught it all on his video camera. He'd gotten the damn thing as a birthday gift and was out there playing around with it when this fancy car comes down the street. He wasn't expecting it to hit my boy, and when it did, he recorded the whole thing. Then two men stepped out. They didn't try to help my son. They dragged his body into an alley like he was a piece of trash. And they left them there to die."

"The kid recorded it?"

"He didn't intend to, but after the car struck...he froze. I only learned about it because after my boy was killed, I did my own investigation. Went door to door near the scene, asking questions. The kid's mom was afraid of whoever they caught on camera—if they killed one boy, they might kill her son. At least, that's what she was afraid of. Can't blame her for refusing to get involved with the police, and I can't blame her for destroying the Mini-DV tape. At least she showed it to me before she did."

Mini-DV tape...used in video cameras from two decades ago.

"If that was true, why didn't you tell the police?"

"I did. In fact, I told them I recognized the guys on the tape; they were prominent figures all over the news back then."

"None of that was in the police reports," I argued.

"And that should, what, surprise you?" He shook his head. "The men who hit my kid were rich. Probably funded political campaigns, and had enough influence to make sure their names wouldn't get tarnished in any public record. Plus, without that video recording, there was no physical evidence to back up my claims."

"Police would at least *investigate* what you said."

"You would think so, wouldn't you? And maybe they did, off the record, but talk about a reality check when you realize your son's life means less than smearing the name of a prominent figure in the community. My son was disposable. Nobody listened to me, and nobody was doing anything about it."

Maybe this guy was a conspiracy theorist.

But I'd learned the hard way not all hunches were documented by police.

Putting down someone's name in the public record of having been accused of killing a kid was a significant step. One that law enforcement could never erase. If they firmly believed Stanley was wrong and they had relationships with the powerful figures in question, they might have withheld the names from official documents.

In this day and age, something like that would probably never happen. But back then, times were different.

"When no one listened to me, I tracked the two men down myself," he said.

"Who were they?" I asked. "Who killed your son?"

Stanley hesitated.

"The person that killed my son was your father."

CHAPTER 47

Hunter

The adrenaline shot through my muscles like a missile, and I charged Stanley, the room blurring as I focused only on him, watching the shock flash in his eyes just before he hit the ground. His gun slid along the stained linoleum floor with a metallic scraping sound, coming to rest six feet away from us.

"You're a fucking liar!" I snapped, climbing on top of him. "You killed my father in cold blood, and you expect me to believe *he's* a killer?"

How dare this piece of shit!

No wonder the police didn't believe him. My father was a successful businessman, an adoring husband, a loving father, and a moral person. He was a hard worker who had never been arrested in his life, and in a sea of cutthroat businessmen, my father held on to the values of my grandfather, treating people with respect and kindness.

Hell, my father went to church every Sunday.

This lunatic was so delusional in his heartbreak that he convinced himself my dad killed his son? If someone ran his child down, he clearly got the wrong guy. Video footage from twenty years ago wasn't as crisp as it was today.

He got it wrong. He got the name wrong, and thanks to his delusions, he broke into my home and murdered my father in front of his child.

His neck was cold and clammy as I wrapped my hands around it.

"My father would never hurt anyone." I began to squeeze.

Stanley's eyes bulged, veins popping as he tried to wrench my grip away. I gritted my teeth so hard, that the pressure stretched all the way to the back of my jaw as I watched Stanley's face turn red and start to grow purple. All while he continued to thrash, his arms frantically flailing about.

In a minute, this would all be over.

I finally found my father's killer.

I stared into his gaze, squeezing his windpipe so hard, that my hands ached.

Suddenly, a searing pain shot through my temple as something hard collided with it, sending stars dancing in my vision. Not enough force to knock me off of Stanley, but enough to dislodge my grip, and as blood trickled down my temple, I spotted the metal door stopper in his hand.

Stanley coughed, wheezing as he found his voice. "If your father had nothing to do with my son's death, then how do you explain the five million dollars?"

CHAPTER 48

Hunter

I staggered back, the weight of his accusations pressing against my certainty. Desperation poisoned my breath as I grabbed his gun and pointed it at his face.

"Start talking," I demanded, my voice trembling with anger. "Tell me everything. Now."

The irony of the situation. The dude was about to blow his own brains out, but now I was going to do him a favor and do it for him.

But if the guy had any heart left in him, he could at least answer my fucking questions before he died.

"They had no business being in our neighborhood," Stanley started. "Shortcut to the interstate or not, rich people like him shouldn't cut through the street to begin with. They never should've been there."

"It must've been one of my dad's business associates or something." It had to be someone else from my dad's company...but not my father.

"When they arrested Payne, I told the police it wasn't him. They wouldn't listen, though. No one would, so I started looking for the phone numbers or addresses of the guys in that car. Started with professional directories first, but eventually, I found the contact for the passenger through a charity event he'd hosted.

"He told me he had friends in the police department and assured me that he would get Payne off. He told me he wanted to go to the police himself to own up to his part in that awful night—that your dad had made him pull my boy into that alley. And that after, your father was stopping him from doing the right thing."

"That's bullshit."

"I wanted to believe—needed to believe him. Especially after he found out my wife had cancer and he cut me a check for five million dollars to help pay for a lifetime of treatment. He swore he'd convince your father to turn himself in. His only request in exchange for that money was my signature on an NDA, prohibiting me from talking to reporters about it—said your dad would dig his heels in more if his name went public, so I agreed. I didn't care about reporters. I cared that your father turned himself in.

"But as time passed, it became clear your father was never going to accept responsibility for what he had done. I showed up at his house once to confront him, but some security guard held me back, and your father refused to see me."

"You're lying," I said. "If my father had struck someone with his vehicle, he would've turned himself in."

"When Payne was formally charged for my son's murder, police still wouldn't listen to me. Going to reporters? The guy who claimed he was trying to do the right thing threatened to retract the money meant for my wife's treatment. I confronted him again. Now he said your father was threatening him. Told me your father was too influential, had too much money, and would hire a team of defense attorneys."

Stanley took a ragged breath. "Your dad killed my son. Then he refused to take responsibility for it and was going to allow an innocent man to go to prison. The guy worked me up until I was in a rage. At the time, I was so vulnerable. I believed every word he said, but I think he played me so I would want to kill your father."

"Why would he do that?"

"My guess is that it was the other way around. That your father was the one about to go to the police and tell them what happened.

After all, Payne's story was all over the news. There were only two people in the vehicle, and if one of them was dead, the other could deny it to their grave. And get away with it."

"You think the passenger manipulated you into murder," I said.

"He lit the match, and I was the fire he invited inside. He told me that your father was going to be alone the next night. And that there was one door always unlocked."

Boom. The explosion.

"Who told you the door was going to be unlocked?" I demanded.

His voice dropped to a barely audible whisper, each syllable heavy with resignation. "Alexander Lockwood."

CHAPTER 49

Hunter

A cold knot tightened in my stomach. There was no way what this guy was saying was true. I mean, this guy might've *believed* it to be true, but it couldn't be.

Alexander was the closest thing I had to a father after my dad was killed. He was a fixture in our family through all those years, particularly in those early days after my father's death. It was incomprehensible to think he did this.

But if this guy was wrong, how could I explain the money? How could I explain Stanley knowing his son was hit by a car when that was never introduced into public record?

Well, not until Payne's recent hearing. Maybe he heard it then?

But how did he know about the unlocked door of our mansion? That wasn't in any police reports or public records either. It was an important clue that police withheld so that, should the real killer ever come forward, they'd know he wasn't faking a confession.

The prosecutor in me sifted through every word he'd said, wanting desperately to poke holes in his belief, to find evidence that contradicted his claims.

But there was none.

In fact, as his confession settled into my soul, a clarity came into focus. Knowing the personalities of my father and Uncle Alexander, I could see a scenario playing out.

I could almost picture it: them driving through the dimly lit suburb, perhaps coming from a business meeting, and then the sudden jolt, the sickening thud. My father would've wanted to call the police, but Uncle Alexander was a force to be reckoned with. My father's older brother must've dragged the boy off to the side, not wanting to get into trouble, not wanting to risk his family fortune and good name to lawsuits for something that couldn't be changed.

He must've been the one Luna's father saw leaving the alley just as he stumbled across the boy's body.

I bet my father was insisting they call for help, but Uncle Alexander convinced him that someone was with the kid—Luna's dad —helping him, and in a moment of panic, my father must've agreed to drive away.

And I bet Stanley was right. That guilt, the image of that injured boy, would've haunted my father. He'd have grappled with the need to confess, especially with another man facing the blame.

But if my father was arrested, Uncle Alexander would be arrested too. Leaving the scene of a crime after a hit-and-run was a big offense. A huge one, if it involved a kid that later died. And if they found out the kid was intentionally moved, they could have argued moving him had caused him more harm, possibly even resulting in his death.

Worse, moving the body might open the door to an argument of intentional homicide. Meaning they could have argued the boy was struck on purpose, and while that might not have been true, Alexander would have known that was a risk.

That he could have been facing a murder charge.

If my father was about to reveal it all, Uncle Alexander would have lost everything. His reputation, his stake in the company. Financially, he probably would've been sued by the kid's family, and most significant of all, he risked his freedom.

We all want to believe that those around us that we love, particularly family, would never be capable of hurting us. But as a prosecutor, I had seen time and time again that statistically, it was the people closest to the murder victim, the people they trusted the most, that often caused their death.

Each revelation snapped into place, shards of a fractured mirror reflecting a truth I hadn't seen before.

My father had killed that kid. He'd struck that teenage boy with his vehicle, resulting in his death, and that was why my father had seemed so solemn in the days before he was murdered.

A memory flashed—our last conversation, the way his eyes had clouded over when I'd said I wanted to be just like him. A hero to me, yet drowning in his own guilt.

Before my dad ever had a chance to repent for his sins, a stranger came into our home and slit his throat.

The memory of my father's lifeless body had poisoned my soul, filling it with a venomous rage, and the injustice of it all had led me to seek vengeance against people who'd hurt others.

Vigilantism is defined as the act of punishing those who perpetrate crimes and doing so without legal authority. While I preyed on the scums of the city, I also hunted the man who'd killed my father.

I never imagined that the man would turn out to be a vigilante in his own right. A man who was seeking vengeance against the driver who had gotten away with killing his son.

"You're telling me my uncle Alexander convinced you to kill my father?"

I still couldn't accept it, no matter how much it made sense. This was a confessed killer, after all.

"He didn't just convince me. He told me how to get into the house. When I got there, I almost didn't go through with it because you were in the room but..." Stanley's eyes filled with tears. "The man killed my child and left him for dead. And there he was, enjoying the company of his own son, living in a mansion like nothing had ever happened. Like my son's life didn't matter."

Stanley shook his head and looked down at the ground.

"I shouldn't have done it, not with you in the room," he said.

CHAPTER 50

Hunter

I aimed the cold, gleaming barrel at Stanley's bloodshot eye socket, watching as the dim light glinted off the metal as he stood in his living room with its peeling wallpaper and stench of stale cigarette smoke.

The shrill ringtone of my cell phone cut through the silence, echoing eerily in the room until it went to voice mail, only to start ringing again.

"Go ahead, son." Stanley's voice was low, the years of nicotine making it rasp.

"Don't call me that," I said through clenched teeth.

I yanked my cell from my pocket, prepared to shut the damn thing off.

Until I saw the number.

I'd asked Grayson to help find the courthouse shooter, who was a threat to Luna. If he was calling me, it might be urgent.

"Everything okay?" I asked.

"You're not going to believe this," Grayson said.

"Is everyone okay? Everyone safe?" I pressed. Anything else would have to wait.

"I found the guy who shot Luna's father."

A jolt zapped through my veins, buzzing my fingertips and toes, my finger trembling on the trigger.

"Are you sure?"

"Positive," Grayson answered. Behind him, there was some kind of low hum.

The gun in my hand lowered a few inches.

"How did you find him?" I managed. Grayson had been gone for a couple of hours. How would he find a shooter that the police had failed to find for days?

"I have some…contacts on the streets," Grayson said evasively. "You were right. It was a contract killer."

Another jolt of electricity, this one shooting through my ribs.

"How do you have contacts with people who know contract killers?"

"You won't believe who this guy claims ordered the hit," Grayson said, skillfully dodging my question. "This guy says it was Uncle Alexander."

Stumbling back, I shook my head, desperate for an escape from this nightmare.

One accusation against my uncle could be doubted, but a second? From an independent source? The facts were becoming harder to dispute.

"I punished him for saying it," Grayson said. "But when I gave the guy some encouragement that was…uncomfortable, he still didn't change his story."

Jesus.

"He's probably lying," Grayson said. "Although I can't figure out his motivation. Or why he'd use our uncle's name, of all things."

The room seemed to spin, and a cold sweat formed on my brow, every beat of my heart echoing the betrayal.

"I'm starting to think he's not lying, Grayson."

As silence stretched on between us, I could again hear a shuffling on my brother's line.

"You serious?" Grayson's voice was tense, but I could hear the heartbreak he was trying to hide.

"I'm with someone right now who's corroborating his story. Pretty compellingly, I might add."

Was that groaning behind my brother?

"He could be lying, too." Grayson grasped at the same thread of disbelief that had frayed for me.

"Could be," I said. "Which is why we need to talk to Uncle Alexander."

"I just talked to him," Grayson said. "He's at his place."

"You talked to him?"

"I didn't tell him anything," Grayson assured. "I want to talk to him in person about this. Told him it was important but didn't tell him what it was about. Want to meet me at his place?"

I couldn't believe this was happening. "Yeah." I glanced at my father's killer. "I just need a minute to wrap something up first."

"Same," Grayson said. "What do you want me to do with the guy who killed Luna's father?"

I blinked. "What do you mean?"

"I have him."

"You *have* him?"

"Tied up in my trunk."

"What the fuck, Grayson? I asked you to get a name, not commit aggravated kidnapping."

"First of all, you asked me to get information by any means necessary. So, save me the speech. Second, you asked me to get a name. I over-delivered, so spare me the theatrics of being shocked and offended and answer my question."

I bit my lip. "You know, when this is all over, you're going to tell me how the hell you know contract killers."

"Do you want to end him yourself or not?"

I stilled.

"What?" I asked.

"He killed your girlfriend's father. Do you need to get revenge out of your system?"

"Grayson, what kind of question is that?"

"I'm standing here with the dude in my trunk, so if you could hurry up and answer me, I'd appreciate it."

"He killed Luna's father, so, no, I'm not going to let him get away with it," I said.

"So, you don't care *who* ends him, just as long as he's dead, then?"

"Grayson..."

Vseww. Vseww.

Silence stretched out for an eternity as my heart launched into fresh shock.

"Grayson, was that a silencer?"

"Can't talk, brother. Need to...dispose of something."

"What the hell, Grayson?!"

"See you at Alexander's," he said. "I'll be there as soon as I can."

My brother disconnected the call.

Leaving me reeling, not only that my brother was far more dangerous than I'd imagined, but also that another person was corroborating this reality that I felt in my bones was true.

That it was Uncle Alexander all along.

He was the one threatening Luna. He was the one who sent her those letters. He was the one who ordered the hit on her father. And twenty years ago, he was the one who set everything in play that led to my father's murder. Uncle Alexander had been responsible for it all and never showed an ounce of remorse. I needed to hurry. When I was done with Stanley, things with my uncle were about to get ugly.

I tucked the gun, still warm from my grip, into the soft lining of my hoodie pocket and reached for the weapon I reserved for special occasions, its cool, sleek form reassuring in my grip.

CHAPTER 51
Luna

"Alexander," I said with raised brows.

"I told you to stand down," the security guard on Hunter's front porch snapped at him.

So that was the arguing I'd heard. I almost didn't answer the door—Hunter would be livid if he found out I did—but the knocking had been persistent, so I looked through the security hole and saw it was Alexander.

"What are you doing here?" I asked.

His eyes, so much like Hunter's, stared back at me, but the skin around them had deeper lines. He had the same strong jaw, the dark hair, too, though his was streaked with a few gray strands.

The vulnerability of seeing Alexander in casual wear was refreshing. Gone was the stern businessman I'd always seen—now wearing a gray T-shirt and black shorts.

"I didn't mean to bother you." Hunter's uncle looked sheepishly at the guard, then back at me. He extended a bouquet of white and purple flowers set in a crystal vase, the soft petals contrasting with the roughness of his hands.

"I came to give you my condolences, but perhaps I should come back another time."

I took the flowers from him, their fresh aroma hitting my nostrils.

"Don't be silly." I stepped back and motioned with my hand for him to come inside.

"He can't come in, ma'am," the security guard said.

"He's not a threat," I said.

"I've known you for ten years, Red." Alexander raised his palms in surrender. "But I don't want to cause any problems."

"Mr. Lockwood said no one in or out."

"He's family," I reasoned. One I hoped to be a part of.

"I'm sorry, but the answer is no," Red, the security guard, said.

The finality of his tone settled on my ribs. I should have felt grateful for the protection, but right now, it felt stifling. I was grieving, alone, and I wanted to talk to the guy who'd gone out of his way to bring me flowers.

The man who was like a father to Hunter.

If Hunter and I were going to be together forever, I wanted his family to like me, and that meant giving them a chance to get to know me.

I tried to wipe the disappointment off my face and gave a slight smile.

"I'm sorry," I said to Alexander. "Thank you for the flowers. You really didn't need to do this."

"I missed you at the funeral. Just wanted to let you know I'm thinking of you."

My throat clenched. His genuine concern, the tenderness in his eyes—no wonder Hunter looked up to him so much.

Alexander looked from the guard back to me.

"Well, I'd best be going." Alexander hesitated, worry etched over his face. "When you have time, Luna, I'd like to ask you something about Hunter. It's important."

My spine stiffened at his ominous tone.

"What is it?"

Alexander's eyes darted to Red for a moment. "Another time. It's… a confidential question."

Crap.

My grip tightened on the vase, the flowers almost quivering. There was no way that he suspected Hunter of being the Windy City Vigilante, right? I mean, even if he did, he was his uncle. He would never turn Hunter in, right?

Right?!

But what if he somehow figured it out? If there was anyone else who would figure it out, it would be someone close to Hunter, like his uncle or his brother.

If Alexander knew, would he go to the authorities? Or tell someone else who would?

I just convinced Hunter to not turn himself in, and now the threat of him being ripped from my arms, just like my father was ripped from my arms, was rising like the swell of the ocean.

Or maybe I was wrong. Maybe his question about Hunter had nothing to do with being the Vigilante.

"Again, I'm sorry for your loss." Alexander offered a sad smile and then turned and began to walk away.

"Wait!" I exclaimed. "He's family. Let him in."

Red planted himself firmly in front of the doorway, his deep-set eyes showing every bit of his resolve. "Ma'am, I've got strict orders. No one goes in or out, no exceptions."

I took a deep breath, frustration evident on my face.

"Red, you've been guarding Hunter and his family for a decade. You know Alexander."

"He might be family, Ms. Payne, but this is about your safety," Red retorted, still blocking the path.

Alexander, sensing the tension, tried to defuse the situation. "Maybe another time, Luna..."

"No," I interjected. I couldn't let Alexander leave here without knowing the risk to Hunter's identity. "Come in."

"I can't let him do that, Ms. Payne."

"Hunter and I share this home now," I said, meeting Red's gaze. "I have a say in this."

Red's chest inflated, and he hesitated for a moment, rubbing his jaw. His gaze traveled in the direction of the other guards stationed around the property and then to the security cameras. There was a weighty pause as he seemed to measure the risks.

After a long pause, he took a deep breath and, with a reluctant nod, finally grumbled, "Five minutes." He pointed a stern finger at Alexander. "Not a second more."

A wave of relief washed over me. "Thank you, Red," I said.

Hesitation flickered across Alexander's face, his gaze darting between me and Red, a silent debate playing out in his eyes—like he didn't want to create a problem.

For a moment, I worried that he was going to decline my offer and leave me wondering what in the hell he wanted to ask about Hunter.

But thankfully, he stepped inside.

"Don't worry," I told Red. "I'll lock up."

CHAPTER 52

Hunter

I pressed my blade against the jugular of my father's killer. He made no move to fight me, resigned, I guess, that this was his fate.

Welcoming it, even.

I'd always wanted to kill the man who murdered my father in cold blood. Ever since I was a kid, I knew the only way to stop this unrelenting torment in my soul—a putrid mixture of guilt, shame, and suffering for not having done something to stop it—was to seek out the murderer and end him.

And yet, as the cold steel of my knife pressed against the warmth of his neck, his pulse quickening and throbbing against the sharp edge, peace didn't feel one slash away.

Killing him wouldn't bring my father back. It wouldn't undo my failure. I had frozen, and sat paralyzed, as this man lunged at my father, slitting his throat.

That guilt would still be there, even if I ripped open his jugular and watched him bleed out. Only, it would be mixed with a different kind of pain.

If I had been in this man's shoes, if someone had killed my child, left him to die, had gotten away with it, and I had come to the conclusion that he would never face the consequences of his actions...would I have accepted that? Would I have moved on with my life, or would that have felt like a betrayal to my son?

In my deluge of grief, would I have also chosen to take justice into my own hands?

I already knew the answer to that.

But I wanted this. I needed this—to see his blood spill from his body, to watch his life force fade to black with my face being the last thing he'd ever see on earth. I needed to feel the vindication of avenging my father's murder, even if it was hollower than I'd fantasized.

But in all my fantasies, this man had been a monster, a beast of demonic proportions, yet looking at him now, I could see he was merely a grief-stricken father who'd done what I probably would have in the same situation.

Save for doing it in front of a child. That was a detestable mistake, but if I put that horrific split-second decision aside, one could argue that this man was more like me than anyone else. Seeking justice where it had failed his family.

Killing him, in some way, felt like killing myself.

But he could have made different choices. He could have gone to the media to make the police listen, if only in the eyes of the public, and accept that the blood money would go away. He could have turned down the money in the first place, no matter how desperate he was for it.

But I suppose that was easy to say now, in hindsight.

When one is suffering the trauma of grief, one doesn't always make rational choices. He was wrong, so very wrong in the string of decisions he'd made, but by the looks of it, he'd suffered every day since.

Which begged the question: When it came to vengeance, what was enough?

But what did it say about me if I didn't go through with this? It said I was complicit. It said my father's murder was acceptable. It said I was okay with it, which was the ultimate betrayal of my dad.

Plus, killing the man I'd hunted my entire life had to be healing, even if it didn't seem like it right now.

I pushed the tip of my knife against his skin until a single drop of blood broke free, giving me a taste of what would come.

Stanley's eyes bore into mine, almost pleading, as the scent of his fear mixed with an odd sense of peace, his shallow breaths carrying a note of acceptance. Welcoming his imminent death.

I didn't want that. I wanted him to beg me for his life, and I would be the one yielding the power to take it away.

Yet my blade remained still against the artery that could end this complicated man. This man wasn't who I thought he was. And now that I found Luna, I wanted to be a better person for her. If even a small part of me felt like this was wrong, how could I go through with it?

My hand trembled, surrendering to the realization that justice wasn't in spilling his blood, but in granting him mercy.

With its serrated whisper fading into the echo of my vengeance, I slowly pulled the blade away.

Honoring my father's memory in another version of justice.

"I'm sorry for what happened to your son," I said.

I stepped back. Stanley Weiss knew my name, and could go to authorities, telling them I'd threatened to kill him. I couldn't control that, but I could control my choices.

Killing a man to protect myself would stoop to the vile level of my uncle.

My uncle.

I balled my hand into a fist, my heart threatening to crack in half. How could he have taken my dad from us? Luna's dad?

All to save his own ass.

Luna was right; her dad must have been killed out of fear that the real killer might be identified. It was unlikely her dad had ever been shown a picture of my uncle in a photo lineup, and while Luna's father admitted it was dark and he doubted he'd be able to identify the person, that wouldn't eliminate my uncle's fear.

Of losing everything.

If he was willing to kill his own brother to protect himself, killing Mr. Payne would be nothing for him.

I could let Stanley live.

If my uncle confessed, could I give him the same courtesy?

With one last look at Stanley's pain-stricken face, I turned around and gripped his gun. Staring at it in my hands.

If I left it here and he went through with his original intent, I could be implicated with my prints on it. If I took it with me, though, I had no idea if the gun was clean or used in other crimes. Should I get pulled over before I had the chance to burn it or throw it in the river, that would pose a big problem.

And I'd made Luna a promise to protect myself.

Plus, if Stanley was committed to ending his life, taking his gun would merely delay it. With a soft breath, I wiped my prints from it and placed it in a nearby drawer before turning to Stanley and saying, "Don't do it, Stanley."

I held the haunted stare of the ghost from my past before ambling out his front door.

The wooden porch groaned under my feet as I made my way down the creaky steps into the fresh air that smelled of distant rain.

Just as I reached the bottom, a sudden, deafening gunshot shattered the calm neighborhood. The raw, explosive sound reverberated through the air, making birds take flight and sending dread racing through my veins.

My feet moved robotically, drawing me to the front window. I looked through the murky glass to see Stanley's body on the ground, the gun in his hand. A dark crimson pool spread from his temple, contrasting starkly against the pale floor.

I had spent so many nights dreaming of this moment, expecting a rush of satisfaction, a sense of closure. But instead of relief, a heavy weight of sadness pressed down on my ribs.

Once, that man had been a young father, cradling his infant son, filled with hopes and dreams for their future together. But a single accident had irrevocably changed the courses of our lives, binding us in a cycle of pain and grief.

I jogged to the car I'd borrowed from my brother—one of his spares that he'd left for me down the street from my mansion—and climbed in.

Ready to face the man who set this dark spiral in motion.

CHAPTER 53

Luna

"I was just chopping watermelon," I said, the sweet aroma of the freshly sliced fruit mingling with the subtle fragrance of the flowers that I set on the marble counter.

He followed me into the kitchen and smiled. "Tasks like chopping have a way of quieting the mind, don't they?"

"I tried reading a book, but..." I shook my head. "Gave up after reading the same sentence thirty times."

Alexander, tall with tan skin that looked too young for his age, positioned himself a few feet from where I stood near the center island. He leaned his back up against the counter—watching the butcher knife in my hand cut another strip of the watermelon.

"Coffee's still fresh," I said, nodding toward the silver holder where steam curled up, catching the soft morning light filtering through the blinds.

Alexander waved it off, crossing his arms over his chest.

Studying me.

I tried to keep my nerves at bay—was he watching my body language for any clue I knew who Hunter really was?

"You said you had a question about Hunter?" I managed to keep my voice calm.

"Where is my nephew?" Alexander asked.

I cut a fresh line down the green strip, having to tug a little to get through the thick of it. The cold, wet flesh of the watermelon slipped against my fingertips as I chopped, doing little to soothe the prickling tension at the nape of my neck.

"He had an errand to take care of," I hedged.

"An errand," Alexander repeated in a low tone. "What kind of errand?"

When I looked up, Alexander's stare was fixed on me. Unblinking. And the warmth that had previously graced his eyes had vanished, replaced by a frozen detachment while he kept looking between me and the knife in my hand. With this look of...was it irritation? Because his tightened jaw made him kind of look angry.

A cold pit settled in my stomach. Just moments ago, he'd arrived with a seemingly genuine smile and fresh flowers.

Moments ago, I'd been the one to get him past security...

"I'm not sure," I lied.

Again, he looked at my butcher knife, his body shifting slightly. Tense.

"He sure seems crazy about you." Alexander's voice was hauntingly calm—his words meant as a compliment, coming off like a warning.

Was I being paranoid, stressed after the ordeal I had been through? Or was my sixth sense justified in telling me to run?

I looked in the direction of the front door.

Alexander pushed off the counter, smirking when I flinched. His shoes tapped softly against the tiled floor as he walked toward the archway that separated the kitchen from the front door and brushed the bouquet with his fingertip.

"That was quite the eulogy you gave at the funeral." He plucked a pedal from the white rose.

I eyed my phone, which sat at the far end of the room. I glanced toward the window, where, outside, security agents were positioned all around this place.

Alexander took a step toward me.

"Hunter looked worried," he said, his tone rigid. "When you got to the part about going after the person who killed your father."

It took me a second to find my voice. "Hunter doesn't want anything to happen to me."

To this, Alexander cocked his head. Took another step. "Then it was probably unwise to provoke the killer, wasn't it?"

I stiffened, a draft crawling up my neck.

"Do you still feel that way?"

He took another step closer.

I stepped back.

"Determined to find whoever did it?"

I said nothing.

"Obsession destroyed Hunter's life. If you're not careful, it'll do the same to yours."

My jaw tightened. "His life isn't destroyed."

"Nonetheless, I have to agree with my nephew on this point."

He advanced another step, and I moved, too, farther away from him, slowly scooting around the island.

"Which point is that?"

Alexander glared at me, all remnants of his pleasant facade finally breaking, replaced by an animalistic look.

"That it was dangerous to threaten someone like that."

Alexander looked at the blade of my knife as he advanced another step.

The cold air seemed to grow thicker, making it harder to breathe.

"Someone like what?" I whispered, tasting the apprehension on my tongue.

To this, Alexander's lips curled up slightly, as if taking pleasure in whatever he was about to say.

"Someone who's been smart enough to conceal the source of those letters."

Ice crackled through my veins. Maybe he knew about the letters because I'd mentioned them in court that day. But Alexander wasn't there.

"How do you know about the letters?"

Had Hunter told him about them?

I sidestepped to the right, putting more of the island between us. But Alexander mirrored me, cutting the distance.

His jaw clenched as he said, "You should have let it go."

And then, with a speed I hadn't expected, he lunged for me.

CHAPTER 54

Luna

I brought the butcher knife up and aimed it at his chest, halting him mid-step.

Panic welled up, hot and tight in my stomach.

"What are you doing?" My voice trembled despite my best effort to sound fierce.

"Put the knife down."

"Don't make me hurt you." I had no idea why Alexander was attacking me, but he was the only father figure Hunter had since he was a little boy. No matter the circumstances, I didn't want to be the one to take that from him.

Alexander inched toward me.

Again, with each step, I matched it with one of my own, keeping the distance between us the same.

Like a morbid dance, we moved in tandem; every step he took, I mirrored the cold weight of the knife grounding me.

"Stay back!" I snapped firmly, but Alexander smirked in response.

With each of his moves, he closed the distance between us, and now, the tip of the butcher's knife was perilously close to his chest.

Outside, there were armed security guards. All I had to do was get to the front door, open it, and run outside. Alexander would be subdued within moments.

I pivoted and took off running.

As I sprinted, the floor stretched endlessly. My lungs screamed, each breath sharp and ragged, while the wooden door loomed so close yet impossibly far.

Finally, I made it to the wooden monstrosity.

Fumbling with shaking hands, I unlocked the cold deadbolt. Every rugged gasp echoed the pounding of my heart—freedom, tantalizingly close, just beyond the door.

But a sharp, stinging pain shot through my scalp, and the world tilted as he yanked my head back.

Still gripping the knife, I tried to twist and spin out of his hold on my hair, but he grabbed my wrist with his free hand to stop me from stabbing him.

"He—" I started to scream, but he let go of my hair, and his sweaty palm pressed hard against my mouth. The metallic taste of my own blood seeped onto my tongue as my lip split against the pressure.

While he used his other hand to pry at my fingers, trying to wrench the knife's handle away from me.

The security panel with its red panic button was only a few feet from me.

Maybe I couldn't make it outside, but with the push of one button, this place would flood with bodyguards.

I jerked my head, trying to free myself from him, but when that didn't work, I opened my mouth.

His skin was salty and rough against my tongue as I bit down hard on his finger, his flesh giving beneath my teeth. He groaned and shoved me to the floor with a grunt.

A searing pain jolted from my hip, hot and sharp, but a flicker of hope ignited as I spotted the security panel just above me.

And my mouth was free once again.

"He—"

Alexander charged at me, the weight of his body crashing into mine. My head slammed into the wall with an echoing thud, stars exploding in my vision, and before I could recover, his hand clamped over my mouth, silencing my desperate cry.

My fingers grasped at the empty air where the knife once was. It was gone, glinting mockingly from the floor, far out of reach.

CHAPTER 55

Luna

Alexander's iron grip hoisted me from the ground, his fingers digging painfully into my arm. As he yanked me backward, my feet instinctively lashed out, striking his shin, but he hardly flinched.

I tried to bite his fingers again, but I couldn't even open my mouth. His hand was fixed across my lips with two fingers tucked under my jaw, so I moaned as loud as I could. I thrashed around in his grasp, but he was far too strong.

He pulled me farther from the front door, from safety, deeper into the downstairs hallway, which led to a panel of doors.

"We can do this the easy way or the hard way," Alexander sneered, his breath hot against my ear.

This time, I grabbed the hand that covered my mouth with both of mine, and I jerked at it until it dislodged enough for me to bite down again.

Alexander roared and pushed me to the wooden floor of the hallway.

I tried to scream, but he punched me into silence.

I held my cheek, which burned in pain, and looked up into his cold eyes. "You killed my father."

He reached for me, but I kicked his hand away.

"You're the one that sent those letters."

"You should have listened to me." Alexander grabbed my hair, but I managed to twist out of his grasp, gritting through the bite of losing some strands.

I tried to get up, to make a run for it, but he shoved me back, and the wooden planks slammed against my chest. I turned over.

"You hired Franco," I accused.

I kicked his wrist, savoring a rush of triumph at the pain flashing across his face.

Alexander was a cold-blooded murderer. But what was his plan in coming here today? He had to know that if he killed me, even if he was arrogant enough to think he could miraculously evade prosecution by police, Hunter would never stop hunting until he found the man that ended my life. Just as he never gave up on finding his father's killer.

Alexander was risking everything.

Unless...

"You're going to kill Hunter," I realized with a sickening dread skating across my bones.

Alexander managed to grab my ankle this time, and when he dragged me closer to him, the grain of the wood scraped against my spine.

"Why?" I demanded. "Why are you going to kill your nephew?!"

"I have no choice."

I kicked him in the thigh with my left foot. I was aiming for his crotch, but he turned before I made contact.

"Help!" I shouted. "He—"

Another punch to my jaw stopped my words.

"They'll never hear you from in here," Alexander taunted.

We were deep in the bowels of the mansion now. I wanted him to be wrong, but I didn't hear the cavalry coming in, either.

He dragged me like an animal down the hallway, but when we passed a doorway, I gripped the frame with both hands.

Alexander tried yanking me away from it by my ankles. When that didn't work, he kicked me in the ribs. My body jolted, and I lost my grip, wrapping my arms around my rib cage as I groaned through the sharp pain.

The pain sent a fresh wave of adrenaline through my muscles. I kicked my ankles, landing a blow to Alexander's hips. He fell to the ground, giving me a moment to jump to my feet.

But he was blocking my path to the front door.

Still holding my pained ribs, I ran down the hallway in the opposite direction, finding a back stairwell.

Alexander's footsteps sounded behind me as I ran up the staircase.

I launched myself up each step, my thigh muscles burning as I charged faster and faster. But suddenly, something locked my right ankle.

I kicked it wildly backward, like a horse bucking, and when it connected with Alexander's forehead, he fell backward down the staircase with a series of thumps and groans.

As I ran up again, I risked a quick glance over my shoulder.

His rage-filled gaze locked on me, and his teeth clenched as he launched himself up.

When I reached the top, it took me a moment to get my bearings.

Bedrooms. I'm near the bedrooms.

Specifically, near Hunter's.

His words echoed in my mind.

"In the unlikely event anything happens and all those fail-safes don't work, I want you to sneak into the weapons room. Close the closet door behind you. And hide there until I retrieve you. You understand?"

I charged into Hunter's bedroom, hearing Alexander stomping up the staircase as I launched myself through Hunter's primary closet, closing the door behind me.

I opened its hidden door on the far side of the space and ran through the secondary closet before opening the door that led to the spiral staircase.

I made it into the damp, earth-scented space, but when I closed the door behind me, it burst open.

Slamming into my chest.

My body flew backward, and I tumbled down the spiral stairs, shoulders, hips, and back taking painful blows.

When I landed at the base, I was on the concrete floor of the amber-lit tunnel, looking up at the man who was now clanking down the spiral steps with his predatory gaze fixed on me.

CHAPTER 56
Hunter

hy isn't Luna answering my calls?

The engine's roar grew louder as I slammed my foot down on the gas pedal and called Red, the security guard positioned outside my front door.

"Red," I said. "Do you have eyes on Luna?"

"Not at the moment. Everything okay, sir?"

"No," I admitted. "I'm on my way to my uncle's."

"Your uncle is here, sir."

My vision blurred for a split second, a dread making my stomach drop.

"Alexander?"

"Yes, sir. I told him he wasn't allowed to go in, but Ms. Payne insisted—"

The putrid taste of panic filled my mouth.

"Red, you listen to me. I just found out that my uncle Alexander is the one threatening Luna. You need to get inside now! Break the goddamned door down if you have to!"

"Yes, sir."

I ended the call, my fingers sweaty against the steering wheel as I pushed the car even faster and dialed another number.

"Grayson," I said. "How close are you to my house?"

"On the property."

"You're *on* the property?" I thought he had a dead body in his trunk.

"Did you know there's a little canal hidden deep on the north end of our property that feeds into Lake Michigan? How did I never know this, growing up here?"

"I need your help."

"I'm disposing of…something right now."

"This is more urgent."

A distant splash echoed over the line, followed by the muted rustling of leaves.

"What do you need?" Grayson asked.

"Alexander's in the house with Luna. She's not answering her phone. Red's going in, but can you please—"

"I'm on my way," Grayson said.

Click.

The engine roared as I pushed it even further, the speedometer creeping past a hundred twenty—the outside becoming a blur.

Every second stretched far too long. *Luna, hold on,* I silently pleaded.

CHAPTER 57

Luna

P anic surged as I scrambled to my feet, every fiber of my being urging me to flee. The dim tunnel loomed ahead, the distance stretching out, seemingly endless. My heavy breathing became erratic as Alexander's menacing footsteps reverberated off the walls, becoming faster and heavier behind me.

If I could make it to the weapons wall, maybe I could incapacitate him long enough to run for it.

As my heart thundered in my chest and my feet slammed against the unforgiving stone, some part of my brain registered the eerie resemblance my desperate escape held. In the depths of this underground chamber, memories of my frantic escape from Hunter surfaced, a stark contrast to the peril I now faced. The corridors seemed to echo with my past fears, but an unsettling clarity pierced through the chaos of my thoughts: Hunter, despite all appearances, never intended to kill me. Yet with Alexander, every instinct screamed, every heartbeat warned of his lethal intent. The two scenarios, though seemingly similar, were worlds apart in the intentions and dangers behind them.

I pushed aside the thoughts and finally charged into the frosty air of the weapons room, snatching a hammer and spinning around.

Watching as the dangerous presence materialized. The echo of heavy footsteps merged with the drip of condensation while the amber lighting cast an eerie glow that carved out the silhouette of Alexander.

His fists, clenched in white-knuckled fury, hung at his sides, promising pain.

When his eyes met mine, his approach slowed, and the charged air between us grew heavier, thick with anticipation—a predator assessing his prey.

He entered the room and stilled, his eyes widening as he looked around the space. At the stone walls residing beneath the earth, a hundred feet from the main house. At the artificial lights positioned along the outer rim, at the large board behind me, where an array of knives and tools sat organized in neat rows.

"The hell is this place?" he murmured.

He glanced behind him, quickly scanning the tunnel he'd chased me down, then returned his focus back to the weapons room.

The smaller tunnel branched toward my right. Surely, there was an outside door in that direction where I could run, hide, scream for help, and run toward the security guards, who were probably looking for us right now since Alexander had never come back out.

I looked back at Alexander, seeing a malevolent spark flickering in his gaze. Before he lunged with predatory speed.

My legs turned my body and pumped in swift retaliation; the cold handle of the hammer pressed into my palm with a promise of protection. The narrow corridor ahead swallowed me into its shadows. It was a tight squeeze, a claustrophobic stretch with barely enough illumination to make out the path.

Alexander's frantic shouts echoed from behind, the ominous drum of his pursuing steps amplifying the dread knotted in my gut.

I was only ten feet from a light ahead that opened into a new space, the taste of victory sweet on my lips.

But suddenly, a force, brutal and swift, collided with my back. Careening forward, I slammed into the stone ground on my chest— sharp aches rocketing through my hips and shoulders.

I rolled onto my back and swung the hammer at the dark figure standing over me, but he caught my arm and wrenched it from my grip. Before grabbing a fistful of my hair and slamming my head against the floor.

CHAPTER 58

Hunter

"What do you mean, you can't find them?" I snapped at Red.

Red ran a hand through his hair, visibly frustrated. "We've gone through the mansion twice. There's no trace of them, but we did find this." He gestured toward a gleaming butcher knife that lay just a few feet away from the security panel.

A dread crept into my bones. The knife was far from its home in the kitchen. A molten anger rose within me, a tightening in my throat. "He attacked her."

"His car's still here," Red said. "They can't be far."

I knelt down and scrutinized the blade. "No blood."

Maybe she got away.

I walked into the kitchen, spotting a cut up watermelon oozing all over the white center island. In the corner of the room, Luna's phone sat on the counter.

"What about the dock around back?" Grayson pressed. He'd helped them look before I'd arrived. "Have we checked the boat?"

"Yes," Red said.

The weight of each passing second pressed down on me, my mind racing to put the pieces together.

"What about the road out front?" I clenched my fists, fighting the urge to pummel Red for letting Alexander in here. "Maybe he had a second car parked out there."

Red hesitated, then nodded. "I'll have my men check again."

"Split your men up," I said, struggling to keep my emotions in check. "Have some go through every inch of this mansion again. Have someone else check the cottage, the boat dock around back again. Every other property on this estate. The surveillance footage. Look everywhere. And call the police."

"Already did, sir. They're on their way."

"Grayson, you and I know this place better than anyone else. You look again downstairs; I'll take the upstairs."

I ran up the steps two at a time.

"Luna?" My voice echoed in the vast expanse, a raw desperation behind it. If she had managed to escape Alexander, she might be hiding, waiting for a sign of safety.

Hiding…

What if…

CHAPTER 59
Luna

Darkness ebbed away, replaced by hazy gray light. Distant footsteps grew louder, each step making my head throb as if a nail was being hammered into it. Slowly, I forced my eyes open all the way, and when they did, my blurry surroundings slowly began to crystallize.

The footsteps ceased just in front of me. "You didn't stay out long," a voice drawled, dripping with irritation.

Coherent thoughts began to punch through the fog in my mind, slowly whipping out memories like a deck of cards, one at a time.

I moved my arm, intending to sit up, but my wrists were stuck. I jerked at them, trying to figure out why I couldn't move them, and realized they were bound together.

"What the hell is this place?" he snarled.

Mingled with my will to survive was also a fierce determination to protect Hunter's secret, especially from this man—a traitor, a wolf pretending to be part of his pack.

"Hunter collects weapons," I croaked, my throat suddenly lined with sandpaper.

Alexander walked to the weapons wall and trailed his fingers along the many tools he could use to end my life.

"Bullshit," he said. "I know people who collect weapons. They don't keep them in a secret dungeon like this."

Why hadn't he killed me when he had the chance?

I wasn't sure, but at least it gave me another chance to get away from him.

It took serious effort to shift my body up into a seated position and prepare for my next move.

Alexander stood to my right, blocking the smaller tunnel, but not the amber tunnel ahead of me. I'd run down the hallway, run up that staircase, and turn my back to the door so my hands could grab on to the handle to unlock it.

The odds were not in my favor, but they were something.

Alexander touched the tip of a knife, his eyebrows furrowed as he glanced around the room once more. Several tense seconds passed, and then in a low voice pulsing with shocked disbelief, he said, "Hunter's the Windy City Vigilante."

A polar frost coated my skin. I shouldn't have come down here; I should have tried to escape out the front of the house rather than risk exposing Hunter's secret.

"That's absurd," I said.

But his gaze studied a specific blade, drawing his fingertip down the metal that glistened slightly. "The news said this is the type of knife the Windy City Vigilante uses."

I looked at the tunnel, wondering if I could use this distraction to my advantage, giving me a better chance at getting away.

"Last time I checked, manufacturers produce more than one. You know, trying to make a profit and all that."

"That was a garage, wasn't it?" Alexander said. "That room at the end of the tunnel I caught you in."

I shifted my feet to the side, together, where they'd have enough leverage to hoist me up.

"On the other end of the property." Alexander continued, "where he could come and go without being detected."

"I don't know," I said. "Why don't you go check and find out?"

"How could I have not seen this before?" Alexander wandered

around the room, talking to himself in a giddy tone, like he was thrilled to solve this mystery. "Mayor Kepler thought it might be somebody in law enforcement or close to law enforcement."

I eyed the other tunnel, calculating my odds of reaching it before he stopped me.

"I mean, look at this place. It's perfect, and it's hidden from the rest of the mansion. I never would've found it if you didn't lead me here."

Guilt settled into my bones.

"You're psychotic *and* delusional," I said.

Alexander squatted in front of me, gripping a serrated hunting knife.

"I was going to do this in the office," Alexander said. "By now, the security guards are probably all over the mansion, but I bet they don't know about this place." He shrugged. "So, I guess we'll have to do it down here."

"Hunter will come for me."

"I'm counting on it." He walked over and retrieved a roll of duct tape. "The security guard will have checked up on you by now and found you missing. I'd imagine it won't be long before Hunter storms in here to save his girlfriend."

I mustered my strength and attempted to push myself up, but his powerful grip forced me down with a thud. My tailbone throbbed with pain as it made contact with the cold earth below. He grabbed my upper arm and dragged me to one of the concrete columns that held up the roof.

I thrashed, I kicked, I fought him, but he overpowered me and wrapped duct tape around my core, anchoring me to the column opposite the main tunnel, so it would be the first thing Hunter saw when he came down here. He might be so fixated on me, that he could let his guard down.

"This is working out better than I imagined," Alexander mused.

"If you kill us, people will know it was you. You're the only one in this mansion alone with me."

"I was going to stage a suicide for you," Alexander said. "You know, grief-stricken with your dad and all that. Same for Hunter, once he found you, but look at this." He motioned with his hand through the air. "I'll say I discovered Hunter was the Vigilante, and you lured me down here so he could kill me."

"I'm tied up, so they'll never believe that."

"I'll untie you before the police find your body. I mean, damn, I had my plan A and plan B, but this, this is so much better. I'll be a hero." He pointed the dagger at me. "You were helping the Vigilante. I discovered you, you attacked me, and then Hunter showed up and tried to finish me. I'll have defended myself. When they see this room, they'll believe every word of it. I'm friends with Mayor Kepler, so he won't question me. He'll have his win, he'll get reelected, and the city will feel safe again once the Windy City Vigilante is dead. Everyone wins."

"Hunter's not the Vigilante," I lied. "Why kill me? Why him? He's done nothing to you."

Alexander's eyes darkened. "Hasn't he?"

CHAPTER 60

Luna

My mind raced back to what he'd said before he'd attacked me—before I'd become overcome with survival.

"You're the one that wanted to make my father's case disappear." But why? "Why would you care about my father's case?" I pressed. "What would you have to gain by keeping an innocent man in prison?"

His lips pursed. "If you'd heeded my warnings, your father would still be alive right now."

The room seemed to close in, and my vision tunneled on him.

"You…you're the reason he's dead. You wanted him silent. Why?"

No response.

My brain scrambled to find the answer that felt like it was dangling within reach, like a word you couldn't quite find when speaking.

Think, Luna. Dad was killed so the case would die with him. The person who would benefit from that case getting buried had murdered to make it happen.

A person who'd kill for it would be…

Oh my god.

"You're responsible for that teenager's death?" I whispered.

"That kid was nothing more than a tragic accident. A Tuesday night gone wrong."

Holy shit.

"You knew an innocent man was charged for a crime he did *not* commit, and you stood by and did nothing?"

"God, you sound just like my brother," Alexander snarled.

My brother?

"Hunter's father knew about this?"

Alexander looked at his watch.

"Was he there that night, too?" I pressed.

No denial.

Did Hunter know this? A bolt of panic flooded my limbs at the betrayal. But, no, there was no way Hunter would have known about this. He was actively trying to find the person threatening me. And if he knew that his uncle was a danger, he would've done something about it. At a minimum, told security officers that Alexander, of all people, was not allowed on the property.

Which meant Hunter didn't know.

"You let an innocent man go to prison."

"Your father was unfortunate collateral damage."

"Because you're a coward and didn't want to take responsibility for it. Even if you wouldn't do the right thing by turning yourself in, you could've helped him. At least provided an anonymous tip, something, to show them that they needed to look into this further."

"If they dug deeper, they could've realized I was involved. I couldn't take that chance."

"You're rich. You could've at least hired a powerful defense attorney for my father that could have given him a fair fight!"

My eyes prickled with tears.

"I wasn't going to take the chance that some defense attorney would figure out what really happened." Alexander's tone was condescending, like any idiot would come to the same conclusion. And any thought process otherwise was childish.

"Did you guys hit the kid on purpose?" I pressed.

"Course not." His head pulled back in offense. "We were driving home after a work thing, stopped for dinner before we hit that kid on *accident* on the way home. He's the one that ran into the road."

How vile to blame the victim, and he still didn't explain, as he put it, "what really happened."

"You went to a lot of trouble to move him and leave him." For dead.

"It's not like we could unhit him with the car." He glared at me like I was too stupid to follow along. "And as I pointed out to my brother, the cops would likely do a breathalyzer."

"You were drunk driving?"

"He was driving," Alexander chided. "And two glasses of wine with dinner didn't make him drunk, but the appearance of hitting a kid after drinking alcohol would prove quite unfortunate for us both."

That poor kid.

And my poor father.

"You sat there and allowed my father's life to be taken from him. He missed out on my childhood! He missed so many milestones, sitting in prison for twenty years for a crime he didn't commit."

The fact that Alexander looked unbothered by this stabbed a dagger through my gut. I don't know what I expected, but I suppose a bit of remorse was the bare minimum, and yet he was void of any compassion.

Of course he was, because, "You killed my father," I repeated.

The sinking reality of it weighed on my shoulders.

"He saw you that night, didn't he?" I choked over a sob.

That's another reason he let my father go to prison. To silence the one person who could pin that kid's death on him.

My father gave a rough sketch to the police, but it had been dark, so it was pretty generic. He couldn't pick any photos out of a lineup, and that amplified police suspicion that my father was lying.

Chances were, my father would never have been able to point out Alexander, but Alexander wouldn't take that gamble, I guess.

Especially if my father was free and coming around Hunter and his family living in that cottage.

Just as the twenty years of my father's freedom were an acceptable sacrifice, so was my father's life.

"You killed that kid," I said. Now he planned to kill me, because I'd never stop hunting my dad's murderer. And he'd kill Hunter, too. How many people would he kill just to protect his own ass?

"My brother was driving, not me," he said with ambivalence.

The remaining puzzle pieces fell into place.

"You're the one that killed Hunter's dad," I said. "Aren't you?"

"He should be here any minute," Alexander reasoned, ignoring me, and looking up at the ceiling. "The security team would've called him by now."

"He's never stopped hunting for his dad's killer," I said. So, Hunter was a threat to Alexander. Especially if I'd wound up dead, too. Hunter would never believe I'd committed suicide.

He'd hunt to the ends of the earth to find the person responsible for my death.

"And he'd have never stopped hunting for mine," I whispered.

CHAPTER 61

Luna

T he sound of the door opening at the top of the spiral staircase was a soft creak as if someone was entering it with caution. Now, my mouth was sealed with duct tape, making me powerless to warn Hunter.

Alexander squatted down, whispering, "A little insurance for distraction."

He winked, and in the next second, the serrated edge tore into my thigh. A muffled scream escaped my lips as hot pain seared through me, blood spewing from the wound. He'd hit the femoral artery—though, by the looks of it, just a nick.

"Better hope he hurries." Alexander smirked, then disappeared behind a curve in the stone wall, waiting to pounce.

With the pungent smell of blood mixing with earth, my lip quivered. Of all the ways Hunter might lose his life, I didn't want it to be like this, and I didn't want to be the bait that lured him to his demise.

My throat swelled in agony.

The steps descending the spiral staircase were soft but urgent.

I jerked my body around, trying to break free from the duct tape that trapped me in its snare. But it was a lost cause.

The atmosphere was thick with the musty scent of mildew and old earth, the humidity clinging to the walls in glistening beads of moisture as I stared down the dank tunnel, where the unmistakable silhouette of Hunter began to take shape in the distance.

He was the kind of man who could make the shadows seem less terrifying to me—someone who'd kill to protect—and more terrifying to those unfortunate enough to meet the wrath of this apex predator.

But he didn't know what was waiting for him.

There was a silent serpent lying in wait, and Hunter was the unsuspecting mouse.

My heart pounded against the confines of my rib cage, a futile plea for escape. A bitter, acid panic rose in my throat, and the sheer terror became paralyzing, like icy tendrils wrapping themselves around my ribs, squeezing until a cold emptiness consumed me.

His form grew clearer with each urgent step, his features emerging from the murk.

A sorrowful howl threatened to erupt from my chest, but it was strangled into a whimper. The cold, hard truth tore at my heartstrings, playing a mournful symphony of impending loss.

And then, when he spotted me, a feral rage rippled through his features.

I jerked my chin to the right, trying to warn him where Alexander was, but Hunter's gaze fixed on my bleeding thigh, and he jogged toward me with panicked eyes.

I shook my head again and moaned. I could only watch as the world I knew crumbled into shards of cruel reality, my heart shattering along with it.

As Hunter emerged into the trap.

CHAPTER 62
Hunter

Crimson life seeped from Luna's thigh, a torrent in sickening slow motion, each droplet hitting the stone like sands of time, emptying the minutes she had left to breathe.

I picked up my speed, my steps rapid and urgent, but suddenly, a mere fifteen feet before I reached Luna, something made me pause.

The look in her eyes.

Wide and full of terror as her gaze shifted slightly, from me to something off to her right, moving her chin and moaning beneath the tape that bound her mouth.

I locked eyes with her and motioned with my finger toward the wall just around the corner.

Luna nodded, her motion so minimal, I could tell she was trying to conceal her movements should he be watching her.

I reached into the soft lining of my hoodie pocket and clenched the knife's hard handle so tightly, that blood was probably getting cut off from my fingers. All I wanted to do was rush to Luna and stop her bleeding, but if he took me down, she'd die.

Barely moving her eyes, she looked off to the side again, and then her gaze returned to me and fixated on the dagger in my hand before looking back up to meet my stare.

I pointed to where he must be standing, then to my blade.

With only a half inch of movement, she gave one nod, her eyes filled with unwavering certainty.

He was armed with a knife, then.

It was helpful information that he didn't have a gun.

It'd play into how I took him down.

What a good fucking girl she was.

I stepped closer to the corner where my uncle was waiting to ambush me and pressed my back to it, just in case he had the bright idea to suddenly lunge for me.

I began to slide closer.

I kept my footsteps light, concealing my location, while Luna stared forward, not looking at me, but rather at the tunnel.

Damn, she was smart. He'd think I was still walking directly in front of her, not up against the wall like this.

She even kept her eyes wide, as if she was trying to communicate to what was actually a blank space.

Approaching the edge of the wall, I clasped the knife's handle firmer, and took two more steps.

And then sprang around the corner.

CHAPTER 63
Hunter

I slammed my forearm to his chest, pushing him against the wall he'd been hiding against, and brought my knife to his throat.

"Drop it," I demanded.

I looked into the eyes of the man who I thought would protect me with his life and watched defiance coat them in rage.

Alexander swung, but I knocked his arm out of the way before he could drive his knife into my body.

He used his other forearm to shove at me. Hard. Not strong enough to knock me down, but it did rock me back on my heels a couple of feet and afforded him the space he needed to charge me.

When his shoulder collided with my ribs, I quickly latched on to his frame and heaved him to the concrete ground. He let out a deep groan, his body stunned by the impact as I stepped on his sweaty wrist, the bone beneath my shoe. His fingers uncurled, dropping the glinting knife that clattered into nothingness.

"You had my father killed," I growled and stomped until his wrist snapped like a twig.

He howled in pain. I had overpowered him, and I could kill him right here and now. I could slit his throat or snap his neck.

I could end him.

Easily.

He deserved it for what he did to my father. And what he did to Luna, her father, and that kid all those years ago.

Or I could go to the authorities and let the justice system prevail.

He could tell them what he'd found down here, though, so yes. Turning him in risked my freedom, but this was the ultimate choice, wasn't it? Even bigger than Stanley.

I lifted my foot and watched my uncle shrivel into the fetal position while Luna moaned, drawing my attention to her.

Shit. Her thigh.

Thank hell I had a belt on.

I ran to her and knelt down, setting the knife aside.

"Hey," I said, pulling the leather from my belt loops.

Suddenly, her eyes widened.

The unexpected force crashed me onto the cold cement, three feet away from my glistening blade. An oppressive load pushed against my back, my ribs aching against the pressure.

Fire surged through my veins. With a guttural roar, I twisted violently, throwing my uncle off.

Clambering onto my knees, I snatched the front of his shirt, pulling him toward me. But he retaliated, his fist meeting my jaw with a jarring crunch. Stars danced in my vision, but my clenched fist found its mark, colliding with his cheekbone with a satisfying crack and momentarily sting to my knuckles.

Before I could land another, Alexander slammed into me with his shoulder. The world spun, and the floor scraped against my skin as I crashed onto my side, watching in horror as my uncle lunged for my discarded knife.

I sprang up, throwing myself at him. We tumbled, my right forearm becoming pinned between my uncle and the cruel stone beneath him. Agony laced up my arm, but I managed to roll him over and punch him in his eye.

My knuckles felt the sting more this time.

His retaliations were desperate, fists flying, but my fists became equally relentless, crashing into his face over and over until he stopped swinging. and he lay there, with blood covering his mouth.

Gasping for breath, I pushed myself off him, my focus now entirely on Luna.

More specifically, her bleeding thigh.

I grabbed the discarded belt and wrapped it around her leg, above the nasty cut. Her pained shriek cut through my heart as I tightened the leather, stemming the flow of blood.

"I'm sorry," I whispered, tightening it beyond any of the existing holes.

I grabbed my knife with its serrated blade and poked a fresh hole at the base, securing the metal clip in place so the tourniquet wouldn't move. Then I ripped the tape off her mouth.

Luna's scream shot through my nerves. "Look out!"

Before I could process the warning, a searing burn ignited in my lower back.

CHAPTER 64
Luna

"**N**o!" I shrieked.

Hunter collapsed to the concrete as a ruby stream trickled onto the stone beneath him—snaking its way around the uneven edges and filling the cracks with its violent hue.

Alexander was slumped behind Hunter, gritting his teeth. In his unbroken hand, he clutched the all-metal knife, and now, he was inching closer to his fallen nephew.

A heartbreaking realization stabbed the chambers of my heart, an understanding of how excruciating this was to watch a killer closing in on someone you loved. Preparing to end their life while you froze in horror.

Is this the terror Hunter felt? This suffocating dread?

It was then that the glint of steel caught my eye. There, barely an arm's length away, lying among the cobbles, was Hunter's knife that had landed near me in the chaos.

It was as if the universe itself had taken pity on my plight, delivering this chance into my shaking hands. The stone was cold against my fingers as I reached out, the metal handle of the knife almost burning in comparison.

I twisted the blade around until it met the bindings on my wrist, where I frantically sawed, not caring that its serrated edge also sliced into my skin. It stung and burned, but I got it free and began slicing through the bindings around my core. Watching in agony as Alexander grew closer to Hunter, who still lay motionless on the ground. His feet were angled toward my body, his head in the opposite direction, toward the main tunnel—while Alexander knelt next to Hunter's right ribs.

Hunter turned his head slightly until his eyes, glassy and filled with pain, met mine.

Just as Alexander raised the blade.

"I didn't want it to end this way," Alexander said, as if that offered any solace.

The last thread of tape broke free, and I hurled myself, shoulder first, into Alex's side. Knocking him away from Hunter.

With all my strength, I thrust the knife into Alexander's right rib cage. The roar of his scream echoed off the clammy walls.

"Luna." Hunter's voice was weak.

I turned to him, alarmed at how ashen his face was.

"Hu—"

A strike to my temple made my vision double, my head searing in pain. Growing as light as a helium balloon while the dizziness made me fall next to the love of my life.

Whose eyes widened in alarm, not at me, but at something looming behind.

CHAPTER 65

Hunter

L una pushed herself into a seated position, blinking away the disorientation, but behind her, Alexander knelt, clutching the dagger's handle he'd slammed against her head.

He turned the blade sideways now, so he'd have the perfect angle to cut her jugular.

It was a haunting mirror image from twenty years ago, a killer lurking toward someone I loved, preparing to slit their throat.

Weakened by blood loss, I tried to shove myself closer but fell back again.

"Luna!" I managed.

But with her unfocused stare and bleeding temple, her movements were too slow.

My uncle slowly drew his arm around her neck and aligned the blade over her jugular.

Luna's precious eyes widened, locking them with me as time seemed to come to a standstill. It was as if instant clarity came over her, the heartbreaking realization that after all we'd been through, after all we'd survived together, this was it.

The end of our love story.

The end of her life while I lay helpless to stop it.

For the second time in my life.

If she died, I'd welcome the flames of hell to consume me for all my days, because I couldn't exist without her.

Luna's lip quivered as she took one last breath and said, "I love you."

In slow motion, the blade indented against her fragile neck.

No.

The word detonated an explosion of adrenaline through my veins. I shot up and grabbed my uncle's wrist—pulling the knife safely away from her—before slamming my torso into his shoulders. Hurling him to the ground, his head cracking hard enough against it to stun him.

"Luna." I crawled to her, drawing my fingers to her neck. "Are you okay?"

"Look out!" she warned.

My uncle tackled me to the ground, the floor grinding into my hip bone as I grabbed his good arm and stopped the knife inches before it sank into my chest. I pulled at his fingertips, his grip weakening until I managed to twist the dagger out of his hand, and wrestled myself above him.

My heartbeat became a deadly rhythm as I looked into his eyes, which were surrounded by faint wrinkles accumulated through the twenty years of life he'd robbed my father of having. His blue eyes once mirrored the ones my loving father had, but now, my uncle's looked like ice, freezing a path to my soul.

"You were everything to me," I began, my voice shaking. "When Dad was gone, it was you who stepped in. It was your shoulders that carried my world."

Tears threatened at the edges of my vision, but I blinked them back, holding his gaze with a newfound determination. His face was a facade, hiding the devil within.

"I looked up to you," I continued, each word a painful knife twisting in my gut. "I loved you like a father. You were my hero."

The chilling echo of my words hung between us.

"But you took him from me," I said, my voice dropping to a bare whisper.

There was silence, a deadly calm that seemed to suspend time itself. His Adam's apple bobbed as he swallowed, the facade slipping just a fraction.

"I won't allow you to take her, too."

"I won't stop until I do," he vowed.

The words lingered in the air, a profound proclamation of the heartbreaking path I was forced to tread.

"It didn't have to be this way," I whispered. It was the final good-bye, a farewell to the uncle I once knew and the father figure I'd lost twice.

And with that, I plunged the knife into his heart.

And then I collapsed.

CHAPTER 66
Luna

"Hunter!" Through my dizziness, a fresh avalanche of adrenaline helped me crawl over to him, terrified to see how ghostly white he'd become.

At least I had a tourniquet on my leg, but there was no way to cut off the blood loss seeping from his deep laceration.

"Hold on!" I peeled the shirt off my body, wadded its fabric into a ball, and pressed it against the warm, slick wound on his back.

He let out a raspy groan—a good sign that he could still feel pain. But his eyelids began drooping as I patted down his pockets and tugged his cell phone out.

Horrified to see it had shattered in the struggle. It wouldn't even turn on.

"Shit!" I leaned down and cupped his cheek.

"Stay with me, Hunter. I need you. I can't live in a world where you don't exist. Do you hear me?"

Hunter's eyes dimmed, but he offered a slight nod and whispered, "I'm sorry."

My throat clenched. *What if this is the last time I ever see him?* And after all he'd been through, having to kill his uncle, too?

"You saved me."

His eyes shimmered with tears as I planted a gentle kiss on his soft lips, which were colder than they should have been.

Reminding me I needed to hurry.

"Hold on," I said.

With immense effort, I got to my feet. I held on to the wall of the underground passage as I stumbled down it as fast as I could, then held on to both cold banisters as I clanked up the metal staircase. Sharp, searing pain radiated from my thigh, sending nauseating waves up my stomach. The world began to blur, and I worried I'd pass out, but I managed to get the door at the top of the steps open. I pushed through it, navigated the secret closet, and emerged into Hunter's bedroom.

Where I ran smack into the chest of Grayson.

Thank God it was him; I trusted him most with what I needed to do.

He gripped my upper arms, steadying me as I wobbled, his hold firm—ensuring I stayed upright as he scanned my body, head to toe.

I could only imagine what I looked like.

Bloodied and beaten, vulnerable, every wound on display. The belt tourniquet seemed a desperate attempt to hold myself together, blood saturating my leg. All while I stood here in a bra, stripped down physically and emotionally.

"The fuck?" he asked.

"I need your help," I whispered, glancing at the bedroom door.

"Why are you whispering?" Grayson growled.

"Because if anyone else sees what I'm about to show you, Hunter will spend the rest of his life in prison."

Grayson's eyebrows pinched together, and he stilled, looking from my left eye to my right. After several tense moments, he nodded his compliance.

"Follow me."

CHAPTER 67
Luna

"What in the actual fuck?" Grayson said as we made our way down the stone tunnel carved beneath the earth. "Was this place here when I was a kid?"

"This way."

Grunting from the immense effort of walking, I grabbed the wall again, my thigh shooting pains down my toes and up my spine.

But suddenly, Grayson's arm came around my back and under my armpit. Supporting my weight. The pungent mix of damp earth and the metallic tang of blood assaulted my senses, a reminder of the grimness awaiting us, while ice-cold air danced across my bare stomach, making my skin erupt into goose bumps.

Every shiver that ran through me was countered by the warmth emanating from Grayson's sturdy form against my side.

When we entered the weapons room, Grayson only afforded himself a second to look around in shock before focusing on the two bodies lying on the floor.

Both were eerily still, the life seemingly drained from them.

"Hunter!" I pulled away from Grayson and dropped to my knees, pressing my fingers against his artery.

"He's still alive," I whimpered.

"My uncle is dead," Grayson said, pulling his fingers off his neck. His voice was unsettlingly calm, lacking the grief or shock I'd expected.

"We need to get Hunter to the hospital," I said.

"You need a hospital, too." Grayson nodded at the pool of blood on my thigh.

"We need to move this crime scene outside."

Grayson stood up from his squatted position and looked down at me. Same broad shoulders as his brother, same intimidating voice as he demanded, "The hell are you talking about?"

"Nobody can find this place. Hunter killed your uncle in self-defense, but if the police find this place, Hunter will go away to prison for life."

Grayson glanced around the room again, his gaze pausing on the weapons arranged on the far wall. His chest inflated before he looked back down at his unconscious brother.

Then returned his stare to me. "Tell me what you need."

CHAPTER 68

Luna

We got seriously lucky. The security guards were not searching the north end of the property anymore, so Grayson was able to drag both Alexander and Hunter into the woods behind the hidden garage.

He discarded the weapons carefully, ensuring they left no telltale signs behind while I spread blood around the crime scene.

If I was looking down on my life right now, I would be shocked. Here I was, taking my skills as a defense attorney and using them to protect my violent, criminal boyfriend.

I'd have to work through that with the therapist some other time. Right now, I needed to get Hunter medical help.

"Ready?" Grayson asked.

The sharp scent of pine mingled with the earthy aroma of soil while distant calls of birds echoed in the warm air.

I nodded.

Grayson took off toward the mansion in a sprint, twigs snapping beneath his steps as he shouted, "I found them! Get over here! We need ambulances!"

My heart raced as I glanced over the hastily crafted crime scene, praying it was convincing enough.

That they would buy the story that Alexander had attacked me. True. I ran from him. True. That I had escaped outside. False. That he was about to kill me when Hunter and Alexander got into a scuffle, Alexander wound up dead, and Hunter and I both suffered grave injuries. True.

Maybe it was immoral of me to leave out the part that it happened in the Vigilante's lair, but all I cared about right now was saving Hunter.

Distant shouting grew louder. Steps thundered along the ground, more twigs snapping beneath their weight, and then the pine trees shook and bowed. Revealing a wave of security guards, their expressions shifting from alarm to determination.

CHAPTER 69

Hunter

B linking against the sterile lights, the cold hum of the AC met my ears as my eyes adjusted to the rigid pattern of the ceiling tiles.

Panic surged with a relentless tidal wave, threatening to drown me.

Where is Luna?

I tried to sit up, but my back stabbed me with a sword of pain, keeping me down, while my heart became a metronome against my ribs.

I scanned the room, the scent of antiseptic and the faint murmurs of distant conversations amplifying my unease.

No sign of Luna.

Not that it would make sense that she'd have been in here—she'd been hurt. Gravely. But she was the only thing on my mind.

What if she didn't make it? What if I'd been too late? She'd lost so much blood.

Fear tightened its grip while the machines beeped relentlessly, indifferent to my torment.

My breath came in shallow gasps as dread churned inside me, and then I saw him. There, huddled in the corner like a harbinger of doom, was my brother Grayson.

"Where is Luna?"

"She's safe," Grayson assured.

I flopped back and let out a deep breath of relief.

My body didn't appreciate it, though, my stab wound burning in response.

"Define safe," I urged.

"She's in a room down the hall. She's going to be okay, Hunter, but we need to talk," he said. "Now, before anyone else speaks to you. You need to listen to me very carefully so that your story jives with hers. Otherwise, both of you will be in deep shit. So will I."

I couldn't hide my confusion.

"Why would Luna get into trouble?" I demanded. "She's the victim."

"Not exactly," Grayson said.

"What the hell does that mean?"

Grayson opened his mouth, but the door hinges creaked softly, and Detective Rinaldi stepped inside. Her aura was authoritative, her movements measured as her gaze scrutinized every detail about me.

Her eyes narrowed, skepticism etched in the furrows of her brow.

"Hunter," she said. "I'm glad to see that you're okay."

But her tone wasn't happy; rather, it was laced with suspicion.

A stone settled in my gut.

I glanced over at my brother and the stern expression he was camouflaging from strangers. The room was heavy with anticipation, the air sticking to my skin like a grim premonition.

"I need to ask you some questions," she declared, her voice puncturing the silent room like a gunshot.

"Of course." I tried to sound unconcerned and hoped I had pulled it off. "But," I said, shifting and grimacing to make a show of it, "I'd prefer to do it a little later."

"Afraid we need to do this now."

"He just woke up," Grayson said in annoyance.

She glared at him. "Most important time to get information. While it's fresh."

"He just underwent major surgery. Let the meds wear off a little first."

Rinaldi's jaw tightened. "Is there a reason you're refusing to answer my questions?"

Grayson took a deliberate step forward.

"He just told you he'll talk, but he's in pain, and he's groggy."

"This can't wait. There are some…discrepancies that need to be examined."

"What discrepancies?" Grayson asked.

"If you could step outside," she snarled. "I have some questions for *you* as well."

"I already gave you my statement."

"I'm aware."

They entered a staredown, but she had us backed into a corner, and she knew it.

I had no choice but to answer her questions. But how the hell was I going to do that without implicating Luna? And evidently, Grayson, though I had no idea what he'd done.

Was he referring to the guy he'd taken out and dumped into the lake? But how would Luna be implicated in that?

Grayson paused for several seconds before grinding his jaw and moving toward the door.

Where a blonde nurse came barreling in, oblivious to tension-fest. She wore her hair in some sort of clip that left a bird's nest of it on her head, little stray hairs escaping down her high cheekbones.

"Mr. Lockwood." She smiled. "How wonderful to see you awake."

A subtle blush tinted her cheeks as her gaze settled on Grayson. She stilled and tucked one of those strands of loose hairs behind her ear, a grin widening to show her teeth.

"It's nice to see you again, too," she said in a higher-pitched tone.

Flirting was as uncomfortable to witness as seeing a stranger change a baby's crap-filled diaper.

Oblivious to Rinaldi's clear annoyance, the nurse's eyes lingered on Grayson a tad too long before she finally turned to me.

"I need to check your dressing," she said. "The nurse in recovery is worried about discharge."

The nurse looked at Detective Rinaldi and motioned toward the door. "This will only take a few minutes."

Rinaldi shifted her weight from one foot to the other, eyes narrowing. Her face was a mask of annoyance as she watched the nurse bat her eyelashes in Grayson's direction.

"Can this wait?" Rinaldi asked her.

"It won't take long," the nurse said, leaving no room for an argument.

I'm going to buy this nurse a Lexus when this is over.

Rinaldi's jaw tensed as she scratched her temple, but after a long hesitation, she reluctantly stepped out of the room.

The nurse locked eyes with Grayson again, her lips curled up into a playful smile.

"This won't take long," she said.

Grayson crossed his arms over his chest and stepped toward her. "Would it be all right if I stayed? I'm family."

If I wasn't so desperate to talk to him alone, I'd call him out for playing into her attraction.

"Is it okay if he stays, Mr. Lockwood?" she asked. Not looking at me—looking at my damn brother.

The hope in her voice that Grayson could stay would be amusing if we weren't in such a pickle.

"Actually, if you could give me a minute," I said. "I need to talk to my brother."

"I don't want her to leave," Grayson said seductively. Making the nurse's feet—I kid you not—roll up onto their balls.

I had never seen Grayson flirt before. It was like watching something on the animal planet—foreign and jarring.

"But I do need to talk to him for a moment," Grayson added. "Could you give us privacy for two minutes?" He glanced at the bathroom door, then back to the nurse before leaning over and whispering something into her ear.

She closed her eyes, appearing to savor his hot breath. But after a second, she wrinkled her forehead.

"I'm so sorry," she said to him.

He whispered something else.

She nodded, locked lust-struck eyes with him.

"I'll be in there." She touched his arm. "Take as long as you need. I'll check his bandage when you're done."

The nurse went into the room's bathroom, shut the door, and turned the sink on, presumably to give us some privacy.

Without risking Rinaldi coming back in. Not that the nurse knew that.

"What did you say to her?" I asked.

Grayson sat on the edge of my bed, which tilted from his weight, and kept his voice low enough where anyone trying to eavesdrop outside the door, or inside the bathroom, couldn't hear our conversation over the running water.

"That in the struggle of defending yourself, Alexander died. That you didn't know yet, and I wanted to be the one to tell you, not the detective."

Grayson leaned closer.

"Now listen. Here's the story."

CHAPTER 70
Hunter

"So, you told your guards you'd search inside, but you ended up outside?" Rinaldi's tone was heavy with suspicion and condescension. Her bun was pulled so tight, even her hair looked pissed.

"Like I said, I started inside, but then I thought I heard something coming from the woods on the north end of the property."

Here's the super-cool thing about massive blood loss: it can legit cause temporary amnesia. When it came to specific details, *I don't remember* became my mantra. I steered her questions back time and time again to the pieces of the puzzle that I could explain away.

But I wasn't sure it was working.

The quiet scratching of her pen against paper broke the silence as she jotted something down in her little notebook.

"You know, it's strange," she said. "Luna's femoral artery had been nicked. Judging by the shape you were in, you suffered significant blood loss as well. Yet there wasn't as much blood as you would expect where we found Alexander's body."

"We were all over those woods," I lied. If this were just about me, I would come clean, to be the bigger man and all that for Luna. But this was about her.

I would protect Luna with everything in my arsenal. Physically, emotionally, and legally. She had been the one to come up with the story, and if I came clean, it would implicate her in lying to law enforcement, interfering with an investigation, faking a crime scene, and destroying evidence. Among other things.

I would lie until I burned in hell if it meant saving her.

"If you comb through every leaf and speck of dirt in those woods, I'm sure you'll find whatever you're looking for," I said.

Her lips thinned even more until they all but vanished. She knew as well as I did that the odds of finding every droplet of blood cast across such a wide net were slim to none.

Still, if she came up empty, she would grow more suspicious, but what other explanation could she come up with?

"We didn't see much of a struggle anywhere in those woods," she countered.

"What are you suggesting?" I asked in a stern tone. Anyone in my position would be offended by her implication, and I needed to play the role of the innocent person being accused of something I didn't do. "We weren't climbing trees and breaking the limbs off," I said. "So, I'm not sure what all you expected to find."

Her chest puffed in offense.

"Strange how you had a team of your trained security guards scour the property and they couldn't find her. Yet, you did. So quickly."

"Lucky is more like it. She was minutes from death."

Rinaldi ran her tongue over her teeth and tried to hide the annoyed shake of her head.

"Where were you today when Alexander showed up at the mansion to find Luna all alone?"

A flare of irritation ignited in my chest. "She wasn't alone," I reminded her, trying to keep my voice steady. "I had security guards positioned outside."

Not that it helped. I'd never forgive myself for that.

"That's not what I asked."

"Okay, that's about enough." Grayson pushed off the wall. "He's lucky to be alive, and so is Luna. They both almost died and are recovering from significant injuries. We just learned our uncle tried to kill her and that he's dead. So, process the scene, but if you have any other *questions*, you can talk to our family attorney."

Rinaldi glared at Grayson. "Hostility often looks suspicious to law enforcement."

"I don't give a crap," Grayson said. "A detective as smart as you can appreciate how offensive it is when the victim is facing accusatory questions. So, if he's not under arrest, there's the door."

Rinaldi licked her lips and glared at me, then glared back at Grayson.

"I'd better go over those woods one more time myself. Wouldn't want to miss *any* clue."

Damn. If they'd uncovered my underground garage in their previous searches, I'd already be in cuffs. My luck might run out any second.

As soon as she left, Grayson approached me.

He must've read the look on my face because he whispered, "That car is a problem, isn't it?"

"So is the tunnel leading from the garage." I kept my tone so low, too, no one would be able to hear us.

"Yeah. Nice dungeon, brother. I have questions, but first, as for the *problems*..." His gaze darted to the hospital room door. "I'll take care of it."

"Grayson, the woods are a crime scene. There's police tape and probably cops positioned less than a half mile from the garage. There's nothing you can do without getting caught."

"You'd be surprised what I'm able to do without getting caught."

And then my suspicious, elusive, grumpy-ass brother winked at me.

"I'll tell Jace and Bryson they can come in."

"They're here?"

"Thought it was best they heard this from me rather than on the news."

"Do they know about Alexander?"

"I told them the *pertinent* information," Grayson hedged. "Now, I have to get going. I'm going to check on Luna on my way out."

CHAPTER 71
Luna

"So, Hunter's really going to be okay?" The backs of my eyes prickled with tears.

Grayson took a moment, as if remembering all the challenges they'd faced together. "Hunter's always been a fighter." His voice held a trace of brotherly pride. "He'll pull through this."

Normally, I hated crying in front of people, but I felt close to Grayson because of what we'd been through.

"Thank you," I said. "For what you did for Hunter."

"I would do anything for my brother."

"He's lucky to have you."

Grayson rubbed the back of his neck, his face stoic.

"You're a really good guy, Grayson."

An unreadable expression came across his face.

"Trust me, Luna. I'm not a good guy."

I could tell by his tone that he wasn't heartbroken or full of self-doubt; rather, he said it factually, as if he accepted who he was and was simply clarifying it for my own sake. And whoever he was, evidently, was someone I shouldn't admire.

Grayson had an ominous aura surrounding him, one I was curious as hell to know more about.

"Care to elaborate?" I asked.

His gaze hardened, and he said, "No," in a tone of finality, ending any further inquiry on the topic.

Which only piqued my curiosity, but if he had secrets, I wouldn't try to draw them out. And no matter what he claimed, he'd always be a good guy in my book.

"Well," I said, "I'm incredibly grateful for what you did. Thank you."

Grayson's teeth captured his lower lip, holding on to it for a moment. "I'm glad you're alive, Luna. You seem good for my brother."

Damn these tears. But in my defense, being accepted by Hunter's family meant more to me than I imagined. Probably after essentially being rejected by everyone in mine, growing up…

After a moment, he turned to walk out the door but stopped when it creaked open. The room's temperature seemed to drop a degree when Detective Rinaldi entered the room, the fluorescent lights humming a little louder, amplifying the tension as Grayson stiffened.

Rinaldi's eyes narrowed, every inch of her stance radiating authority and suspicion as her fingers tapped against the notepad she held, an unsaid challenge hanging between her and Grayson.

After an eternity, she swept her gaze to me.

"I'm relieved to see you are doing so well." But where her tone had once been warm and inviting, it was now laced with a hint of frustration.

"Luna is under the protection of our family now," Grayson said. "You have questions, you can contact our attorney."

My gaze shifted uneasily between her and Grayson, like a hesitant pendulum, caught in the silence that hung heavy in the air.

"You and I both know guilty people are the ones who lawyer up, Luna. This is a bad look," she said.

"You and I both know you'll say almost anything to keep people talking, and a lawyer stops your ability to do that," Grayson said. "Look at Luna's father. Proof that innocent people get accused of crimes they didn't commit."

Guilt strangled my voice at using my father's injustice as a means to protect us from our sins.

"As I told you in Hunter's room"—Grayson stepped in front of me, shielding me with his body, every line of him poised like a guard dog ready to defend—"I'm not going to allow you to victimize them further. Process the evidence because that's all you're getting."

Judging by the tightness of her jaw, the evidence was weak as hell. And evidence of what, exactly? Suspicions that the attack didn't take place exactly where we described it?

All of the injuries were consistent with the struggle we had endured, and all of the relevant details had been the truth. Alexander was killed in a case of self-defense.

Hopefully, the only thing Rinaldi would ever have were her suspicions.

"You know we still haven't gotten to the bottom of who the Windy City Vigilante is," she warned.

"Lawyer," Grayson barked.

Guilt wove through my ribs at lying to a law enforcement officer.

I had made my decision to protect Hunter, and that wouldn't change, but it didn't expel the moral person that also inhabited my body.

"I'll be in touch," Rinaldi said.

"With our lawyer," Grayson added.

CHAPTER 72
Luna

I awoke from my nap to a ruckus outside of my room. The hospital door was open, and the murmurs of several nurses' high-pitched voices mingled together. The two that were in my view had their gaze fixed on something down the hallway.

Smiling, they straightened their scrubs as they froze in place, waiting for whatever was coming.

I pushed the button on my bed so I could sit up straighter, wishing my thigh hadn't been sliced through the muscle, so I could simply walk out and see what was going on.

The sound of metal scraping against the linoleum grew louder, joined by a groan that echoed along the walls.

"You should be in a wheelchair," a female voice said.

But the metallic clinks continued, the moans increasing with what sounded like agony.

"Perhaps we should try this another day," a female voice, a nurse, I presumed, said.

But the walker made another clank against the ground, and another groan emerged.

"You shouldn't overdo it," she said.

Another clank.

Another grunt.

"I'll get the chair ready," another nurse chirped.

A thin blonde with her hair in a bun waltzed into my room with a wheelchair, which she positioned next to my bed.

And then, a pair of strong, masculine hands gripping a walker came into view, their knuckles white with the strain.

The hands I'd thought I'd never get to hold again.

With a ragged breath and determined push, he revealed himself.

"Hunter!" My voice broke, and the floodgates of relief and love opened, blurring my vision with tears. It was as if I'd been holding my breath for an eternity, and only now could I finally breathe again.

The corners of his eyes crinkled, a small smile gracing his lips—a smile that spoke of battles fought and a love that survived against all odds. But then, with each painstaking step he took toward me, his face contorted with effort and pain.

My heartstrings tugged at the sight of him fighting against his injuries, pushing through every ounce of pain just to be closer to me.

Hunter grunted and groaned his way to the chair, where two nurses helped him sit down.

It was unsettling to see such a powerful man stripped down to a hospital gown and a walker, but somehow, he made it look sexy as hell —his muscles not getting the memo that he had been gravely injured.

The nurses wheeled Hunter closer to me and looked between us before one cleared her throat.

"We'll give you some privacy," she said. "Push the red button if you need anything."

And then she shut the door.

Hunter's gaze swept over me, lingering on every cut and bruise, a storm of relief and concern dancing in his eyes.

"Hey, Little Leopard." His hoarse voice was full of warmth.

"I was so scared you…" My throat closed, cutting off my words, so I settled for squeezing his hand. Then I linked my fingers through his.

The warmth of his skin and the pink hue dotting his cheeks were reassuring, stark contrasts to the ghastly white and cold version of him I'd seen last.

Hunter leaned his frame down and pressed his lips to my hand.

"You saved my life," I said through a sniffle. "Again."

"You saved mine. And protected...*other things* in the process." His voice was full of admiration and gratitude.

Relief settled into my bones that, for now, it seemed Hunter might not be in legal danger.

"My brother told me what you did." Hunter studied my eyes and drew his knuckles up to my jaw.

I gave a small gasp at the touch I'd feared I may never experience again.

"None of it would've been possible without Grayson," I said.

Hunter's gaze swept to the hospital room door, then back to me.

"That guy has more skills than I realized. He managed to take care of something that should've been impossible."

I didn't know what he meant, but I sensed it had something to do with concealing evidence.

"But you're forgetting something." Hunter's voice was low and grainy. "None of this would have been possible without *you*, Luna." He pursed his lips, as if weighing how much detail to get into, and then settled with, "I don't know what I did to deserve you, but what I do know is that I'll spend every minute of every day making you feel how much I cherish you."

And just like that, my world, which had tilted dangerously since the attack, seemed to right itself.

His gaze was an anchor, flooding my soul with the overwhelming relief that he was alive, his presence a promise of our future—his love the balm to my battered heart.

"Tell me it's all over," I whispered. "Tell me we get to leave the hospital together and put this all behind us."

Hunter drew his fingers up to my temple and back down again, his stare a beautiful mix of hope and optimism.

"Thanks to you," he said, "I think we have a decent shot at that."

The conviction in his voice, the steadfast promise in his gaze— they were silent oaths to a shared dream of a life beyond the nightmare we'd just woken from.

CHAPTER 73
Luna

Alexander didn't deserve his nephews. Three of the Lockwood brothers carried his casket at the conclusion of the funeral to the waiting hearse while Hunter trailed behind, still healing from his injuries.

Though we'd been discharged with promises of a full recovery, the emotional scars ran deep.

My gaze flitted over to Hunter, who seemed lost in thought.

"You okay?" I asked, sensing the weight of the day as we drove to the cemetery.

Everything Hunter had learned about his uncle and the role he played in his father's murder had to be weighing on his soul. And while it sounded like his father had been gearing up to do the right thing by confessing to the police his part in the hit-and-run of that teenager, it still fractured the perfect image Hunter had carried of his father for all these years.

It's hard to let go of the innocence we once saw in someone.

Hunter paused. "I'll be fine," he murmured, "as long as I have you."

I hoped he could find peace with this someday. As much peace as you can, given this terrible turn of events.

"It was nice to see your other two brothers again," I said. "I wish it were under different circumstances."

Hunter squeezed my hand. "I'm sorry I didn't figure it out sooner, Luna. I'm sorry I left you and allowed my uncle the opportunity to get to you."

"It's not your fault," I repeated. "I'm still in shock from everything your uncle did. Attacking us, letting an innocent man rot in prison, orchestrating the murder of your father and mine. Not to mention convincing your dad to leave a teenage boy to die."

Hunter looked out the window as the ground rushed beneath our sedan's tires.

"Looking back on it now, it shouldn't have been such a surprise that he convinced my dad to go along with it," Hunter said in a pained tone. "Even though they grew up in the same household, he and my father had very different views on the world. My father was grateful for our fortune, and he never saw us as better than other people because of it. My uncle, on the other hand..."

Must've seen that lower income teenage boy as less than.

"But him arranging my father's murder"—Hunter scrubbed the side of his face—"the prosecutor in me gets it. People are capable of terrible things when it comes to saving their own ass. But the nephew in me..."

Would grapple with that for quite some time.

"I'm so sorry, Luna." His voice cracked slightly. "I'm sorry it was *my* uncle who was responsible for your father rotting in prison for twenty years. For the suffering it caused you and your family. And that it was my uncle who had him killed."

"Hunter..."

"And then to come after you..." Hunter hesitated. "If you hadn't survived..." He glanced at the partition that separated us from the driver—his tone growing dangerously dark as he whispered, "I would have hunted every person who ever caused you an ounce of pain. Your ex. Every bully from school. Every acquaintance of Franco's. I would have made a list and never stopped killing."

I swallowed. It had been a lot for me to reconcile the killer with the protector, but I was grateful that, in the battle for his soul, the protector won.

"Are you really okay with giving up being the..." I eyed the partition, nervous to finish in case it wasn't as soundproof as Hunter thought.

Hunter took my chin between his thumb and finger, staring deeply into my eyes.

"You're my reason for existing now, Luna."

His words echoed through my ears and glued the fractures in my heart.

"I don't want to do anything to jeopardize what we have. You've suffered enough with having your dad in prison all those years. Last thing you need is for a repeat."

Dang, this man knew how to put my heart into the microwave and heat it instantly.

I laced my fingers through his, overwhelmed with gratitude for having him in my life.

The scent of pine filled the air as our sedan wound through the tree-lined road and arrived at the cemetery, where fading sunlight painted the tombstones in hues of gold and orange with long shadows creeping over the manicured grass. The scent of freshly turned dirt mingled with the subtle aroma of flowers left on graves while the distant chirping of crickets and the soft rustle of leaves punctured the hushed whispers of people.

During another short service, Hunter and his brothers paid their last respects to his uncle.

He was the murderer of their father, and I knew Hunter, for one, debated on even coming to Alexander's funeral. But he said he needed the closure of seeing him put into the ground.

The brothers didn't allow Alexander to be buried near their father, though. They chose a secluded plot, where Alexander would decay beneath the earth alone.

When the ceremony was over, Hunter held my hand and walked over to his parents' headstone. The massive granite stone was engraved in white letters, and at its center, surrounded by intricately carved flowers, was a family photo. The Lockwood brothers—children ranging in age—smiling, with their mother and father behind them. Looking at them with adoration. Oblivious to how soon their world was about to shatter.

Hunter released my hand and knelt before it, placing his hand on the granite—connecting with the man who lay beneath.

"I'm sorry, Dad," Hunter's voice was barely a whisper, a heartbreaking mixture of grief and shame.

My lip trembled as the strong man I loved appeared as fragile as a lost child, his shoulders hunched, bearing the weight of years of pain.

With a shaky exhale, Hunter continued, "But I can let you go now." The breeze seemed to still, waiting for his next words. "I can finally let you rest in peace."

I wiped a lone tear as Hunter was silent for several seconds before standing up. He stared at his mother and father's names, the dates of their deaths moments in time that changed the trajectory of his life. And then, with one last sigh, Hunter let go of his past and claimed his future by wrapping his hand in mine.

"They loved you, Hunter. Remember the good times, not just the end."

He seemed to consider this for a moment before nodding his head.

"Come on. Let's say goodbye to the people who lingered."

We ambled back to where the funeral had been held, and after waiting until most other people left, Elizabeth Wood—the lawyer who'd offered me a job the day Dominic died—approached me and Hunter.

She glanced around and then stepped close enough to ensure no one could overhear us.

"Police haven't found any other evidence to contradict your version of events," she assured. "Other than the lack of blood at the crime scene, all they have are suspicions."

After what happened with the family accountant, Jeff—who'd hidden secrets from the Lockwood family—Hunter cleaned house and started over. New family accountant, new lawyer, to avoid any other secrets or allegiances.

Elizabeth and her entire firm were now the official Lockwood attorneys with Elizabeth being our point person. We'd told her everything.

Well, save for the Vigilante, the injuries and death occurring inside the house—because explaining that would risk exposing the Vigilante situation—and whatever the heck Grayson had been up to right before Alexander got to me. Two family secrets they'd speak about if absolutely necessary, but Hunter didn't feel it was necessary to confess all the family sins if law enforcement wasn't asking about them.

"I learned the hard way that sometimes it doesn't take too much for people to be convicted," I reminded her.

"They have nothing, and while that might change in the future, for now, things have settled down. They did ask a few questions about something else that occurred on the same day as the attack."

Hunter and I said nothing.

"They find it curious that the father of the teenage boy who was killed—the one that murdered your father—committed suicide on the same day that Alexander attacked Luna. But all the evidence supports suicide, so they have nothing."

I felt so bad for the father of that kid, that he endured so much tragedy, that he couldn't take it anymore.

"I'll let you know if anything else comes up, but even if it does, you have the full weight of our firm behind you."

Elizabeth securing the Lockwoods was a career high for her, and her firm was already getting more clients because of the accolades. Which meant the Lockwood family was in exceptional hands.

It should have made me feel happy.

And it did. In part. But I couldn't help but feel a twinge of pain, too.

While we'd told the police Alexander had been behind it all—the hit-and-run, the death of Hunter's dad, the conviction, and subsequent murder of my father—when it came to the Vigilante stuff, we were guilty of lying to law enforcement. We had obstructed justice;

we had altered a crime scene, among other offenses. We were guilty, yet we had an army of high-powered criminal attorneys behind us.

While innocent people remained in prison. It wasn't right.

And doing my part to prevent it from happening no longer felt like enough.

"I want to start a chapter of the Innocence Project," I declared.

Hunter and Elizabeth looked at me.

"I'll figure out how to finance it," I said. I knew Hunter would offer to provide the money, but I didn't want all of my happiness to come from him.

I wanted to build this on my own from the ground up. Starting with securing the money.

"Elizabeth," I said, "what would your firm think about earmarking a percentage of their profits for pro bono work? To fund a chapter of an Innocence Project, led by me?"

She tilted her head, her eyebrows knitting together thoughtfully. "I do believe they'd consider it. But I need to be honest; it's not solely out of altruism. There's been chatter within the firm about our public image. When a firm becomes as sizeable as ours, there's always the risk of being seen as just another bunch of high-flying lawyers only interested in their next big paycheck. The partners expressed interest in countering that public perception."

"I don't care *why* they do it, so long as they would be willing to commit to funding." I would be the heart of the project. I would make sure the people we defended got the very best they deserved.

"I'll talk to my boss tonight." Elizabeth smiled.

"Thank you," I said.

Elizabeth nodded to me, to Hunter. "I'm sorry again for your loss."

And then she wandered toward the parking lot, high heels sinking into the grass as she passed Barry Mansfield, who approached us next.

He shook Hunter's hand. "I'm sorry for your loss."

"Thank you," Hunter said. "For everything you did."

Barry scratched his chin. "Wish I'd been the one to identify your uncle's role in all this." He put his hands in his pockets. "Not to mention the kid's dad. I'm sorry I didn't solve this faster."

"You did more than all the police and PIs combined," Hunter assured.

Barry's mouth curled up, but the disappointment weighed his shoulders down that he hadn't officially been the one to solve this case. Still. He had to take solace in having played the most instrumental role in it.

He offered me a nod. "Glad you're okay, Luna."

"Thanks, Barry. Any chance you'd be willing to help me with some Innocence Project work?"

He grinned wider. "I'm afraid I already have my next client lined up."

Probably more like a hundred.

"Well. If you ever change your mind," I said. "Thank you for everything you did."

He nodded. "It was good working with you, Hunter. I'm glad you got the closure you were seeking, but I'm sorry it came with such an" —he looked at the grave—"unfortunate ending."

Hunter glanced at his brothers, who stood together. "Maybe something else good can come from this." His voice was quiet, speaking more to himself than us, I think. "I'll be right back."

CHAPTER 74

Hunter

Grayson, Jace, Bryson, and I stood near our uncle's grave.

I hated that we stood in silence for a bit, struggling for words. Because it wasn't the grief stealing them from us; it was because in many ways, after Mom's death, we had grown apart, into strangers. And not just because of things like Grayson's mysterious absences or my secrets.

Hell, I got the vibe we all had secrets from each other.

But secrets were one thing.

Being emotional strangers at a time like this accentuated just how distant we were on the daily.

I guess over the past few weeks I'd confided in Grayson more—about my feelings for Luna. That was something, at least. A step in the right direction. But one that would vanish like a fog if we didn't push ourselves to keep moving forward.

And it didn't include my other brothers.

It was time we changed that—we were all we had.

"First our parents," I said. "Now our uncle."

"I can't believe he's the one that had Dad killed." Grayson clenched his fists.

"And then he tried to step in like the noble father figure." Jace shoved his hands into his pockets.

"I've been replaying the last few years in my mind," Bryson said. "And something struck me. He was supposedly trying to be a father figure to us, but when Mom died, she had one wish: that we would never grow apart. Yet every time we turned around, Alexander was doing the opposite of trying to keep us together."

"He inserted himself into our conversations with each other," Jace agreed.

"And started taking us out of the house to supposedly get our mind off things, but he'd only take one of us out at a time," Bryson said.

"Making him the sole person we leaned on. Instead of each other," Jace added.

"He was too busy working on the Lockwood image to actually care if we stayed a family unit." Grayson glared at the grave.

"Maybe he didn't want us to be close," Jace suggested. "Gave him more power over each of us. He had a huge secret to protect. Keeping us apart would make us easier to control."

"Easier to influence," Grayson agreed.

"And we let him do it," I said. "We broke our promise to Mom."

My throat swelled at our failure. While we hadn't avoided each other per se, I wouldn't count what we had as a close relationship, either.

"Maybe it's about time we put in an effort to start keeping that promise," I said.

We could step up for each other, and it would be cool to get to know my brothers more.

My brothers' eyes swept over each other's faces, and after a solemn silence, all three of them nodded in agreement.

CHAPTER 75
Hunter

"You're not going to believe my first case."

Luna's smile reached her eyes. I think it was the first time that happened since her father died, and I can't describe what that did to my heart.

I grinned and followed her as she walked up the grand staircase into *our* bedroom and into *our* closet. All the while chatting so quickly, the words tumbled out of her mouth like they were falling down a staircase.

I crossed my arms over my chest, watching her take her business suit off, hanging it on her side of our closet.

Well, her side was my original closet. The big one—which was now filled with designer clothes that my personal shopper had picked out for her. Clothes that Luna had fussed about, saying she didn't need anything like that, just as she'd fussed about the car I'd bought her. She said she didn't want material things, she just wanted me, but whether she liked it or not, I was going to spoil her rotten every day of her life.

Clothes and a car were just the beginning.

My half of the closet was the smaller closet that had once

contained my Vigilante attire. I'd knocked down the secret door and had it converted.

And had closed off the secret tunnel after cleaning out the weapons room.

I'd be lying if I said there were days I didn't miss that life, but all I had to do was touch Luna or see her smile, and any lingering urge would evaporate.

When you find someone you love more than the air you breathe, you gladly give up old habits. Like murdering assholes, for example.

"I'm proud of you," I said. "After what happened to your father, you could've let the grief suffocate you, but instead, you're living each day with purpose and meaning. You're helping people. People just like your father. I know he's proud of you."

My words made her still, her gorgeous eyes shimmering in the incandescent light.

"Working the Innocence Project is even better than I could've imagined," she eventually said. "And guess who they found to replace me as the public defender?" I walked up and stroked her cheekbone with the pad of my thumb. "A Harvard Law School graduate. The underserved and vulnerable are going to get an amazing defense."

"And you're going to get a lot of innocent people out of prison."

God, look at the way her face lit up anytime she realized that.

But even in her light, I could still see her worry for me in the lines on her forehead, hear it in the long silence she let pass before clearing her throat.

Studying me and checking in on me like she did often.

"Are you okay?" she asked.

It would take time to fully get over everything that happened. And even then, I probably never would, but every day that I had with Luna was a gift. One I would never waste.

"With you in my arms, I have everything I've ever wanted, Luna."

CHAPTER 76
Luna

"Hey," I said, plopping down in the diner outside the city.

The chrome-trimmed clock, a relic from a past era, hung just above the entrance. Its neon letters declared *9:06 AM*, a stark contrast to my heavy heart.

Rows of shiny red vinyl booths hugged the windows. Regulars, families, and lone wanderers filled the seats—their faces, half illuminated, caught in the soft morning light. Speckled white-and-black tiled floors gave the space a retro appeal, and strong, rich scents of freshly brewed coffee mingled with the sweet notes of maple syrup.

The soft murmur of conversations filled the space, punctuated by occasional laughter, while the clink of ceramic mugs battled with the chime of the cash register and the quiet hiss of the coffee machine.

"It's good to see you," Mom said.

Since I'd graduated high school, we saw each other once a month or so, but our relationship, I would argue, was surface level. When someone has hurt you and broken your trust, you can still love them, and still spend time with them, but it's an empty shell of what it once was.

After Dad's funeral, however, I was hoping to change that. I'd lost the most important person in my life, and I didn't want to have this strained relationship with my mom anymore; she was all I had left, and I wanted to be part of her life.

But I wasn't sure if I could get past the resentment from her trying to stop me from seeing Dad for all those years. Lecturing me about wasting my time trying to help him. Abandoning him in his time of need.

I wanted to. A good person would find her way past it.

So here I was. Ready to finally confront her about it, all in hopes of turning the page on a new chapter.

We made small talk about the weather and her job, ordered our food, and then settled into the real conversation at hand.

"You visited him in the beginning." I looked down, trying to hide the anger burning through my gaze. "Those visits slowed, and then you just stopped going."

Mom's fingers trembled slightly as she brought her coffee to her lips, her eyes avoiding mine as she took a long sip. Her tone was almost a whisper as she said, "I know. I'm sorry for that."

My hand tightened around my mug, heat rising to my cheeks. *Sorry? Sorry is for when you accidentally door-ding someone.*

I took a shaky breath, trying to calm the whirlwind of emotions threatening to break free.

"Why did you stop?" I pressed, desperate for some semblance of understanding.

"It was a long time ago," she said.

"And why did you try so hard to convince *me* to stop going?" Once I was out of high school, she couldn't stop me.

She glanced away, wringing her hands. "We've been over this, Luna. I just...I thought you deserved a chance at a life without the false hope of someday seeing him free from behind those walls."

I crossed my arms over my chest as I tapped my foot. I don't know what I expected, but I'd hoped for something more than the same lines of bull she'd been feeding me for years. You don't give up on the love of your life—you just don't. If Hunter had gone to prison, I would have visited him...every. Single. Day. And he was *guilty*, for God's sake!

After experiencing that kind of love, I couldn't imagine abandoning him.

But Mom did, and she did so after she'd had a child with Dad.

"He needed us," I said. "We were all he had, and he needed our love.
It was the only thing he had left."

"Luna—"

"Be honest, Mom. Tell me the truth; otherwise, I don't know
how…" *To move forward. To look at you without resentment.*

Mom stared into her coffee for several long seconds and took a
deep breath while she shook her head.

"Luna, he asked me…" She hesitated, tears brimming in her eyes.
"He asked me to stop visiting him."

A cold shock raced down my back.

"He what?"

"About a year into his sentence, he even asked me to move to
another state and bring you with me. And never let you see him
again."

Bile rose up my esophagus, and my lungs pumped oxygen so fast, I
was growing lightheaded.

"Why?" I whispered.

"He wanted to minimize the damage of the tragedy. He suffered
the weight of it, and he didn't want it to spread into our lives."

My throat tried to close up with a ball of despair lodged inside.

"And he thought we would what?" I said, the backs of my eyes
pricking. "We'd just forget about him?"

Mom's gaze faltered, retreating from mine. "I think he was hoping
we would move on with our lives instead of letting his circumstances
hold us back."

His circumstances?

My ribs started to fold in on themselves at the sacrifice my father
had made to save us from further heartbreak.

"He did it for you," Mom said.

The taste of agony was bitter and cold on my tongue.

Maybe I didn't want to hear this. Maybe it was easier to keep my
mom in the role of the villain. In that role, it was me and my dad

against the world, and in that role, I didn't have to re-examine the past through a different lens.

I'd seen how hard that had been on Hunter, and I wasn't sure I was strong enough for it now.

"When your father and I had you, we both made a vow to put you first. No matter what. He told me keeping you away from the prison and trying to force you to move on with your life was the last thing he would ever ask of me."

Dammit, Dad.

That was why my mom had stopped taking me to visit him. It wasn't until I was older that I bulldozed my way into the prison, ignoring the pleas of my father to stop coming. I thought he didn't want me there because it wasn't a place for a young lady, what with all the inmates.

And when I showed up anyway, that's why he kept changing the topic from his trial. That's why he tried shifting every conversation to *my* life, insisting I make plans and get out there and live. Maybe he didn't have the heart to reject me when I'd shown up for our visits, but he sure as hell tried to use them to convince me to give up on him.

And save myself.

"How could he sacrifice the only thing he cared about? Us?"

"Because your happiness meant more to him than his own."

A single tear slid down my cheek, anchored by the weight of my father's sacrifice.

A memory surfaced, solidifying one of his last sacrifices for me.

The echo of laughter from years ago filled my ears.

"Oh my gosh!" I squealed, the world full of wonder as I dashed into the backyard, my pigtails flying.

"Careful," Dad said. "They're not sanded yet. You could get a splinter."

"I thought you said we couldn't afford to build a tree house?!" My smile was so wide, that it probably touched my ears. "I thought you had to save up for a car?"

"Well"—Dad adjusted his baseball cap—"I got to thinking." He put his

hands on his hips. "You've been wanting a tree house for a while. The car can wait, but you're growing up so fast, this can't."

"But—"

He held his hand up. "Getting to work faster is a small thing. Making one of your dreams come true is big, Luna. You deserve this."

"Thank you, Dad!" I ran up and slammed my arms around him. He picked me up and kissed the top of my head.

As the scent of Dad's cologne dissipated, replaced with cooked bacon, I wiped a tear from my cheek.

"But once I started to visit Dad," I said, "why didn't you start visiting him, then?"

Mom looked down. "He was hoping if I remained away, eventually, you might give up, too." She paused. "I'm sorry," she said. "I thought I was doing the right thing, but if I could go back in time, I would make different decisions."

For the first time in years, the knot in my chest loosened, the sharp edges of my resentment toward Mom beginning to blur.

I might disagree with her decisions, but the real question was, could I accept her apology?

I'd learned that rescuing my father from prison hadn't changed the injustice going on in this world, and now, I was realizing there was an injustice going on right here, with my mother.

A mother and her daughter strained over tragic circumstances.

And if I were being honest, outside the strain relating to Dad's incarceration, she had always been a wonderful mother.

She held down multiple jobs and did whatever it took to keep food on the table. Not an easy task. She attended every school function that her work schedule would allow, every parent-teacher conference, and stayed actively plugged in and engaged with her child.

I met her gaze.

One conversation didn't heal years of hurt, but Dad wouldn't want me to push her away. He'd want me to wrap my arms around her and forgive her.

To reestablish the bond we'd once shared.

Taking a deep breath, I reached across the table, placing my hand over hers. "Maybe we can start over, Mom," I said. "With a fresh slate."

My mom's lower lip quivered. "I'd love that, Luna." Her voice was thick with emotion, bridging the years of distance with those simple words.

I smiled, and took a sip of my coffee, feeling lighter than I had in a long time.

"Maybe after we eat, I can take you back to my place. I'd like to introduce you to my boyfriend."

It felt like everything was falling into place.

Today, Hunter would spend time with my mom. Tomorrow, we were meeting with Sean.

I could only hope *that* meeting would go as well as this one had...

CHAPTER 77

Luna

"I do not want to do this," Hunter groaned.

"He doesn't suspect you anymore," I assured.

After hearing about Stanley Weiss's suicide—a manner of death confirmed by a top-notch medical examiner and corroborated with letters Stanley had mailed to relatives the day *before* he died—Sean reasoned Hunter couldn't be the Windy City Vigilante, because if Hunter was the Vigilante, he would have killed Stanley himself.

He'd been right there, facing his father's killer.

Hunter had admitted to talking to Stanley that day about the missing money from all those years ago but had left before the gunshot sounded.

His alibi had been backed up by eyewitnesses—neighbors who had seen Hunter outside when the shot went off.

Sean's suspicions of Hunter were severely reduced after that.

Ironic, by the way, that Hunter's ultimate choice of letting Stanley live probably saved him from prison.

While Sean's suspicions hadn't been completely eliminated with that alone, the Vigilante's vehicle mysteriously turned up in downtown Chicago, wiped clean and the inside bleached. Nowhere near Hunter's home or any location he'd ever been to, and in reviewing surveillance footage from the courthouse killing, it was again confirmed that the Vigilante was at least twenty pounds heavier and three inches taller than Hunter Lockwood.

So, there went Sean's lingering doubts about Hunter.

Rinaldi—whose hunt for Franco Hopkins had gone cold—was still mildly suspicious of Hunter, but there was no other evidence to turn over, and she had other cases taking priority now that the Vigilante hadn't attacked in a while.

Reporters were having a field day with that—wondering if the Windy City Vigilante had been killed or was in prison. Or if he was lying in wait.

Mayor Kepler convinced the public that the Vigilante had likely been driven out of town due to the pressure he had put on him. And he pivoted his reelection campaign to take credit for solving the murder of Hunter's father.

We knew he had nothing to do with solving it, but his constituents didn't, and he was reelected.

Meanwhile, Sean's interest in solving *who* the Windy City Vigilante was had dwindled, in part, because he no longer suspected it was someone close to me. That, and because Hunter Lockwood had agreed to talk about his dad's murder for Sean's podcast.

The first public interview he'd ever given on the subject.

"I thought you said this wasn't too painful?" I asked. "If it is…"

"It's not that," Hunter said, tugging his tie's knot. He glowered across the room. "It's *him*. I still want to punch him in his jaw."

I cocked my head.

"He let you pre-approve every single question and is abiding by the legal contract you made him sign." That gave Hunter full rights to the audio and the right to walk off if he felt uncomfortable.

Hunter exchanged a look with me as Sean walked over and clapped his hands.

"Ready?" Sean motioned for him to take a seat.

Hunter glared at the microphone like it might give him a rash while Sean introduced Hunter Lockwood and started a respectful, noninvasive podcast—but an exclusive one that Sean was thrilled to get.

When it was over, Sean thanked us profusely and got to work breaking down the equipment.

"Not punching him is harder than giving up murder," Hunter mumbled.

I smirked and kissed my ex-killer on the cheek. "Thank you."

Just as Grayson's number came across Hunter's cell phone screen.

CHAPTER 78

Hunter

"What's going on?" I asked, an anchor sinking my heart as I took in my brother's tense posture.

Grayson sat hunched at the dimly lit bar, nursing a scotch, his every movement betraying unease.

But now that I was looking closer, he'd been talking to someone.

"Hunter," Grayson murmured. "Didn't expect you so soon."

Grayson's gaze shifted to the figure to his left, and they locked eyes before the mystery man stood up and slapped his hand on my brother's back.

"Phone's always on," the guy said to him, then looked at me.

I narrowed my eyes, recognition flickering. Then blazing on.

"Hunter, this is Dillon," Grayson said. "Dillon, this is Hunter, my brother."

Dillon extended his hand and held it there for several seconds before putting it back down.

"Why are you talking to *him?*" I scowled, pointing my finger at Dillon.

Grayson shot me a look, his eyes sharp with a silent warning.

I glared at the guy. "You were that criminal kingpin all over the news." Not active anymore, supposedly, but the guy had a lot of dead bodies he'd racked up. The only reason he hadn't fit my code was because the people he'd killed had been violent criminals.

But what the hell was he doing with my brother?

"I'll see you later, Grayson," Dillon said. "Good luck."

Good luck. With what? Me? Or whatever the hell Grayson had brought me here to talk about?

I watched in repulsion as Dillon McPherson ambled out of the bar, off to do god knows what.

"You know who he is?" I demanded.

"Yes."

"What are you doing, talking to a guy like that?"

Grayson raised an eyebrow. "A guy like what?"

I balled my hands into fists.

"You know what he's done?" I asked.

"We didn't come here to discuss Dillon."

"How do you know him?"

"Look, our paths crossed during a work thing once, but I don't have much time, and this isn't why I asked you to come."

A work thing?

Suspicion and fear churned in me. "Grayson, are you running drugs?"

"What? No."

"That guy was the most wanted criminal kingpin in the country."

Grayson sighed and flagged the bartender down. "He'll have a scotch."

I ground my teeth, but after a few seconds, I sat down.

My brother had picked the two seats at the far end of the bar, out of earshot of everyone. In theory.

To be safe, I kept my voice low. "If you're not involved in narcotics, then what *are* you involved in?"

How did Grayson have mysterious contacts with contract killers and seem unfazed when killing a man and dumping his body in the waterway behind our property? So skilled, I might add, that the police never found it.

"Here you go, sir."

A wiry bartender with tattoos snaking up his arm set my drink down and walked off.

"Do you really want to get into this?" Grayson leaned over, putting his mouth by my ear. "Because I never did ask you about your secret underground room. Or why you'd go to prison if anyone found it?"

"I kept it from you, so you'd have plausible deniability," I said.

A slow smirk crept onto Grayson's face. He lifted his scotch, letting the amber liquid swirl for a moment as he looked deep into it before taking a deliberate sip and setting it down with a clank.

On the television in the corner, some story was running about the Windy City Vigilante. I couldn't hear what they were saying—perhaps talking about how there hadn't been an attack recently. But my brother looked at the screen, then back at me with knowing eyes.

"It wasn't hard to connect the dots," he said.

I didn't deny it. No reason to, so instead, I let the unspoken confirmation settle in the space between two brothers.

Grayson scrubbed his jaw. "I have to take off for a bit. Will be out of touch."

"For how long?"

Grayson shrugged. "Hard to say. Some jobs take a couple of days; some take a couple of months. The job I just got hired for sounds complicated…"

"Hired to do *what?*" I pressed.

"Nothing I'll tell a lawyer." Grayson's mouth curled up. "I'll be in touch when I can."

He got up, but trepidation yanked my stomach to the ground, wanting to pull him back to me, and beg him to stay. I had a bad feeling about this—he'd never given me a heads-up before one of his disappearances.

"Grayson," I said before he could walk away. "Will you be safe?"

Grayson put his hands in his pockets. "Safety's an illusion, Hunter. No one in this world is truly safe."

A sudden rush of fear gripped me, making the words come out more as a desperate plea than a statement. "Grayson, don't go."

He paused, his eyes searching mine. "I'll see you soon, brother."

But his voice betrayed his doubt, and he wouldn't have said goodbye for the first time if he was certain of that. Leaving me wondering what in the hell my brother had gotten himself into.

And if I would ever see his face again...

Extended Epilogue

HUNTER

"Okay kiddo, you know the drill," I said. "Scoot your butt over."

"I'm all the way over!" Amelia claimed.

"Mr. Snuggle Muffles—"

"Snuggle Muffins!"

"Is taking up half the bed. Tell him to scoot over so I can sit down."

Amelia smiled—damn, that smile brought me to my knees every time—and moved the huge elephant I'd given her for her birthday to the foot of the bed. Affording me the space I needed to sit by her hip.

I brought her flowery pink covers up to the base of her chin. Her whole room was pink with white drapes and accents. Stuffed animals. A dollhouse in the corner that was bigger than my first car. Luna worried we were spoiling her, but she had no idea how many things I'd almost bought my daughter already.

I thought I'd be a tough dad. Strict, especially with money, because nothing irritated me more than entitled brats whining to their parents.

But the universe has a sense of humor. Because what happens when you don't get an entitled kid? What happens when you get the sweetest one on the planet, who is grateful for a 99-cent pack of crayons? Well, when said kid is in a store and her eyes light up over a trinket and her tiny hand is wrapped around her billionaire father's finger?

Billionaire father crumbles. Every time.

So here we were. In a room that looked like a toy store vomited in it. And this was the most *humble* home we owned. Out in the country, a great place to spend a weekend.

"High and low," I reminded her.

"Why do we do high and low again, Daddy?"

"Because," I said, rubbing her arm, "my daddy did it with me, and you'll do it with your kids someday. Each event is a learning opportunity. The ones that make us sad or upset. And the ones that make us excited."

She put that adorable finger to her chin, looking up in thought.

"Oh! The high was when I saw your car pulling up the driveway after work!"

Fuck. Me.

If a heart can melt, this kid held the flame.

I smiled and kissed her cheek. "That was my high, too, baby. I missed you so much."

Sometimes I wondered if I was making the right decision, staying on as a prosecutor—since doing so meant not getting home until dinner each night. Sometimes later. But I'd cut back my hours and wanted to do everything in my *legal* power to put the scum of Chicago away.

"The low was, I almost got a dog. I was so close! But I didn't get one."

"Really?" That surprised me. Luna was an animal lover, but we had several family vacations planned this year and had agreed to revisit the dog debate next year. Knowing my daughter, I'd walk out with an entire zoo of them.

"Yeah!" Amelia shuffled to her side, tucking her little hands beneath her cheek. "This man had a whole car full of them! He was going to give me one!"

On the outside, my smile remained frozen so I didn't scare my child.

But on the inside, a fury of rage boiled through me.

"What man?"

"This man was driving by and saw me riding my bike on our driveway, and he rolled down his window and said he had four puppies inside he was trying to find a good home for. He asked if I'd help him by taking one."

I ran my tongue over my teeth.

"Where was Mommy?"

"She ran inside to go potty for a minute, so she missed it!"

More like this man was stalking my fucking daughter, waiting for a brief opportunity. Luna was a great mother and, if anything, was called "overprotective" by other moms. She'd never leave our daughter in harm's way.

"Did the man know your name, honey?" Was this targeted at the prosecutor's kid or a Lockwood family grudge?

"No," she said.

In theory, this was just some sick asshole, out hunting little girls, then.

"Does Mommy know about the puppies?"

I was surprised Luna didn't call me. She'd have freaked the hell out.

"Mommy told me to stay in the garage," Amelia said. "I thought he'd be mad at me if she found out I was on the driveway." Guilt tained her freckle-covered cheeks.

"You can't ride your bike without us," I said. "That man could have been a tricky person."

We'd had the tricky person talk. The new age way of the stranger-danger talk. I couldn't believe my ears that my daughter had left the safety of our garage, even for a minute, let alone that she'd engaged with someone.

Where did we slip? Every warning, every lesson, and yet…

My heart churned in my chest, what-ifs flashing before my eyes, my stomach tense. Later, I'd have a meltdown over this. I'd beat the shit out of my boxing bag. Luna would freak the hell out. It was going to be a bad night emotionally, and tomorrow, we'd be left reeling.

All the safety measures we took. All our talks. And this happens.

But my daughter was only four. A man in a car claiming he had puppies who needed a home would bypass all of those talks, wouldn't it? If some asshole wanted a kid bad enough, he'd practice over and over and over until he got it right.

I clenched my fist so tight, that my nails tore at my skin.

"What did this man say to you, exactly?"

"That the puppies were going to starve if he didn't find them good homes. I know I'm not supposed to talk to strangers, but he was a nice man who was trying to save puppies."

Mother. Fucker.

"And then what happened?" I managed through a forced smile, my teeth clenched so tightly, one might've cracked.

"Well, he asked if I wanted a puppy. And I said I'd have to ask my parents. And he said to come look at the puppy so I could tell you what kind of puppy it was, since that would be your first question…"

I bit my cheek until I tasted blood.

"So, I started walking toward him, but before I got to his car, he looked at Mr. Kemp's driveway and sped off."

Russel Kemp. Next-door neighbor. An elderly man who lived alone.

So, the asshole saw an eyewitness and sped off.

"I see. We'll have to talk more about this in the morning," I said. Not now. Not with the rage building inside me.

"You're not going to tell Mommy, are you?" she asked with round, pleading eyes.

"Time for bed." I kissed her forehead, wishing I had the energy to ease her worry about getting into trouble with Luna, but I could barely contain my anger. And I refused to explode in front of her.

I stood up and walked toward her door.

I should call the police. An attempted child abduction would be taken very seriously. They could get a make and model, possibly from Kemp or from surveillance images. Maybe even a plate number if our camera or others in the area caught it. And get the description of the child predator from my daughter.

Even with the police's limited budget—limited compared to mine—they'd work their asses off trying to catch this guy.

But even if they succeeded, I knew how this would play out. A child's eyewitness testimony was shaky. And it was the only evidence they had of whatever almost happened. There was no physical evidence of an attempted abduction because he hadn't even gotten out of his car. It was suspicious activity, at best.

There was a chance a jury would see the truth.

But there was at least an equal chance, if not greater, they wouldn't.

And that was if they even caught and charged the guy in the first place.

Still, I needed to let the police handle this. My Vigilante days were behind me.

But this fucker went after my child.

My little girl, who I held in my arms when she'd taken some of her first breaths. My little girl, who was the sweetest soul on this planet, her heart so big, she'd see past red flags if an injured animal was at play.

If anything had happened to her, I wouldn't have been able to bear it.

Nor would Luna.

I stood at her door, telling myself to walk out. To call the cops. But my feet were cemented in place as I swirled my wedding band on my finger.

Once.

Twice.

Three times.

And then I turned around, plastering my fake smile back on and asked my daughter one final question.

"What did the man look like, sweetheart?"

Thank you for reading SILENT VENDETTA! Grayson's getting his story next, but while you wait…

Wondering who Dillon, the guy at the bar with Grayson, is? Don't miss Dillon's **stand-alone** **Enemies-to-Lovers** Romance in **FATAL CURE! I had no idea that the criminal kingpin I've been hunting, the one I vowed to make pay for decimating my family, is the man I've fallen in love with…**

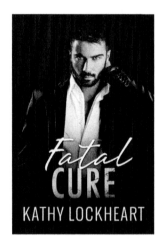

⭐⭐⭐⭐⭐ *"One of the BEST books I've EVER read!"*

One-click FATAL CURE now!

And don't miss Grayson's story—**get notified** when it's released (https://kathylockheart.com/graysons-story-notification/), but meanwhile…

. . .

What **shocking revelation did Grayson unveil** in his jaw-dropping conversation with Dillon at the bar? Find out in this **EXCLUSIVE bonus scene** from the Vendetta Duet. Oh, and please enjoy an additional bonus spicy scene, too! **Don't miss out on these thrilling exclusives!** (https://kathylockheart.com/vendetta-duet-bonus-scenes/)

Finally, I'd love for you to join my VIP TEAM! Sign up here: https://kathylockheart.com/join-my-vip-team/

Also by Kathy Lockheart

Immerse yourself in this **bestselling, unputdownable romance series** where desire and danger collide. Four couples, four **stand-alones interconnected** by a deliciously dark thread of romance, action, mystery, and shocking twists…

. . .

Deadly Illusion She was able to hide the bruises from everyone...until an MMA fighter came along. Now he'll die to protect her, maybe even kill...

Fatal Cure She'll risk everything to annihilate the enemy who decimated her family. But what happens when that dangerous enemy turns out to be the man she's fallen in love with?

Lethal Justice Chicago's most wanted criminal has fallen for the wrong woman. She's his hostage in a heist, and if he leaves any witnesses, his colleagues will kill them both.

Grave Deception Her new neighbor is a scorching hot police detective—one she has a massive crush on, but she never wanted to get his attention like this: as the apparent victim of an attempted murder.

Equal parts rapturous and intense, this roller-coaster series will leave you begging for more. **Binge these stay-up-all-night romances if you dare...**

"An amazing, gut-wrenching...out-of-body experience."
"Raw, emotional, and beautifully written."
"This is the kind of fairytale that would change our lives."

Acknowledgments

First, **I'd like to thank you, the reader.** You have a ton of options when it comes to books, your time is incredibly precious, and you gave *me* a chance. From the bottom of my heart, THANK YOU. Readers mean the world to me, and I'd love to connect with you! Please find my social media links at www.KathyLockheart.com.

Thank you to Susan Staudinger. Your developmental and content editing, combining with our amazing virtual sessions made this book far better than it ever would have been without you.

To Amy and Kristen, my formal beta readers. Thank you for helping make this story even better.

To Valentine and the entire team at Valentine PR—I'm so very grateful for all your help making the Vendetta Duet what it is today!

Thank you to my husband for showing me the beauty of true love and being my biggest cheerleader. Thank you to my children for giving me a love I didn't know existed until you were born and for inspiring me to be the best *me* I can be. Always go after your dreams.

To my family for enveloping me with love, encouraging me, and embracing my idea to become a writer.

To my friends, for your never-ending support.

To my editor Jovana, your attention to details polished this story and made it the best it could be! To my cover artists, Hang Le, and Sherri with Wild Love Designs, for bringing such beauty to this novel!

To all the authors who came before me—your success paves the road for new writers to do what they love. Thank you.

~ Kathy

Let's connect!

The easiest way to connect with me is to go to my website, <u>www.KathyLockheart.com</u>, and find my social media links. I interact with readers, so don't be surprised if you see me reply to your post or invite you to join a reader team!

Xoxo

Kathy

amazon.com/Kathy-Lockheart/e/B08XY5F2XG
bookbub.com/profile/kathy-lockheart
facebook.com/KathyLockheartAuthor
tiktok.com/@kathylockheart_author
instagram.com/kathy_lockheart
twitter.com/Kathy_Lockheart
pinterest.com/kathylockheart

Printed in Great Britain
by Amazon

45867680R00209